GU00832379

Wolf

Book 2 in the Loma_ _ _.._ ...._

First published in 2017

Mendus Harris

ISBN: 978-1545446973

Wolf Man

Mendus Harris

DEDICATION

Noreen and Tony Harris

Prologue

"Chumshkev will kill him."

The statement hung in the stale and fetid atmosphere as the speaker, a blond man in a pin stripe suit, paused for dramatic effect. His blue eyes swivelled before coming to rest on an enormously fat man sitting on a large, reinforced chair, a silver-topped cane clasped in his fleshy hands.

"I'm telling you," the man insisted, his smooth English accent purring, his left hand gesticulating. "I'm telling you, if word leaks out about this, it'll mean the end of Lomax and Lomax Enterprises."

The fat man swivelled in his chair to focus on the only other person in the tiny room. "What do you think Jeremy?" he asked in high pitched Cockney.

Surprised by the mention of his name, Jeremy sat up straight and tried to remove the mask of boredom from his handsome tanned face. "I don't know," he said in a languid Home Counties drawl, careful not to agree or disagree. "I worked for Lomax as Head of Africa Operations for five years; he's very clever at smoking out the opposition. How do we know Lomax hasn't put these two idiots up to telling us this story?"

The speaker ignored Jeremy and instead appealed directly to the fat man. "Mr Snodgrass, you sent me out to find a way of bringing down Lomax. These men represent our best hope of doing this quickly and efficiently."

The one called Snodgrass nodded but said nothing, preferring instead to look around the room. Eventually his eyes rested on Jeremy. "I've known Lomax as a business associate, rival and enemy for nearly twenty years," he said, "and I don't believe the man has enough subtlety to set us up like this. If what I've heard is genuine we have a unique opportunity to deal with him once and for all."

Jeremy nodded his head but did not respond.

Snodgrass lifted one buttock and shifted slightly. "What's happening at Lomax Gold Mine in Ghana?"

Once again Jeremy looked surprised, but his initial confusion was soon covered over. "Things aren't good. Lomax has misunderstood the extent of your influence. He believes that you have the miners' union in your pocket so he's set about ridding the mine of them. I've heard there's been mass sackings."

Snodgrass nodded his approval. "I always enjoy hearing of union bashing. And what of his main henchman, James Allen? Does he remain an important cog?"

Jeremy smiled. "Lomax has made him Manager of Geology, he's now on the board of mine management."

"Excellent."

Silence. Snodgrass looked up at the speaker. "Thank you, we now need to discuss what you've said."

Realising he was dismissed, the man opened a door and light flooded into the small space from a bar room illuminated by afternoon sunshine that glinted off mirrors and white plastic cladding. When the door shut again and the small room was plunged back into gloom, the two remaining men said nothing for a while. Then Snodgrass banged his cane on the floor, making Jeremy look up. "Cat got your tongue?" he asked.

Jeremy screwed up his face in annoyance. "What does

that mean?"

"It means that I want your opinion on whether we should go ahead with this operation."

Jeremy sniffed and looked away from Snodgrass and into the corners of the room as if he was expecting to see somebody crouching there. "I don't think it's advisable," he said. "Lomax has a way of being the last man standing when it comes to arse-kicking contests. Unless you're absolutely certain of where all the balls are going to land, I wouldn't bother."

Snodgrass struggled to his feet, an action that required some heavy lifting on his cane. "I understand where you're coming from, particularly after what happened to you at the Lomax Gold Mine."

Snodgrass's voice was soft and Jeremy looked up at the corpulent figure, scorn etched around his eyes and mouth. "What do you mean by that?" he said.

Snodgrass smiled. "I mean I understand that you might feel intimidated coming up against your old employer."

Jeremy said nothing.

"He was lucky, that's all," continued Snodgrass. "That friend of Greg Boston – Ed Evans or whatever his name was - turning up like that and frightening the game."

Jeremy's lip curled. "Have you killed him yet?" he asked.

"Of course not," replied Snodgrass. "I'm somebody who needs a reason to kill, I'm not a complete savage. In any case, he could be useful, particularly if we can turn him against Lomax. Of course, I'm having him watched, I've started the process of intimidation. I don't think it'll take much to turn him."

Jeremy sniffed dismissively. "What about Forge?"

"Dead," replied Snodgrass. "A mercy killing. If he'd recovered from that beating he took there was a chance he would talk. He was the one who knew the most about what we were up to at Lomax Mine. Kojo and Bismarck weren't really aware of my involvement. Besides, Kojo and Bismarck are almost impossible to find; they've disappeared into the African woodwork."

Furrowing his brow in confusion, Jeremy looked up into Snodgrass's piggy eyes. "I don't understand why you're bothered with Lomax."

"It's the Great Game. In order to win it you've got to be in it." Snodgrass put his hand in one of his jacket pockets and produced a small object which he rotated in his fingers. Jeremy looked in fascination. "Recognise it?" Snodgrass asked.

Jeremy nodded, now looking un-nerved. "It's a fossil trilobite," he said. "One of the ones I brought back from Africa."

Snodgrass beamed in approval and tossed the fossil in the air. "Of course I don't blame you for all of the fiasco with the trilobites. At times it seemed like a pea and thimble game at a fairground. But you were careless. A very careless cat." He stopped, shifted the trilobite back into his pocket, changed hands on his cane and sidled from the room, shutting the door behind him.

A sneer broke out on Jeremy's beautiful face as the vast bulk of his business partner disappeared. He found it difficult disguising his true feelings about the man; so common, so uncultured. But soon he'd be able to move against him, usurp the organisation Snodgrass had developed, and bend it to his will. Then all this obsessing over Lomax would be at an end. In fact, first thing he'd do would be to make peace with Lomax, offer him a partnership. Needless to say, the price of any settlement would be the disposal of James Allen and Ed Evans and any others who had humiliated him.

A second later he heard a small click. In any other place

except the quietness of this small room he would have dismissed the noise as part of the central heating, but in a sound-proofed space it was utterly alien. A wave of coldness emanated from his chest and began to spread down his spine. Breathing had suddenly become more difficult.

Rising from his chair, he grabbed the handle of the door. It was locked. He pulled more vigorously and it came away in his hand. A subtle smell of almonds had entered the small space. A few seconds ago he had thought it might have been a residual scent, left by Snodgrass's perfume. But now it was growing stronger, beginning to overwhelm his senses.

He started to bang on the door with his fists, then screamed at the top of his voice for somebody to open it. He scrabbled at the wall until his fingernails bled. In panic, he stood back and ran at the door with all his might, so hard that he felt something in his shoulder give way.

Falling to the floor, he began screaming at the thought that he was going to die. His voice was disembodied, like he was hearing it underwater. He needed to get up. "Let me out, you've had your fun," he shouted. The almond smell intensified, it was now overpowering all his senses, making him dizzy. The dim light in the room extinguished, plunging him into utter darkness and bringing a fresh wave of panic.

With an enormous effort, he jumped to his feet and kicked out at the door, but his footing failed and he fell to the floor. He picked himself up and stared into the utter blackness, head spinning. Kicking out again, his foot connected with fresh air and once more he tumbled to the floor.

But this time it wasn't so easy to stand. A wave of nausea hit his stomach so that he vomited. With a final, almighty effort, he stood. But it was no good, he subsided sideways and crashed head-first into the wall.

The Inquisitor

Less than five tube stations away, one of the elements of Snodgrass and Jeremy's conversation, Edryd (Ed) Evans, sat in a room lit with a single desk lamp. He nervously moved his right hand down the faint scar on his cheek and then pushed it through his short brown hair.

On the other side of a large wooden table was a man with small rimless glasses who eyed him with keen interest. "I am a professional inquisitor," said the man eventually. "It doesn't mean that I use thumb screws or matches under the nails, but I am paid to find the truth. That means I like to discover reasons and motivation for people. I produce reports which detail whether or not I think somebody should be employed, whether they are of sound mind." He stopped and looked at Ed carefully. "Do you understand?"

Ed hesitated and then nodded.

"It means that I need to know everything, and you must give it willingly. If I detect that you're holding out on me then I will include that in my report and it is likely that your application will be ditched forthwith. I would guess that Mr Lomax is offering you a lot of money; I myself do not come cheap, so if you wish to be employed you must first convince me." He pushed up his glasses and read a few lines. "I understand that you have suffered from some psychiatric illness recently. I need to warn you that any attempt to understate or exaggerate the effects of this illness will be duly noted and will form an important part of my report. I urge you to make a full and frank disclosure." He glanced up. "Do you agree to this arrangement?"

Ed nodded his head.

"In particular," continued the man, relentless in his quest to explain procedure. "I will be trying to investigate the relationship between yourself and Greg Boston. We understand there is a history between you and Greg and between you and Greg's wife. We want to establish whether this might prevent you from carrying out any of your duties should you succeed in securing the position."

The man shuffled his papers importantly and placed a finger on the top part of the first page. "Let's start with the army, shall we? You did well; I've been told you were offered commissions and extensions, lots of pats on the back and hints about how far you might travel up the ladder. Why d'you give up?"

"I knew there'd always be a limit. I'm from a council estate in Garston, my ancestors are poor Welsh peasantry, not army. I hadn't the tradition or the upbringing of those around me, and most of all I hadn't a degree."

"And that's why you decided to study? And where better to do a degree than in your home city." Looking down at his notes, he adjusted his glasses and continued. "You bought a flat and shared it with Greg Boston, your childhood friend and once your grandfather's farmhand, who happened to be doing the same course." He looked up and peered at him over the top of his glasses. "Was that difficult?"

"Not really, Greg needed a straight man, somebody who wouldn't compete with him, who'd be dour and unreadable." Ed stopped and then grinned. "That's what he liked to say, anyway."

The inquisitor ignored Ed's attempt at levity. "After you graduated, you never considered re-joining your old unit and resuming your army career?"

"Sure I did, but I wanted to stay on at university and do research. Unfortunately, the year I graduated there was no money. "

"So you decided to become an exploration geologist?"

"Somebody whispered in my ear that geologists could make good money in West Africa exploring for gold. I had an agent who got me some work with a metal exploration company for six months, extended for another six months. After that, much of my working life was centred on metal exploration in West Africa, based in mines or camps." Corralled behind barbed wire and armed guards, he might have added, where men would throw punches for no other reason than to break the tension.

"And Greg followed you into Exploration." It was a statement, not a question, and Ed did not feel the need to respond. "And Alice," asked the man. "How long have you known her?"

"All my life; her aunt lived close to my grandfather, we'd hang around together during school holidays. But we really got to know each other a few years after I'd stopped being a student. She answered an advertisement to flat-sit while Greg and I were away in West Africa. She was a nurse at the Royal Liverpool and needed cheap accommodation while she looked around for somewhere to live. She was escaping a rotten marriage."

"And you accepted her at once, of course."

"Once I'd established there was no chance of her former husband coming to look for her. Apparently, he'd gone off with another woman. She was the most suitable candidate of all those who applied. And besides, it was like finding a long-lost cousin. I'd have let her sit in the flat even if the husband was likely to turn up and rip the place apart. I handed her the keys and told her I'd be back in a couple of months. 'That's all I need to set myself up in my own flat', she assured me. In fact, I returned after only a few weeks. I told her she could stay and I'd take the spare room. She was none too pleased at the arrangement but she had no alternative."

"How quickly did it grow more serious?"

Ed shrugged. "After a night in the pub, which had started as a quick sociable drink, we sort of came together."

"And what did Greg have to say when he learned you were now an item?"

"I told him, of course. I said he needn't get any ideas about her."

"And what was his reaction to that?"

"He shook his head and said he liked his women more sporty-Porsche than family-Ford."

"Did that reassure you?" he asked. "Make you feel comfortable when he was in the flat alone with her and you were away in West Africa?"

"Not really. It was the challenge and the competition that mattered to Greg."

"But from then on your relationship with Alice blossomed," the man prompted.

"Absolutely it did. We discussed marriage, but she'd been there before and didn't want to make the same mistake."

The man seemed to want more. He gazed intently, light glinting off his glasses.

"So, I said we'd discuss it again, after I got back from my latest trip to West Africa."

"But you didn't return after a month," interjected the man, examining his notes. He removed his glasses and swung them around. Then he fixed them back on his nose and began to read in earnest. "According to your statement, you'd gone with a small exploration team into a remote area where your plane came down. Your life was saved by foraging tribesmen who took you back to their village. When you'd recovered, you set about trying to return but the area had been over-run by rebels. It took you some time to get home, by which time you'd been posted as 'missing, presumed dead'."

He lifted his eyes from the sheet of paper and looked at Ed. He seemed to have memorised the next section of the report. "On landing, you rang Alice at work; she was silent when you told her you were back from the dead and that you would be at the flat in under forty minutes." He took off his glasses again and then threw them onto the manuscript. "And that's when you learnt that she had married Greg."

Ed nodded, the blank words on the page could never portray the mind-numbing disappointment, the howl-at-the-moon madness.

The inquisitor continued. "You hid yourself away in your grandfather's old farmhouse in the Welsh Borderland. Tell me about that."

"Nothing to say," said Ed dismissively. "I fell apart, had a bit of a breakdown and Sophie came and sorted me out."

"Sophie?"

"Alice's aunt, she lives down the hill from me; she knew what had happened and kept an eye open. When I didn't appear for a week, she came up to see me. She kept popping in, brought me beef tea, books to read, talked about Taid, my grandfather, the old days."

The inquisitor made a note in his report before continuing. "So then you had the call to go back to Africa and work in Lomax Mine in Ghana, to replace Greg Boston who had been reported missing." He looked up and stared.

"What possessed you to go?"

Ed shrugged. "I needed money. Greg had been a close friend, my grandfather's farmhand. I felt I owed him something, if he was in some kind of trouble…"

"But still," insisted the inquisitor. "He'd married Alice, surely he was your enemy now."

Ed considered the statement and remembered how he had felt when he received word that Greg had disappeared. He veered towards a purely emotional explanation for his actions. "While I was alone in my farmhouse falling apart, I realised that I had nobody else but him and Alice, and Sophie of course."

The inquisitor looked incredulous but noted Ed's reply in the margin of the report. It was clear he didn't believe the explanation, perhaps it was too glib and pre-meditated.

Ed performed a mental shrug. He was unsure himself about why he'd gone back. Maybe he wanted to make sure Greg was dead and that his route back to Alice was clear. On the other hand, he wanted to escape the darkness of the Welsh winter and his lonely mountain-top existence.

"So when you returned from Africa, you went to see Alice and explained that Greg was almost certainly dead. What was her reaction."

Ed toyed with telling the man that Alice was nothing to do with him, or Lomax. Eventually he said, "They'd been estranged, my return from the dead had caused strains in the marriage. Besides, Greg was a philanderer, Alice is not a sporty-Porsche and never will be."

The inquisitor decided to back off, he shuffled his pages and moved on. "I'm obliged to tell you that Lomax Mine is recruiting again. James Allen, the new Manager of Geology, has particularly requested you to help him. If you were to be offered the position, would you be inclined to accept?"

"Yes," said Ed, with a confidence he didn't feel.

The inquisitor gazed at him over his glasses, open disbelief written across his face. "Sign here then," he said proffering the report.

The meeting broke up and they walked out of the room in silence, into the bright office beyond. At the escalator door, the inquisitor stopped. "Is there anything else you want to tell me?" he asked.

Ed contemplated confessing the events of the last few days, the phone call from Papua New Guinea in which James Allen had pleaded like a condemned man for Ed to come back to Africa, or the appearance of fossil trilobites around his farmhouse in places which were impossible to access without a key. They'd turned up in his favourite cup, on the mantelpiece and kitchen table, underneath his favourite hat. Only somebody who knew the circumstances of Greg Boston's apparent death would understand why Ed found them so disturbing.

"Why is James Allen in Papua New Guinea?" Ed asked, suppressing all mention of trilobites.

"He's interviewing two new recruits who Lomax wants to employ at Lomax Gold Mine."

In the quiet of the elevator, Ed heard Allen's voice in his head, implying that he might be in trouble unless he came back to Lomax and helped sort out the mess. Ed's protestations that it was not his mess in the first place had been brushed aside. "For your sake, and Alice's, you need to spend a month back in Lomax. That's all it'll take. Something's happened."

* * *

From London, Ed went straight up to visit Alice in Liverpool. "But I don't understand," she said. "What's the big deal? You've only just returned from Africa."

13

Shrugging his shoulders, Ed sat down at her kitchen table and nervously traced his cheek scar. It had more or less healed over, only obvious as a groove in his facial stubble. Not for the first time he felt out of place in Alice's beautiful flat with its carefully chosen ornamental furniture and its smell of vanilla and peach blossom. He looked down at his dull shoes, straightened his half-mast tie and rubbed an excess of debris from a scuffed leather jacket that had seen better days.

Looking up to gaze in her soft hazel eyes, framed by curling auburn hair, he sensed confusion, even distress. He tried to reassure her. "All I'm saying is that I think you should keep an eye out."

"For what? For God's sake." She placed hands on hips and formed her face into a frown.

"Anything unusual. Things which don't seem quite right. Phone calls, unusually attentive strangers, trilobites left in strange places. You may want to note down registrations of cars parked outside, and cars that follow you."

Alice's eyes widened. "Are you being serious?" The hint of anger had turned to outrage. "And for what possible reason would anybody wish to leave trilobites, or follow me around?" Arms were now crossed, leading with her chin.

Saying nothing, Ed crossed to the window that looked out onto the expanse of Sefton Park. "Easy to keep watch," he said eventually.

"I beg your pardon?"

"You can be watched from the park," he said, turning his head.

"Are you going to tell me who might be watching?"

"Same people as last time. Greg's lot."

Sitting down, she put her head in her hands. When she spoke again it was in a resigned voice. "What should I do if I see anything suspicious," she asked. "I can't just up and leave my job, I need to eat. And where should I go?"

"Your Aunt Sophie's."

She gave a mirthless laugh. "No way."

"My place is just up the hill, there's a good track, you could go up there if she gets too much."

"Won't they be watching your place as well? I mean if they're watching mine…"

She had a point, he thought, rubbing his chin. "They'll know I'll be in Africa and probably won't bother. In the old days, you always used to come up the track in the dark."

"That was when I was young and foolhardy. When I still thought knocking about with boys like you and Greg exciting." She folded her arms again. "I'd have been better advised never to have gone near you two."

"But none of this is my fault, it was Greg who…"

"Don't give me that," she retorted. "It was you who went and stirred this hornet's nest, not Greg."

"You're wrong," he replied after several moments.

But Alice was no longer listening, she was buttoning her coat. "My shift starts in an hour and I expect you have planes to catch, so I won't detain you any longer." She lifted her eyes and gazed into his. They were cold. "I need to set the alarm," she said, pointing at a console in the wall next to the front door, "so I'll see you outside."

"I'll let Sophie know," Ed said as he hovered nervously around the front door. "That you may need to go there and lie low, incognito." He could see she was too angry to reply, fumbling with her bag, dropping the keys. "I'm not saying it'll be necessary," he continued, "but I'd feel better knowing you have somewhere safe to run."

She strode off down the path at a fast pace, swinging her handbag. "Goodbye," she shouted over her shoulder so loudly that several people in the park turned their heads.

* * *

Alice's angry tones followed him all the way back to his home in the Welsh Borderland. He drove his four wheel drive up the long track to his farmhouse and then looked out across the long slope that stretched down to the valley bottom. Not far below, in a small coppice of stunted oak trees was the small white-washed cottage that belonged to Alice's aunt, Sophie. A thin plume of smoke rose from her chimney.

On entering the kitchen, he found two new trilobites on the kitchen table. After placing them on the mantelpiece he sat down on his favourite seat and stared at them until he started to get tunnel vision. Something needed doing to give Alice a chance if anything happened and she required help. Without realising it, Ed found himself on the old overgrown path that led down to Sophie's old cottage.

Sophie had been his confidant ever since she had found him at death's door two years ago. She knew everything about what had gone on in Africa, about Greg and Snodgrass, and Lomax. She had a sharp mind, and was surprisingly worldly-wise for somebody who had lived half way up a mountain in Wales for much of her life.

His gentle knock provoked a loud barking followed by the sound of a stick banging against stone floors. After a few seconds the barking stopped and there was the slam of an interior door which suggested the dog had been safely stowed in a convenient room. A small eye appeared at a window, and then the door was flung open to reveal a small, grey-haired woman in her sixties, hale and hearty, dressed in a neck to floor black woollen dress.

She blinked at him for a few moments, then her face broke into a smile. "To what do I owe this honour?"

"I want to make sure you remembered our agreement

about Alice," he said.

Nodding her head, she pulled him into the hallway. "Brandy and chicken wings," she said after pecking him on the cheek. "It was your grandfather's favourite. Popped in here quite a lot when he was alive. 'Course that was after your Nain died. Great man your grandfather." This was her mantra whenever Ed visited.

Busying herself around the kitchen, sucking on a couple of empty teeth, she found tea cups in the sink and then walked to her kitchen table where she poured brandy from a teapot covered in a chicken-shaped cosy. "To the dead," she said, raising her cup. "May they rest in peace and trouble us no more." It was an incantation, more of a spell than a toast.

Sitting down next to her large range she made herself comfortable, thoughts of eating chicken wings temporarily consigned to history. "I'm guessing your trip back to Africa is something to do with Greg, I can tell by the constipated look on your face." She lifted her nose slightly and sniffed, like she'd just smelled dog shit. It was the expression she usually saved for when Greg was mentioned. "Knew he'd come to a sticky end, used to tell your grandfather all the time. Gives me no pleasure that I was right."

Ed hesitated, but Sophie hadn't finished. "It's your capitalist friend," she said, betraying her left-wing roots. "Lomax, or whatever his name is." Smacking her lips, she pointed him to a plate covered in an old doily. "Chicken wings in there. Pass them over." As Ed produced the plate and took off the cover, Sophie eyed him. "Or is it Snodgrass?" she asked softly. "He's come back for a second bite of the cherry?"

"Looks that way," said Ed.

A huge snort erupted from her. "That little toe-rag, Greg. What the hell was he doing getting involved with the likes of Snodgrass?" Ed opened his mouth to protest, but Sophie was in no mood to be interrupted. "You seem to have forgotten that I knew Greg since he was the young tear-away your grandfather recruited as his farmhand. Just the sort of boy to take advantage of a girl when her defences are down." She'd moved onto her favourite topic, Alice and Greg's marriage. "Why she should have married such a one is beyond me."

"You said it yourself, she was vulnerable. I'd gone missing, presumed dead and I suppose Greg presented himself as the next in line."

A beady eye fixed him from out of her wizened face. "Greg never did anything unless there was something in it for him. I daresay he took an interest in Alice because she was useful to him at that moment. Sex and so forth."

Shaking his head, Ed took another sip of his brandy. "You've got it wrong…"

He was interrupted by a sharp sucking of teeth. "Just the same as your grandfather," she said contemptuously.

Sophie was becoming belligerent. Time to leave. But before he could stand, she leaned forward and grabbed his forearm, her voice less accusative. "Did Taid ever tell you about how he met Nain, your grandmother?"

Ed shook his head.

"Pity," she said reflectively. "She was raped, y'know. She was in service, working in a country house in West Wales when her employer took a fancy to her. I'm only telling you now because I've decided to investigate. You might think it's all in the past. He's dead and so is your grandmother, but I think I owe it to her and your Taid."

Ed said nothing so she leaned back in her chair and sighed. "You never know where these things might lead. Greg used to have dealings with Nain's people. Taid introduced them to him."

She stood and offered Ed more brandy, but he needed a clear head for the afternoon when he would be packing for Africa. Besides, he wasn't in the mood to hear her spitting acid about Greg, somebody she'd been completely one-eyed about since he was a small boy.

"You tell Alice she's welcome anytime," she said, realising that Ed was determined to leave.

These words were why he had visited and he was pleased that she'd repeated the offer. Although she was getting on in years, she was formidable. He remembered when she managed to "accidentally" touch Greg with a cattle prod and then stood on his face.

Ed had once asked her how she earned a living. "Social work," was her answer. Further questioning had elicited little more.

'She runs a charity,' was what Taid had said once. 'Her sister died at the hands of her own husband. I think she's into direct action, red hot pokers and the like.' He'd smiled, nervously.

"I'll collect your mail," Sophie called after him. "I'll put it in the plastic tub in my greenhouse."

Ed waved his thanks and set off up the path back to his own house.

Back in Lomax Township

As the Lomax Gold Mine service bus entered the outer conurbations of Lomax township, Ed's spirits were low; they always were after long and exhausting journeys. When he'd left this town a few short months ago, he'd been determined never to return. He'd sworn there was nothing that could drag him back, not even if they'd found a mound of gold sticking out of the ground.

He gazed at the teeming humanity that lined the long thoroughfare that led straight to the gates of Lomax Gold Mine. Many of the women wore bright colours, orange, blacks and yellows. They moved around in packs, babies pinioned tightly to their backs. Men congregated at the entrance to alleyways, gesticulating and shouting. A few wore the green uniform of the mine, but most were in t-shirts and shorts. And everywhere there were children, ducking in and out of alleyways.

He longed for the journey to stop so he could find somewhere quiet where he could have a shower and lie down. But he knew that when he arrived there would be the usual welcoming circus in which he would be expected to maintain a fixed smile of gigantic proportions that would make his face ache.

Shouts from his fellow bus passengers brought his attention back to the window. For several moments he wondered what was going on. Then he spotted, just ahead, the three-metre high razor-wire fence, watchtowers and vast wrought-iron gates of Lomax Gold Mine; journey's end.

The bus came to a sudden halt and people rose from their seats, gathering belongings. He waited until they'd all left before stepping from the bus onto the scorched brown earth. He smelt fly-struck meat broiling in the sunshine. Clenching his hands, he forced down the bile that was making its way into his parched mouth. He was back. James Allen had better not be exaggerating about this being a matter of life and death.

Retrieving his belongings from the bus driver, he turned and stared at a sign, 'Welcome to Lomax Gold Mine; a Lomax Enterprises Company'. It was hammered to the enormous wrought iron gate about one hundred metres from where he stood. Beneath its vast letters patrolled heavily armed men clad in khaki.

He remembered the sign from his last visit. Since then it had been repainted and a slogan added 'Every Gram Is Jam'. Smiling to himself, he hoisted his rucksack, wondering if the slogan was an elaborate joke, or an attempt by the new mine management to engender a corporate image. Almost certainly it was an idea of Miriam, wife of the new Mine Manager, who was Jam and Jerusalem to the core.

To get to the gate he would have to push his way through a large throng that had gathered to shop at a makeshift market, the source of the meat-smell. Dust rose in billows around the stalls, blown on a strong wind that caused tarpaulin to flap violently. Cyclists with bread in the front basket rode through the crowd shouting for trade, some followed by small children trying to insert sticks into their spokes. Voices were lifted to yells, competing to be heard amid blaring radios and beeping car horns. The entire crashing crescendo assaulted his ears and caused him to close his eyes.

Hunching his shoulders, he ignored the shouts, the attempts to drag him this way and that, and prepared to set off. Once he was inside the mine, he would be protected by guards and barbed wire, but right now he was in a no man's land, a westerner ripe for the picking.

He put down his head and stepped out of the shadow of the bus and was immediately hauled backwards as a taxi emblazoned with the slogan 'All Gods Condemned' rattled past, kicking up a cloud of billowing dust. His eyes stung and began to water, and he felt his throat contract as he swallowed a consignment of particulate matter.

It took him a while to realise that somebody was shouting his name, one voice amidst the many that rang above the tinny noise of the stallholders' radios. It came from a man, taller than the rest, who had pulled him to safety. With a feeling of trepidation, Ed blinked up through tear-stained lashes and found the dark brown eyes of Frank, his former driver, dressed with his usual sartorial elegance in an open-necked Hawaiian shirt.

Shaking hands so their fingers clicked, Frank evinced surprise at Ed's return. "Made me an offer I couldn't refuse," Ed wheezed. "And what about you? Still driving for the mine?"

A sad shake of the head. "They say I'm too lazy, never where I should be, always hiding." His face saddened and he bit his lip.

"There's a few notes if you can get me to the gates," said Ed, shoving yet another grasping hand off his shoulder. "I'll need a driver as well, but no promises."

Linking his arm around Ed's, Frank forced a hole through the enveloping crowd and shouted imprecations at anybody foolish enough to approach.

"Don't forget," he said on delivering Ed safely to the guard hut at the main gates.

Ed reached inside his shirt and produced several notes. "I'll see what I can do."

Frank nodded gratefully before walking back into the crowd.

Watching him go, Ed wondered how he earned a living now he wasn't a driver. Then, with a shrug of his shoulders, he turned and showed his papers to a guard and walked through into the comparative serenity beyond.

Behind the gates were rows of Toyota Land Cruisers parked higgledy-piggledy in a large car park. To his right were stairs that led up to a series of wooden offices linked by a communal balcony and with windows that stared down at the main gate. Beyond the car park were white, plaster-clad buildings with floor to ceiling windows and large verandas arrayed in ornate, black ironwork.

He remembered first arriving at this mine and being surprised to see period, colonial houses. He had subsequently learned that they had been built in the early twentieth century at around the same time as the main shaft, Lomax 'A' had been sunk. In those days, the mine was called 'Andrews' after the man who had discovered what the locals had known for many centuries, that this area was ripe with gold seams. After Independence, the mine had been renamed 'Strength through Progress' but there had been significant difficulties and eventually the Ghanaian government had decided to sell to Lucky Lomax, a London-based city tycoon.

Lomax and his henchmen had gone about their business in typical ruthless fashion and dragged the mine into the modern era. But the price had been high. "When you dance with the devil, the devil leads," as Allen had once said to him. "And Lomax couldn't give a stuff about the conditions in his mine or the polluted environment in which the miners and their families live. So long as he makes a good return, that's all that matters."

The note in his pocket said he was required to report to Engineering, in the white villa directly opposite. But he knew he was most likely to find Allen at the top of the stairs to his right. Without thinking, he found his feet climbing steps. On reaching the top he strode down the communal balcony wondering why half the rooms he passed were empty and dark.

On reaching the office in which he'd worked during his previous visit, he pressed his face to the window and cupped his hand over his eyes. The room hadn't been touched since he'd pulled the door shut several months ago. He saw his old desk at the far side of the room, still with its pen and pencil holder. Closest to the window was the desk that had belonged to Dave Smith. And to the left, set against the interior wall, was the desk that had belonged to Paul Forge, former head curator of drilling information.

Forge had been beaten to a pulp and airlifted back to Britain. Ed wondered what had happened to him, whether he'd survived or had succumbed to his injuries.

For several moments, Ed gazed at his desk with its collection of beautifully lacquered trilobites. Then, lifting his eyes to the wall, he saw shelves crammed with large, neatly-labelled volumes. This was the drilling data gathered by Forge during his thirty-year tenure as Head of Drilling in the mine. He'd jealously guarded each and every page so that the volumes had become known as 'Forge's Drilling'.

Letting his eyes linger, he marvelled at the array of trilobites that shared the shelves with Forge's Drilling. Their hard eyes glinted at him through the gloom, like miniscule guards daring him to approach and defile Forge's precious work.

Hoisting his rucksack higher on his back, he walked along the balcony to the next room. This had been Bismarck's office, a place that had been full of family pictures, holiday snaps, rock specimens, drill core, posters on the wall. But now, as he gazed through the window, he realised that the place had been stripped. Even the desks and chairs where Joe and Kwame had sat were missing.

The scene made him draw breath; he wondered why Forge's room had been spared but not Bismarck's? Both had been equally culpable as members of a syndicate that had sought to swindle Lomax Mine out of tens of millions of pounds. Presumably Kojo's offices had been stripped as well. Unlike Forge, both Kojo and Bismarck had escaped without a scratch and they'd taken at least half of the syndicate's money with them.

With a feeling of foreboding in his stomach's pit, he headed up a second flight of stairs. Here he was confronted by several more doors, the nearest with a sign saying 'Manager of Geology'. This had been one of Kojo's rooms. From behind this door, Kojo had ruled the geology section with the same benevolence as a father watching over his children.

On knocking and entering, Ed's eyes were blinded by the low light so that he could see only vague shadows cast against blank wooden walls. "'Tis yourself." The Irish American voice exploded across the gloomy silence. And then a man stood behind a large desk. "Coffee, Adzo, my love," he shouted, apparently to nobody, before moving into the light, revealing curling sandy hair, a grin with plenty of bright white teeth and twinkling, translucent brown eyes.

Instinctively, Ed stretched out his hand. Allen knocked it away and tried instead to give him a hug, but the rucksack prevented him. Unfazed, he stepped back and grabbed Ed's hand in two of his own and led him across to a chair. "Really appreciate you coming," he said. "I've been a bit stretched."

There was silence while Allen made his way back to his own seat. "How was your journey," he asked. "No accidents?"

"A few near misses," Ed replied with a smile.

"And Alice?"

"She's fine."

"I bet she wasn't too happy about you coming back here. Still, it's only for a month, and then you can go home and never darken my doorstep again."

Ed smiled, unconvinced. "What's so urgent?" he asked.

"Same old, same old," replied Allen. "We're still clearing up the mess from the last time."

"Any news on Kojo?"

Shaking his head, Allen seemed sad. "Nothing. The new Mine Manager ordered that his offices be cleared and he gave me the keys, but somehow I can't bring myself to move in. This was always Kojo's room, it's imbued with his presence."

"And what about Bismarck? Any news?"

"Nothing."

"But surely…" insisted Ed.

"They've both disappeared into thin air. Gone to earth. There's not a sniff. Lomax has had their families watched and all known associates have been questioned. He's even offered a reward of one hundred thousand US dollars for information leading to their arrest."

"So they must have left the country. Sunning themselves somewhere, drinking cocktails on the beach," said Ed.

"Not a chance," replied Allen. "Can you imagine Kojo doing that? The man lived for his work. I reckon both he and Bismarck are still here. Neither will be moving far from their families."

"And what about the money they stole? Any sign of that?"

A shake of the head. "I think that's what worries Lomax most."

"A few tens of millions? He can't be that worried, he's got a few more quid left in his back pocket."

"It's what it might be used to buy. Bismarck's a firebrand, he now has money, and he has Kojo who's former Manager of Geology, a first-class bureaucrat. Together they could be quite a formidable pairing." Leaning forward, Allen jabbed his finger on his desk, emphasising the point. "You can be as sceptical as you like, but Lomax is right, the miners' union and the Galamsey together are bad enough, but imagine if they had Bismarck's brains and Kojo's organisational ability, plus tens of millions of quid."

A booming silence filled the room as Allen sat back in his chair. A nearby door slammed; there was a sound of clicking high heels and the door to the office was thrown open letting in sunlight and hot tropical air. A woman in her mid-twenties with large gold earrings and a tight-fitting orange and black skirt walked noisily into the room carrying a tray. Immediately Allen and Ed jumped up. "Always a sight for sore eyes, and the coffee's welcome as well," Allen said taking the tray and winking at Ed.

"Welcome back," Adzo said to Ed. It was the first words she'd ever spoken to him. Then she proffered a cheek to be kissed before turning and walking out.

When the door closed, Ed picked up his cup. "Galamsey still causing trouble?" he asked. The Galamsey were illegal miners who lived in the jungle surrounding the mine. In the past, Allen had described them as African hillbillies, people who kept to the old ways and who spent much of their time waging a low-grade guerrilla war against Lomax mine.

Nodding, Allen sat back down at his desk. "Raiding the open pits, signs of voodoo magic everywhere, intimidation of the workforce." Ed took a sip of his coffee and remembered a time when, not so long ago, he and Allen had stood on a hill overlooking the mine and watched five hundred Galamsey invade one of the open pits, carrying off large sacks of gold ore. Mine militia had arrived and opened fire.

"And the miners' union, what of them?"

Allen screwed up his face and for the first time looked genuinely angry. "There's been wholesale sackings. Anybody suspected of union membership, or in any way associated with Kojo or Bismarck have gone. That means most of the geology section. I've been left with a few raw recruits. It happened after I was sent half way 'round the world to Papua New Guinea so I could interview some geologists Lomax was keen to employ."

"But that's crazy," replied Ed.

"That's Lomax," said Allen. "It's in revenge. He suspects that Bismarck, Kojo and the union, were 'consorting with his business enemy, Snodgrass, to bring shame and ruin on his organisation'. At least, that's what he says; whether he believes it or not is another matter."

"And what's been the reaction?"

"Too early to say. Lomax gave the order a week ago, around the same time as I got in contact with you. I've only just got back. From what I hear they were given thirty minutes to clear their desks and they were then escorted off the premises with an AK-47 jabbed in their back."

He slurped his coffee and put it down on the desk. "Brutal," he said.

"Why don't you resign?"

Pushing his head back so he could look at the ceiling,

Allen gave the impression that he was on the verge of saying something unguarded. Then he suddenly whipped forward and rested his elbows on the table, beckoning Ed toward him. "I'll tell you," he said in faint whisper, "but not here and not now." He lifted his eyes to the wall behind Ed's head, nodded and then leant back again. He began to speak in a normal voice. "I told Lomax I was only prepared to work if he reinstated some of the men. I've submitted my list and he's thinking about it. At the very minimum we'll need men who can take over running the geology section. I'm not going to stay as Manager of Geology for very long and you're here on a month-long rolling contract. We need Joe and Kwame at the very least, individuals who can take over when we're not here."

Neither man spoke for a moment. Ed took the opportunity of changing the conversation. "Went past Forge's old office on the way up here," he said.

"Yours now," said Allen.

"Always Forge's," Ed corrected him. "I'm not going to change a thing. I quite like the trilobites."

Allen nodded, waiting.

"Is he dead?"

"Yes," said Allen. "He died in some London hospital."

"And I'm guessing he died with his secrets intact?"

Another curt nod from Allen, and this time he pursed his lips.

"So it's important that nothing in his office is disturbed," said Ed. "Probably best to treat it as a crime scene."

Shrugging his shoulders, Allen got to his feet. "That's for you to decide." He looked at his watch. "I gotta get goin'. I'm meeting the new Mine Manager in ten minutes. I'll organise a car to get you back to the compound."

"I saw Frank at the gate," said Ed, refusing to stand.

"Who's Frank?"

"The man who drove me last time. You remember? Gold jewellery and Hawaiian shirts?"

"What about him?"

"He's been sacked. I said I needed a driver and I'd put in a good word."

Frowning, Allen moved to the door. "If he's the man I'm thinking about you've no chance. He was using company vehicles to run a taxi service around town. Never there when you wanted him. They also reckon he was running messages for the union."

"Shame," replied Ed.

"I'll ask the Mine Manager. See what he says," said Allen, then opened the door to the office and let them both out. "The meeting'll be no more than an hour. I'll pop along to the compound later for a drink and a bite to eat, discuss what you'll be doing."

"What about these men from Papua New Guinea?" asked Ed, not wanting to leave while Allen was still so talkative. "The ones you were meeting when you called me?"

"Billy's good, but Brett's barely more than a bushwacker. Lomax's idea, God knows where he dug them up. But he was adamant that these were what we needed. I have me doubts. They'll be coming tomorrow. Billy'll work with you and I think we'll send Brett out to Chiri's exploration department."

Chiri, the Exploration Manager was a power in the mine, as Ed recollected only too well from his last visit. Sullen and aggressive, he had a number of followers (acolytes) who accompanied him everywhere and did his bidding. He made Ed extremely nervous.

"Is that a good idea?" he asked.

"There's nobody keeping an eye on Chiri anymore, not

since I was made Manager of Geology and moved to the gatehouse. Brett seems to have all the attributes necessary."

"What d'you mean?"

Allen gave a huge beaming smile. "Wait 'til you meet him. Believe me you won't want him 'round here."

They moved off down the stairs together and reached the landing with Forge's old office. As they walked, Allen whispered to Ed, "I was delighted when you agreed to come back, can't tell you how pleased."

They stopped by Forge's office window and looked in. "Hadn't much choice, really," said Ed.

For a moment they gazed at the files and gleaming lacquered trilobites lined up across the entire width of the room. "I knew I'd never get any peace until this whole thing is resolved once and for all."

"What d'you mean?"

"Trilobites on my mind all the time," Ed said nodding at the winking fossils. "I see them everywhere. And it's not because I'm getting a fixation like Forge. They turn up at my house on the gate posts, arrive in boxes at the door, in the glove box of my car. I've collected twenty in total, all left in places which I would consider private."

He turned to look at Allen. "I came because I'm being watched all the time and somebody is trying hard to scare me. I've tried lying low so I can catch them in the act but I've never succeeded."

Allen's face was a picture of shock.

"Must be somebody who knows the significance of trilobites, linked to Lomax Mine in some way..." He stopped and gave Allen a piercing glance. "It's not a ruse by Lomax to get me back here is it?"

Allen shook his head vigorously. "Snodgrass's lot? Doesn't make any sense, though," he continued. "Why would he be sending people after you to surreptitiously give you trilobites?"

"Maybe he thinks I'm unfinished business. Softening me up. After all, I switched Forge's trilobites so Lomax got the correct ones. Or had you forgotten." He turned and made his way along the wooden balcony toward the steps that would get them down into the car park close to the gates.

"But the trilobites you gave Lomax didn't work either," insisted Allen following in his wake. "They're still in that shop window and nobody has enquired about them let alone claimed them. We're still no further forward in knowing what Forge did with his share of the money."

"Does Snodgrass know that?" asked Ed.

"I don't know," said Allen. "I suppose these things get around, on the grapevine. He probably does know, yes."

"Well, why is he ordering somebody to leave trilobites around my little farm?"

They'd reached the bottom of the steps by now and Allen was looking around for an available driver to take Ed to the compound. On the far side was a smart white pickup; he walked across and rapped on the window to wake the sleeping driver, then he pulled Ed aside.

"So you think you can stop the trilobites arriving by doing something here?" he asked.

Ed shrugged. "I'm less likely to get my throat cut one night," he said. "And also, your phone call was so urgent, I thought it and the trilobites must be related."

"No," replied Allen softly. He fidgeted with his hands as if he was nervous. Then he realised what he was doing and put them by his sides. "And what about Alice, is she in danger?"

"I don't think so," said Ed, rubbing his chin. "But I've made arrangements, just in case."

By now the driver had loaded Ed's bag into the pickup and was waiting for him to get into the passenger seat.

"Are you going to tell me why you thought it was urgent for me to return?" he asked Allen. "I've told you why I decided to come back."

But Allen had turned his back and was walking away. "It'll soon become obvious," he said. "You'll have to trust me for now."

The Faces at the Compound

As the driver made ready to leave, Ed traced the route to the contractors' compound in his head. He envisaged dusty-dry soil, rutted roads, neighbourhoods of rusted corrugated iron shacks, children playing chicken with passing vehicles. High on the hill overlooking the town stood large villas with high walls, the glass of innumerable windows glinting in the strong tropical heat. These were the scenes he associated with Lomax township, a place where the very poor and the very rich lived cheek by jowl.

But as they left the car park, the driver avoided turning through the main mine gates and into town; instead he turned right and headed into the surface mine. Ed recollected that there was an easy route through the mine which involved a shortcut through the golf course and a detour around Lomax 'A' shaft. But the driver zoomed straight past the golf course turn off and headed for the open pits.

Ed was surprised; he recollected Frank saying that the drivers generally avoided the surface mine where the movement of vast haulpaks, the size of small houses, kicked up dust and were driven with a reckless abandon. As they drew near, Ed saw a vast parking area full of huge haulpaks.

"The open pits have just blasted," explained the driver.

"They are waiting for the militia to give the all clear before they set off."

Ed nodded his understanding; he knew the all clear meant that the militia had checked and there was no Galamsey raiding the pits to steal visible gold. "It'll be nice to see the mine again," he said. It would add an extra twenty or thirty minutes to the journey, but Ed didn't mind much.

As the pickup crested a rise and the complex of huge holes that marked the Lomax surface operation materialised before his eyes, the vastness of the scene overwhelmed him. His first glimpse of this two-kilometre wide zone of devastation had been with Bismarck, and that journey came back to his mind. Bismarck had been proud to show off this most visible evidence of the mine's industriousness. But at that time, Ed's imagination had been unable to cope with the enormity of what he was seeing through the windscreen. And during his time away from the mine, he'd somehow buried this ruined and eaten landscape in a part of his sub-conscious where he kept things he couldn't quite comprehend. That familiar griping sensation returned to his stomach, the one that he experienced whenever he realised the immensity of what he was up against. How could he, Edryd Evans, a boy from the back streets of Garston, possibly influence an organisation like Lomax Gold Mine which had enough resources to demolish an entire mountain range.

They plunged down the other side of the rise at breakneck speed, jolting Ed's already-tensed stomach. He shut his eyes as the pickup skirted the edge of sheer drops, kicking up dust from the roadway and causing pebbles to fly away into the abyss. Occasionally they passed blue armoured scout cars carrying heavily armed men in mine fatigues.

After climbing to the highest point of the surface mine and pausing to look over the edge of the largest pit, Ed spotted the frame of the Lomax 'A' winding tower and its concentrically arranged collection of small wooden offices. He'd been underground with Bismarck when the shaft had been put out of operation by a massive explosion. It had taken them many hours to get back to the surface, an experience Ed was unlikely to forget. However, the wheel atop the tower was spinning again. Ed gesticulated excitedly, "Is the shaft in operation?"

The driver nodded but did not care to elaborate.

As they passed through screens of trees that separated the surface mine from the shaft, a series of scaffold terraces came into view, that climbed toward a new double decker cage suspended within the A frame. A sign that advertised 'Quality Underground Mine Transport' was plastered across huge metal fencing. Here too there were armed guards, but they were without the hard stares and fixed, determined faces of those they'd encountered in the surface mine.

They zoomed past guards who lurked at the 'Lomax A' mine gates and rocketed into the streets of Lomax shanty town with its tin can and mud brick houses. Pretty soon the contractors' compound came into view, its modern concrete façade, grassed lawns and spreading tropical hardwood trees an oasis of luxury in the grinding poverty.

"Tomorrow morning, eight o'clock," said Ed when the driver dropped him in the car park. He slammed the door on the frigid air conditioning and turned his back so he could run his eyes over the familiar geography of the compound.

To his right, along a short gravelled path, was the sprawling, white-washed accommodation block where each room was a carbon copy of the next; two small windows, an air conditioning unit, narrow beds with a hook for a mosquito net, TV with no reception, a long, thin bathroom with a shower that trickled rather than sprayed. He felt the now-familiar tightening of his stomach as he pictured the plush red carpet and the large polished wardrobes; utilitarian decor that was miles away from the shabby, welcoming interior of his kitchen and living room at home.

In front of him, on the far side of a manicured lawn, beneath a gazebo strung with globe lights, was the bar. Several men in white shirts were hard at work sweeping the concrete floor, wiping tables or polishing glasses, getting ready for when the contractors finished their day and this place would become a hive of activity.

Turning to his left, he pushed open glass doors and entered a wood panelled room dominated by a large desk where a man bent over a book. Behind him, standing respectfully to one side, was Moonlight, one of the compound staff. Her face broke into a smile full of bright, white teeth. "Mr Evans," she said, "Welcome back. We got confirmation of your stay this morning."

The man turned and fixed him with penetrating blue eyes; it was clear that he knew Ed and was not pleased to see him back. Ed reached into his memory to find a name. "Bill?" he asked.

"Peter," came the reply. He turned his back and completed signing off something in the diary before walking out. As he passed, he looked away, like Ed had some kind of unmentionable disease. Ed watched him go, trying to catch him in his memory, seeing the same deep blue eyes and curly brown hair conversing with Forge at the golf club bar in the mine.

Shrugging his shoulders, he turned to Moonlight who was waiting respectfully behind the desk, beaming from ear to ear. Throughout his previous stay, Moonlight had waited at the tables in the dining room, silent as the grave and about as attentive. "You're in room 42," she said in a high pitched squeaky voice, producing a key from behind her desk.

But before Ed could receive the key, a man appeared from a door in the far wall and took it. Ed hesitated, he could probably find his own way to room 42 and he only had a small rucksack for luggage. The man gestured urgently for Ed to hand across his rucksack; DIY at the compound was not optional, everything had to be done by the staff or not at all, and of course the staff required tips.

After being led to his room, across the plush lawn, through glass double doors and down a dark corridor, Ed sat on his bed thinking of Peter's strange reaction. Maybe he'd been offended at being called Bill, it had been a mistake to guess the name. Or perhaps there was an entirely different reason for Peter's hostility, such as the death of Forge. In mines like Lomax where men had nothing better to do but drink the night away, fiction very quickly becomes fact.

Sighing, he unpacked his meagre possessions and worried about what Peter's reaction might mean for the rest of his stay.

After a quick trickle shower, he wandered around his room feeling the cooling touch of water on his skin, thinking that his fair complexion was too sensitive for the heavy duty climate of Africa. Lying on his bed, looking up at the ceiling, his thoughts turned to Allen. Allen the outcast who went out of his way to ensure he was treated differently, even going so far as to spread rumours about himself. 'No imagination,' he'd said of the men who inhabited the compound bar. 'They've an inability to see further than the next beer.'

And it was true, many of the men who inhabited the bar were dull; outcasts from large mining companies, victims of the hire and fire culture that they determinedly espoused at every opportunity; free marketers every one of them. They were nevertheless resentful of the men who had sacked them on the grounds of efficiency and corporate governance, blaming the people rather than the system for the shoddy way in which they'd been fired. Lomax represented their best offer of work, six months' contracts with money paid direct into tax-free offshore accounts to help maintain the school fees and hefty London mortgages.

It was time to head to the bar to meet Allen; he was looking forward to questioning him again. When they'd been together in the office, Allen had been on the verge of telling him something important, something about why he'd rung from PNG with a voice that had been edged with panic.

Presumably Allen's panic was because of the purge of the union and the ensuing chaos that was bound to occur. He'd rung Ed because he needed somebody he could trust, who was known around Lomax; a safe pair of hands. The likes of Peter would always be watching for an opportunity to slip the knife into Allen's ribs and Allen would need somebody to watch his back.

But the more Ed thought about it the less likely this theory seemed. At the time of the 'phone call Allen could not have realised that the union members had been marched off site, and if he had known what Lomax was planning surely he would have mentioned it to Ed during the phone conversation.

He needed to confront Allen, ask him exactly why he had so desperately wanted Ed to return. Dressing quickly, he let himself out of his room and down the deserted corridor, out into the tropical evening of the compound gardens and its open-air bar. He paused to admire an array of orchids that grew close to the razor wire fence defining the perimeter. Tiny hummingbirds flitted around between the large blooms, their wings a blur of motion. In the fading light, their delicate dance brought to mind fairies in a magical garden. For a precious moment the knot in his stomach relaxed and he felt glad that the long journey from his home was at an end. In his mind, he ticked a box which said 'back to farmhouse in one month', and then continued his walk across the compound gardens.

Looking around, he recognised faces from his last visit, all of them engineering contractors, like Peter. They looked right through him as he walked past, as if he was some phantasm. Approaching the counter and ordering a beer, he looked back and noticed that they had all put their heads together. He didn't want to know what they were saying about him, their blank stares said everything he needed to know.

Shoving down his annoyance, he turned to the barman who gave him a big beaming smile. "Welcome back, Mr Evans."

Somebody pleased to see him. "Thank you Jimmy, bottle of the best Ghanaian."

Allen appeared at his shoulder and winked at the barman. "What did you call them fellas?" he said indicating the group of engineers who had blanked Ed.

"The Faces," replied Ed taking a swig of his beer.

He chortled. "That's right, 'cos you could never tell any of them apart."

"They seem more hostile than I remember," Ed commented.

"You were never very popular. Too stand-offish."

"And too friendly with you," Ed reminded him. "So what's the story? They're looking at me like I was a criminal."

The barman arrived with their beers and levered off the

tops. Only when he'd gone did Allen speak. "Many of them find it difficult to believe Forge would do anything wrong. There are loads of rumours suggestin' that you and Forge had a feud and that you trumped up charges against him. It's why you left so quickly, 'cos you were part of the gang who attacked him. The best one I heard was that you hijacked Lomax's helicopter and flew to Liberia where you are now shacked up with a couple of seamstresses." He sniggered and then took a swig of his beer.

"And I daresay you never bother to correct them," replied Ed.

"On the contrary, if anybody asks me I tell them that you were responsible for unmasking a conspiracy involving Bismarck, Kojo and Forge and that when the job was done you lost no time in getting off home to your quiet farmhouse. But I'm afraid that doesn't really satisfy their craving."

The light had faded so that the bar was now in darkness. Far off they could hear a sclerotic cough as a generator was cranked to start, then a full-throated roar, settling to a constant rhythmic rattle. Above them, globes strung on ropes started to emit a sickly glow.

As they drank, a group of men who Ed didn't recognise arrived in the bar. He watched as they approached the counter and ordered beer in unmistakeably Australian voices. Most had the paunchy look of heavy beer drinkers, except for one who was tall and lean, like an athlete, a mop of curly blond hair lying carelessly across one eye.

"Australian drillers," said Allen quietly. "Emergency deployment from one of Lomax's mines in northern Queensland."

"What's the emergency?"

"He's sacked all the drillers for being in the union. Madness."

For a moment they gazed in silence, watching the drillers as they wandered to an empty table and sat down. They were instantly joined by a group of women from the town.

Smirking, Allen turned to Ed. "Didn't take long."

"Are you going to tell me?" Ed asked suddenly.

"Tell you what?"

"About exactly why you haven't resigned. You said you would tell me. You got all conspiratorial."

"It's quite simple, Lomax said he would reconsider employing some of the staff, the ones who were closely associated with Bismarck and Kojo; to give me something to work with."

Ignoring Ed's stare, Allen ploughed on. "And one of the things he promised was that Forge's room would be left in one piece until I'd been able to properly investigate. But I don't have the time to do it myself, which is why I insisted he employ you. I need somebody I can trust to go through all those drilling volumes and find out what he's hidden."

"That's not what you implied in your phone call," said Ed. "And earlier, in your office, you came over all shifty."

For a moment, doubt entered Allen's eyes and then he smiled. "I've told you before, I'm Lomax's man."

Ed wanted to ask why he was Lomax's man but he knew the response would be the first bullshit answer that came to Allen's mind. Rumours abounded throughout the mine about Allen's past, including that he was a terrorist, an arsonist, a thief and a bankrupt. Most of these stories had been put about by Allen himself. Only Lomax knew which, if any, were true, and he wasn't saying.

"So what d'you expect me to find in those volumes?"

"Forge was more of an accountant than a scientist," replied Allen wiping some excess beer from his upper lip. "Everything had to be neat, lined up in rows. You and I know that's not how nature works. I want you to find strangeness and follow where it leads. You should go underground, do a bit of geology, satisfy yourself that everything adds up."

"And what if it doesn't?"

"Come and show it to me."

"And what if it all looks fine?"

Allen pursed his lips. "I'm willing to bet there'll be something. For the last twenty years Forge had an iron grip on the drilling department and made sure nobody had access. We'd be irresponsible if we didn't check what he'd been doin' all that time." He took a swig of his beer and then placed it carefully on the table. "Particularly when we have evidence about the extent of his dishonesty."

Allen looked around to make sure nobody was overhearing. He gazed at the drillers and their seamstresses, then at the bar and finally at the compound dining room. Then coming forward again, he whispered, "The money he stole never did turn up and Forge didn't say anything before he died. Lomax is keen that you search. You're the person who worked with Forge most and knew his horrid little ways. You're the person best placed to work out what he did."

"There's a lot of files," said Ed, trying to make sure Allen had realistic expectations. "It'll take longer than a month to go through them all."

But Allen waved his hands at Ed's doubts, as if he was waving away flies. "You'll have Billy as an assistant. I've met him and I think he's exactly what we need. He's meticulous. Joe'll be with you as well. Joe's a Ghanaian, he's a good guy. Lomax sacked him because he used to share an office with Bismarck, but his loyalties are elsewhere."

"You mean he's not a union man?" Ed found it difficult to believe that anybody could share an office with Bismarck and not come under his influence.

"He is a union member," Allen said with a nod of his head, "but he's well connected. Lomax must realise he's made a mistake by sacking him. I think we'll be able to get him back. He'll be destined for great things, perhaps not a Mine Manager, too much of an academic, but certainly Head of Research."

"So that's why you were so desperate to get me back here," said Ed. "Because you need somebody to audit the drilling. It sounded much more urgent on the phone, like I was in imminent danger of death."

Allen smiled mischievously. "Perhaps I did lay it on a bit thick, but I knew you wouldn't come unless I made it sound convincing. Anyway," he said dismissively, waving a hand, "you're here now and that's all that matters."

Biting back a retort of frustration and annoyance Ed took a sip of beer. Perhaps Allen was right, it was important to establish what Forge had been up to for all those years. After all, the tens of millions he'd managed to embezzle from the mine with Kojo and Bismarck might just be the tip of the iceberg.

Finishing his beer, Allen rose from his seat and shook Ed's hand. "Thanks for coming," he said. "Got to get back to my house, early start tomorrow. We'll have a meal some time when Billy arrives from PNG."

He made his way through the tables and the assembled Faces, nodding his head at one or two, ignoring most others. Then he was out into the night, beyond the weak beam of the globes. Ed rose as well and decided to head for bed, walking around the edge of the gazebo, avoiding the knots of Faces.

The night was still, and but for the constant rumble of the generator it would also have been silent. Whether the hummingbirds continued their hunt for tropical blooms in the blackness Ed couldn't say, but the smell from the orchids was just as pungent as during the day.

As he wandered along the crunching gravel path, near to the car park, a hiss sounded in the darkness. His foot hovered in mid-air, fearful that he was about to stand on one of the local poisonous snakes. But the hiss stopped immediately and was replaced by the whispered sound of a voice. "Hey," it said.

Looking around in the darkness, Ed could see nothing, just the outline of flowerbeds and shrubs. He'd been surprised by a voice emanating from shadow once before, very close to this exact spot. On that occasion, it had been one of the seamstresses who inhabited the compound bar. She'd wanted to sell him one of Forge's trilobites. It was this incident that had set him on a search for trilobites, and which had ultimately led to the unravelling of a conspiracy.

"Hello?" he said.

"Mr Kojo sends you a message," said the voice. "You should leave this place. You should finish your business and be gone within five days. Beyond that he will not be responsible for the consequences."

"How is he?" Ed asked. "I would like to speak with him. Please tell him."

There was no answer.

"Please tell him I would like to speak with him, tell him that I am trying to get his old geology section restored." He made sure he sounded out his words so there could be no misunderstanding

Silence.

For the next few minutes Ed blundered around in the dark trying to locate where the man might be hiding. But he was too well hidden, or more likely he had already gone.

Standing, frustrated, gazing into the blackness, he wondered if he'd just had a waking dream. A simple message recounted by a spirit of the bushes who had turned into a hummingbird and flown away.

Billy Barker Arrives

Billy turned out to be several years older than Ed; a small man with a mop of curly, ginger hair and tiny, round glasses which were held together with sellotape. When he arrived in the office unannounced, he looked down at Ed's outstretched hand and then risked a suspicious glance at him before finally agreeing to be touched. "Thanks very much," he said for no obvious reason.

To Ed's surprise, Billy spoke with a slight Liverpool accent. It was subtle, and few who worked in the world of mining would have placed the flattened vowel sounds. Ed indicated that he should sit at one of the two desks occupying either end of the room.

Blinking, Billy looked around and then walked to the desk furthest from the window, the one Ed had once occupied. His metal-toed boots stuck out of the enveloping flesh of his khaki trousers like a nascent toe. And the heavy cotton of his shirt hung like sack cloth from his shoulders. Ed was forcibly reminded of a small woodland animal walking warily into a glade.

He wordlessly placed his rucksack on the floor and then turned to look at the shelves. His glasses gleamed from the bright lights of the windows. He blinked again, like a miner emerging from long hours down a hole, then he shuffled toward them. "D'you mind?" he asked, picking up one of the shelf trilobites.

"Be my guest, they're not mine, they belonged to Paul Forge, previous occupant of this office."

Reassured, he pushed his glasses back onto his head in order to take a closer look. "Glasses useless for close work," he mumbled in explanation, examining the specimen in detail before putting it back on the shelf and returning the glasses to his eyes. "Quite a collection," he said looking the shelves up and down. "Forge was clearly passionate about his fossils."

"Forge was an obsessive," Ed said dismissively.

"Aren't we all?" he replied walking back to his desk and sitting down. "One man's passion is another's obsession. I've been called an obsessive, many times." Then, pulling his rucksack toward him he rummaged around inside one of the side pockets and produced a packet of wipes, pulled one carefully from the plastic wrapper and began polishing his glasses. He extracted a small box from the same pocket and placed the used tissue within, clipping the lid firmly into place.

"I tend to chew on a pipe," he said eventually. "Hope you don't mind. Helps me concentrate. Don't smoke anymore of course." He produced an old-fashioned walnut pipe from the other rucksack pocket and stuck it in his mouth where it rattled around for a few seconds. "Stopped smoking many years ago," he said through his teeth, "but I find I need to do something with my mouth. Chewing is a disgusting habit and boiled sweets rots me teeth." He removed the pipe. "Tell me if it annoys you and I'll tuck it away."

"I'm sure it'll do just fine," said Ed. "Has James Allen briefed you about what you'll be doing here?"

"He said something about putting the drilling in order."

"That's right, this drilling," said Ed waving his arms at

the rows of files lining the wall. "There's thirty years' worth of drilling records here with full chemical analysis."

"Just you and me?" he asked. "Or will we be having assistance from Brett for instance, the guy I usually work with?"

"'Fraid not, he's detailed to work with Chiri over at Exploration."

Billy leapt to his feet and gave a shrill giggle. "Tell me what we're going to do then, in more detail."

"Did Allen not tell you when he came out to see you in PNG?" asked Ed. He was surprised at Billy's reaction to the news that his partner would be working elsewhere, he'd expected a complaint, maybe an attempt at haggling.

Shaking his head, Billy smiled. "He was very vague, and to tell you the truth I was so glad to get out that I never stopped to ask about details. He said something about a man named Paul Forge and putting drilling in order, tracing through a chronology."

"That's right," said Ed. "We need to audit the drilling and establish what's missing and what may have been hidden. I think the best approach will be to start right at the beginning. Find the earliest possible drill hole and establish what decisions were made at the time and where they might have drilled next as a result. Make our way step by step."

"Why?"

Ed narrowed his brows, perplexed that Billy should question him. "Because we're looking for where and when Forge might have acted dishonestly."

A strange sound like water passing through a plughole emanated from Billy's pipe. "Wouldn't that be something of a waste of time? I mean, surely it'll become obvious as we work through."

"Go on," said Ed, folding his arms.

Eyes glittering, Billy leaned forward. "Allen says there's

only a simple engineering model for this mine. It's so rich in gold there's never been the impetus to do anything more imaginative."

"What's your point?"

Walking around his desk Billy approached him. "Allen tells me that the richest seams are worked out and that they're all a bit clueless about where to look next. That the only idea they've got is to go deeper, and that's really expensive. We could build a scientific model using all of this data, we could find places they've missed and at the same time discover where Forge might have deceived them."

"That's not what we've been asked to do," said Ed cautiously. "What you're proposing is something far more extensive…"

"Not at all," said Billy, interrupting Ed in his enthusiasm. "Don't you see, we'll be doing what we've been employed to do and much, much more." For the first time Billy looked him full in the face, then blinked and went slightly pink. "I'm not going back to PNG, never, never. And I'm never going to work with Brett again." He paused and combed his hair with his fingers, looking away. "I need this job to work. This is my big chance and I'm not going to mess up." He leaned away from Ed and went back to his desk, all the time sucking on his pipe. He dipped into his package of wet tissues, wiped his glasses, placed the waste in the plastic box, closing the lid with a click.

"Tell me about Brett," Ed asked in a quiet voice that barely carried above the sound of the air conditioner. He was unused to people he met being so forthcoming so early. Usually there was some kind of fan dance, a probing of the other person's attitudes and abilities. In Lomax, knowledge of a person meant you had power over them. In some quarters – and here the Faces at the compound came into his mind – the gush of information emanating from Billy's lips would be tantamount to admitting weakness.

Billy seemed to realise his mistake in giving away too much too early. Sitting down he shook his head, and for the next few minutes the office reverberated to the strange sucking of his pipe. In time Ed would come to recognise this noise as the weather barometer of Billy's mood. Fast and sharp for anxiety, slow and long for pleasure, with a myriad of different rhythms and notes for all the shades of humour between.

For the rest of the day the two men looked through the large drilling volumes so they could get used to the way in which Forge had curated the data. Each mine had its own methodology and it took a newcomer some time to decipher the method for encoding information. They rarely spoke except to discuss the meaning of different hieroglyphs or about the location of a particular drill hole.

By the end of several hours, both agreed that they needed somebody who was familiar with the conventions of the mine in order to interpret what the different numbers and acronyms meant. "But Lomax has sacked them all," explained Ed. "Let's hope that Allen is successful in persuading him to re-employ Joe, otherwise it'll take forever to put all this together."

A sharp rap on the window caused both of them to turn. A tall man in a Hawaiian shirt with a large chunky medallion on his chest stood outside. In his right hand there dangled a set of keys and on his face was a big beaming smile. Billy looked alarmed at the apparition, he retreated to his desk and sat down. Smiling, Ed crossed to the door and beckoned Frank across the threshold.

"My orders are to take Mr Billy Barker to the compound first," said Frank, "then take Mr Evans up to see the Mine Manager."

Billy grabbed his large rucksack and hoisted it onto his back, waving Frank away when he tried to take it from him, and walked out of the door. Watching them both disappear down the steps and get into the waiting pickup Ed was left to ponder his first meeting with Billy. The word for him was incongruous. He belonged in the research faculty of a university, or the scientific civil service, somewhere he would be free to be as eccentric as he liked. In all the gold mines at which Ed had worked none but a very few had ever put mental curiosity at the forefront, beyond the pursuit of making money. Perhaps this was why Lomax had instructed Allen to go half the way around the world to interview him.

The Mine Management

Frank took an hour to drop Billy, and by the time he returned, his beaming smile had been dropped in favour of a sombre, professional face. "I have the job on Mr Allen's say so," he said.

"Well, don't be running a taxi service," said Ed climbing into the cab, "or we'll both be in the deep shit."

Nodding his head and curving the edges of his mouth upward, Frank kicked the pickup into reverse, turned the wheel and bounced out of the car park. There was only one main road artery in this part of the mine and it led inexorably toward the Mine Manager's residence. It was flanked by Engineering plus some other significant buildings that acted as accommodation for permanently employed staff. Various sub-arteries split off, the first to the mine hospital, the next to the golf course, the third to the open cast pits and a fourth that headed off to the west, presumably to skirt the western boundary of the mine.

At this fourth junction, the main road started to climb up the steep hill to where the Mine Manager's residence commanded views across the rugged coastal range. On clear days, the sea could be glimpsed, on one memorable occasion on his last trip Ed had even heard it far off. Atop the hill the temperature was lower than around the other mine buildings because a constant breeze acted as an evaporative air conditioner. If it was not for the glimpse of the A frame and shanty town far below you could be in southern England on one of those hot summer days when the wind blows strong from the south.

As they began climbing the jungle–clad slopes of the hill, Ed remembered the first time he had taken the road, when he'd been summoned to meet Jeremy, Lomax's Head of African Operations, to give a report on how far the investigation into Greg's disappearance had progressed. Jeremy had shouted a lot, been thoroughly obnoxious in the way of a badly-behaved over-bred spaniel. His attitude made Ed clam-up, refusing to divulge any of his half-digested thoughts and surmises. Which was fortunate, because Jeremy turned out to be the prime mover behind Forge's conspiracy.

Jeremy had assumed control of the mine soon after this meeting, a position he had held until the conspiracy had been unveiled and Lomax had acted. Since then, the mine had been managed by John Price, the old Chief Engineer, a man who was notable for having a wife who was far more charismatic than himself.

Emerging out of the jungle, a vista of well-cut lawns and beautifully maintained flower beds came into view. In the middle of this picture of sylvan beauty was a three-storey colonial-style villa with wrap-around verandas and cream-coloured, clap-board cladding. A woman stood on the ground floor veranda leaning on an ornate, black railing, looking out at staff who were working on one of the flowerbeds. She turned her head at the sound of the vehicle approaching.

There was no other word for Miriam, except formidable. As she walked toward him, long pleated dress flowing in the wind, she looked like a Valkyrie floating across the Rhine. But Miriam was from Northern Ireland, not

Germany, a handsome woman in her sixties.

When they'd last met she'd occupied one of the villas at the foot of the hill, surrounded by tasteful silk and lace decorations, mistress of everything she surveyed. As the wife of the Chief Engineer to the mine it was known that she had considerable influence over everything from employment policy to the design of new buildings. Now her husband had been promoted to Mine Manager her opinion on anything that mattered would be unassailable.

Her smile was ingratiating as she lifted her hand in greeting, her arm streaming with flowing silk. "Mr Evans, how nice to see you again."

Resisting the urge to bow and swear fealty, Ed took her hand somewhere around chin height and gave a quick shake. "Thank you," he said. "I've come to see the Mine Manager. Is he in?"

"I believe he's in the drawing room talking to some people in London. He won't be long."

She took him by the arm and walked him away from the house into the garden. "I'm glad I've got a few moments with you," she confided. "James Allen has been up here asking for some union people to be reinstated. John is considering his request but I think he's rather unsure about what to do. What's your thoughts on the matter?"

"I think we need to reinstate as many as possible."

"Really?" She answered, shock on her handsome face. "Won't that mean reintroducing trouble?"

"No, I don't believe so. In any case, we can't run the place without them. I've just been looking through all the old drilling and neither I nor the new man, Billy, can make head or tail of it. Forge made everything as hard as possible to understand. We need people with local knowledge."

"I suppose you're right Mr Evans. The real intention of the mass sackings was to separate the wheat from the chaff.

John always intended to re-employ the best of them afterwards."

"Allen seemed to think the policy of sacking came direct from Lomax," said Ed.

"Well, he was certainly in favour, or at least he didn't resist very much. 'On your head be it', was what he said in the meeting."

Miriam decided that she'd had enough of talking about mundane matters. "How is Alice?" she asked. On one of their previous meetings Ed had been pressured to name a partner, his mind had gone blank and he'd blurted out, 'Alice' as the first name that entered his head.

"She's a nurse I think you said. You should make an honest woman of her, and then bring her out here."

Smiling, Ed nodded his agreement but privately thought that Lomax Gold Mine would be the last place on earth Alice would think of living. But he was saved the bother of replying because Miriam had changed the direction of the conversation again, back to James Allen.

"I can't tell you how surprised I was when Lomax promoted James Allen. Of course, John protested about Allen's promotion, but Lomax wouldn't change his mind. And then he's brought in these new people from Indonesia or somewhere. What are they like, Mr Evans?"

"I've only met one of them. He seems like a good man. Very pleased to be here and not PNG."

"It was a most unusual appointment," continued Miriam. "We were only told yesterday that two new people would be arriving. There was no vetting or interview, I can tell you that John is quite upset. That's why he's on the phone now, trying to find out what's going on and who these men are."

"Allen said he flew out there to interview them, on Lomax's orders…"

"So he said," interrupted Miriam. "But one can never tell with James Allen. He's demanded the reinstatement of all the geology section, despite knowing that they were heavily infiltrated by those Trotskyiite revolutionaries. I'm not ashamed to say that I'm suspicious of his motives and I want to know about these men he's importing from PNG. You know my theory about James Allen…"

But before she could march down the well-worn path of her belief that James Allen was a former member of the IRA, the bald-headed gnome-like figure of Miriam's husband appeared at the door of the villa and beckoned. Seeing his chance, Ed launched himself across the lawn leaving Miriam in his wake. By the time he reached the grand entrance of the villa, and looked back, she had given up the chase and had decided to hector one of the gardeners who had not been quick enough at getting out of the way.

Entering the coolness of the hallway he saw the Mine Manager disappear to the right through a doorway. From his previous visit to this exalted place he knew that beyond that door was the drawing room, full of fine furniture and Persian carpets. Letting his eyes grow used to the dark, he looked around at the polished mahogany floor bedecked with fine porcelain perched on period English furniture. On a wall facing the door was a large ship's clock, otherwise it was exactly as he remembered.

His eyes lingered on the clock, it had once rested on the wall in the Chief Engineer's house at the foot of the hill. It had belonged to Miriam's father, a ship's captain and later a senior man in the Northern Ireland police who had eventually been killed by an IRA bomb. It went some of the way to explain Miriam's paranoia that Allen was IRA, an assertion that was given credence by Allen's habit of wrapping his past in a cloak of misinformation.

Sniffing the air, he detected polish and bees wax. Its smell brought to mind the last time he'd been here, when the whole conspiracy to defraud the mine had been unmasked. There'd been a standoff between Lomax and Jeremy, his Chief of African Operations. It was into this hallway that Ed had been brought, at gun point, while a helicopter had been made ready outside so Jeremy could escape.

A head appeared from around the door and beckoned. "Time is money," it said, and disappeared again.

The drawing room turned out to be much the same as he remembered, except for the addition of silk and lace curtains. They looked odd amid the leather armchairs and fine walnut cabinets that were so reminiscent of a London gentlemen's club.

On entering, Ed realised that the Mine Manager had not bothered to sit down and was standing to attention next to his desk. He was a head shorter than Miriam and had a bristle moustache that was closely cropped to reveal over-large lips. He looked more like the caricature of a librarian or an administrator in a town hall than manager of one of the largest gold mines in Africa.

Ed stood to attention so that he towered over him.

"Welcome back, Mr Evans," he said curtly. "I believe you are reporting directly to Mr Allen."

Catching the sniff of a point being made, Ed shrugged his shoulders. "James Allen said I was the interim Head of Drilling and I was to report to him in the same way as Forge used to report to Kojo."

"That's not what I understand. You're doing a special project and all of the results will bypass Engineering and go straight to Lomax in London. I'll only see things if Mr Lomax deems it necessary."

He ground his teeth for a moment and then indicated

the phone perched on the desk. "I've talked with Lomax personally about this and told him I'm unhappy at the thought of special projects that are outside my jurisdiction. I also said I was unhappy about having personnel foisted on me."

There was an awkward silence, Ed thought that he was being invited to comment. "What did he say?"

"Tough titties, or words to that effect. He said I had to re-employ half the geology section."

Ed's non-committal nod did not seem to calm the Mine Manager's temper. He ground his teeth again and brought his right hand up to smooth non-existent hair on his head. "I told him that thanks to the inaction of previous Mine Managers we are now knee-deep in revolutionaries and that I would not be held responsible for the consequences if we were to allow these neo Trotskyites access to sensitive data."

"So what d'you intend to do?"

"I have no choice but to re-instate the people who Allen wants. Over the last few months the miners' union and the Galamsey have made common cause and not a day goes past when there isn't some kind of sabotage. So, I'll be checking Allen's choices thoroughly to ensure they're not active ring leaders."

He paused for breath, still standing to attention, his little hands bunching up into fists by his sides. "You've met the leader of the miners' union I believe." It was a statement, not a question.

"That's right," replied Ed. "I think your predecessor as Mine Manager – the one before Jeremy - had tried to negotiate with the union and I was nominated as a go-between."

"Why you, I wonder?"

"I suppose I wasn't part of the mine, more like a

contractor. I think Bismarck and Kojo must have recommended me as somebody who was reliable and trustworthy. I had no choice in the matter."

"What was he like?"

"Sorry?"

"Herman the Helmet, leader of the union, what's he like?" said the Mine Manager fists bunching together more aggressively, small spots of pink appearing on his cheeks.

"Bit of a gangster, surrounded by his heavy mob. Smoked a cigar and wore a silk dressing gown. I'd say he was pretty bright. Got a head shaped like a helmet."

A strange calmness seemed to come over the Mine Manager, he stopped clenching his fists and instead of standing to attention he leaned back and perched on the edge of his desk, arms folded. "He wants you as a go between again," he said.

"Me? How the hell does he know I'm back? I've not been here more than a day." Ed's stomach, which had relaxed since he'd had a good sleep, began to tighten into a knot again.

"We are beset with spies," said the Mine Manager. "I can hardly make a phone call in this place without the whole content of the conversation being broadcast around town."

"But I thought you didn't negotiate with unions, by order of Lomax."

"We don't, but an emergency channel of communication is wise. I need to know from you if you're willing."

"I have no choice in the matter," said Ed. "Herman's henchmen'll walk straight into my room in the compound and force me into a pickup, like last time."

"I'll let it be known then," he replied. "And now, unless you have something you want to say to me I think our meeting should end here."

The Mine Manager escorted him out of the villa and up
to the waiting pickup in which Frank sat. "I'd still like to
know why Herman wants you and not another contractor."

Ed could see the Mine Manager disliked him, was
suspicious of his motives. He had probably been listening
to the whispers of the Faces in the bar. He had a gut feeling
that he needed to come clean, to tell the Mine Manager why
he was back. Allen might think it clever to keep everybody
in the dark but Ed had never seen this as a good way of
getting cooperation. Without thinking very clearly about
what he was doing he took the Mine Manager's arm and led
him away from the pickup.

"No doubt you've not be told the truth about what
happened last time I was here," he said. "When I had to
leave in a hurry and there was all that trouble with the
union?"

The Mine Manager gave him a suspicious glance. "I've
heard a few things, all unconfirmed and therefore
unreliable."

"Well, I'll tell you," said Ed. "There were two halves,
Kojo, Bismarck and the union on one side, Forge, Dave his
assistant and a man nicknamed Golf Club on the other."
He turned and looked directly at the Mine Manager. "I'd
appreciate if this was kept strictly between us two."

A nod of the head.

Ed continued, hesitatingly, wondering if he was doing
the best thing. "Uniting the two halves was Lucky Lomax's
Head of Africa Operations, Jeremy."

"Jeremy?"

"Has Lomax not said? He was the man behind the
whole shambles."

"Lomax just said that Jeremy'd found alternative
employment, with a rival businessman named Snodgrass."

"Well, that's true," said Ed folding his arms. "But

Jeremy's been working for Snodgrass for more than a few months. Snodgrass has contacts in the City of London and supplied legitimacy to what the two halves were doing."

He looked around to check if Frank was within earshot. "If you were ordered by the Head of Operations to falsify data, to make exploration prospects less attractive so they could be sold off at rock bottom prices, what would you do?"

The Mine Manager shrugged. "Never happened to me. I'd like to think I'd tell him to get stuffed."

"Well, Forge didn't. He must have known what he was doing was illegal, of course. I assume at the beginning he thought the whole thing was sanctioned by Lomax. But as time went on he probably realised that this was not the case and it was a piece of private enterprise by Jeremy. By then he was in too deep."

"How did Kojo and Bismarck get involved?"

"Not sure," said Ed quietly. "Maybe they found out, threatened to go to Lomax. But I think it's more likely that Forge or Jeremy brought them into the group. Together they could pull the wool over everybody's eyes."

"And the union?" asked the Mine Manager. "What was their involvement?"

"Muscle, pure and simple," said Ed. "Once Chiri started to smell a rat he started to throw his weight around using the mine militia. Allen told me that Chiri's like minor royalty and to certain sections of the local populous his word is law. The group needed some kind of muscle and the union supplied it."

The Mine Manager nodded. "Chiri's got his own power base, all right," he said, an edge of bitterness in his voice. "So the group made money by selling off prospects cheap?" said the Mine Manager, frowning. "Doesn't sound like a great money spinner."

"Quite right," said Ed. "But the prospects were all sold to a single company called Tremendous Resources of London, principal shareholders unknown, but probably Jeremy, Forge, Bismarck and Kojo. Within a space of a year four minable deposits were found and the share price of the company went through the roof. Lomax had to buy the company lock, stock and barrel or face having a rival mining company competing for resources on his doorstep. The gang made somewhere between fifty and one hundred million dollars."

The Mine Manager whistled. "I remember it well. One hundred million? Is that how much they made?"

"That's right," confirmed Ed. "When Lomax did an investigation into the company and found the name Snodgrass he knew there was something strange going on. This is a man with his fingers in many pies, he's very cosy with the Press Oligarchs in Britain, he makes and breaks reputations. If you want to do any dirty work, like have a rival bumped off, launder money, disguise your identity in a dodgy deal, he's your man. He has a price, of course, and he won't work with anybody except apparently legitimate business people. So when Lomax found out Snodgrass was involved he went ballistic, knew it was an inside job."

"The trilobites. Why were they important? I remember some furore over them."

Ed looked over his shoulder again to make sure Frank was still in his pickup and that the gardeners or Miriam hadn't encroached within ear shot. He leaned in closer and whispered, "I think Forge knew he'd got in over his head. As far as Jeremy and Snodgrass were concerned he was a 'little' person, completely disposable. He'd be left as the scape-goat while everybody else rode off with the cash. So he bought some insurance in the form of four trilobites, one for himself, one for Golf Club, one for Dave and one for Greg."

"Greg?" asked the Mine Manager. "You never mentioned he was involved as well."

"He came later. If you remember, I replaced Greg. In fact Greg was brought in by Allen and Lomax specifically to find out what was going on. But when he discovered the truth he assumed the whole thing was being done at the behest of Lomax and threatened to tell the press unless he was cut into the deal as well."

"My God," said The Mine Manager in a loud voice. "I had no idea."

"The syndicate acted quickly to protect their investment, and that's why Greg disappeared."

"So the trilobites," insisted The Mine Manager, now thoroughly absorbed. "Where are they now?"

"Forge didn't trust anybody. When the cash was divided at a meeting in London, he set up a post office system. If you put one of your trilobites in the window of a particular shop and left your calling card with the shopkeeper, eventually a third party (unknown) would ring you up and tell you where your money was stashed. But Dave, Golf Club, Greg and eventually Forge, all died before they could do this. We found out which shop but we don't know who the third party is."

"So have you done it?" asked The Mine Manager, his eyes agleam. "Have you put these trilobites in the shop window?"

"Yes."

"And?"

"Nothing, not a sausage. As far as I know all four trilobites are still in the shop window and have been for months."

"So it's a dud," said the Mine Manager, disappointment etched in every syllable.

"I guess so," replied Ed. "Allen and Lomax think the trilobites might have been a red herring to throw everybody, including Snodgrass, off the trail. That's one of the reasons why they're keen for us to look through all the drilling. This is Forge's life work, if he hid anything it was in there."

The Mine Manager returned his gaze to the huge villa. Ed was silent.

"And Forge said nothing before he died?" asked the Mine Manager.

"He was in a coma for most of it."

"All that time I was in meetings with Forge, Kojo and Bismarck," said the Mine Manager suddenly, "And they were working to undermine everything we were trying to do." The bitterness of the words made Ed look across. "It was a cabal."

He reached his hand across to Ed. "Thank you for telling me this."

Brett Walsh Arrives

Arriving at his office half an hour later, Ed was surprised to find the door ajar. Pushing carefully at the handle, he entered, staring around at the gloom. He could smell stale tobacco, and there was a shadow on the far wall rocking backwards and forwards on a chair.

"Hello?" he called.

Silence.

"I guess you're Brett," he said.

Silence.

Reaching over to his desk lamp he threw a switch and resisted the temptation to throw the beam of light directly onto the rocking figure.

Brett was thick-set, dressed in khaki with large metal-toed boots. Ginger and black whiskers covered most of his face and on his head perched a Kookaburra hat. Standing up, he wordlessly handed a piece of paper across. Dumbfounded, Ed found it to be a letter of introduction, signed by Lomax himself, assuring the reader that Brett Walsh had been appointed as an exploration adviser at the Lomax Gold Mine.

"Welcome aboard," said Ed, then cursed himself for sounding so lame.

Brett snatched the letter back, removed his hat to reveal a completely bald head and pushed Lomax's contract into the top before replacing the hat carefully on his head. Walking backwards, he regained his seat and resumed rocking backwards and forwards. From nowhere he produced a tin of rolled tobacco and a packet of cigarette papers.

"I bin told to come here," he said. "I needed to pick your lock 'cos I wasn't goin' to wait around outside in the heat." He had a slow drawling voice which Ed placed in New Zealand rather than Australia.

"I'd rather you didn't smoke in here," said Ed, indicating the shelves of folders along the wall. "This lot is irreplaceable."

Ignoring him, Brett took out a paper and expertly placed tobacco along its curled middle. "You gotta name, or shall I call you the trilobite fetishist."

"Ed."

"Like the horse?"

"That's right," said Ed, finding the first hint of irritation.

"Apparently Chiri'll be along presently to pick me up and take me out to the Exploration Department. I'll be working there for the duration, but Sucker'll be here with you."

"Correct."

"You met Sucker yet? He's got brains but no balls. Does all sorts of things like embroidery and carvin' and stuff. You two should get on really well."

Ed tried to give a smile. "Have you worked with Billy a long time?"

"Longer than Sucker'd like. But you work in places like PNG you gotta have somebody like me otherwise you're likely to end up on the menu."

"So you were like his bodyguard? Not a geologist then."

A slow nod. "Course we took up together in Western Australia. He was working on some prospects for a fly-by-night and I was his roustabout. Then we heard o' the rich pickings to be had in PNG so we went out there."

The sound of banging boots on the walkway brought Ed's attention to the window. A feeling like cold sweat started to erupt across his body as he realised that Chiri would soon be walking in through the door. Brett must have picked up on Ed's apprehension because he quickly finished rolling his cigarette and placed it in the side of his mouth, then he pulled the hat down over his eyes.

Six unsmiling faces appeared at the window and Ed felt his pulse start to race even harder. As if in anticipation of Chiri's appearance he began to smell roast meat and chilli in his nostrils, the scent he would forever associate with the man and his minions after a terrifying night in the mine hospital when they had appeared in his room, silent, watchful and intimidating.

The door was pushed and in strode a large figure dressed in the mine fatigues of green with yellow trim. Chiri never smiled, except on special occasions, which Ed reflected was just as well because the scars he wore on both cheeks gave him an especially menacing aspect.

But he was smiling now, though Ed couldn't think it was in welcome. And then he laughed, like a hyena on the savannah. "Mr Lomax said he'd invited you back," he said as if not able to believe his eyes. "And here you are. And you've brought somebody with you who will be keepin' me and my guys company."

By now Chiri's men had entered the office and, in characteristic style, had spread themselves around the room, leaning against walls or perching on desks, the better to fill the space with their baleful presence. None of them looked at either Ed or Chiri, their entire focus was on Brett.

Still with his hat down low over his eyes, Brett struck a match and lit his cigarette.

Silence.

Gradually tilting back his hat he looked at the assembled crowd, face registering nothing but a haughty disinterest. Only the plume of noxious smoke drifting lazily from his mouth suggested a slight misgiving.

"This is Brett," Ed said. "Just arrived from PNG."

Chiri's smile remained on his face, but became rather more fixed than when he'd seen Ed. "I've had word from Mr Lomax that we're to look after you," he said, addressing Brett directly.

Brett transferred his gaze from the acolytes straight onto Chiri, his cigarette glowing orange at the tip. He stood up and removed his Kookaburra hat and tipped out Lomax's letter before handing it to Chiri.

Eyes narrowed, Chiri looked at the paper before placing it in his top pocket. "I think I'll keep this," he said.

For a moment it looked as if Brett was about to argue, but then he shrugged and replaced the hat on his head. "I suppose we betta get goin'," he said to the room. He went behind Billy's desk and took hold of a large rucksack which he thrust onto his back.

Silently, Chiri led the way out, followed in strict order by his acolytes and then Brett. Their feet clumped noisily down the balcony and then onto the stairs. From the window, Ed watched them climb into a pickup in the car park and zoom through the gates into the town.

Chiri was the terror of the mine; he and his acolytes were known to control the mine militia for and on behalf of Lucky Lomax. They were the enforcers, the bully boys who faced down the Galamsey from their fortress in the middle of the jungle. Surely they'd make swift and certain work of a brute like Brett Walsh.

From the slight quizzical expression on Chiri's normally impassive face, Ed had detected a hint of uncertainty. Brett clearly represented something slightly different from the normal western contractor. He was trouble, Ed could see it, Allen could see it, even Chiri could see it. So, what the hell was Lomax up to, sending such a man to a place like this which was already stuffed to overflowing with trouble?

Dinner with Brett Walsh

As arranged, Allen arrived early at the compound bar that night. He said he wanted to get to know his new charges better. There was no sign of Billy in the dining room or the bar so Ed went to find out if he wanted to join them. "I've had dinner," he said. "Ordered one of those club sandwiches. Hope you don't mind if I try and get some rest. Travelling always tires me out." He shut the door, leaving Ed with the impression of a small mole scuttling back into his hole for safety.

Brett shared none of his partner's reticence, he appeared half way through the meal with his hat perched defiantly on his head and an unlit roll up in his mouth.

The other diners, all Faces from the bar, turned to look at Brett as he swaggered past their tables. They too noticed that there was something different about this man, the way he looked straight ahead with his eyes fixed on something only he could see, the way arrogance exuded from him like a noxious smell.

"You said you were from New Zealand," Ed asked politely after Brett had sat down in one of the vacant seats opposite him. Uncharacteristically, Allen was being silent and watchful in the presence of a stranger.

Brett grunted. "Sheep shearer, originally, up in the Canterbury hills. But I gave it up and went to Australia."

"Why was that?" asked Ed.

"Better money, 'o course," he replied, lip curling in contempt.

Finding himself flustered, Ed ploughed ahead. "I mean there was no other reason except money?"

Suspicion replaced contempt, "What other reason could there be?"

"I don't know, relationship breakdown perhaps...." He was going to add some other reasons such as death of a parent, debt, a brush with the law, but Brett interrupted him.

"That's right, relationship breakdown."

Exchanging glances with Allen, Ed decided to let the subject drop. "How did you get on with Chiri this afternoon?"

"Nosy bastard."

Exchanging glances with Allen again, Ed leaned forward. "Did I hear you right?"

"I said he and his mates are nosy bastards. Want to know where I'm from, what I've done. Man has a right to privacy. That's what I told them and they left me alone."

At that moment Brett's order arrived and Ed was saved having to make conversation. Not that Allen had helped. Normally Ed couldn't get a word in edgeways, but right now Allen seemed content with silence.

Half way through wolfing down his meal, Brett stopped and took out a small bottle of whisky. After a large swig he wiped excess food from his beard and gave a loud, satisfied belch. "I cannot tell a lie," he announced suddenly. "There was a reason I left New Zealand. Some bastard of a farmer didn't pay the rate he promised for each sheep I was to shear." He turned and looked directly at Allen. "So the next day, I cut every other throat. I got through to lunchtime before he noticed."

Ed stood up, disgusted, his meal was finished in any case. "I'm going to the bar," he said. Looking down at Brett, he saw amusement.

Walking from the dining room he kicked himself for having reacted so badly to the story. It was clear that Brett was trying to build his legend as a rough and ready bushwacker who chose to live on the wrong side of the law. By reacting, Ed had signalled that he could be wound up with tales of simple cruelty. From now on he could expect Brett to pepper their conversation with filthy savagery.

Allen arrived soon after. "Wow," he said, "Chiri's going to have fun."

"What the hell is Lomax doing," asked Ed, "offering that man a job?"

"I think it's more that he wants Billy." Allen said, winking at Jimmy the barman. "It's like one of those supermarket offers, buy one get one free, only Brett comes taped to Billy."

"Billy seems a good guy," agreed Ed. "Got a funny habit with a pipe. According to Brett he does embroidery and carving, is that right?"

Allen nodded. "Did it all the way through the interview in Port Moresby. Really good stuff as well, really professional."

They took their beers to a table and sat in silence, waiting and watching for Brett to appear from the dining room. Eventually two guards entered, AK-47s slung over their shoulder. They reappeared a few minutes later behind Brett, who had a lit cigarette dangling from this mouth.

"Looks like he's got on the wrong side of your Faces," said Allen smiling. "They're very particular about smoking in the dining room."

Brett walked across to them. "I just got myself banned from the dining room," he said with a scowl. "Gotta take my food in my room or out here, otherwise I get thrown out." He looked mystified rather than upset. "I'm gonna sit with some of my own kind," he said indicating the table of Australian drillers.

"With pleasure," said Allen.

"How long d'you think he'll last?" asked Ed as Brett walked away. "Before Chiri's had enough, I mean."

"Chiri'll have no trouble dealing with Brett," said Allen. "If Brett decides to give him woe there'll be a bullet or a knife in the back courtesy of the Galamsey. And good riddance."

Ed was surprised at the vehemence with which Allen expressed himself. "Bit extreme," he said, "couldn't Chiri just ask him to leave? Dispense with his services?"

Allen seemed to regret his words. "I expect you're right, but I can't help thinking that it might be difficult to ask Brett if he'd mind leaving. I've met characters like him before in mining camps, they've a keen eye for opportunity. Whatever the problems in Lomax, it's a hundred times better than the place in PNG he was living."

"Describe it then," demanded Ed.

Smiling, Allen took a sip of his beer. "I never saw it, he and Billy came to Port Moresby for the interview. The way Billy describes the place, he had to keep a loaded gun under his pillow every night; constant tribal warfare, fighting between government forces and local bandits, typhoid, cholera, a myriad of other water-borne tropical diseases. I doubt Brett will return there willingly."

They watched as Brett settled himself down at the table of Australian drillers, tipping his hat graciously at the seamstresses who crowded around. There were only ten or so drillers at the tables tonight. No doubt the rest had gone elsewhere for their entertainment, outside the perimeter razor-wire fence of the compound.

"Hardly a warm welcome," mused Allen, observing how the drillers stopped their conversations and turned as one to Brett, hard looks on their faces. One of them, a large, bullet-headed man, leant toward Brett and talked to him. The others listened and occasionally nodded their head. Brett was motionless, silent, a sneer on his face.

"Wonder what they're saying to him," asked Ed. "Hardly a way to greet one of their own."

Then Brett stood up, his chair toppling backwards and slamming to the floor. The drillers stood as well, closing ranks around their bullet-headed companion. Jimmy the barman had realised what was happening and reached down to grab the baseball bat that Ed knew was kept amongst the store of empty beer bottles. Conversation suddenly ceased as the Faces turned as one to watch what was happening.

Brett's face had a look of calculation, his eyes flicking across his adversaries, like he was contemplating how he might win the forthcoming fight. But then he smiled, tipped his hat and turned on his heel. As he swaggered across the grass back to the accommodation block, the eyes of the entire bar on his back, he waved his hand in farewell.

The drillers watched him until he was out of sight before returning to their seats. They looked shaken, like they'd just faced down a beast of the jungle. They talked to one another in agitated whispers, the seamstresses forgotten for the moment in their quest to compare notes.

Ed stood.

"Where are you going?" asked Allen.

"I'm going to ask what they said to Brett."

Allen laid a restraining hand on Ed's arm. "Not just yet, they look a bit battle charged, they're likely to tell you where to get off. I'll ask Jimmy, he's the fount of all knowledge around here. My round in any case." He stood and went across to the bar where he engaged Jimmy in conversation for quite a while before returning.

"Looks like there's history between the drillers and Brett. They told Jimmy to be prepared for trouble tonight. Brett's meant to have threatened one of them back in Australia. Fights like a cornered dingo."

Ed nodded but thought he might ask the drillers in person rather than relying on second hand information. But the drillers decided that they'd had enough beer for the night, stood as one man and left, leaving the seamstresses to mutter angrily amongst themselves.

Watching their retreating backs, Ed was reminded of the previous night when he'd been accosted by a voice from the shrubbery as he made his way back to his room. It had been on the tip of his tongue to tell the Mine Manager in his garden earlier that day but he had stopped himself, deciding that some things are best left unsaid. But now, with a belly filling with Ghanaian beer he decided to confide in Allen.

"Leave in five days?" said Allen in surprise. "Why five days?"

Ed shrugged his shoulders. "The man disappeared into thin air before I could ask him. One moment he was speaking out of a bush, the next there was silence."

"Do you think it was somebody using his name in order to add weight to the threat?"

"Why?" asked Ed, puzzled that Allen should have doubts.

"Because if it really was from Kojo then it's proof that he's back in the area and scheming."

"I know," said Ed, "that's why I didn't tell the Mine Manager this afternoon when I talked with him. He seemed jumpy and paranoid enough, particularly with Miriam constantly chirruping in his ear about Trotskyite revolutionaries under every bed."

Allen nodded his agreement. "Also," he said, sipping his beer and then leaning forward to whisper. "I think if the threat was genuine it would come from Bismarck."

"What d'you mean?" asked Ed, leaning forward himself.

"I mean that Bismarck is the man of action, the one who would be issuing orders. Kojo's the organiser, the one who sits in the background. Chiri's most afraid of Bismarck, you'll notice how he never mentions Kojo when he's charging about looking for insurgents in the mine, always chunters-on about Bismarck, like he was the devil incarnate."

For several moments neither spoke, then Allen decided to conclude the evening. He stood up and stretched. "No doubt we'll find out more. In the meantime, I wouldn't worry too much. Bismarck and Kojo had it in their power to kill you a few months ago and stayed their hand. It was more than they did for Greg and Forge." He reached out a hand, "I think they must like you."

Joe Arrives

At breakfast the next morning, Ed arrived early to find Billy already finishing his first cup of tea. Sitting down opposite him he received a cheery hallo and smile. "Lovely tea," he said. "Normally I'm forced to have coffee or nothing at all. Brett doesn't like tea."

"Not very much he does like," said Ed.

"True," said Billy, smiling again. "Beneath that rough and gruff exterior beats a heart of pure hatred."

"I don't understand, you've been partners for years…"

"We have this mutual loathing," he interrupted. "For most of those years we've had a simple understanding that he'd be roustabout, dealing with drillers and locals, driving the truck and maintaining the camp, and I'd do the exploration; the bit that required brains and subtlety."

"Well, we don't need roustabouts here, we have Chiri and his merry acolytes," said Ed.

"Yes, but to get me, Lomax had to sign a contract with Brilly Consultants, that's our company name. When they got me they also got Brett. He'll soon get bored and go back to PNG, it's where he knows best."

"Not Australia?" Ed asked distractedly. The waitress had brought his tea and pineapple.

"Why would he go back to Australia? He's from New Zealand."

"I know," replied Ed. "But he sat with the Australian drillers in the bar last night."

"Australian drillers? There's Australians here in the mine?"

"Course there is," said Ed, surprised by Billy's naivety. "The mining industry is full of them."

"Even in Africa?"

"You got a problem with Australians?"

For a moment Billy looked confused, slightly panicked by the presence of Australians, but then he recovered himself. "Of course not, I naturally assumed that the African mining industry would employ people from South Africa."

"Not at all," Ed said, pouring himself a cup of tea from the pot that had been plonked on the table by Moonlight. He added milk and then placed it against his lips, blowing the froth to the far side. "There was a bit of an altercation between Brett and the Australians last night, they seemed less than welcoming."

Billy peered at him through his small, round glasses. He looked like a vulnerable miscreant caught in the act of lying. "They probably recognised him, he's got a reputation for nastiness, not a nice person to have around."

"You don't seem to mind having him around," said Ed.

"No," said Billy. "Perhaps I'm more tolerant than many others."

Neither man spoke for the next few minutes as both ate their breakfast. Only when they'd finished did Billy speak again, thoughts on Brett banished from the conversation. "What should we do today then, boss?"

"Hopefully we'll have some help," said Ed, happy to let the conversation revert to work. "Yesterday the Mine Manager told me that he'd re-employed some of the geologists."

"Explain why they were sacked again?" Billy asked. "You did explain but I like to get the details sorted in my head."

Thinking that the subject of the union might not be a good one to discuss in the middle of the dining room where one of the Faces could be listening, Ed leaned in. "They were sacked for being in the union. But the idiots who run this mine discovered that they can't run the place without them so they're intending to re-employ some of them."

"Serve them right if they said no," said Billy. "I think I'd be tempted to tell them where they could stick their job."

"Precisely," replied Ed. "But there aren't that many jobs around, particularly if you've just been given the elbow for being in the union. They'll have no choice but to come back. I'm hoping that we'll get a man named Joe. He worked in the same office as Bismarck, the main union organiser. Allen reckons he's really good."

The door to the dining room opened and then closed. The hubbub that was a normal part of breakfast died and Billy's face took on a blank look. Turning, Ed saw that Brett had arrived, an as-yet unlit roll up in the side of his mouth.

Moonlight pushed herself through the kitchen door and disappeared.

Brett walked up to their table, all eyes of the room on his large frame. "Aye, Sucker, missed you last night. There was quite a kafuffle in here, they chucked me out for smoking. The gentlemen who dine don't like smoke." He looked around the room at all the Faces and leered.

"I thought you weren't allowed in here anymore," said Ed.

"Not allowed in a lot of places," he replied with a sneer. "Doesn't stop me. It's a free country, I can do what I like."

"In that case, I'll be going," said Ed, standing up. "You better be quick because Chiri and his men will be along to pick you up."

"They'll have to wait 'til I've had me breakfast."

Billy joined Ed on the way out. "How did you stand that for so many years?" asked Ed.

"No choice," Billy replied. "We're bound by the same chain."

As Frank drove them into the mine offices, Ed reflected on Billy's reply. Once or twice he leaned across to ask what he'd meant but felt that he should wait for Billy to tell him in his own time.

"What should we do this morning?" Billy asked.

"Can't do much until Joe arrives," Ed said. "He'll be able to procure maps of each level showing the position of the drill holes. Once we have that we can start trying to find inconsistencies between what's in the computer and what Forge archived. Don't forget Forge was responsible for overseeing data entry into the DataMine system so any discrepancy between the two will almost certainly be deliberate."

"And when will this Joe turn up?"

"Don't know," shrugged Ed. "Allen said last night that he'd located him and hoped he would be coming in this morning."

When they arrived in the office there was no sign of Joe. Billy walked over to his desk and then stuck his pipe between his teeth. "Shame to sit here and do nothing," he said. "I always feel the need to work with my hands." He produced a piece of cloth from his bag and placed it on the desk. "Don't mind if I start my tapestry?" he asked.

Ed smiled then shook his head. "I guess I'll go and find Allen, ask about Joe."

But Allen was in meetings, his room locked. For several

moments he wondered whether he should walk over to Engineering and introduce himself. But then again, why bother? He was answerable to Allen alone, and through him to Lomax.

When he returned to the office Joe had arrived and Billy was attempting to engage him in conversation. But Joe's eyes were narrowed, his face set. Ed could judge the thoughts of resentment which must be coursing through his mind. After several moments, Ed coughed to let both of them know he'd arrived. Joe turned to look at him and Ed had a vision of the slim, happy face that had once shared an office with the owl-like Bismarck. Now there was no trace of the levity, just a blank, staring face beneath a completely bald head.

"Welcome Joe."

Joe nodded his head then screwed up his face like he had a sour taste in his mouth.

"Thanks for agreeing to come back." He thought it better to strike a more conciliatory note. "I know Allen is working hard to convince the Mine Manager and Lomax that we need to re-employ the entire geology section. You're just the start." This wasn't a lie, he assured himself.

Joe's face remained impassive, like he knew that words were cheap. Ed cast around for something else to say. "Allen wanted you back first because he's spotted you as somebody who'll be able to take over the drilling section. Do Forge's job. But he wants everything in order before you start. Us three: you, me and Billy, we'll go through everything first, find places where there might be discrepancies and put them right."

Joe nodded his head, still unwilling to speak, then turned to face Billy. It was clear that he resented the presence of an unknown white contractor. Ed attempted to reassure him. "Billy's not been employed to do the work of one of the sacked geologists. He's here because he's an expert in the interpretation of drilling. Like me. He'll be gone within a few months."

Billy gave a weak smile and then put his empty pipe to his mouth. The sound of sucking soon filled the room.

"Has Allen spoken to you about what you'll be doing?" he asked.

A shake of the head.

"I guess it'll be better for you to get it from the horse's mouth. I think he's in a meeting at the moment." He hesitated, licked his lips and ploughed on. "Probably trying to get those people re-instated."

No smile, no words.

Billy started to thread a needle with cotton causing Joe to turn and look at him.

"Got our very own seamstress," said Ed and winked at Billy, who grinned back. "Billy's just flown in from Papua New Guinea with his business partner. As well as drilling he does tapestry and carving."

"Business partner?" asked Joe in his deep West African drawl. "Where's he?"

"Entertaining Chiri out in the jungle, name of Brett."

Nodding his head, Joe stood up. "I'll go and find Allen then," he said. "I guess I'll get the desk by the window. Dave's old desk."

It was clear that Joe was still extremely doubtful of the arrangements.

"You'll have Forge's old desk, I'll take Dave's," said Ed in a flash. He wondered why he hadn't immediately offered this on entering the room. "Sit in the chair, see if it fits you."

But Joe wasn't to be won over so quickly by the offer of the best seat in the house. Standing, he stretched his muscles and walked to the door. "I'll find Allen, see what he says." The door closed behind him with a click.

For several long seconds the room was filled with the noise of a sucking pipe; Billy was having a think. "Beads and mirrors," he said eventually, pulling the needle up through his tapestry cloth

"Sorry?"

"The Native Americans were bribed with beads and mirrors and they gave away large tracts of land." He plunged the needle back into the cloth, refusing to look up. "They betrayed their birth right and their friends. You're trying to bribe Joe with a desk and a chair so he'll betray his friends."

"What nonsense."

Billy continued sewing, sucking the pipe between his teeth.

The Miners' Diner

For lunch Ed decided to take Billy to a small cafeteria kept for managers and their guests called the Miners' Diner. Frank had assured him that he knew the way and that it would only take five minutes. The pickup zoomed out of the front gates and sped along the main Lomax thoroughfare before turning left and climbing a small hill flanked by corrugated iron shacks. At the top Frank made a sudden sharp right and entered through a narrow gateway that was guarded by men with AK-47s. Skidding to a halt he indicated with a relaxed flick of the hand that they had arrived.

Through the windscreen they could see a large villa surrounded by many cooling trees and well-kept lawns. Billy leapt out and walked eagerly to a set of steps that led up to wide open doors.

Ed followed at a more sedate pace looking at the assembled pickups for a sign that Chiri had arrived with his acolytes. Reassured that he would not have to steel himself for a confrontation with the exploration department, he climbed the steps.

The dining room was tiled in blue and white with large bay windows at the far end that looked out onto the wide expanse of Lomax shanty town. He could see the mine gates, the processing plant, Lomax 'A' winding tower and the substantial razor wire fence that enclosed the entire site. Not for the first time he was able to appreciate the sheer scale of destruction that open cast mining had wrought on the geography of the area. Several large hills must have been razed to the ground and then put through the grinding mill. And down-wind of the processing plant chimney were mountainsides devoid of vegetation, poisoned by the arsenic that had been vented as part of the gold extraction process.

It was, he reflected, a very industrial landscape, where the generation of enormous wealth was juxtaposed against extreme poverty.

After selecting several items from the self-service hot plates, he joined Billy at an empty table adjacent to the large windows. "Quite a view," Billy remarked. "You don't realise the size of the town until you get up here. All those people living down there with no sanitation and running water. Must be hell."

Ed shrugged his shoulders. "Can't say it'd suit me. I daresay it's worse than some places and better than others. Must be a bit like PNG."

Billy finished his meal, then pushed away his plate with a contented sigh. "Delicious," he said producing his pipe from his left pocket and tapestry from his right. Before long he had extracted a needle from somewhere in his shirt and had started to sew.

"What are you making?" asked Ed.

"It's part of a much large tableau which I'm gradually stitching together, either a wall hanging or throw for a bed. Every year I have a different theme. I once did an Outback scene. I broke down the view from my camp and did every small section in detail. Took a year to do. I did the night sky first so I got a snapshot of the southern constellations, then the trees, and finally the campfires." He sat back and sighed, drifting off to somewhere in his head.

"Why'd you leave to go to PNG?"

Billy snapped out of his day dream. He looked shocked, as if Ed had caught him off guard. "I left to find work," he said.

Ed gazed at him for a moment, wondering whether he was being serious. "With a choice between the Australian Outback and the jungles of PNG, I know which one I'd choose."

Billy refused to meet his gaze and eventually returned to his tapestry. "We all make mistakes," he said. "I've made several in my life."

"Why don't you just go back to Australia?"

"I haven't got citizenship. I can't go back."

"But you must have been resident in Australia for several years, doesn't that make you eligible?"

For several seconds, Billy didn't reply. Then, pricking his thumb with the needle he yelped in pain and ran across the dining room and into the toilets. On returning he indicated to Ed that he'd meet him outside in Frank's pickup.

Billy was morose for much of the afternoon. Not until Joe returned, this time with a grin on his face, did he seem to cheer up.

Allen turned up soon after. "Joe's fully in the picture with everything," he said. "Anything you need, Joe'll be able to fix up. He's quite a whizz on the computers so anything you want from DataMine, he's your man."

Beckoning to Ed, he disappeared out through the door onto the balcony. "Bernie's around," he said in a quiet voice when Ed joined him. "She arrived this morning to cover the mass sackings of union members. Late as usual, but I guess that's the media in this part of the world, hardly twenty-four hours."

"I wouldn't have thought Lomax would want it known,"

said Ed, he knew Bernie to be in the pay of Lomax while ostensibly working freelance for a number of large multinational newspapers.

"Lomax likes to have the news managed. He's probably sent her out here because other news outlets have got wind of what's happening. You know the sort of thing, 'get your side of the story out first, muddy the waters, make the opposition work a bit harder'."

"So what's the problem? You look uncomfortable about her."

"Bernie's good at sniffing out a story and I don't think we should subject Mr Sheep Slitter and the tapestry man to her. She's likely to start digging. So, if she comes after you trying to sniff out a story send her in the opposite direction. Tell her you've been asked to be the go between with the union, rabbit on a bit about how disappointed you are that so many men have been sacked, tell her nothing of any substance." He hesitated for a few seconds. "You could even tell her about the message from Kojo. Not been in touch again has he?"

Ed shook his head. "Not a dickie bird last night, nor this morning."

They returned to find Joe and Billy examining some of the trilobites that lined the walls. "These two'll get on real well," said Allen, regarding both men with a fatherly eye. "I've persuaded Joe to take you both underground tomorrow for the sake of orientation. There's a new and safer cage since the accident."

"Accident?" asked Billy, turning suddenly.

"Ask Ed," replied Allen. "He was actually there, saw it all unfold." He winked at Ed and then walked out.

Ed sidled over to his desk. "If we're going underground," he said to Joe, "you'll have to go into DataMine and print off a level plan so we can plot anything of interest."

"I'll go now," Joe said, "before the computer room closes."

When he'd left, Ed returned his attention to a drilling volume which lay open on his desk and Billy took out his tapestry and started to suck on his pipe. "What happened?" he asked after a while.

"The accident you mean?" replied Ed sitting back in his chair wondering how much to say. A sudden vision of flame, the sound of wind in his ears as he looked down the shaft, the screams of men dying in a diesel inferno.

"They were moving a locomotive between levels using the lower deck of the main cage. When they loaded the engine, it sprayed diesel over a group of miners on the upper deck. There was a spark from metal grinding and..." He stopped for a moment, remembering the carnage and then swallowed. "The fire got into the locomotive fuel tank, it exploded and took out the main cable."

The words tripped off his tongue like he was reading from his own report of the incident. He remembered at the time that there had been a suspicion of sabotage. Herman the Helmet, leader of the miners' union had threatened that he would be hitting Lomax where it hurt, in the pocket, unless his demand for better pay and conditions were met. The accident in the shaft had crippled the mine, there had been millions of dollars' worth of lost production and it was only now getting back into full operation.

Billy's face was a mask of shock. "You mean the cage got loose and plunged down the shaft?"

"That's right, took all the poor sods in the upper deck with it, two and half kilometres straight down. Not that they knew anything about it, they'd all been burnt to a cinder before the explosion happened. On the way down, the cage failsafe took out the explosives cage and over a ton of ammonium nitrate followed it down." He mimicked an explosion with his arms. "Boom. A huge ball of flame came all the way up and blew the top off the shaft, like a cork coming out of a bottle."

The sucking on the pipe grew in intensity. "I guess health and safety isn't a big deal over here."

"Ha! That's the understatement of the year. Not sure what it's like now but Health and Safety practice used to be encouraged by a man named Golf Club."

"What happened to him?" asked Billy, a slight tremor in his voice.

"Beaten to death with his own golf club," said Ed. "Probably on orders from the miners' union."

The Open Pits

"I'd like to visit the open pits," said Billy several hours later when they were making ready to go back to the compound. Joe had gone home and they were alone in the office. "I'd like to see the ore zone up close. Difficult to be sure what you're looking at underground. Nothing like seeing the real thing in broad daylight."

Ed scratched his chin thoughtfully. "We can ask Frank, he knows his way around. The geography of the place changes rapidly because of the mining process, new roads driven through, old ones blocked off, I wouldn't know where I was half the time."

A quick meeting with Frank revealed that he'd been for a trip around the open pits the day before. "Not been much change lately," he said

Climbing into Frank's pickup, Ed reflected that the first time he'd entered the surface workings of the mine it had been with Bismarck. He leaned across to Billy and related the story. "Some witch doctor had tried to curse the ore body, there were chicken guts and the head of a dead cockerel on top of it. Bismarck said that nobody in the mine really believes in the old ways, but it still sends a shiver down the spine."

Frank joined in. "Galamsey are on the prowl, we'll stick to the eastern side."

Billy felt in the top pocket of his shirt and produced his pipe. "What do they want, these Galamsey?" he asked through clenched teeth.

Ed leaned over. "It's mostly cat and mouse," he said in low voice. "Allen reckons they're better explorationists than Chiri and his acolytes. They tend to know where's best to plant crops and build their shacks. Chiri moves them off using AK-47s and bulldozer blades and then the mine gives them negligible compensation. The consequence tends to be violence and more disruption."

They passed the golf course and the beautifully laid out greens and then turned left onto a road that had been cut through scrub. Before long they'd crested a small rise and the vista of the open pits opened before them and Frank stopped.

"What a size," said Billy. "I've never seen anything like it, not even in Western Australia."

"We'll keep to the right, on the town side," said Frank pointing out a plume of smoke that looked to be rising several kilometres away on the west side of the open pits. He gunned the engine and shot down a steep road kicking up plenty of dust in the process. As they descended, Ed kept his eyes on the inky-black plume of smoke. He'd seen one like that before, when one of the massive mine lorries had been set on fire.

"Perhaps we should go straight back to the compound," said Ed. "We don't want to be caught out."

Billy agreed, so Frank took the next turning to the right. They were now travelling away from the plume of smoke toward the Lomax 'A' winding tower.

A cloud of dust rose ahead of them on the road, not smoke from a burning vehicle but signs of an approaching vehicle. "Militia," said Frank. "We'd better get off the road so they can get past." He manoeuvred their pickup across a small gully so that the left wheels were on the bank and right on the road. They waited for the convoy to pass, eyes focussed on the bend in the road in front of them.

A white pickup sped into view waving wildly from side to side. It was followed by two other vehicles only a few tens of metres behind. As they approached, Ed could see that the white pickup was full of men in t-shirts, some wearing bandanas. They were looking back and clutching AK-47s close to their chest.

The following vehicles had men dressed in the uniform of the mine militia. One or two of them were checking their firearms as if getting ready to start shooting.

Then they were gone up the road in a cloud of speed and dust. As Ed listened to the receding noise he heard the sound of sucking from the back seat, and then a voice through clenched teeth. "I guess the Galamsey are into stealing mine vehicles as well as setting them alight."

"There're a lot of thefts at the moment," Frank agreed.

Billy laughed. "If it's not nailed down, it's abandoned. That's what they used to say where I was brought up."

Ed was slightly more concerned. "Not a joke."

Frank grinned, then he turned out onto the road. They made their way out of the mine through the gates at Lomax 'A' shaft.

Bernie Arrives

After dinner Ed retired to his room, tired after a day in which he had done very little. As he'd wandered across the grounds he wondered whether there was going to be another message from Kojo uttered from the middle of a bush like some biblical announcement. But the night was still and devoid of any noise but the mumbled conversation of the Faces and the distant cough of a generator.

Billy had decided not to join him for dinner, claiming that he had a migraine. He'd scuttled off, brief case in hand and pipe in mouth, waving a hand over his head. Ed knew that Billy's room was only just down the corridor from his own and it crossed his mind to knock on his door and check he was okay.

But the thought of an early night made him pass Billy's door and head for his own. He hesitated, key poised to enter the lock when he heard the rustle of cloth behind him and realised that somebody was following him down the corridor.

Turning, he saw a tall blonde woman, mid-thirties, dressed in a safari suit. She walked with a calculated swing of the hips, her attention entirely fixed on Ed. "Hello Bernie," he said sliding the key home and opening the door. "Didn't think it would be long before I saw you."

"Howdy," she said, accentuating her broad American

accent. "I didn't think you'd be back here so quickly," she countered, pushing past Ed into his bedroom, swinging a large leather shoulder bag and striding confidently to a soft armchair perched in the corner of the room. She turned to look at him coquettishly, her blonde hair carefully pinned so that some fell across her face while the rest fitted perfectly in place "You wanna drink? My duty free or yours?" She smiled, revealing polished teeth that glinted in the room's gloomy light. She batted her blue eyes playfully, then sat down and crossed her legs.

"You been abroad?" said Ed, closing the door.

"To London, tryin' to visit Lomax." She removed a bottle from her bag and pulled out the cork. "They give you glasses in the place or am I goin' to have to drink from the bottle?"

"How is Lomax?" he asked handing across two toothbrush cups perched beside his bed.

"Not so good. Couldn't get near him. Security's tight at Lomax Towers. You gotta exit at the nineteenth and climb to the twentieth where you're frisked by gorillas. He refused to see me."

"Why?"

Shrugging her shoulders, she began to fill the glasses with whisky. "I guess power's slippin' away. Lomax Gold Mine ain't the only sick child in the stable, there's been rumours about problems in Indonesia. Seems he tried to send in mercenaries to dig out a group of local bandits who were makin' one of his copper mines inoperable. Became a bit of a blood bath. Really pissed off the local government."

"But why the security? Somebody trying to kill him?"

"These tycoons get paranoid," she said handing over the whisky. "But the word is doin' the rounds that he took out a contract on Jeremy, his old Head of African Operations. And in return Jeremy did the same. He who lives by the sword, dies by the sword. Jeremy has deeper and darker allies in the London underworld than Lomax."

"Snodgrass you mean?"

She nodded and took a gulp of whisky before crossing her legs. "It's said that the fat man himself has taken an interest in bringing down Lomax." She dug into her bag and lifted out a picture. After gazing at it for a moment she handed it across. "Seen this man before?" she asked.

Ed took the photograph and gazed in shock at the image of Brett Walsh, Mr Sheep Slitter. "Not sure," he said, "Might have seen him. Why?"

"You lie badly," she said smiling, sniffing her whisky. "Brett arrived here yesterday. The moment Miriam clapped eyes on him she rang me."

Ed shrugged and then lay back on his bed nonchalantly. "If you know he's here why bother trying to trick me?"

"Because I want to know if there's a story to his sudden appearance," she replied. "He's a known felon, not that Miriam knows it. But I've got to credit Miriam, she can sniff a criminal at ten thousand paces. I looked up Brett on the international police list, and bingo!"

She smiled, put her glass down on the table and leant forward. "There was a brutal murder of two German tourists in New Zealand around ten years ago, had their throats cut. Brett was suspected but he did a runner before police could catch him. There was a large manhunt throughout New Zealand and Australia but they couldn't find a trace. Then, about five years ago a hitchhiker on a lonely road in Western Australia was brutally murdered. The local police had a number of suspects, but there was one in particular who they thought might have been more likely than the others. When they sent his details to the federal authorities they found that this suspect was none other than Brett Walsh. They flew by helicopter to the camp where he was working as roustabout only to find that he had fled with another man. Once again, the trail went cold."

By now Ed had propped himself up on an elbow. "You can't be serious," he said. "Why the hell would Lomax be employing somebody like that?"

"Just what I want to know," replied Bernie.

"But you're a Lomax employee," said Ed. "Doesn't he pay you a retainer or something, to keep him informed?"

Bernie picked up her glass again, her face a picture of annoyance, then she waved a hand. "He pays me for information every now and then," she said dismissively.

It was a little more than that, thought Ed. He remembered Bernie coordinating the chase for Kojo and Bismarck, ordering Chiri and his acolytes to search offices and on one memorable occasion to search Ed. "Nevertheless, won't he be a bit dis-chuffed if he finds you lifting lids on cans of worms?"

She smiled, but there was no look of amusement around the rest of her face. "Lomax is trapped in Lomax Towers, in fear of having a bullet through his brains. I don't think he knows or cares what's going on in Lomax Gold Mine. It's not Lomax who's employed Brett Walsh, it's Allen."

"Why would Allen employ a suspected murderer?" asked Ed.

"Precisely what I want to know," she shot back. "And you've convinced me that there is more to his sudden appearance than mere chance. I think I'll dig deeper, see what I can discover."

Heart sinking at what Allen would say of his feeble attempt to divert her, Ed tried to throw her a bone to chew. "I've been asked to act as go-between again, between the mine and the union."

"Oh?" Bernie visibly pricked up her ears. "Why is that I

wonder? Since arriving all I've been hearing is the sound of attitudes hardening on both sides."

Shrugging his shoulders, Ed took a sip of his whisky before replying. "All the more reason for a go-between."

"Why you, though?" she asked, rolling her glass around in her hand. "I'd have thought after your stay in Herman's cellar you'd have been shy of getting involved." She plunged her hand into her handbag and produced the bottle of duty free.

"I am shy," he confessed. "It's at the insistence of Herman the Helmet; he's the one who's thrown my hat in the ring and the Mine Manager is happy to accept my nomination. I had no say in the matter."

She poured out a second glass of whisky, then offered him the bottle. Ed, wanting to keep a clear head for his trip beneath ground the next day, shook his head. "Kojo's been in touch as well," he said, "a voice spoke to me from a bush the day before yesterday."

Bernie looked surprised. "I thought you stayed clear of the bushes around here," she said with a smile. "What did it say?"

"That I had five days to clear out," said Ed.

"Five days?" she said, "Why five days?"

Ed said nothing.

"I mean," she continued, "why not 'clear out tomorrow', or 'get the next bus out of town'. And why would he want you out of town in any case? I bet none of the other contractors have had this sort of personal treatment."

She rose from her seat and threw back the last of her whisky. "Thanks for telling me all this, you're a love." She blew a kiss at him and walked to the door. "Say hi to Allen for me, I'm finding it difficult to track him down at the moment, always in meetings or too busy to stop."

Going Underground

Sleep was difficult again that night as thoughts of Brett and his awful crimes circulated in and out of his mind. When he did manage to sleep, he found himself dreaming of trilobites in his farmhouse. Kojo's face swam into view, happy and smiling, explaining that he must return otherwise the trilobites would take over the world. Several times he woke and went back to sleep, the final time to dream of Alice before she'd married Greg, when they'd been an item. After that, sleep was impossible; he kept remembering her in the flat they'd shared, things they'd done together, her beautiful curves, lithe and enthusiastic.

Eventually, sitting up in a chair he started to compose an email to her, but then found that words sank without trace. He wanted to say why he'd come back to Africa, to say the things he'd wished he'd said at her flat. For an hour he hacked about, seeking a way through to fully explain why he'd returned, but every time he read back his words they sounded self-justifying and weak, almost like he was unsure himself why it was necessary. Alice would take one look at it and become annoyed again.

So instead he wrote an account of what had happened since he'd arrived at the mine, the welcome of Allen, the wholesale sacking of the geology section, Billy and Brett. He didn't mention Brett's terrible past, or the warning from

Kojo that he should be gone by the end of tomorrow or else face the consequences. He finished by saying he would be able to return to his farmhouse very soon and expressed the wish that she would join him there for a day or two.

He settled back in his chair and pictured the path that wound down from his farmhouse. In their youth, when Alice visited Aunt Sophie's during school holidays, she would come up it, wading the small stream, passing through the coppice of stunted oaks and the waist-high bracken before hopping across the fence. She'd been happy to help around Taid's farm, particularly as she had the undivided attention of both himself and Greg. But she'd chosen Ed above Greg in those days. Ed wasn't sure whether this was because he was older or whether Aunt Sophie had forbidden her Greg.

He showered and dressed, then took his laptop to reception where he was able to log in to the compound's internet link and access his email account. Trying to do this from the mine network would be impossible, there was a strict ban on employees accessing their own email accounts. Communication in and out of the company was done through a strictly controlled mine email system.

As he waited for his laptop to establish a link and then download all the waiting, unread emails, he looked around at the notices on the desk. One notice proclaimed that employees were no longer restricted to working in their offices but could access their files direct from their rooms. Grimacing at this thinly veiled attempt to squeeze more juice from an already dry orange he saw that his emails had finished arriving and that he was free to proceed.

There was nothing in his inbox but circulars or reminders about bank statements, no worried emails from Alice or Sophie.

When he arrived in the breakfast room Billy was sitting

on his own sipping a cup of tea. He was pale, like he'd not slept either. "Got up late," he said, "I think that club sandwich I had in my room last night didn't agree with me." He fixed his pipe in his mouth. "I spent most of the night running between the bathroom and planning out a new tapestry," he said through clenched teeth. "Made a few preliminary sketches. It might be a quilt with each square depicting a different scene."

"Great," said Ed nodding at Moonlight who had appeared from the kitchen. "Bernie arrived at my door last night."

"Oh?" said Billy taking a cautious sip of his tea. "Who's he?"

"Not a he, a she," replied Ed. "Beautiful, buxom, Bernie."

Billy grinned. "All right for some," he said.

"She's a journalist from Accra with an unhealthy appetite for scandal," continued Ed.

This wiped the smile from Billy's face. "A journalist from Accra?" he said quietly. "What did she want?"

"Scandal, as usual." He gazed at Billy's pallid cheeks and staring eyes, his instinct told him he needed to hold off, maybe Billy would get offended and storm off, refuse to talk, become obstructive. It wasn't in Ed's nature to be confrontational. "About Brett," he said cautiously. "Something about a murder in Australia?"

Sucking sounds came short and sharp from Billy's pipe, so loudly that the Faces on the surrounding tables turned to stare. "I'm going to get my bag," he said, standing quickly and pushing back before striding from the room leaving his tea un-drunk and the question unanswered.

Watching him disappear, Ed felt his stomach knot in frustration. He could sense concealment, and not just from Billy. Allen too must have known about Brett's past, otherwise why try and warn him off speaking to Bernie?

Moonlight brought his toast and pineapple and for the next few minutes he set about filling his aching belly, wondering about why clever and erudite Billy would link his lot with Brett.

When he arrived at the car park to meet Frank and their pickup there was no sign of Billy, nor Brett. Only when Frank arrived did the small form of Billy emerge from a nearby building and approach, pipe firmly clenched between his teeth. Ed had the feeling he'd been there for a while, watching and waiting.

"Where's Brett?" asked Ed. "Nobody's seen him this morning, he didn't turn up to collect his breakfast from the dining room."

Shrugging, Billy climbed into the back of the pickup, averting his gaze from Ed, preferring to look at a sketch drawn on thin tracing paper. Ed looked wonderingly at the back of Billy's head before climbing into the passenger seat. "Need to get kitted up for the underground," he said to Frank. "Know where to go?"

Frank nodded and zoomed off toward the Lomax 'A' gates. "We'll have to hurry," Frank explained swinging the pickup around corners, narrowly missing men who were filing through the roads leading to the mine. Ed watched in alarm as people threw themselves out of their way by jumping over deep water-filled ruts, or flattening themselves against the walls of buildings. After getting through the Lomax 'A' gates, Frank made for a series of low wooden buildings that were set back from the rest. They'd been recently painted, and when Ed opened the pickup door he was greeted by a strong smell of creosote.

"We'll be back at the surface by late morning," he told Frank, "Don't do anything that'll get you sacked."

Frank smiled and nodded.

"I'm not joking, Frank," Ed insisted, leaning through the pickup door. "It'll get back to the Mine Manager, I'll be in trouble and you'll be out of a job."

In front of the pickup was the wooden shed where equipment for the contractors and engineers wishing to go underground was distributed. Pointing his finger, Ed led Billy through a plain wooden door into a room that had a section curtained off to allow privacy for men changing into their overalls. He was confused for a few moments. On his last visit, there'd been battered wooden benches, flaking green paint and stale cigarette smells. Now there was a set of brand new plastic seats, whitewashed walls with prominently displayed posters detailing health and safety when going underground.

"Kit for two, please," said Ed to a young man in green mine uniform who stood to attention behind a polished serving hatch. There was no sign of the stores attendant Ed had met on his previous visit, an old man in a string vest who smelled of rancid meat. The new attendant reached above the hatch and brought down lamps and batteries, then he disappeared behind a partition, reappearing seconds later with overalls clasped in his hand.

"More changes," Ed said to Billy through the side of his mouth as they both dressed. "Last time I had to bribe the store attendant before he'd give me equipment that worked."

On exiting the stores they walked around a corner and stopped. A sea of men met their eyes, the night shift going in one direction and the morning shift in the other. Billy reached for his pipe. "Not anywhere near here," hissed Ed. "They're likely to hose you down if they suspect you're smoking." Billy quickly placed the pipe back in his top pocket, sucking on his teeth.

Joe appeared beside them, already kitted out with lamp

and overalls. "We'll make our way to the other entrance," he said walking off briskly.

As they traversed the expanse of tarmacadam that surrounded the Lomax 'A' winding tower Ed had a query for Joe. "The man doling out the hard hats and lamps is different from the last time I went underground."

They'd reached the edge of the huge crowd waiting to enter cages and go underground, there was a loud hub-bub of shouting and laughing. Joe led them around the edge of the crowd and got to a side entrance which allowed access up steps.

"That guy was sacked," he said as they nodded at guards.

"Was he in the union as well?"

Joe shook his head. "After the accident, the new Mine Manager thought that anybody employed at the shaft was suspect, knew more than they were letting on. He sacked most of them."

Ed decided to let the conversation lapse, it was not a good idea to be discussing the union in front of armed guards. "Geologists and engineers have priority," he said to Billy through the corner of his mouth as they mounted the steps up to a raised platform. "We go on the upper deck and the miners go on the lower."

At the top he nodded to several Faces from the compound before following Joe to where five African geologists stood. Joe shook each by the hand and spoke softly in Twi, the local language. Turning to Ed and Billy, his face had a mask of annoyance. "Hand-picked by Chiri," he said before walking off to another section of the platform.

With the arrival of the cage the engineers and geologists sauntered onto their upper deck while down below the miners where pushed, shoved and kicked onto the lower deck by Kalashnikov-toting guards until they were stuck like sardines in a tin. They shouted good natured imprecations at each other and at the guards, although Ed could hear an edge to many of the voices.

Nudging Billy he pointed to a sign outside the cage that gave the total number of shifts that had elapsed since the last fatality. It was set at thirty. "Not bad," he commented, "When I first went underground it was zero."

His comment was meant to reassure, but Billy made instinctively to twiddle the bulge in his pocket.

As the cage started to drop, Ed switched on his lamp and looked down through the wire flooring at the crammed miners below. They had finished laughing and shouting and now waited, faces blank. After only a few minutes the cage began to slow, then with a great shudder and clank of metal it ground to a halt at a brightly-lit level. The scent of paint was strong above the pervasive smell of diesel and with a jolt Ed realised that this was probably the level in which the fire and explosion had happened.

The cage door opened and the miners poured out like molasses and headed down the tunnel, beyond the influence of strip lighting and into the darkness beyond. The doors clanged shut and the cage set off again.

It took another five minutes before the cage slowed again, by now the heat and humidity was making the atmosphere thick enough to slice with a knife. As the cage ground to a halt and the great doors were flung open there was an overwhelming smell of diesel. Two bright gleaming eyes of a massive locomotive were fixed on them from the darkness beyond the strip-lighting. Licking his lips Ed tasted salt from his own sweat and the mild, sickly flavour of the diesel fumes. "Let's get going," he said to Billy and Joe. "They look as if they're about to take the locomotive to a different level."

Billy quickly skipped off the cage and stood to the edge of the tunnel as the enormous engine came rattling into view. Then he set off at a fast pace down the dark tunnel, leaving Ed and Joe to bring the maps and sampling equipment.

Catching up several minutes later they found Billy with a compass in hand measuring features in the wall of the drive under the weak glow of his torch helmet. For several moments nobody spoke.

Silence, except for Billy's loud breathing and the unmistakeable drip of water somewhere close-by. During his time as a geologist Ed had experienced silence in the way that many people never did, whether in windless forests of northern Canada or in the vast open landscape of Australia. But silence on the earth's surface is never as complete as underground where there is no buzzing insect, breath of wind or creaking tree to disturb the emptiness. There is auditory blackness, an absence of noise, and here, a kilometre beneath the ground, he could tell they were completely alone.

A loud buzzing reverberation started. Somewhere near at hand the unmistakably sound of drilling had erupted.

"I thought the drillers in the mine had been sacked," said Ed, looking at Joe.

"They have, those are the Australians," replied Joe.

We'd better go and see how they're getting on." He and Joe plodded off, leaving Billy to his measurements.

After five minutes as the noise grew progressively louder they reached the cuddy in which two Australians, sweat pouring in torrents from torsos that were stripped to the waist, swapped around drill casings and bits. Ed recognised them from the compound, particularly the tall blonde man with film star looks. The other man was much shorter, both wore ear protectors and didn't notice them approach.

The short one jerked backwards in shock when Ed tapped him on the back. He swivelled around and looked at him, face filled with a wild-eyed fear. Then, leaning against the wall of the cuddy and putting his hand over his heart in the universal sign of shock, he took off a leather glove and, after wiping off excess dirt and sweat, offered it to Ed and then Joe.

Slapping the tall blonde on his bare back he made a slashing motion across his neck, a lever on the drilling equipment was pulled and the rattling of heavy machinery subsided gradually.

"I'm Alfie, this is my assistant Sandy, known as Surfin' Sandy to his many friends and admirers. Many fellas think Alfie and Sandy sounds like a couple of pooftas, that's why they call me Auntie Alfie." He gave a smirk and winked at Joe.

Surfin' Sandy nodded his head.

Alfie was like many men Ed had met in the army, the barrack room character, glue to meld and bind a group of men together. A fleshy face and fried egg eyes suggested a lifestyle of drinking sessions and too many late nights. "What can I do for you blokes?" he asked.

"Just wondering how you're getting on," said Ed.

Alfie exchanged a look with his partner. "We're just fine," he said eventually.

"Anything we can do to help, anything you'd like to tell us?"

A broad grin spread across Alfie's face and he winked at Sandy. "Plenty," he said. "Stuff that'd make your hair stand on end." He laughed, and so did Surfin' Sandy.

"Like what?" said Ed.

"Like some of our kit goin' missin'," said Alfie. "It's like you turn your back for a moment to stop one fella filchin' only to find somethin' else has gone while your back's turned. Screws, bolts, grease for the drills, beer, clothes." He leaned forward and pointed at Sandy. "I keep the boy close in case they nick him as well."

"You been threatened?" asked Ed.

"Nah, not really. The miners say stuff in their own language so we can't understand, and I keep hearing the word scab mentioned, but that could be part of the local lingo."

Ed turned to Joe, who shrugged noncommittally.

"But they bin' quite welcomin'," Alfie continued, "particularly those girls at the compound bar. We went out last night 'round the town, ended up in a place called 'We Don't Mind Your Wife Spot'. You notice how they like to call their bars 'spots'? We had a great laugh with some of them." He turned to his companion. "Didn't we Sandy?"

Sandy nodded.

"How are you finding things Sandy?" asked Ed.

Sandy looked to Alfie, his beautiful face a mask of confusion, then he turned to Ed. "Fine," he said.

Alfie leaned close to Ed. "Sandy ain't the quickest on the uptake," he said quietly. "Looks like an Adonis, great at surfin', the lads like to keep him close 'cos he attracts in the local wildlife." He winked knowingly. Then, addressing Sandy directly he said, "It's like tuna 'round a bait ball with you, ain't it, they all want a piece of you."

Sandy nodded.

As Ed and Joe walked back down the drive they found Billy coming toward them, head down looking at the plan of the level which Joe had printed off the previous day. "I need to go all the way along here and take measurements," he said, "particularly several hundred metres either side of the drilling cuddy along this section."

"There're two drillers there now," said Ed. "Surfin' Sandy and Auntie Alfie."

Billy stopped in his tracks. "You what?" he asked, his face taught.

"Sandy and Alfie, they're two Aussie drillers. You must have seen them at the compound, there's a big gang of them from Australia. Part of Lomax's effort to replace the men he's sacked."

"I haven't seen any Australian drillers at the compound. I haven't been to the bar."

"Nevertheless," said Ed, wondering why it mattered.

"We need to go back to the shaft," said Billy backing away.

"But I thought you said we had to do some measurements?"

Billy hesitated and was on the verge of turning back when Joe caught him by the shoulder. "They don't bite," he said. "We've talked to them, no need to stop, we'll walk straight past them."

"That's right," said Ed, mystified by Billy's allergy to Australians. "If they attack we'll tell them where they get off. I thought you'd lived in Australia for years, you must know loads of Australian drillers."

But Billy was still reluctant. It was only after Ed led the way down the drive and Joe brought up the rear that they managed to get him to move.

As they approached the drilling cuddy and the noise of the men's voices were obvious, talking about what they would do once the contract was finished – a night out in Perth, Billy moved to the side of Ed and turned his face to look at the wall. When they'd moved well past the cuddy, Billy came to himself again and started measuring foliations in the wall of the drive.

If Joe thought Billy's behaviour was odd, he made no comment about it. He watched in fascination as Billy took measurements. "Why do you do that, Billy?" he asked eventually. "There's no gold in those rocks."

Turning to face him, eyes and face lost in shadow, Billy held up the level plan. "Why is there no gold in these rocks?" he asked.

"The gold is behind us and in front of us," said Joe, pointing at small tunnels that ran at right angles to the main drive. "Down there is where the stopes that contain gold are located."

"I know that," Billy said patiently, "But if I can understand why these rocks have no gold then I might understand where not to look. Mining people are too quick to dismiss negative data, they assume that if a drill hole contains no gold that it's a waste of money. They're as valuable as those that intersect gold."

"I'd like to hear you try and persuade a mining engineer about that," said Joe. "I remember Bismarck was always muttering darkly about such things and he would often say…." But Joe pulled himself up, aware that he was about to quote a man who was vilified and portrayed as an enemy of the mine.

For several seconds there was silence. "I'd like to meet this Bismarck," said Billy, gently rolling up the map. "Perhaps you can introduce me to him one day."

They walked on, stopping every twenty steps for Billy to take a measurement. Eventually he announced that they must be very close to the end of the drive and that they should now go back. "You fellas don't mind if I suck on my pipe for a while do you?" he asked. "Nobody around to chuck buckets of water."

They were at the limit of ventilation from the shaft, the air was moist and hot, Ed was feeling his chest wheeze from lack of oxygen. "Does the mine have a problem with carbon monoxide?" he asked Joe.

"Particularly on the lower levels," replied Joe, nodding.

"Right down at the end of the drives, when the locomotives have been busy, some men have been killed, they just lay down and lose consciousness and never wake up. When they're found they look like they're sleeping."

"Is there a chamber?" asked Billy sucking his pipe agitatedly. "I mean where you can escape when the carbon monoxide alarm goes off," he said to Joe's uncomprehending look.

"There ain't no alarm down here," said Joe.

"But how will people know?" he asked.

"When they feel sleepy," said Joe, smiling. "Men know from experience when it's dangerous and they can warn others."

Billy's pipe started to work overtime. "Once the carbon monoxide rises there's nothing you can do," he said eventually. "You can't outrun a gas, you may as well try and outrun the wind."

A shout from in front of them made Billy stop, remove his pipe and slink behind Ed and Joe. It was Alfie.

"I'd recognise that noise anywhere," he said. "That's got to be old Sucker, sucking on his blasted old pipe." He appeared out of the shadows, Surfin' Sandy behind him, grinning. "Knew you had to be somewhere around when I saw the Wolf Man at the bar." He took a step forward. "It's me, Auntie Alfie, the driller's best friend. I was your best friend at one time, remember? Till you took off with the Wolf Man."

Ed stepped out of the way so that Alfie's torch light fell on Billy's face. He screwed up his eyes and put his arm up to his forehead.

"Bet you're surprised to see me here," continued Alfie. "Surprised more than pleased I guess. Managed to slip out of the way of the Wolf Man last night, wondered if you were still with him. In fact, I wondered whether he'd finally done you in as well. Glad that's not the case."

Billy didn't answer.

"Last I heard was that you and the Wolf Man had headed off to PNG."

"That's right," said Billy at last. "Spent a few years working out of Port Moresby. Until this job came along. You know how it is, an old friend got in touch and flew out to meet me. Said he was desperately in need."

"Great," replied Alfie. "We'll have a beer then tonight, when the Wolf Man's not about, catch up on old times."

Billy said he'd love to. Both men shook hands on the arrangement and the party of Ed, Joe and Billy walked on down the tunnel. None of them spoke, not even when the sound of the drill erupted again in the darkness and there was no longer any chance of being overheard.

On reaching the shaft, Joe picked up the phone and placed a call to the winch man. "They're sending the explosives cage," he said, putting the instrument down.

Under the brightness of the strip lighting Billy looked ashen-faced and shaken. Whether because of being underground, or due to the shock of seeing old friends, Ed couldn't say. "Perhaps you shouldn't tell the Wolf Man you've met Auntie Alfie," said Ed. He contemplated telling him about Bernie's visit the previous evening but was saved making a decision by the intervention of Joe.

"You didn't say you were an old friend of Allen's," he said, almost accusingly.

Removing his pipe from his lips, Billy gave a sheepish smile. "Allen thought it better if we kept it quiet. Nepotism and all that."

"Where did you meet him?" asked Ed.

"He was my post graduate supervisor." Shrugging, Billy put his pipe back in his mouth and started to suck. It was an agitated suck.

Computer Code

That afternoon, in the comfort of the office, Billy started to plot out his measurements on level plans while Joe went to the computer room so he could generate more data. "I'm not absolutely certain what I'm looking for at this stage," Billy confided. "However, I did notice that the layering in the rock changed its orientation as we went along the drive."

While he continued working, Ed went to the shelves and took down volumes containing data from the holes drilled along the drive. He found the exact distance of the ore body from the drill collar then returned to Billy and placed the information on the map.

Billy nodded to him and then stuck his pipe in his mouth and started to suck. "Assuming the layering is folded," he continued after a while, "we might be able to predict the form of those folds by projecting." He looked up at Ed and smiled.

"All the ore bodies are dead straight, they're not folded, what's more they all point in the same direction," Ed said, unable to understand why Billy was bothering.

Billy popped his pipe back in his mouth and started to suck. "I'm not suggesting the ore bodies are folded," he said producing a knife from his pack so he could sharpen his pencil. "Quite the opposite. I'm saying that the layering that hosts the gold is folded."

"Amounts to the same thing in the end," said Ed, shrugging.

"Not really, not if the folding came before the gold." He bent over again and started to carefully project his layering marks out into the walls of the drive toward the location of the ore body.

"Why did Alfie call Brett the Wolf Man?" asked Ed.

A moment's silence passed before Billy was ready to answer. "You've seen him, the man has a face full of whiskers, looks like a wolf."

"Only I got the impression he was talking more about Brett's nature than his appearance."

Removing his pipe and sitting back, Billy took the opportunity to further sharpen his pencil. He chipped away thoughtfully before answering. "Wolves are mis-understood," he said eventually. "They're shy creatures who live away from people and only attack when cornered, provoked or hungry."

"So you're saying Brett isn't as bad as he seems?"

Billy was thoughtful again, seeming to weigh his words carefully. "No, I'm saying wolves have a bad press. If I was to name Brett according to his nature, I'd probably call him Fox Man. He's a loner who kills without conscience and then keeps on killing because it's what he does."

Leaning forward, apparently unaware of the impression he had created, Billy continued to pencil in his interpretation. Before Ed could continue to question him, he banged the table with his pencil-free hand. "If you want more information, you'll have to see Allen. He said you'd get curious and start to dig."

It was the first angry words Billy had ever spoken to Ed and a tense silence descended on the office. Eventually he withdrew his pipe from his mouth and threw it down on the table and stood up. "Goddamn it, I can't believe I said that to you." He looked over at Ed and fixed him in the eye. "I'm really sorry," he said. "I've been trapped with Brett for so long that I think some of him is rubbing off on me."

"That's all right," replied Ed from the desk where he'd retreated. "I understand." But he didn't, not really. He understood that Billy had something to hide as well as the Wolf Man but what that thing was he couldn't possibly guess.

"Thank you," said Billy sitting down again and grabbing his pipe. "Now," he said with impatience, "I'd like to have ten minutes' silence while I finish this work."

Suitably admonished, Ed turned away and looked out of the window. The usual scene met his eyes; armed guards in the shade, armoured scout car blocking the entrance to the mine, and in the distance the town of Lomax with its myriad of higgledy-piggledy houses.

"Tell me why you came here," said Billy suddenly. "To make money, I suppose?"

"I swore never to return here," Ed said, thinking that perhaps he should give part of himself if he wanted something from Billy in return. "I came back because Allen pleaded with me. He put me in this office with you and made sure Brett was sent to hell with the devil Chiri. I'd like to know why."

This was not the response Billy wanted or expected. "I can't help that. If you want to know more see Allen. I haven't a clue why he wanted you to work with me."

"Okay then," said Ed. "How about a trade. I tell you something about myself if you tell me something about yourself."

"Sounds a bit like going behind the bike sheds," replied Billy, grinning. "I was never attractive or brave enough to do that sort of thing at school."

"I came here a few months ago to find Greg, an old friend who had disappeared. I found out that he'd become involved in a plot to defraud this mine with a man named Forge who used to sit at that desk." He pointed at Joe's desk. "And who used to collect trilobites." He pointed at the shelves.

"Did you find him?" asked Billy

Ed shook his head. "Dead, probably."

"You're not sure?"

"I found out where the miners' union kept him after he was kidnapped. Nobody could survive in there for very long. I expect he died of dysentery or malaria or both."

"Why did the miners' union kidnap him?"

Ed shrugged. "To protect their assets inside the mine. Lomax feels the union was the vehicle by which his business rivals ripped him off. That's a large part of the reason why there's such an anti-union feeling around the place."

His contribution finished, Ed sat back and folded his arms. "Now tell me why you stick with the Wolf Man," he said.

"I still don't understand why you returned to this mine," Billy said. "All you've said is that you've come to investigate the drilling and that you're sure that somewhere along the line Forge was dishonest."

"That's correct," said Ed.

"Why are you concerned about whether Forge lied?"

Looking down at his crossed arms, Ed had sudden visions of trilobites left on kitchen tables and fence posts. "Your turn," he said. "I've told you something about me, now you need to tell me something." Confessions about trilobites could wait, he felt.

Billy slowly reached into his bag and produced his

tapestry. Then very deliberately took out a set of very thick glasses which enabled him to thread a needle. "I suppose," he said, carefully bringing the thread to the needle, "the story starts in Australia around ten years ago. I'd been working as a gold mining geologist out of Kalgoorlie for quite a few years."

He put the tapestry on his knees and shut his eyes. "I'll be honest, those years before Brett turned up were the best of my life. I'd get contracts to interpret drilling all over the Outback. I'd lie out on my iron bedstead and look up at the stars. The southern night sky is beautiful, and on clear nights it's almost three dimensional. I'd lie by myself around my own fire and look out at the drillers' fire a hundred metres or so away and I imagined myself in my own solar system, far away from the cares and worries of the world."

He picked up the tapestry and gave it a long stare. "Always been alone," he said, shaking his head. "Dad disappeared when I was young and mum entered a mental asylum not long after. I've never found people very helpful or appealing."

With needle in hand he carefully pierced the cloth and pulled so that a piece of thread gradually tightened. "Anyway," he continued. "One day, some interfering busy body politician decided that being out on your own was a safety risk and set about demonstrating how much he cared about us folks in the Outback by outlawing the practice of singletons. I was forced to have an assistant, a roustabout. I had no say in who that was to be, the company who employed me simply sent somebody along. Brett Walsh."

He poked the needle back up through the cloth carefully. "I was about to resign, but then found that Brett wasn't too assiduous. He would sometimes disappear for days or weeks on end. He'd appear occasionally, and then only if he'd run out of money. I'd give him some dollars and he'd go off again."

A sigh escaped from his lips and he placed the tapestry back down on his knee. "I was back in Perth for some leave. I used to keep a small flat in a place near to Herdman's Lake, close to the railway station. I would go to Freemantle to the fish market and stay in a café all day reading a book, looking at all the pretty girls, getting used to being around people. On this occasion one of the pretty girls came up to me and engaged me in conversation."

He shook his head and put his pipe in his mouth and started sucking, then bent over his tapestry. "That's another reason they call me Sucker, always a sucker for a pretty face. Fancy me, Mr Knobbly Knees, King of Scrawn, being of interest to a classy-looking woman like that." He put his head on the desk for several seconds before picking it up and calmly continuing.

"She turned out to be a reporter interested in illegal aliens living in the Outback. People without citizenship or a visa. I had neither. She published an expose on me, a sort of case study. Brett came into the camp with the newspaper clutched in his hand and said I'd better leave. He said he knew people in PNG and that he was tired of Australia and he'd come with me."

"And that," he declared, "is how come I'm with Brett Walsh."

The story had a partial ring of truth, but from what Bernie had said last night it was the Wolf Man who was the fugitive, not Billy. Ed wondered what details had been omitted. And there was the relationship with Allen that had not yet been explained.

"So when was it that you met Allen? You mentioned to Alfie that he was an old friend."

Billy cursed under his breath. "Allen's not going to be

happy," he said. "He was adamant that I should keep that quiet. I'd be grateful if you wouldn't spread it around."

"Why?" asked Ed. "What's there to be afraid of?"

"Nepotism," said Billy. "This job wasn't advertised, Allen doesn't think it should be known that we have a connection, it could make difficulties for him."

"But my job wasn't advertised either. And in any case, there aren't that many people banging on the door to come here, they're desperate to get anybody they can."

Billy put down his tapestry and picked up his pencil, a signal that the conversation was at an end. "You'll have to ask Allen why he doesn't want anybody to know," he said. "If you don't mind, I'd like to finish what I'm doing."

When Joe walked in from the computer room, Ed was busy examining drill core returns and Billy was putting the final touches to his map of layering. "I've gone for simplicity," Billy said to the room. "There are several details I need to figure out by doing some more measurements, but at least we have something which we can use to test Forge's drilling.

He'd interpreted a series of Z-shaped folds. "The gold occurs in the middle limb of the Z but where the layering turns there's none."

"What does that mean?" asked Joe.

Billy shrugged his shoulders. "It's an observation which we need to investigate, find out if the gold is hosted in similar situations throughout the mine. It'd be nice to go further south tomorrow, have a look at some of the other ore zones."

They began planning the next day's work by transferring all interesting features from Forge's drilling onto the plans of the level which they were to visit.

"This is odd," said Joe as he opened a new volume. "Some of these pages are just 0s and 1s."

"Strange," said Ed after a moment. "Why would Forge include that?"

"By mistake?" asked Billy.

Joe shook his head. "Not Forge, everything he did was deliberate. If this data was printed out by mistake he wouldn't have bothered including it."

"Not even to pad it out?" suggested Billy. "Make the drilling volume look larger, more impressive?"

"Not even to do that," said Ed. "Not the Forge I knew."

"It looks like compiled computer code," said Joe turning several pages. "But there isn't enough here to run even the smallest sort of program."

Billy interrupted. "Could it be an image?"

"Could be," agreed Joe. "It could also be a binary-encoded message," he said looking up at Ed. "But it doesn't explain why Forge would have printed it off and placed it at random in a drilling volume."

Unclipping the binder and removing the pages, Ed handed them across to Joe. "You're the computer expert, you tell us what it's all about."

"You think this could be significant?" asked Billy. "Surely it's just a mistake."

"We've just explained that Forge did nothing by mistake," replied Ed returning to his desk. "We don't really know what we're looking for. This might be very important." He looked out of the window in time to see Chiri's pickup arrive in the car park. He swore very loudly, bringing both Joe and Billy to the window.

"Only one pickup today for the entire crew," said Joe thoughtfully. "Normally they come in a convoy of three."

"And Chiri does not look best pleased," said Ed, as the Exploration Manager jumped from the vehicle.

Joe and Billy went back to their desks leaving Ed to

watch Chiri's procession mount the steps. He knew from past experience that the order in which Chiri's acolytes moved was carefully controlled by the man himself. The most favoured were closest to him and the least favoured were at the back. It was therefore no great shock to see Brett at the tail of the column, hat on head and roll-up steaming away from his mouth.

As they approached the landing on which the Drilling Room was located, the acolytes looked as if they were bunching together. A few threw nervous glances behind them at Brett's advancing figure. It looked more like the acolytes were running away from Brett than following Chiri. Before long they heard the heavy footfall that signalled Chiri's arrival on the Drilling Room balcony. Ed leaned back in his chair, ready for the invasion.

When the door swung open, Chiri marched straight up to Joe. "I heard but I couldn't believe," he said. "And there are plans to re-employ more of you."

Joe said nothing, his eyes wide and staring.

"Joe's here because I particularly requested him," said Ed. "If you have any issues you need to address them to Allen or the Mine Manager." He was pleased to hear his steady voice did not betray the beating heart within.

"It's Allen I need to see now," said Chiri without concern that Ed had spoken to him out of turn. "We have been attacked, one of our vehicles was stolen and we were forced to destroy the other one chasing the criminals."

"Oh?" said Ed. By now the acolytes had arrived in the room and distributed themselves around the available desk space and walls. For a moment Ed hesitated seeing Brett appear at the door; he had never knowingly clapped eyes on a multiple murderer let alone shared a room with one. The acolytes nearest the door moved away once he arrived, to join others on the other side of the room.

"Yes," continued Chiri. "We had to come here in only one vehicle and we were ambushed on the road through the jungle. Shots were fired and we were very lucky to escape without one of us being injured."

Ed tried to look shocked but all the time sensing that the acolytes were not behaving in their usual sullen way. The atmosphere was timorous rather than threatening and this impression was enhanced by the way they all bunched together, as far away from Brett as possible.

"I need more vehicles," said Chiri. "I cannot carry out my duties without them. I need to see Allen."

"He's in a meeting with the Mine Manager," said Joe. "I talked to him just now. He was on his way up there."

Chiri curled his lip at Joe. "Where's Bismarck and Kojo?" he spat.

"No idea," replied Joe.

Chiri made a dismissive sound in his throat and then marched to the door where he intersected Brett lighting a new roll-up. He pushed past him angrily and then thumped down the balcony. The acolytes charged for the door en masse and dived past Brett like rabbits encountering a fox and followed their master toward the steps. Brett said nothing, and after lighting his cigarette walked calmly after the group.

As Chiri and his acolytes trooped down the steps and climbed into the pickup, Ed watched Brett make his way calmly to the car park and re-light his rollup. The pickup waited for him, there were no cat calls or angry shouts for him to hurry up. Once his cigarette was lit he put away his lighter and moved slowly over to the waiting vehicle and then climbed gracefully onto the flat bed where he took a space on his own.

Billy joined Ed at the window. "I see the Wolf Man is working his dark magic," he said. "Good luck to them all."

He went back to his desk, shoulders hunched, and picked up his pencil.

* * *

Billy decided to join Ed in the compound bar that evening when they returned. He was fidgety, constantly sucking on his pipe. Only when he reached into his bag and produced a section of tapestry did he begin to relax. The Faces noticed after a while what he was doing and kept watching, transfixed, as he carefully pulled needle and thread through the material.

"Ever tried knitting?" asked Ed.

Shaking his head, Billy put his work down and reached for his beer. "Never worked anywhere cold enough to need woollen clothes. Mind you," he said picking up his tapestry, "it gets quite cold at night in the Outback at certain times of year."

For several moments neither man spoke. Ed searched his mind for something to say. He really wanted to ask more about Billy's relationship with the Wolf Man and why they were still together, but he knew that Billy would be likely to stand and walk off. He looked around the bar and noticed that Alfie and Sandy hadn't joined their fellow drillers for the second night in a row, nor was there any sign of the Wolf Man.

"It's the fifth day of my stay tomorrow," he said, voicing another of his anxieties.

"So?" said Billy.

"I was warned that I should leave within five days of arriving."

Billy looked up, eyes narrowed. "By who?"

"Somebody purporting to speak for Kojo, the old Manager of Geology."

Billy blinked and stopped pushing his needle. "Is he still around?" he asked in a small voice. "I thought he and Bismarck had disappeared for good."

Ed shook his head. "I don't think so, and neither does Allen. I'm telling you to keep your eyes and ears open. The warning was non-specific, he didn't say what would happen, just recommended that I leave."

"Why five days?"

Shrugging, Ed grabbed his beer bottle and took a drink. "No idea."

"Why are you still here then?" Billy pressed. "You should be preparing to leave."

"No, I don't think he was referring to me specifically, it was in the manner of good advice that I would be wise to follow."

"So, why don't you?"

Here was a question that Ed couldn't answer. He'd asked himself the same thing many times and kept coming back to the same response; he needed to find out why somebody was leaving trilobites at his farmhouse. The solution was here, somewhere at Lomax; he wasn't going to leave until he'd found answers or until the threat was so serious that he had no alternative. "I don't like a mystery," he said. "I want to know what Forge did with the money he stole. The answer's somewhere here, I need to find it."

"It is money then," said Billy, resuming his sewing. "There are things more important than money, you know, like your health."

"No, not just money," replied Ed, stung by Billy's sanctimonious tone. "There are other reasons."

"Such as?" asked Billy, not looking up.

But Ed did not feel ready to confide in Billy, not when he knew so little about him. He drank the last of his beer and stood up. "I'm tired," he said. "I had no sleep last night and I need to turn in early. I'll see you at breakfast."

Meetings

When Ed arrived in the breakfast room next morning it was busy with Faces. They avoided Ed's gaze, making it quite clear that he was an outcast. He wondered if their hostility was not just because he was too closely associated with James Allen, but had to do with Brett the Smoker. Deciding that he didn't really care, he found himself an empty table and waited for Moonlight to bring him his breakfast.

'Today was the day,' he thought. A visit to Allen would be essential. As Ed contemplated the best way of contacting the new Manager of Geology he heard a cough from behind. "Excuse me, sir." It was Moonlight the waitress. "Your tea, and a note from Mr Allen."

Smiling, Ed thanked her and reflected that yet another of Allen's qualities was his timing. Unfolding the note he saw it contained an instruction not to accompany Billy and Joe underground but come and see him straight away. Putting the note into his pocket he helped himself to the tea and sat back.

Billy arrived, his face flushed, and helped himself to tea from Ed's pot. "Going to be a warm one today," he said. "Probably best to go underground."

"I've a meeting with Allen. An urgent note just arrived. Joe'll look after you."

"Wonder what he wants?" asked Billy. "I bet I can

guess." He took a sip of his tea. "No more messages or final warnings last night?"

Ed shook his head. "Nothing."

Leaning across conspiratorially, Billy beckoned Ed to come closer. "Alfie came around last night for beers. There's a lot going on at the moment, stuff going missing, sabotage and the like. And several tons of explosives have gone walkabout."

"Why?"

"Obvious isn't it, it's the union exacting revenge for all the sackings. Alfie and the other drillers are thinking of pulling out, they were accused of being scabs when they came to the surface yesterday afternoon, had death threats. They're worried that the explosives might end up in their vehicles."

"I'll ask Allen about it when I see him," said Ed. "What about the Wolf Man? He wasn't in the bar last night, or did he arrive after I left?"

"Wouldn't know about that, I left straight after you, but he did call at my room just as Alfie was leaving. Quite an awkward moment."

"Oh?" asked Ed.

"They hate each other; Alfie's genuinely frightened of him."

"What happened when they met?"

"Brett curled his lip and Alfie scampered away. It was most unfortunate timing, almost like Brett had been keeping a watch, waiting for Alfie to appear. I asked what he wanted and he told me he'd be accompanying Chiri and his men on an expedition; they'll be spending the next few nights out in the jungle. They're apparently going to be visiting some outlying prospects."

"That's unlike Chiri," said Ed thoughtfully. "Never heard of him going off into the jungle for more than a few hours."

Billy's breakfast arrived and they sat in silence for the next few minutes. When they'd finished, Billy took out his pipe and fixed it between his teeth. By now the Faces had realised that Billy didn't smoke, merely made strange sucking noises; they gave the pair dirty looks and carried on eating.

When they arrived in the car park, Frank was fiddling with the audio system of the pickup. His music was pitched so loud that Ed could feel the gravel vibrate under his feet as he approached. Spotting them through the windscreen, he smiled and then turned the volume down and jumped out. "I'm to take you to see the Mine Manager as soon as possible," he said, almost standing to attention.

"My day to be popular," said Ed. "It'll have to be after we've dropped off Billy and I've seen Allen."

When they arrived at the Lomax 'A' shaft, Allen was waiting in front of one of the large wooden sheds. He waved at Ed and disappeared through a doorway. "See you at the office later," Ed said to Billy. Then he turned to Frank. "Wait here, I won't be long."

Walking quickly to where Allen had been standing, he knocked respectfully on a door labelled 'Manager of Geology'. On entering, he realised he had been in here before, when Kojo had been in charge of the geology section. Like his office close to the front gate, this room was also bare. The tramp of Ed's miner's boots echoed as he made his way across the huge expanse of floor to Allen's desk.

"Sit down," said Allen pointing to a wooden chair which was off to the side. "Joe says he found something strange in Forge's drilling yesterday," he continued, ignoring his usual habit of asking after Ed's health. "Some kind of binary code."

Ed nodded. "That's right, could be something, could be nothing, but worth investigating."

"Definitely," said Allen. "I persuaded Lomax that the secret of Forge's millions is in his drilling volumes, this is exactly the sort of thing he'd like to hear. Anything else of interest?"

"Billy was recognised yesterday by those drillers from Australia."

A slight cough. "I know, I went to see Billy yesterday and found him with that Alfie bloke. We need to make sure it goes no further. Nobody must know he's here, it's most important."

Ed laughed. "Why, for God's sake?"

"He has something of a history." Allen licked his lips and Ed could see him picking his words carefully. "I guess he told you that I was his post graduate supervisor? That means I know something of his past. He was a bit of a radical, got himself into a lot of trouble with the law. Direct action and all that."

"So?"

"With all this union activity going on…it's probably something that needs to be kept under wraps."

There was a loud knock on the door and Adzo walked in carrying a tray of coffee. She smiled warmly at Ed, plonked the coffee on Allen's desk and walked out, stilettos clicking on the wooden boards.

When the door shut behind her, Ed leaned forward. "Bernie came to see me a couple of nights ago. She says Miriam's been sniffing around and has clapped eyes on Brett Walsh. She thought he looked a bit shifty so immediately got on the phone to her. Bernie did some digging of her own and discovered stuff about Brett, stuff which you neglected to tell me, stuff like he's wanted for murder." He folded his arms and glared at Allen.

Allen took the news calmly. "We'd better tell Lomax that Bernie's interested, he won't be happy," he said.

"Already told Bernie Lomax wouldn't be happy with her digging about. She brushed me aside, said Lomax had enough problems at the moment without worrying about Lomax mine."

"She probably thinks power is slipping away from him," said Allen pursing his lips. "She's looking to move on and curry favour with some of his rivals."

Anger flared inside Ed's head; for a moment he thought of taking out his frustration by shouting at the top of his voice. But almost as quickly as the emotion appeared, it began to dissipate. His future health and happiness was bound up with Allen. The threads that bound Lomax and Allen together also entwined around him. Instead of shouting he decided on the emotional approach. "Why don't you trust me?" he asked.

"I do, of course I do. What makes you doubt me?"

"You never told me Billy was an old friend, I found that out by accident. It was Bernie who told me that Brett was wanted for murder and that Lomax is under siege in his London headquarters. At every stage I find things out by chance, never from you."

Allen started to shape his face into a surprised expression, but then stopped and started to grin. "You're right, I'll tell you everything straight. But not now. I think you've got an urgent appointment with the Mine Manager so there's no time." He rose from his chair and indicated the door with his hand. "You gotta trust me on this. I need you to be strong for the moment and go about your business as usual. If I tell you what I think might be happening..." He stopped. "Well, let's just say it's best if we go about our business as usual."

They both walked to the door. "You know what day this

is?" asked Ed, feeling like a wife chastising her husband for forgetting their anniversary.

Allen looked at him quizzically.

"It's the fifth day since I arrived." Then, when he saw this meant nothing to Allen he pressed on. "Kojo's warning that I should leave for the good of my health."

Allen's eyes lit up in recognition. "I hadn't forgotten," he assured him. "When I arrived in the office this morning and heard the news I immediately thought of you and Kojo's warning."

"What news?" asked Ed feeling that Allen was once again holding out on him. "Has something happened?"

Allen nodded his head gravely. "Mine Manager was on the phone first thing, he wants to tell you personally; there's been an incident, the Australian drillers are pulling out." He pushed Ed out of the door and locked it. "I need to get over to the main office, there'll be meetings all morning. I honestly can't tell you; if I do the Mine Manager will go ballistic."

As Frank drove him to the Mine Manager's hilltop residence, Ed could feel his insides knotting with frustration. He would give Allen an opportunity to make good on his promise of full information, but if he prevaricated for too much longer, then Ed would be packing his bags and going home to brave the blizzard of trilobites.

Emerging out onto the hilltop he felt the familiar cooling breeze and smelled the vague undertone of ozone that was reminiscent of the sea. Far off to the south he saw a dark blue line between the green land below and the wispy sky above. Although only a smudge on the skyline, the thought of the sea made him forget his troubles for a moment and he could feel his spirits rise.

"Don't forget to wait," he told Frank as he got out of

the pickup. "Don't want to get out of the meeting to find you've gone to pick up a fare."

Frank nodded and gave a big beaming smile. "I'll be right here, sleeping."

"Welcome, Mr Evans," said Miriam as Ed entered the cool hallway of the Mine Manager's villa. She advanced toward him in her usual green silk, shoes squeaking on the wooden floor. "The Mine Manager is busy for the moment, he's asked me to come and greet you." She led the way into the drawing room where Ed had met the Mine Manager on his previous meeting. Miriam took a side saddle seat on one of the leather arm chairs and indicated that Ed should sit in the one directly opposite.

"I ordered tea the moment I saw your vehicle coming up the drive, it won't be long. How are you settling back into life at Lomax?"

"Oh fine," said Ed. "There's all these changes. Makes my head spin."

"I believe Joe is working with yourself and this new man Billy," she said. "I must say I was very dubious about employing Joe. He was Bismarck's friend and bound to be a big union supporter."

"I've never asked him about his union affiliations," said Ed. "He seems assiduous and hard working. Rather astute, in fact."

"And Frank? Is he behaving himself? I gather he used to be the union messenger, carrying packages and so forth. You must make sure he doesn't fall back into his old ways. There should be no hint that he's using mine vehicles and facilities to further union business."

The door opened and a waiter in mine fatigues brought tea on a patterned wooden tray. Miriam waited until the man had left and shut the door behind him before she continued. "This whole house is full of union eyes and ears," she said. "I wanted wholesale changes up here as well."

Ed said nothing, Miriam was not a woman with whom you argued.

"I must say I'm deeply unhappy with the two men Allen has brought over here from PNG. The one looks like some kind of Australian drifter and the other reminds me of Trotsky. What do you think?"

Taking a sip of his hot tea, Ed decided to place the cup on the table perched close to his right hand. "Bernie came and visited me the other day," he said carefully. "Told me of your concerns. She said she'd be going away and looking into his past."

"She hasn't got back to me yet," Miriam replied. "But I've done some digging of my own, not about this Brett man but about Billy Barker. Lomax sent across his CV for us so we have a back story."

"I never knew his second name," said Ed quietly.

"No, there's a lot that Mr Barker wants to keep quiet, but I've found out quite a lot. It seems that he was in university during the early eighties in London. One of the polytechnics." She sniffed in an unlady-like fashion. "I asked a friend to investigate, she's the wife of one of the senior faculty men."

"Which polytechnic?"

"I'm afraid I'm not at liberty to say, but it's converted to a university and it's doing its best to come up in the world. When Billy went there it had the most horrendous reputation for radical loonies, Trotskyiites, Maoists, every ism that ever existed congregated there."

"And what has your friend found out?"

"Nothing yet, but she's digging very vigorously. I'm sure it won't be long until I have complete information." She sipped her tea thoughtfully. "But while we're trying to deal with the local loonies I'm not sure it's healthy having somebody wandering around who is indoctrinated in the arts of agitation. I don't know what Allen was thinking when he brought him over here."

"Allen said it was Lomax's idea," said Ed. "Besides, the early eighties were a long time ago; Billy's been working in Australia for ages, in the Outback. People change, they move on."

"Mr Evans, people do not change their nature just like that, they just suppress their urges for a while until the opportunity presents itself. Look at Burgess and McLean in MI6. I don't like the idea of that man in the mine."

"I'll keep an ear open," Ed said. "If I hear anything which might be construed as being detrimental to the smooth running of the mine, I'll let you know."

She rose from her chair and smiled at him. "I'll go and see if the Mine Manager is available."

Ed listened to Miriam's retreating footsteps as she squeaked down the hallway and wondered what would happen when she discovered that Allen had once lectured at the Trotskyiite polytechnic. He was amazed by Miriam's grasp of detail, even down to the identity of his driver. He went to the window and gazed out at Frank, asleep in the pickup. She kept referring to her husband as Mine Manager, which was odd. She'd used 'I', 'we' and 'us' a lot as well when talking about mine policy. To Miriam, the mine was a toy and the miners were accessories, stick figures rather than real people.

Miriam's husband squeaked into the room. "Mr Evans," he said. "Glad you could come. I was down below in a meeting, there's something of a crisis." He put his head around the door. "Tea in the drawing room," he shouted to the house.

Striding across to his desk, he sat down heavily in the

seat and placed his briefcase on the ground. "Please sit down Mr Evans," he said gesturing to the seat Ed had just vacated.

Rummaging around in his briefcase he produced a small envelope and pulled out a document. "You probably don't know this, but there's been rather a lot of damage done to vehicles, and mine property has been stolen. All by the union of course."

"I did hear something of it," admitted Ed.

"What you probably don't realise is that one of the drillers we brought across from Australia was killed by them last night."

"I beg your pardon?" asked Ed.

"One of the drillers from Australia was killed by the union last night."

For a moment Ed's head began to swim. It didn't seem to make sense. "Why do you assume it was the union?" he asked.

"These people are terrorists, it's in their nature," said the Mine Manager looking at Ed as if he'd gone mad.

"But you're sure it's them and not some vendetta between drillers?" insisted Ed.

The Mine Manager looked down at the piece of paper in his hand. "The driller's name was Alfie Sanders, he was found dead just outside the compound in the early hours of the morning. He had clearly struggled with his assailants and been overpowered before being dispatched with a machete. Once on the floor the word 'scab' was carved on his forehead."

Silence. The Mine Manager crumpled the sheet of paper in his hands.

"Scab?"

"Yes, the term used for strike breaker. You may be unsurprised to learn that all the Australian drillers are now making plans to leave for home. Can't say I blame them, but it does present us with some difficulties because we need drillers for the mine to run efficiently."

Ed's brain was still catching up. "Alfie Sanders? Is that Auntie Alfie?"

"No idea. I do know his drilling partner is called Sandy."

The Mine Manager turned away and placed the file with the report of Alfie's death on his desk. Then he pulled open a drawer and started to compose a letter using a very old fashioned looking fountain pen. Ed listened to the scratch of the nib as it glided across the page. He remembered the same noise in the silence of his grandfather's kitchen. Taid had inherited his father's fountain pen and kept it clean and working all his life.

The silence allowed him to pull himself together. "Why did you want to see me?" he asked.

"Surely it's obvious. You're the go between with the union, I want you to take them this letter and I want to find out what the hell is going on."

"But how am I to set up a meeting?"

The Mine Manager turned around and looked him in the face. "You're driven around by Frank and you work in the same office as Joe. Can't be that difficult to set up a meeting."

He handed Ed the letter. "This letter contains a reminder to the union that they're on borrowed time. Unless their activities cease forthwith we will take action. Hand it to Herman in person. And now," he said standing up, "I have a meeting with all of the mine management." He gestured with his hand for Ed to leave and walked him to the front door of the villa.

"I need hardly say that we take this sort of thing very seriously," he said, as if addressing the press. "There's no doubt in my mind that the union is involved and they will be punished forthwith." And having delivered his statement, he withdrew inside the villa.

Ed stood on the threshold, too shocked to move. He saw the face of Alfie lit by torchlight in the underground, its features blunted and coarsened by years of hard living and exposure to the sun. The implication of what the Mine Manager had said was that Alfie had been chosen at random for retribution; he was a western contractor located at the compound and in the eyes of the union he was a legitimate target in their high stakes game with the mine. It could have been Ed, wandering around after dinner, in the dark of the compound garden, who had been targeted. In fact, it probably would have been Ed had he not decided to go to bed early and lock his door.

With a sudden thrill of horror he realised this was what Kojo had warned him about. Kojo must have known that a killing was planned, might even have been part of the planning for the outrage. His mind rebelled against the notion that the man he had known as the first Manager of Geology could have been part of a pre-meditated plot to kill. Not happy, laughing Kojo, in his freezing cold office, drinking freezing Coca-Cola with a belly like a pregnant woman. It would be like hearing that Father Christmas had organised a hit.

If Kojo had known about the plan it was presumably because he was privy to what the union intended. In which case Allen and Lomax were right to be worried that the union now had a man with Kojo's organisational ability in their camp.

C.R.A.P.

"This Miriam is married to the Mine Manager?" asked Billy.

"She's the power behind the throne," said Allen, who'd popped his head around the door to find out how Ed's meeting with the Mine Manager had gone. "Not to be trifled with."

"And she knows something of your past and is continuing to investigate," said Ed.

It was late morning, Billy and Joe had spent only a few hours underground and then been picked up by Frank and brought to the Drilling Office. Joe had told them he wanted to spend a little time in the computer room sorting out maps for the next day.

Billy had gone pale when he'd heard the news of Alfie; for several minutes he'd been unable to speak. Ed had been seriously worried that he was about to go into shock, but then he emerged from himself, brought out his pipe and started to produce long, slow, mournful sucks that reverberated around the office. "Must have happened straight after he left my room," he said to nobody in particular.

For the next half an hour they'd all three discussed the death of Alfie the driller before moving on to the matter of Miriam's investigation into Billy's past. Billy glanced at Allen for a fleeting moment and then looked away to the plan laid out on his desk. Ed thought a message had been communicated between the two men and was keen to find out more. "Is there anything else I need to know?" he asked.

Silence.

"What is Miriam going to find out?" he persisted.

Neither of the men said anything for a moment. Then Allen smiled. "I don't see why we can't tell Ed what went on," he said. "It was a long time ago after all, a lot of water has flowed under the bridge."

Billy looked up at Allen in alarm. "I'm not sure…People today won't understand."

"I think Ed's a man of the world, he knows what it's like." He sat down in Joe's chair and leant back. "He's from Liverpool after all; must be pretty familiar with far-left groups." He looked up at Ed, grinning. "Isn't that right? Militant Tendency and all that."

"Not my scene."

Allen pointed at himself and then at Billy. "Believe it or not we were both cadres in a revolutionary communist organisation. I was the group's leader, founder and chief recruiting sergeant and Billy made the tea." He looked across at Billy and winked.

Billy grimaced and stuck his pipe in his mouth.

"What were you called?"

"The Campaign for Revolution and Peace. We were so humourless in those days we didn't realise the acronym was CRAP. We changed it when we realised, but it was too late. So, throughout the revolutionary world we were known as the Crappers."

Billy produced his tapestry and started to suck on his pipe. They were long drawn out sucks, not the short and sharp sucks which he made when agitated.

"Anyway," continued Allen. "We were probably on the

more esoteric end of the spectrum when it came to revolutionaries, more likely to be putting forward specious arguments than taking on the police or the far right. That's not to say that we weren't averse to the odd bit of a scuffle outside the local watering hole."

Allen stopped and looked across at Billy. "That's pretty much as I remember it," he said. "Billy decided after a while that he'd had enough and headed off for Australia and then I eventually calmed down as well. Even went back to America for a while."

"I didn't know that," said Billy, his eyes narrowing. "I'm amazed you weren't arrested on the spot."

"I suppose even America forgives and forgets," said Allen looking down at his hands.

"I don't understand," said Ed. "Why would you be arrested?"

"He's a draft-dodger," said Billy triumphantly. "Has he never told you? When we were at college he never stopped going on about how he'd done a tour of duty in Vietnam and then refused to go back." Billy's face was shining with joy at telling the story. "He quoted the Nuremburg Judgement at his trial. They told him he had forty-eight hours to quit the country and never come back."

A small smile reached Allen's lips. "It's not something I spread around anymore. People here would not see it as a badge of honour." He gave a little wince. "Could you imagine if Miriam got hold of that information? She'd have me hounded out. Bernie would make sure it was headline news." Turning toward Ed, an earnest look in his face he said, "Perhaps you understand now why I haven't been as straightforward with you as I would have liked. I have to keep this under wraps."

"I can see that," said Ed. "Only I still don't think you've been quite straight with me."

There was a tense silence in the room, almost like Allen and Billy were holding their breath.

"For instance, how did you get the lecturing job, just like that?" He clicked his fingers. "How do you arrive on a plane from America and walk into a job? Doesn't make sense."

Ed had never seen Allen embarrassed, he even went red in the face and looked down at the back of his hands so he didn't have to look at Billy. "I got connections in the States. My family made a few phone calls and got me the job."

Billy's pipe fell silent. "I never knew that," he said.

"Not the sort of thing you'd tell the Crappers," said Allen. "If you remember one of our hatreds was inheritance and the 'Old Boys' Network'. I'm hardly likely to tell everybody that their leader was part of everything we were supposed to hate."

Allen rose from his chair. "Anyway," he said. "Enough reminiscing, I have work to do, and you boys need to crack on as well."

When he'd left, Billy got his head down and started to plot his data on the level plans. "I'd wondered why the drills were still today," he said quietly. "I can't believe Alfie's dead."

"Do you think it was the union?" asked Ed.

Billy looked up from his desk and gave him a quizzical look. "How should I know? I'm no detective. If the Mine Manager is convinced it was the union then who am I to argue?" He maintained his gaze long enough for Ed to register his doubt.

"You said the Wolf Man visited you last night, just as Alfie was leaving. Did they talk?"

Billy shook his head.

"So there was no altercation?"

No response from Billy this time, not even a shake of

the head.

"You see the point I'm trying to make?"

Picking up his pen again and leaning over the plan, Billy started to draw lines. He worked with such care and concentration that Ed didn't want to pursue the question. Instead, he turned back to the drilling volume he'd been studying. For the next few minutes he tried to focus on the words on the page, but they kept slipping through his mind like sand slips through hands.

"Alfie and Brett never did get on," said Billy eventually.

Ed waited, pretending to concentrate on the drilling information.

"Alfie was the one who informed the police that Brett was missing from the camp the night there was a murder of a hitchhiker in Australia. The Wolf Man tried to kill him but Alfie hid, then slipped away into the night."

Prickles started to erupt on Ed's neck. They made their way down his spine to his lower back. "So he had a motive to kill Alfie, had even attempted to do so before last night, is that what you're saying?" Ed said, not turning around.

"That's right," said Billy in a small voice that shook either in fear or emotion. "He hasn't killed in a while. They do say that men like Brett are compulsive."

Turning around, Ed stared into Billy's face. It was grey, as if the death of Alfie had only just hit home. "We should tell the mine," said Ed. "They need to know about the Wolf Man."

At this suggestion Billy went from grey to white. "That'd not be a good idea. They might find out about me…" He hesitated.

"What about you?" asked Ed. "They're not going to worry about some immigration irregularities in Australia. If we're right and Alfie was killed by the Wolf Man, then people ought to know before the mine does something rash in retaliation against the union."

Further Revelations

Later that afternoon, Joe took Billy to visit the drill-core shed leaving Ed alone in the office. Ed had much to think about, not least the revelation that Allen had been head of a revolutionary organisation. Not that it bothered Ed, but the situation might get fraught should it be discovered by Miriam.

Leaning back in his chair he wondered whether Lomax knew of Allen's student politics and whether Allen might be anxious to prevent him learning of it.

Rubbing his eyes, he looked down at the drilling book open on his desk. There was so much to go through and he hadn't even begun to scratch the surface. The phone began to ring and he did a small jump in his chair. He had never heard the sound in this office, not even when it had belonged to Forge. Probably a call for Joe, he decided, and picked up the receiver.

"I need a word," said Miriam's voice. "Please come across to the Chief Engineer's villa directly." The line went dead.

"Next time I'll pick up the phone and then switch it off before anybody can say anything," he said through clenched teeth. He wondered whether he could ignore a direct order from Miriam. After all, she wasn't actually the Mine Manager.

When he arrived at the Chief Engineer's residence he was greeted by a man in a green mine suit who ushered him down a dark mahogany corridor and into a large, light room with many lace curtains that danced in the wind blowing through floor to ceiling windows. Miriam was sitting in a chair, side saddle, and opposite her was Bernie.

For a moment Ed was nonplussed. During his last visit to the mine, this had been Miriam's room, where she greeted people and took tea. He'd assumed she'd have moved her centre of operations once her husband had become Mine Manager, but this was clearly not the case. She must have hung onto this room, annexed it from the wife of the new Chief Engineer.

"Welcome, Mr Evans. I believe you know Bernie. She's a journalist."

Bernie smiled at him. "Sure he does, we've met many times before," she said.

"Please sit down, Mr Evans. We have some information which we need to discuss with you." She gestured toward a sofa upholstered in green material with gold braid.

"I'm very busy actually," said Ed walking squeakily across the dark, polished floor.

"Nevertheless, we would appreciate your opinion on a matter that has just cropped up." Her face was set.

Reluctantly, Ed took a seat, legs bent, ready to spring and run away at the smallest excuse. He remembered being in this room before, full of Miriam's delicate china ornaments and display cases full of porcelain.

"How is Billy Barker?" asked Miriam, her eyes locked onto Ed's face.

"Fine. He's gone to check out some drill core with Joe. He's working very hard, producing excellent results. Why?"

"I probably told you I was investigating his friend, Brett Walsh," said Bernie. "Turns out he's an uncomplicated soul, known as the Wolf Man in Australian mining circles. Likes killing people. Men like that are simple to understand, they kill because they like to have control. But Billy is a much more sophisticated type of character."

She turned her head to a pile of papers on her lap and started to pick her way through them. "Miriam gave me some details about Billy and I did a bit of digging. You may remember that when the Wolf Man fled Australia after he'd killed the hitchhiker, there were reports that he'd left with another man, I presumed that was Billy."

"It was," said Ed. "I asked him about it. He said he had to leave because he had neither a visa nor citizenship. There was some article published in the local papers about it and he felt obliged to leave."

"Is that what he said?"

Ed nodded.

Bernie looked down at her papers, a look of barely concealed triumph on her face. "When I rang up a journalist friend in Western Australia he remembered the case very well. He put me through to a colleague who had written an article on Billy Barker. She was very interested to know where he was now living." She stopped and smiled. "Very interested indeed."

"What's he supposed to have done?" asked Ed.

Bernie reached across and took a grape from a fruit display on a beautiful, polished table, her sense of satisfaction palpable. "He's quite a guy," she said, her American accent very strong.

"Billy's no killer."

"Oh yes he is," said Miriam forcefully, maintaining her side saddle stance but managing to lean forward. "He is wanted for the murder of a journalist in London. A man who was investigating his sordid little group of revolutionaries. He came too close to finding out about them so they beat him to death and then threw his body in a lake."

"Billy's no killer," repeated Ed.

"How can you be so sure?" asked Miriam. "Killers come in all shapes and sizes."

"I just feel that Billy's too…too 'other worldly'. His whole kick with revolutionary politics was an intellectual exercise, I don't believe he took it seriously."

"If he didn't kill the man, why did he spend so much time hiding out in Australia? Why, when the police were coming to arrest both the Wolf Man and him, did he decide to run?" – this from Bernie.

"I don't know," said Ed, annoyed that he was being forced to defend Billy. "I suppose because he was worried that the charge was trumped up and that justice for revolutionaries in British courts could be very summary."

"Not because he was guilty, then?" said Miriam.

"More likely he doesn't have much faith in the British justice system, Birmingham Six, Guildford Four and all that," countered Ed.

The silence that followed showed that the two women had not expected Ed to be so willing to take Billy's part. Miriam bridled at his suggestion that the British police and justice systems weren't perfect. "Are you suggesting that judges are biased or that policemen deliberately lie?"

Ed pulled himself back, a simple yes was likely to be counterproductive. "I haven't talked with Billy about his attitude to police or the courts, but his political beliefs are unlikely to give him a positive outlook."

Miriam shot back quickly. "You said his days as a revolutionary were a long time ago and a lot of water has flowed under the bridge."

"And as you pointed out, old habits die hard." He stood up, annoyed at the way he was being interrogated about something he knew nothing about. He would certainly be having words with Allen and Billy. Yet again he'd been left in the dark.

"I will of course be asking Billy about what went on when he was a student," he said nodding at both women. Through his teeth he heard himself saying that he was grateful that they had told him what they'd discovered about Billy. He gave a carefree smile, walked across the room and down the dark corridor that led to the main doors of the villa before either woman could call him back.

Chiri was standing outside, talking quietly with his acolytes. When Ed appeared, he gave one of his cheerless smiles so that his cheek scars became more prominent and threatening. The smell of meat and chilli was overpowering, again bringing Ed unpleasant memories. He was determined that his racing heart and adrenalin would not betray him. "Hello," he said, as if bumping into Chiri was a happy coincidence.

Chiri's smile faded into a frown. "Are you seeing Miriam as well?" he asked.

"That's right, we often have tea during the day." Ed grinned to show he was making a joke, then moved out of the way so Chiri could enter the building. But as he did so he glanced at the acolytes and a thought occurred to him. "Can't see Brett," he said, holding out a hand to prevent Chiri making progress.

Chiri looked down at the hand, as if it held a knife, then he looked carefully at Ed. "He has decided to stay at Exploration headquarters."

Ed was surprised. "He said something to Billy about going out into the forest to do some exploration. He said he would be going with you lot."

"We are not doing exploration this week," replied Chiri, "We have many important matters. But I have allowed

Brett to stay in headquarters because he is frightened ever since this man was killed by the Galamsey or the union. He says he cannot return to Australia or New Zealand; some matter of sheep stealing or cutting the throat of sheep, so I have allowed him to stay in his office for now."

There was a round of knowing laughter from around the group of acolytes.

Ed withdrew his arm and nodded. "I see, that makes sense," he said. But before Chiri could enter the villa he threw out another question. "Has he been threatened personally by the union?"

Chiri looked at him seriously. "Indeed he has been threatened, he has been very lucky not to be killed. There's a nasty mark on his face from a fight with one of them, he barely escaped the attack that killed this unfortunate driller."

Watching them troop into the Engineering villa, Ed was in a quandary. The mine, in the form of Chiri and its militia, were about to take some action in response to the death of the Australian driller little knowing that in all probability it wasn't the union who had perpetrated the outrage. For several moments he thought of rushing after Chiri, but just as he moved back to the door he stopped. Miriam knew full well what Brett had done in Australia, she was already deeply suspicious of both him and Billy.

Even so, he would go to Allen again and ask him what the hell he was doing allowing Lomax to employ somebody like the Wolf Man. And while he was about it he would find out from Billy about this murder.

When he returned to the office, Frank was waiting for him. "Mr Allen has invited you and Billy back to his house for a meal this afternoon," he said. "I need to go and get Mr Billy and then take you both."

Ed remembered Allen's house on the outskirts of

Lomax from the previous time he'd been at the mine. It had beautiful gardens and a high wall that was useful at excluding the noise of traffic and shouting neighbours. Inside, the house was tiled in blue and white ceramics to give a cooling aura. The whole effect was rather too shiny for Ed, a bit like living in a bathroom. "It's Lomax's," Allen had said when Ed had asked how come he'd such beautiful accommodation. "He decides who lives here, not the mine management, otherwise Miriam would have her claws in it."

On arrival, Allen indicated to Billy and Ed that they should sit in the living room while he made lunch of beer and sandwiches. As both men sat back on the sofa listening to the bang of plates and clink of glasses emanating from the kitchen, Ed wondered whether to tell Billy about his conversation with Miriam and Bernie. But he decided that Billy was too fragile, he would be likely to take Ed's interest as an accusation; better to wait until Allen was present as well.

His eye fell on photographs perched on a large bookshelf that took up part of one wall. "That's Allen's sister," he said indicating a framed picture featuring a pretty European woman. Allen had shown him the photograph on his previous visit and related the story about how he and his sister had been adopted to separate homes in America."

Billy walked over to the bookcase and took down the picture. "Is that what he said?" he asked.

"Sure he did," said Ed. "They were split up when he was very young, after his mother and father died in a car crash. His sister's in some religious sect."

Billy put the picture back on the shelf and glanced over at the kitchen, where activity had ceased. "I think we're going to have food soon," he said, picking up another photo. "Who's this African woman?" he asked

"Adzo, his secretary," said Ed smiling.

Allen charged in holding bottles of beer and plates of sandwiches. "Tuck in, folks. Plenty more where this came from."

Billy sat down again and took the offered bottle of beer. Nothing was said for several moments, but Ed could tell that Billy was agitated. It was in the way he kept searching for his pipe, taking it out, putting it back in his pocket, taking sharp sucks at his beer and leaving the sandwiches untouched. Eventually he said, "One of the greatest surprises of us meeting again is to find you without Cat. Whatever happened to her? I thought you two were made for one another."

Allen stopped chewing and sat back in his chair, bottle in hand. "Cat and I split soon after I went back to America," he said. It was evident he was picking his words carefully. "She found some preacher. As far as I know she's in a kind of sect that believes the apocalypse is upon us and we must all give away our earthly possessions."

Billy screwed up his face. "I'm sorry," he said.

Allen shrugged. "I think she's happy," he said.

"And Kitten?" asked Billy.

Allen stood up and strode across to the picture Billy had been holding moments before. "Kitten is with her mother," he said. "I haven't seen her for over ten years. She must be thirty by now." His voice was low. Ed could tell he didn't like Billy's intrusiveness.

"Do you never communicate?" asked Billy taking his pipe out and finally placing it in his mouth.

"No. No communication is allowed with non-believers. I keep a tidy sum in case she ever needs help, and Lomax has been good about it as well."

"What d'you mean?" asked Ed.

"Lomax's son is in the same community." He gazed intently at the picture. "Lomax has agents on the ground watching them, waiting for the moment when his son needs help so he can spring him. He's promised to do the same for Kitten." He hesitated and gave a little grin. "I think Kitten and Lomax junior are married."

"So that's how come a former revolutionary works with a capitalist like Lomax," said Ed nodding his head. "Nice to know that money's not the only thing Lomax loves."

"And that you haven't totally sold out," said Billy, through the pipe between his teeth.

"I sold out ages ago," said Allen, his voice full of a bitterness, even a self-loathing that Ed had never heard before. "It was all a mirage. The collapse of the Soviet Union demonstrated that."

"You're wrong," said Billy. "We just didn't have enough faith that we were correct."

"If I'd needed faith I'd have become a Christian," said Allen, his voice slightly raised, sharp as needles.

Billy looked through narrowed eyes, sucks coming short and sharp.

Ed looked from one to another and decided the time had come to tell them of his conversation earlier that day. "Miriam and Bernie have discovered Billy's being hunted for the murder of an American journalist."

Billy's normally flushed cheeks drained of colour. The sucking on his pipe re-doubled.

"She's not yet found out that you two were close associates when the murder was committed," continued Ed, "but I don't expect it'll take very long for that to fall into place." As the silence from the two men grew, Ed decided to speak his mind. "Yet again I'm finding stuff out about you two from other people." He directed this remark at both Allen and Billy. "You assured me before that there was nothing more to find out."

"There is nothing to find out. We were framed," said

Allen.

Ed looked at him sceptically. "Go on…"

"By one of our former members, Sonny Jim."

Ed waited for elaboration, but Allen seemed completely unaware that further explanation was required. "Who was Sonny Jim?" he asked, feeling the nascent anger build in his chest and develop into something more aggressive.

Allen sensed that Ed was beginning to lose his temper, and he held out a placatory hand. "A real fanatic. He saw American agents everywhere, he even thought I was an American agent." He turned to Billy. "We were in our favourite pub when we heard the sound of breaking glass, d'you remember?"

Billy was gripping the bowl of his pipe and sucking hard, he gave a small nod of the head, his face still drained.

"We were afraid to leave," Allen continued. "Chances are the mob would have turned on me, they were smashing anything and everything to do with America. After the riot an American journalist by the name of Ledger was missing. When the police investigated, Sonny Jim had an alibi, he claimed he'd been calming the mob and that the last thing he'd seen was Ledger running away. There were several witnesses who backed up his story. Then he came up with some bullshit that he'd been at a Crappers meeting where we'd discussed killing Ledger. He let it be known around the campus that we were responsible."

"And you really expect me to believe you're innocent?" asked Ed. He turned to Billy. "Is what Allen just told me a pack of lies or the real truth?"

Billy averted his eyes, continued to suck on his pipe. Ed turned back to Allen. "I hardly know who you are. There are rumours about you being a terrorist, an arsonist, a fraudster. Now there's soon to be a new legend: James Allen the rabid revolutionary who kills nosy journalists."

Allen looked hurt. "I admit that I dabbled in revolutionary politics, but we're innocent of everything they accused us of doing," he said.

"Then why did Billy run?" asked Ed. "Miriam and Bernie believe that this is the conclusive evidence that he was the murderer; you'll all have to have a reason for why you didn't just turn yourselves over to the law."

"I told Billy to run and keep running until I could sort everything out," said Allen. "I thought I could persuade the police that we were miles away and that Sonny Jim was seeking to deflect suspicion away from him and his crazies. But nobody listens to reason. The police had plenty of circumstantial evidence, like we were in the area at the same time Ledger disappeared."

"There must have been more reasons why the police suspected you," said Ed. "Even if they were prejudiced against people like yourselves, why pick on the Crappers rather than any other crackpot organisation?"

Allen was ready with the answers; he had moved smoothly into overdrive where every suspicious fact had a ready explanation. For a moment Ed wondered about where Allen had developed this facility, was it the sort of thing you could learn or was it innate?

"Ledger had been investigating the Crappers because of our links to an East German cultural exchange organisation. He claimed we were being trained in sabotage techniques and espionage. The police claimed we'd killed Ledger because he was getting too close."

"So you had the motivation," said Ed. "You were in the area at the time and you probably had the means with which to carry out the act."

Allen nodded his head sadly. "As the net started to close I escaped to America and lay low for a while."

Ed eyed him suspiciously. "So a draft dodger with links

to a far left revolutionary group, suspected of killing an American citizen, arrived back in America and disappeared." He waited for a moment to see if Allen's face was about to break into a grin, to confess that he'd told an untruth and change his story. But Allen said nothing. "And you expect me to believe that?"

Allen shrugged. "I've got a very influential family, they found me, Cat and Kitten a place to hide out in a remote religious retreat in California. Course that's when the trouble really started. I think Cat decided she liked the cloistered life and took up with the head man of the place."

Ed turned to Billy, to see if he was willing to verify what his old comrade was saying. "So you've been on the run all your life, waiting for the knock on the door from the policeman."

"Ain't no doors where I've been livin'" said Billy. "Only miles of Outback where you can see a man coming."

Then, Ed had an insight. It came to him almost as if he'd been seeing it in front of his face but it had been too obvious to take seriously. He lay back in his seat and looked at Allen with his eyes wide open, heartbeat slightly raised. The more he looked at the solution and turned it around his mind, the more obvious it seemed.

"What?" asked Allen, alarmed at Ed's sudden stillness.

"You're being blackmailed by Billy and Brett," he said. "That's how come you went all the way out to PNG to find them. They threatened to expose you as the murderer of this American journalist unless you offered them a job, somewhere far away."

Allen said nothing.

"And you went and persuaded Lomax, who was too preoccupied with his own problems to care very much." He jerked forward suddenly. "Or did Lomax fear what would happen to his crumbling empire once it became known that his main man in West Africa had links to revolutionary groups and had apparently killed a member of the press corp?" He looked sharply at Allen. "Perhaps Billy and the Wolf Man are actually blackmailing Lomax as well as yourself."

"Billy's not blackmailing anybody," said Allen, pink spots growing on his cheeks.

"The Wolf Man then," said Ed. "He'll have known about Billy and the murder of Ledger and made it his business to find out about accomplices. Lomax Mine would have been in the news recently and no doubt he would have seen your name, he'd have taken his opportunity."

Ed turned to Billy. "Is that how it was?"

Billy exchanged a glance with Allen, who shrugged his shoulders. Removing his pipe from his mouth and placing it on the table, he took a tissue from his pocket and began to polish his glasses. Ed felt a swooping dizziness as if he were experiencing the first stages of flu. He was right, or as nearly right as made no difference.

"The Wolf Man killed Alfie the driller, you do know that?" he said to Allen, standing up so he could breathe more easily. "He killed Alfie and made it look as if the union did it. I saw Chiri disappear into Engineering for an interview with Miriam. He had his serious face, the one he keeps for special occasions." He turned to look at Allen. "You've got to tell them that it was the Wolf Man, not the union."

"We don't know that," said Allen. "The union has threatened retribution and the union are the main suspects."

"That's not true," said Ed, his voice raised. "People believe it's the union because that's what they want to believe."

"There's also Kojo's warning," said Allen. "He told you

to get out within five days, he knew that something of this nature would happen. This was a premeditated act by the union to disrupt the work of the mine, and it's worked, all the contractors are clamouring to go home."

Sitting down heavily, Ed put his head in his hands, the events of the day had pushed Kojo out of his mind.

The sound of wheels crunching gravel came from outside and momentarily knocked Ed out of his thoughts. "Who's that?" he asked jumping to his feet.

Allen walked swiftly to the door and looked out. "It's Frank," he said. "Funny, I told him to come back here at five-ish." He looked at his watch. "It's only four o'clock." Without looking back, he walked out of the house.

Glancing at Billy, Ed saw that he had recovered some of the colour in his cheeks. He was rocking backwards and forwards slightly, arms hunched at his sides. 'Was this a man who would commit a murder?' Ed asked himself. Was this a man haunted by what he had done all those years ago?

Frank appeared at the door with Allen, his Hawaiian shirt flapping in the afternoon breeze, medallion swinging backwards and forwards in agitation. "Herman wants to see you now," he said breathlessly.

Allen walked back into his house, a smile on his face. "I think we should make him wait until we've finished our beer and sandwiches," he said. Frank hovered at the threshold, wondering whether he should enter or go back to his pickup. As he backed away from the door, Allen shouted for him to come in. "You want a beer?"

Frank moved from foot to foot, then advanced cautiously to the threshold. "I think we should be going," he said. "Herman doesn't like to be kept waiting."

But Allen ignored him. "Come in here and take a seat, there's something we want to know."

Frank was suspicious, but he obeyed and sat down cautiously. "What is it?" he said when Allen had returned from the kitchen carrying enough beer for everybody.

"The union, did they kill the driller? What's your opinion," asked Allen handing him the beer.

"Probably," said Frank. "Who else would it be?" He looked confused by the blatantly obvious question. "Why else would he have scab carved on his forehead?"

"Perhaps somebody else killed him and then carved scab on his forehead to make it look like the union. Perhaps it was a rival part of the union, a more radical wing, not under Herman's control."

At this remark, Frank's discomfort increased. "A more radical wing?" he asked. "I don't understand what you mean."

"Surely it's obvious," said Allen. "With all these sackings, there's bound to be people who feel that direct action is the way to go. Negotiation has failed, all of the active members have been sacked, why not take the fight to the mine? All these thefts, the sabotage, the missing explosives, it speaks to me of a more militant wing of the union taking control."

Frank took a swig of his beer and shrugged.

Allen continued. "And who would be leading this new, more militant wing? Bismarck and Kojo? They were, after all, senior managers in the mine, used to giving orders, and they have at their command those who have been sacked, their former colleagues. I'm not suggesting that all of the former geological staff are part of this group, but there would only have to be four or five to make it work. Men with a high level of education, well organised, determined. They'd have to get extra help, of course; some muscle which they could boss about and do their bidding."

Putting his beer down on the table, Frank reached

across and took a sandwich. "Is that what's happening?" he asked carefully.

"You tell me," said Allen. "Bismarck and Kojo have disappeared with quite a considerable sum of money if the rumours are to be believed. Lomax thinks they're still in the area, we have some evidence ourselves that Kojo is around." He looked at Ed and nodded. "Rumours abound that there's internal strife in the union and that it's split from top to bottom. Herman is in danger of being overthrown by a new young upstart."

Frank continued to chew slowly on his sandwich. "You may be right," he said after swallowing. "There is a challenge to Herman," he admitted, "but I couldn't say where Bismarck or Kojo have gone. I certainly haven't seen them."

Meeting Herman the Helmet

After a thirty-minute drive to the other side of the Lomax township, Frank and Ed arrived in a large piece of dusty orange waste ground. Ed had been here before, several months ago, kidnapped from his room in the compound and driven to this very spot. In front of him was a large corrugated iron fortress. The only access in and out was through small enclosed alleyways.

They'd held him in a stinking cellar somewhere beneath this ramshackle structure. It had been Bismarck who'd liberated him, led him past a gang of people and out through small alleyways.

"You wait here," said Frank. "I'll get Herman, see if he wants to talk."

Ed looked about him and saw the small shack where he and Bismarck had hidden when the mine militia had arrived. Bismarck had pulled a gun on him and demanded that he handed across a couple of Forge's trilobites, it had been this action that had confirmed for Ed in his belief that trilobites were significant.

The mine militia had opened fire and Bismarck had fled. It had been the last time Ed had seen him.

The sound of loud voices made him turn back to the fortress. Several people were emerging from an alleyway, one of them dressed in a silk paisley dressing gown with a cigar stuck in his mouth, eyes bulging messianically and head bulging at the back and at the lobes. Here was Herman the Helmet, boss of the miners' union and local strongman who was said to control much of the criminal activity in the town of Lomax. As he walked forward, cigar smoke billowing in the wind, his entourage spread out behind, gazing suspiciously at the surrounding shanty town through dark glasses.

"I am glad to have this opportunity to talk with you," he said, after coming to a halt in front of Ed and looking him up and down. "After the sad misunderstanding when you were kept in my cellar." He blew cigar smoke from his mouth and then blinked his bulging eyes twice. "You may have got the wrong impression about me, that I am a gratuitous bully. Nothing could be further from the truth."

He looked around at his four large friends. They nodded obediently.

"In addition, I feel the need to talk with your Mine Manager, man-to-man. I will be sending you back with a mobile phone which he should keep charged at all times. I will ring it when I need to talk, and he should likewise ring me. We are both facing problems and perhaps working together will help solve them."

Wind whipped at Herman's dressing gown as a dusty cloud enveloped the group. Everybody turned away, putting their hands over their eyes. When Ed turned back, Herman was looking at him, cigar puffing in his mouth, waiting patiently.

Ed reached in his pocket and produced a note. In discussion with Allen they had decided it would be best if he read out a prepared statement. That way, if Herman didn't like anything he heard it would emphasise that Ed was only the messenger. "The Mine Manager wishes to know why the mine is being sabotaged and equipment stolen, why you have ordered one of the replacement drillers to be killed and mutilated."

The rumbling of a growl came from Herman. "How dare you. I'm not the boss of some criminal gang."

For a moment Ed was wrong-footed. Strange, he thought, how people very rarely perceive themselves as others might. Nevertheless, a straight denial had been foreseen.

"As for the sabotage," continued Herman, "I have not given orders for this to happen, despite the severe provocation from the mine management. These breakages and thefts are a spontaneous outbreak of anger on behalf of men who are sick and tired of being denied their basic rights as workers."

"And the murder?"

"As I said, nothing to do with me. And I reject completely that it could have been any of my men who did it, even in the face of outrageous provocation."

"I see," said Ed, gazing past Herman's ear at the tin can town behind. "And these problems you speak of, that both yourself and the Mine Manager face, what are they?"

"They are not for the ears of a simple messenger. But you might want to tell him that I am not happy with the extent of thefts that are occurring in the mine. I want him to know that the explosives that have gone missing are not in my keeping. We are both threatened by this."

Ed gazed down at the letter the Mine Manager had given him. He banged it thoughtfully against his hand and then handed it across. Herman looked surprised; he extended one large hand and then ripped open the envelope. His brows narrowed as he read down the page, then he looked up at Ed and there was something akin to outrage in his large bulging eyes.

"I'm only the messenger," Ed reminded him holding up

his hands.

Herman ripped up the letter and threw it in the air where the pieces spiralled across the empty waste ground. "You can tell your Mine Manager that I am the only thing that stands between him and total chaos. He should not be threatening me, he should be thanking me."

Turning on his heel he marched angrily into the alleyway from which he'd emerged, followed quickly by his entourage. After a few seconds, Frank appeared from around the corner and made his way across. "We better get goin'," he said. "I don't know what you said to him, but he's angry. He may send out some of his men to teach you some respect."

Ed needed no second telling, he climbed into the seat next to Frank and gripped the ceiling bar as the pickup sped away up the slight rise that led to the town-proper. "Let's go back to the mine, I need to get a few things before goin' back to the compound."

Frank acknowledged the instruction, then said, "How'd you make him so angry?"

"Don't know, he seemed okay until I gave him the Mine Manager's letter. Up until that point he was full of the joys of spring, even wanted me to take a mobile phone to the Mine Manager so they could have cosy chats."

"You got the phone?" asked Frank.

"I think once he read the letter he decided to withdraw the offer."

"Wonder what the letter said."

"Nothing good," said Ed. "I think we can definitely be certain about that."

As they rushed back along the main Lomax thoroughfare, Ed was worried. The unspoken agreements that governed the relationship between the mine and the union was beginning to break down, he could sense a growing hard line attitude from both sides.

"Park at the main gates, will you, I want to pop into the Drilling Office," he told Frank as they approached the mine.

Frank swung the wheel and stopped briefly at the main gate to show his pass and then zoomed into the car park. "I'll be two minutes," said Ed, jumping out before the pickup had come to rest. He hurtled as fast as he could up the stairs and let himself into his office. He waited, blinded by the low light level, before grabbing his briefcase from the floor and his room key from the top drawer.

There was a note on the table, written in a neat cursive hand. "Come to the Miners' Diner, important we meet, Bernie." It had the time written at the top indicating that she had been there only thirty minutes before. He sniffed the air and detected a faint smell of her perfume.

Cursing loudly, he flung himself out of the office and back down the steps. "Miners' Diner," he said to Frank. "I have a quick meeting to attend and then we can go back to the compound and you can go home."

They retraced their tracks through the main gate, this time getting less than a cursory glance from the guard, and then belted back down the main highway before taking the road up to the Miners' Diner. "This better be good," he mused to himself, it was probably just another fishing trip by Bernie to find out how the meeting with the union went. Bernie somehow always got to the news first. On the other hand, she may have discovered Allen's connection to Billy. Either way, it would be useful to know where she was digging.

When he walked into the eating area of the Miners' Diner he was surprised to see that Bernie was the only customer. She sat at the window staring out at the Lomax shanty town, dark glasses perched on her face. When he approached her table she barely noticed that he'd arrived.

Normally this restaurant would be full with contractors having their evening meal or having a well- earned beer. He was puzzled, until he realised that after the death of Alfie most of the western contractors had decided to go home and were lying low until they could organise travel arrangements.

"What's so urgent?" he asked.

She looked up at him, eyes hidden. He could tell she was still distracted. Then she pulled herself together and indicated a chair opposite. "Mr Evans, thanks for coming."

Wondering why she was being so formal, Ed sat down. Then returning her gaze to the large windows and the sweep of the shanty town, she said, "Not a place I'd like to live. You wonder why people flock here in such numbers."

"They've come on the promise of getting rich," said Ed.

She nodded her head as if acknowledging the truth of his remark. "But you and I know that that's hardly going to happen. The wealth of this mine flows to Accra and then out of the country to shareholders in London. Nobody who actually works here is ever going to get wealthy."

"I suppose so," replied Ed, wondering what she was driving at. "But it'll buy them a tv or mobile phone."

She smiled. "Sometimes you can understand the miners' union and their stance against mine management."

Ed was silent, he sensed a trap. Bernie looked around at him, her face inscrutable. "Can there ever be a justification for violence?" she asked. "Taking the life of another person can never be right. Look around here," she said sweeping her arm. "By taking the life of a single man the miners' union has managed to paralyse the mine, they have won a tactical advantage in their battle with Lomax."

Ed cocked his head to one side. Bernie should have been dancing about with joy at the current situation. The chaos would have thrown up all sorts of human stories which would have generated acres of copy.

"Don't tell me you've started to get a conscience. You're not going to turn into one of those agonised correspondents?"

She shook her head.

"Good, because I don't think you could pull it off very well."

The comment shook her and she removed her shades so that Ed could see piercing blue eyes full of anger. "I've just had an email from London," she said. "I wanted to know a little bit more about this murder that Billy committed."

"Accused of committing," Ed corrected. "There's no proof. Billy said he was a nosy American journalist who kept poking his nose where it didn't belong. But when he was murdered, Billy and his mates were at a rally several miles away. The Crappers weren't the only ones this journalist was molesting, there were plenty of others far more dangerous."

"The Crappers?"

"Didn't your source tell you the name of Billy's organisation? They were known as the Crappers. Don't think much of your source if he didn't even know that."

Her eyes flashed with anger again. "The Campaign for Revolution and Peace. Yes, I know the name of their organisation but I didn't know the short hand. There were three men on the central committee Billy Barker, my source and James Allen." She stopped and glared at him. "Did you know James Allen was the leader of the gang?"

"Yes," said Ed.

"But you decided not to tell me. Does that mean you're part of this left wing cabal as well? You've got a suitable profile; from Liverpool, working class origins, family members killed in the North Wales coal field." She smiled at him. "Yes I know about the Evans's and their support for mining unions."

"You know nothing but the paranoid bleating of Miriam and her husband who believe there's a Red under every bed," said Ed angrily.

Bernie's voice grew low, her most soothing and unctuous tones. "Miriam bores me rigid but I like to keep in touch with her. She talks rot and has a way of trying to twist the world into a shape that suits her. She's typical of the sort of person who reads the stuff I write."

Ed had finally had enough. He began to rise out of his chair. "I think I'll be going. I'd hate for you to think such things about me."

"Oh no, quite the opposite," she said soothingly. "You're the sort of unimaginative jackass that scares my readers. You and this Billy, and James Allen of course. Educated men intent on preventing progress because of some crazy set of beliefs."

Ed laughed and turned to leave, but Bernie hadn't finished.

"My source was at the Crappers meeting where the journalist's death was planned. He was a police agent named Sonny Jim, reporting their every move. James Allen pulled the trigger and Billy disposed of the body."

Ed stopped but didn't turn around.

"The journalist wasn't really a journalist," she continued. "He was a CIA agent who was investigating the Soviet infiltration of far left groups in Britain. The Crappers were known to have been taking money from an East German cultural and scientific organisation. If you come and sit down..." she said.

Ed still hadn't turned around. He could feel Bernie's eyes bore into the back of his head. The waitress was approaching with lemonades, they looked large and inviting. Shoulders hunched, he turned around and walked back to the table not looking her in the eye.

"Thank you," she said.

"Better be quick and straightforward," he said, "otherwise I'm outta here."

The waitress deposited the drinks on the table and left.

"We're both people of the world," she began. "We don't dream of a new World Order. Tell me what motivates Billy and Allen."

"Tell you the truth I don't think much motivates them at the moment except preparing for a comfortable retirement. And of course Billy wants to be rid of Brett."

"Nothing else? No latent revolutionary feelings? No overt sympathy for the miners' union?"

"Not overtly sympathetic, no. But I daresay if you scratched beneath the surface you'd find more than a little sympathy."

"In what way?"

"In the way that the mine management and Lomax have managed to radicalise men who were hitherto fairly moderate in their outlook."

She nodded. "I agree, but Miriam believes in shooting and flogging. She'd have the gibbet back if she could. In her world view, Bismarck and Kojo would be hanging on either side of the main gates as a warning to those coming to work about what dissent achieves."

Sipping his lemonade, a thought suddenly occurred to him. "You told Lomax what you've found?"

She shook her head. "I'm still wondering what to do about it. Lomax is usually so sure-footed. He'd've known about Allen's past before employing him. And he'd certainly have appreciated that Billy and Allen were old comrades in arms."

"What's your point?"

"Why bring them together? If Billy had stayed in PNG and Allen in Africa I would not now be sitting in this place with the story. It's almost like Lomax is punishing Allen for something."

"Or Billy," commented Ed. "Except Billy's delighted to be out of PNG. He's desperate to stay here if he can."

"In which case, perhaps the idea of coming here was Billy's idea," said Bernie.

"Like a cry for help you mean?"

"That's right, help me escape the Wolf Man or else I'll tell all to the next journalist who crosses my path."

Ed fiddled with the dew on his glass, making trails that dribbled down to the wooden top of the table. He could imagine Billy getting desperate to be away from the Wolf Man, so desperate that he might try to blackmail Allen. "Didn't you say that Lomax was having trouble with one of his Indonesian operations?" he asked. "Something about a use of military force which went wrong?"

Bernie swung her head around. "That's right. He's got himself into real trouble over that. There's been a lot of unfortunate publicity." Her eyes were suddenly searching. "You're about to ask whether Billy and the Wolf Man had been operating near there?"

Ed shrugged.

"I'll go and get it checked out," she said.

They both drank their lemonades in silence for a while. It occurred to Ed that her manner was very strange. He'd seen her rampant, ordering Chiri around, seen her as a smouldering seductress trying to get Ed to be her spy, but this new guise of earnest soul searcher was entirely new.

"I hear you've met with Helmet," she said.

Ed nodded but said nothing.

"You two must know each other quite well by now, you're always popping over there for chats."

"Hardly," said Ed.

"What did he say about the murder? Did he seek to justify why it was necessary?"

This was why she wanted to see him, he thought. She was trying to be earnest because she wanted Ed to think that she was concerned for the miners and their cause. With a sense of relief that he was not going to be confronted with yet another surprise, he gave a smile. "You want to know what we talked about?" he asked.

"Certainly," she said. "If you don't mind."

"He completely denied that he had anything to do with the murder and he also denied that he had anything to do with the theft of materials from the mine, including several tons of explosive."

"And do you believe him?" she asked.

"I'm just the messenger," he shrugged, "Not for me to offer an opinion."

"I promote you to chief negotiator," she said. "Was this man lying?"

Ed took another draught of his lemonade to give himself time to think. "I'd say Herman's hand is not as strong as he'd like us to think. He's a worried man, but not because he's afraid of the mine but I think he's afraid of something within his own organisation."

"There's a leadership challenge you mean?"

Ed nodded.

"So who is this new leader, what's his name?"

Ed shrugged. "A certain name jumps to mind. Bismarck."

She laughed. "Bismarck's no leader. The man looks like an owl and talks like a thesaurus. Hardly a miners' pin up."

"I suppose you're right," he said and fell silent, stung that Bernie should think of Bismarck in such a way.

"So who is it?"

Ed tutted angrily. "I've told you who I think it is."

"But why? He's an academic, not a leader."

"He wants you to think he's a bit useless and impractical and that's because he lives in a world that contains Chiri and Herman."

So your theory is that Bismarck's thrown off the whiskers?"

"Not just my theory. Allen thinks that as well, and so does Lomax. They're terrified Bismarck and Kojo are running around the place with tens of millions of pounds radicalising the people of Lomax. I think Herman's worried about it as well; he wanted me to take a phone so he could have a direct line to the Mine Manager."

"So it's Bismarck who organised the killing of this Australian driller."

"That's where my surmise falls down. Bismarck isn't the sort of person who'd be into torture and mutilation."

"On the other hand, if you're correct in what you say, some of his followers would see it as entirely justified."

Ed said nothing, just stared into the depths of his glass. He reflected that if he was right and Bismarck was making a bid for the leadership of the miners' union why wasn't there more signs of what was happening. All he had was shrugs from Frank and wild surmises from Allen. There were no posters around town saying Bismarck for President, no whispering behind hands. All there seemed to be was stolen vehicles and explosives.

"Penny for them," said Bernie.

Ed looked up and gazed at her for a moment. It went without saying that she was inherently untrustworthy and if he told her what he really thought it might be counter-productive. He leaned forward conspiratorially. "Have you managed to interview the Wolf Man yet?"

"Brett Walsh you mean? No I haven't. Tell you the truth

I'm a bit nervous of approaching him."

"Very wise. But maybe you should try. Ask him where he was on the night that driller Alfie was killed."

"Why?"

"Surely it's obvious," said Ed. "I haven't seen him since Alfie died, he's gone to ground with Chiri's exploration department." He coughed nervously. "Billy tells me that Alfie and Brett have a history. It was Alfie who dobbed the Wolf Man into the police after the murder in Western Australia, blew his alibi out of the water. The Wolf Man swore to kill Alfie in front of several witnesses."

Bernie flicked open her notebook. "Just for the record, you're saying that Brett had reason to kill Alfie and had made threats in the past?"

"That's what I'm saying."

She finished making a note and then looked up. "So just to be clear, you think that the union had nothing to do with the murder, that Brett mutilated the body to make it look like the union was responsible?"

Ed didn't bother to reply, it was clear what he thought. "Chiri says that Brett was threatened by the union and that he's scared."

"And what do you think?" she asked looking up from her notes.

"I don't think he's been scared of anything in his life."

She shut her note book and looked thoughtful. "Might be good to go out and see him. Perhaps I could put some of your suspicions to him. I could ask him how he was threatened by the union, make out that I've been deputed by the Mine Manager to investigate."

An Eventful Day

Ed woke to a loud banging on his door. The noise bounced around the inside of his head before pushing him out of his dream. He'd been thinking of Alice again, when they'd gone on a winter trip to Scotland. It had rained constantly, but they hadn't cared, trapped in their cheap cabin with a roaring log fire.

"Hey, Ed, we gotta get goin'," came the voice again. He struggled to think who it might be and what they might want at this time of the morning.

"Hold on," he said and swung his feet out of bed and put them on the floor. He felt dizzy, disorientated. "Who is it?" he shouted.

"It's Allen, something's happened."

Staggering to his feet he went to the door. Through the spy hole he could see the unmistakeable features of Allen, magnified and distorted so he looked like the victim of a horrible growth disorder.

Allen rushed through the door when it opened. "They've found Bismarck."

"What? Who've found him?"

"The mine militia. They went in this morning with bulldozers and cleared away the union township. Most of the residents fled, but they found Bismarck in a cellar, hiding."

"I'm sorry?" said Ed, trying to keep up. "They flattened the union township? Had they the right to flatten homes?"

"They can do what they like," snapped Allen, "You know how this place works. They had an order condemning the shacks as unfit for human habitation, it was served last month and the union refused to recognise its legitimacy. Did you not know that?"

"No," replied Ed. "You didn't tell me and nor did Herman the Helmet."

"Herman probably thought it was an empty threat, not worth considering seriously. The deadline expired midnight last night and the bulldozers moved in at one minute past. It caught them all unawares, Herman was arrested and so were some of his Lieutenants. They were just mopping up, seeing if there was anybody else dead or hiding underneath the wreckage when they found a locked door leading down to a cellar and there was Bismarck."

Ed frowned. "Unless you've forgotten, I was held a prisoner in a cellar somewhere within the confines of that small township," he said.

"What's your point?"

"Are you sure he was hiding or was he being held prisoner by the union?"

"I never considered the possibility," said Allen, scratching his head. "Why would the union hold one of their own as prisoner?"

"Don't know. Perhaps we should talk with him?"

"Not likely," said Allen. "He's in the local lock-up surrounded by militia. The only one with automatic access is Chiri."

"What about the Mine Manager?"

Allen shook his head. "It has nothing to do with the Mine Manager. This is being treated as a matter of simple criminality. Chiri only has access because his word is law with the militia. He's got an agenda as well, he wants to humiliate Bismarck for what he did to the mine."

"So is Bismarck likely to survive?"

Allen shook his head. "Don't forget it was Chiri's reputation, as Head of Exploration, that Bismarck damaged the most. I'd say his only chance is if the miners' union is able to spring him from the lock-up. But if, as you suggest, he was a prisoner of the union, then even that slim possibility has gone."

"And Kojo?" asked Ed. "Any sign of him?"

"Nothing."

"So if we haven't a chance of talking with him, what are we going to do?"

"We need to get down to the gates, see what's going on. I've already contacted Frank, he's on his way in the pickup. You get dressed and I'll raise Billy."

A trickle shower and a set of fresh clothes later, Ed walked out into the morning sunshine and found Frank waiting in the car park. Instead of sitting in the pickup where he could benefit from the air conditioning, he was outside, leaning against the bonnet, face set in a serious expression.

"Heard the news?" asked Ed as he approached.

Frank nodded.

"Do you know of a way of getting in to speak to Bismarck? I'd like to make sure he's okay, not being ill-treated."

Frank shook his head.

His conversation with Frank was cut short by the arrival of Allen and Billy. All four climbed into the pickup and they set off. Frank decided to go via Lomax A shaft and the golf course so that they did not have to enter the mine by the main gates which were known to be clogged by militia.

When they arrived, armoured personnel carriers were

drawn in a crescent around the outside of the gates. The watch towers that overlooked the approaches to the mine were manned with men aiming heavy machine guns and yet more uniformed guards were preventing anybody entering or leaving.

"Not taking any chances," commented Billy. "Where'll they be holding him?"

Frank pointed at the guard post where a dozen uniformed personnel milled around. "There's a concrete building inside where they put prisoners. He'll be in the deepest and darkest cell."

Leaving Frank inside his vehicle, the three men walked up the steps and into the Drilling Office. To their surprise Joe was at his desk, head thrust in a drilling volume.

"Came by the Lomax 'A' entrance, my usual route," he said after they questioned how he'd got through the security.

Joe stood and went to the window when they told him that Bismarck had been captured and was probably being held at the gate house. "Where did they find him?" he asked.

"In the union township," said Billy.

"I guess Herman and the union leadership will be in there with him as well," said Ed.

Joe came away from the window and sat down at his desk, apparently supremely unconcerned. "None of them are going to take this lying down," he said. "It'll all end in more bloodshed."

Somehow his words caused a thought to stir in Ed's mind. Where was Kojo? "We'd like to get in to see Bismarck," he said. "You wanna come?"

"Why?" asked Joe, looking up. "What would you like to find out? If you're after the location of the money he and Kojo stole he'll never say. Herman's been trying to do the same. He's been sweating Bismarck in that bunker under the township, if he'll not say anything after living in that godforsaken hole he certainly won't reveal it to you."

"True," said Ed, amazed at Joe's knowledge of the situation. "But maybe we can do something for him, buy him time."

"Why?"

For a moment Ed was stumped. "Because he's a friend of course; as he was your friend as well."

Leaning back and arching his fingers, Joe looked as though he was thinking. "Bismarck changed after he got the money, he got to be power hungry. I guess some people see money as a way of buying stuff to put on their fingers or in terms of the amount of land they can buy; with Bismarck it was power. He wanted the money to buy himself power and influence."

He looked up and stared into Allen's eyes. "Even as he was sitting in the office and attending meetings he was plotting his path to power. He had a plan to overthrow Herman and install himself as boss of the miners' union. Fortunately for everybody Herman caught up with him before he could put it into action. But there's a faction who're still loyal to Bismarck, led by Kojo."

'At last, the truth,' thought Ed.

Silence in the office, while everybody considered what Joe had said.

"He won't try and blast his way through all that armour," said Allen pointing with his finger out of the window. "They'd all be cut to shreds."

Joe gave a little grin. "All the guns are pointing in one direction, toward the town. I saw you arrive from Lomax 'A', same way that I came; maybe Kojo'll come that way."

There was thumping of feet on the steps leading up to the Drilling Office. Billy went to the window and looked out. "Shit, it's Chiri." He headed back to his seat and waited for the inevitable crash of the door.

Chiri arrived in a state of great excitement, his usually narrowed eyes were wide and gleaming, his voice sharp and gleeful. "We've got them," he said. "And Bismarck'n'all." He surveyed the room and its occupants, waiting for a reaction.

"That's great," said Allen. "We guessed something of the sort. They're in the lock-up?"

Chiri confirmed with a sharp nod of the head. "They're shouting their mouths off about rough treatment, all except Bismarck." He stopped for a moment. "We've taken him to the hospital, he's in a bad way, seems to have been badly treated." He looked at Allen. "Lomax wants him in good health and he wants you to question him."

"Me?" asked Allen.

"Says you're the one he wants, you've been briefed to negotiate." Ed could see that Chiri was curious about what these negotiations might entail. "I've told Mr Lomax that I don't want any deals done with Bismarck, not after what he did, he needs to be made an example. I want to know where Kojo has gone, I want both of them." His acolytes had all trooped into the office and arranged themselves around the room, an appreciative audience for Chiri's utterances. They murmured agreement and nodded their heads. "I need to be present at his interrogation so the interests of the Exploration department can be represented."

Allen folded his arms and sat down on the edge of a desk. "At some stage I'm sure we can get you involved," he said.

The way Chiri's acolytes shook their heads indicated that this was not acceptable. A tense silence ensued. Ed noticed Billy pull his pipe from his shirt pocket and place it in his mouth. Next second the room was filled with a series of loud sucking noises. The tension in the room broke as the acolytes turned to find out from where the sound was coming.

"The Sucker," said Chiri delightedly, and all the acolytes burst out laughing. Billy flushed red to his hair roots and swiftly stowed his pipe back into his pocket. "And where is your sewing, Brett tells me you do tapestry like some bored widow."

Billy looked stumped for something to say, and he turned to Ed for help. "Billy's very skilled at all sorts of things, including drilling," said Ed. "He's doing a great job sorting out Forge's volumes, he's organising the mapping of the underground as well. Perhaps you'd like to go underground with him?"

Neither Chiri nor any of his men had been known to go underground, and Ed knew it. "We'll leave such matters to the Drilling department," said Chiri, smirking.

"When can we see Bismarck?" asked Allen. "Can you arrange for us to go straight there?"

Chiri nodded his head. "He's in a really bad way but I'll talk to the captain and see if we can do that," he said moving to the door. "I'm sure he'll be more than happy if I ask him."

After Chiri had left to negotiate with the captain of the militia, Joe stood up and walked to the door. "I'm going to the computing area, have another go at that strange binary code of Forge's."

"The Wolf Man wasn't with them again," said Ed when Joe had left. "You notice that?"

Allen ignored him, his thoughts were more immediate. "What the hell is Chiri playing at, pretending that it's the captain who's in charge and not him? I think he just wants to have us wait, keep us guessing and make us sweat."

Allen looked as if he was correct when Chiri did not send word until well over an hour later. By then Allen had already chewed out several mine employees who had gone past the Drilling room making too much noise. And he'd reprimanded Billy for sucking too noisily on his pipe.

Eventually one of Chiri's acolytes arrived at the door and told Allen he could go down to the hospital. "You coming, Ed?" he asked leaping from his chair.

"Me? But Lomax only asked that you question him."

"I need you to be there as well. You know the circumstances, you know Bismarck, I need to have a witness."

Ed got to his feet. "It'll be interesting to see Bismarck," he said scratching his chin. "We didn't part on good terms."

They wandered down the steps to the car park and glanced at armoured vehicles guarding the gate and troops of militia gathered around the gatehouse. "All this muscle at the gate, there must be nothing protecting the rest of the mine," said Allen under his breath. "I bet the Galamsey can't believe their luck."

The mine hospital was past the Engineering section and down a side road. As they walked they talked about what they might find. Ed was adamant, "Bound to be in a bad way, locked up in that basement for a length of time. If it was the same place as I was kept I'm amazed he's still alive."

"He's tough," agreed Allen. "He's a survivor. He won't talk to us about what Lomax wants, even if we put on thumb screws. We might threaten his family, but Lomax knows that I'll have no part in that and nor will the Mine Manager. Chiri wouldn't think twice, but he's happy to obey Lomax."

"So why are we going to see him?" asked Ed.

"Friendly face?" said Allen, and then smiled. "Let him

know that he's not yet been abandoned to Chiri. Playing the good cop to Chiri's bad cop. I honestly don't know what I want to achieve, but I'll have an idea by the time we get in to see him."

"Well one thing's for certain," said Ed, "he's not working for the union."

"And why should that matter?" asked Allen.

"Don't know," said Ed, thinking hard. "Kojo's warning to me about leaving within five days. Maybe he wasn't warning me about Alfie's death. Perhaps it's Kojo who's been stealing and stockpiling material. He could've been getting ready for an assault on the union township to rescue Bismarck? Trucks, ammunition, explosives, heavy lifting gear. Maybe he was warning me that a full-scale war is about to break out."

Allen stopped walking and turned to look at Ed. "Go on," he said, "it's a bit far-fetched but you've got my attention."

Ed moved closer, his voice low and urgent. "Herman denies his men have been stealing from the mine, he also denies that he's responsible for the death of Alfie. Supposing he's telling the truth, supposing Kojo and Bismarck cooked up a plan to oust Herman, for that they'd need men and material. Herman's a gangster with serious muscle at his beck and call."

Allen began to move again. "So what you're saying is that we should ask Bismarck whether he's mounting a challenge against Herman and whether it's he and Kojo who have been pilfering stores from the mine." He took another few steps. "And maybe we can ask him whether there was a plan to kill a western contractor as well."

He began to quicken his pace, voice suddenly urgent. "If you're right, I'd say the moment Kojo hears where Bismarck has been taken he'll be planning to rescue him."

By now they'd reached the hospital. "As well as establishing whether or not he's challenging Herman for leadership of the union, ordering all the thefts and the murder of Alfie, we can also have some fun pulling Chiri's plonker."

He winked and entered the main doors of the hospital. "According to Chiri's message boy, he's in the same room as you occupied when you had that bout of malaria." They walked along the hushed corridor to a room guarded by four men clutching AK-47s. "We're here to speak with Bismarck," Allen told a man who had walked part way to meet them, his hand held up in the universal sign for halt.

"I'll have to check that," the man said and plucked out a radio.

"He'll be telling Chiri we've arrived," Allen said, not bothering to keep his voice down, "so he should get ready to listen in on those microphones he planted an hour ago."

The man came off his radio and nodded to indicate they could enter the room. One of the seated guards rose and pushed open the door, and they were ushered into a hot, gloomy room.

For several moments Ed stopped to allow his eyes time to adjust. A gurgling came from the air conditioning unit in the corner, bringing back bad memories of dark, lonely nights when he lay on this same bed with nothing to do but listen to his whirring thoughts. Looking around he noticed the same green paint on the walls and dusty old wardrobe in the corner.

Gradually he began to notice a form lying in front of him. Only the slight rise and fall of the chest indicated that life still continued, otherwise the body was inert, head thrown back as if struggling for breath, naked arms motionless at the side. His lasting impression of Bismarck had been a happy, smiling face with large glasses that made him look like an over-friendly owl. Now he was cadaverous, a man of skin and bones. Allen took the chair beside the bed, leaving Ed hovering nervously close-by, staring at Bismarck's head.

"I know you're awake," said Allen after a few moments. "I can see your eyes glinting."

The figure stirred slightly but didn't speak.

"I have Ed here as well, he's over there, keeping a low profile." He looked up at Ed and winked before turning his head back. "You've led everybody a merry dance, Lomax has been on the phone every day wondering whether you've been found yet. He's quite frightened of you. I think Chiri'll be on the phone to him as we speak telling him what a good boy he's been."

Allen leaned across and grabbed Bismarck by the hand, his voice suddenly low and urgent. "'We're all enslaved by money,' isn't that what you said to me? 'And Lomax is the high priest of the Money religion.'" He kept his eyes on Bismarck's face. "'Money begets power and only those who have it can be free.' I didn't understand what you were saying to me until I realised you were behind the scam to liberate tens of millions of dollars from Lomax."

For several moments Ed was certain that Bismarck's head moved, but his face remained impassive, his withered arms motionless on the bed covers, hand limp inside Allen's. Ed wondered how long he'd been locked in Herman's cellar. He was visited by memories of a hot, dark, stinking hell into which dirty water from the union township constantly poured. His own captivity had been no more than a few hours, and afterward he'd emerged a broken and desperate man. To turn Bismarck into this virtual corpse may only have taken a few days.

"I have the power to intercede on your behalf with Lomax," continued Allen. "I can call off the dogs. Lomax isn't that interested in the money you stole, but he wants to protect his investment. So, here's what I'm going to do, I'm going to ask you a few questions. There is every chance that Chiri is watching and listening to us. Squeeze my hand once for yes and twice for no." From his pocket Allen produced a clean, pressed handkerchief which he flapped out and placed over Bismarck's hand.

"Do you understand what I am asking you to do? Squeeze once for yes, twice for no." There was a pause while Allen received the signal, if any, from Bismarck.

"Is Kojo still alive?" He paused looking earnestly at Bismarck's face.

"Is he close by?"

"Thank you," said Allen after a while. "The next question concerns yourself and Herman." He turned and looked up at Ed, a grave look on his face. "Was there a plan to kill a contractor from the compound? Once for yes, twice for no." Allen put his head down and closed his eyes, apparently waiting for Bismarck's response.

"And what about the thefts from the mine or vehicles and explosives, was that you and Kojo?" A pause. "Are you and Kojo working together?"

The door of the room crashed open and the guard marched in, AK-47 raised and pointing straight at Allen's chest. Standing quickly, Allen pulled his hand out of Bismarck's and smiled. "Can I help?" he asked.

The guard threw a nasty look at Ed and then nodded his head to indicate that their interview with Bismarck was at an end. They both left quickly, Allen winking at the guard before leading Ed down the corridor and out into the bright sunlight. He walked quickly up the road toward the Drilling Office, not speaking.

Slowing after half a minute, he allowed Ed to catch up. "Bismarck's playing doggo, he doesn't want to go into the cells with Herman and his mates. But he also wants us to know he's not quite as helpless as he seems."

"What were his responses?" asked Ed who had been bursting to find out.

"Kojo's still alive and he's close by, exactly as we thought."

"I don't understand," said Ed. "Why would he give you that information? If it was me I'd tell you he was dead, or failing that was somewhere far away."

Allen stopped and looked at him. "Bismarck wants us to know that there's somebody on the outside who's working hard to get him free." He started to walk slowly. "Kojo is out there somewhere, we all know it, Chiri knows it, Lomax knows it. He's armed and dangerous."

"We are talking about the same person?" asked Ed. "Kojo the old Manager of Geology, the man who laughed most of the time, who pushed paper around. I don't see why we're all so worried."

"I'm worried because he's armed and dangerous and thanks to Chiri we've incarcerated a close friend and member of his wife's family. He's likely to see that he has very little to lose."

"Even so…"

"Not so long ago I remember a man lying in the very same bed as Bismarck and declaring that he would be turning this place into a 'bloody slaughterhouse'."

Ed flushed red at the memory. "I was ill, under stress. You remember how we stood on the hill and watched Chiri's militia kill all those Galamsey…?"

"I know, I remember well," said Allen. "You were angry and frustrated, sickened by the way this mine exploits people, how Chiri seems to have a grip on the place."

They walked on for a further few metres, and then Ed grabbed Allen's arm. "Why are you here?" he asked forcefully. "You hate this place as much as I do. I've told you why I've had to come back."

Allen looked at him blankly.

"Why are you here?" he asked again, a note of pleading in his voice. "What keeps you taking the Lomax shilling?"

Allen gently removed his elbow from Ed's grasp. "I'll tell you why," he said and began to stride away. "But it'll become obvious to you sooner or later if things keep going as they are."

"Then tell me," Ed shouted after him. But Allen pretended not to hear. He bounded up the steps to the Drilling Office and disappeared along the balcony. For a moment Ed thought about running after him, but the idea died as quick as it rose. Even if Bismarck had told the truth with all the hand squeezing, there was no guarantee Allen would. As he approached the Drilling Office door he wondered yet again whether he should pack his bags and leave. The situation was getting hot. People had died and more would die in the near future.

On entering the room, he was greeted with an explosion of noise. "Look at this," said Joe, sitting at his desk, several sheets of paper covered in binary 0s and 1s in front of him. Ed sighed and walked over, annoyance at the recent conversation with Allen ringing in his ears. "I think a pattern's emerging," Joe said placing his pen at the top of the page and drawing a line down the middle. "Compare left of the line and right of the line. What d'you see? Is there more clumping of the 1s to the right than the left?" he asked.

Ed gazed intently. "If I shut my left eye and screw up my right, there might be some slight difference," he said.

"Tchah," said Joe in disgust and threw down his pen.

Billy, who'd been watching from his desk came over, took out his pipe and began to suck. He picked up one of the pieces of paper and squinted at it, then picked a second paper and compared the pattern of 0s and 1s. "It's random, mate," he said finally.

Pinching his eyes and nodding his head Joe stood up and walked to the window. He gazed for a moment at the gatehouse and not for the first time Ed had a sudden urge to ask where his loyalties lay.

"What a mess," he said eventually, turning away and coming back to his desk. "It's either machine code for a small program, a part of a picture, or an encoded message." The statement had become something of a mantra.

"I'd say it must be a message," said Billy. "Why else would Forge have put it in the file? If it was a picture or a program it'd be much bigger, it'd probably fill one of those volumes."

"So how would we go about decoding it?" asked Joe. "It's not simple ASCII or Unicode, so if it's a message then it's been encrypted." He picked up one of the sheets of paper. "I've assumed both a four bit, seven bit and an eight bit pattern and in all cases it turns out to represent just a jumble of characters, numbers and arcane formatting symbols."

"What about a One Time Pad?" said Ed.

Both men looked at him as if he'd gone mad. "Say again?" said Billy. "A what time pad?"

"You can encrypt one message by using another message," said Ed. "I found loads of messages to do with Bismarck, Forge and Kojo encrypted in this way. It was Bernie who was able to point out how it had been done. You add together letters to get a new letter." He smiled at Joe's look of incomprehension. "You take a letter, like a, then you add b and you get c."

Joe looked across at Billy to see if he had a clue about what Ed was talking about. "I remember reading about that somewhere," said Billy. "Wasn't it used during the war? They'd use a passage from the bible or something."

"That's right," said Ed. "Same thing was used in this mine. As I remember it was a passage from Romans or something. Once Bernie knew which passage was the cipher key she was able to take the encoded message and work out what it meant."

Joe looked down at his pieces of paper and there was a hopeless look on his face. "I don't see that helps me much. Even if we're correct about this being encoded text we have no idea about the cipher text."

"We could look through his emails," said Ed.

"Allen's been through them," said Joe. "I've been through them as well."

"Perhaps he had webmail," suggested Billy. "Something only he could read."

"Can't use the web here, not allowed," said Joe. "In case we send messages or data we're not supposed to send. There's the intranet and your own email address and that's it."

Billy took his pipe out of his mouth and laughed. "Are you telling me you haven't found a way around that?"

Joe gave a sheepish smile. "Of course I have, but I doubt if Forge will have found a way around. Unless somebody told him." He shook his head. "Even if he did have such an account we'd need to know his password."

"Any name of a trilobite followed by 01," said Ed. "I found that out when I worked in this office with him."

"But there're thousands of trilobites," complained Joe.

"True," admitted Ed. "But there are only ten directly in front of you on the desk. Those specimens were in front of Forge when he was using the computer. You'll find that each trilobite has a serial number on the base, and," he walked across to the shelves of drilling and picked one apparently at random, "you look up the number in this volume to find the trilobite name, where it was bought and how much it cost."

Bemused, Joe took the volume from Ed and flicked through. Billy came and stood behind him. "Obsessed," he said in fascination as he watched the pages of trilobites fall open. Then he flung out a hand to stop Joe turning the next page. "A page of noughts and ones," he shouted indicating a picture of a trilobite.

Ed came around the desk and examined the page. "Where?" he asked.

"Underneath the trilobite."

Then Ed saw what Billy was indicating. The trilobite in the picture was resting on a series of papers which were filled with 0s and 1s. "Are they the same pattern?" he asked, a feeling of excitement bursting into his chest.

For several tense minutes both men feverishly searched through the pages, comparing them with the fragment of paper sticking out from beneath the trilobite. At one point Joe grabbed a trilobite from the desk and held it against the page. He didn't have to say anything, it was clearly the specimen in the photograph.

"I'd say it's the same pattern," said Billy. "Close enough that makes no difference."

"So this trilobite clearly holds a key," said Ed. "Forge's obsession with trilobites again." He returned to his seat, head whirring with ideas. "Forge, Bismarck and Kojo weren't the only conspirators," he explained. For a moment he stopped and looked at Joe, wondering how much he should say. If he told Joe, could he rely on his discretion? Did Joe have his own agenda?

Joe looked up at him, an enquiring look on his face.

"There were others," said Ed. "Trilobites were used as calling cards, to identify members of the gang. Perhaps they were also used to create cipher keys. Rather than using passages from the bible they could have used the name of the trilobite to encrypt."

Joe looked down at the page again. "I'll have to create a program of some kind to find out. It'll take far too long otherwise."

"Do it now," said Ed. "I'll ask Allen if you can have time off from the drilling. I'm sure he'll agree." He broke off as the sound of running boots came from outside and the door crashed open.

It was Allen, he was looking pale and distraught. "Billy, a word," he said leaning on the handle.

Billy looked up from his work in surprise. "What is it?" he asked.

"A quick chat, it's really urgent," said Allen and disappeared back onto the balcony.

Reluctantly, Billy stood and followed Allen out of the door. Ed looked at the two of them through the window, he had never seen Allen so flustered. The conversation became quite heated before Billy grabbed Allen by the shirt front and started shaking him backward and forward. He started to shout about broken promises, Allen tried to calm him down, his mouth forming the word 'sorry' several times.

Suddenly, Billy broke away and marched back to the office, he threw open the door and stormed to his desk where he grabbed his day sack and swung it on his shoulder. "I need to go back to the compound," he told Ed in a shaking voice. "Mind if I borrow Frank?"

"He's your driver as well," said Ed. "What's the matter?"

"I've got to leave, go back to PNG," he spat, "with the Wolf Man." He crashed out of the office and bashed along the balcony before hurling himself down the steps and into the car park.

Allen walked slowly back up the balcony and climbed the stairs to his room like the weight of the world was on his shoulders.

"I'll go and see what's going on," Ed said to Joe.

Joe nodded, "I think you better had."

On entering Allen's office, he saw a single light glowing at the far end of the room. Allen sat with his head on the desk as if listening to it, his gaze fixed on his single office window.

"What's going on?" asked Ed, alarmed at Allen's supine posture.

Lifting his head from the desk, Allen gave him a baleful stare. "The shit's just hit the fan," he said. "Miriam's told the press that Billy and the Wolf Man are here and there's a pack of journalists on their way. She's pissed that Lomax told her to mind her own business."

The breath caught in Ed's throat. "Does she know about you yet?"

"I don't think so. When she called me just now she made no mention of it. Bernie's presumably saving that juicy detail for the right moment." He leaned back in his chair. "I can't think at the moment, there's too much going on." He paused. "I need time," he said desperately. With a sudden burst of energy, he walked to the window and looked out. "Nothing is ever as it seems, Ed, just remember that. I'm not saying that I'm proud of everything I've ever done but I can say, hand on heart, that I did my duty." He turned and looked at Ed and there was real sorrow in his eyes. "Poor Billy, I love him like a son, like I love Kitten, and I've managed to use and betray him because my duty always came first."

Ed was confused. "How have you betrayed him?"

Allen shook his head. "I need you to watch out for me, Bernie seems to confide in you; you need to keep me informed." He looked back again. "Take me on trust."

Ed scoffed.

"As a friend. Just don't abandon me, whatever you hear over the coming hours and days. I was following orders, I had my duty to perform."

"And what about Billy?" asked Ed. "You're throwing him back to the Wolf Man…he's never going to survive."

"He'll survive, I'll make sure of it. We'll go and find the Wolf Man now, tell him what's happened. Frank'll be able to take us."

"He's just taken Billy back to the compound, we'll have to get another driver."

Allen looked taken aback, "Back to the compound, why's he done that?" A flicker of uncertainty crossed his face, then he shifted gear again and marched across the room. "I'll find a vehicle and another driver."

Allen knew the route out to the Exploration Office well. Before he'd been made Manager of Geology he'd been based there overseeing Chiri, checking that he was doing his job properly. This was in the days before Forge, Bismarck and Kojo had been unmasked and there was widespread paranoia about why Lomax Mine was losing ground against its competitors.

He directed the driver through the less well-known cut-throughs, instructed him to 'step on it because this is where the Galamsey lie in wait for vehicles', and slow down at bends in the road where children sometimes played. Half the journey was through pristine jungle, dark enough to switch on the pickup's head lamps. Allen related how the Exploration headquarters had been built this far out of town as a sign to the Galamsey that the mine's remit ran throughout the territory and not just in the town of Lomax. Over the years there'd been innumerable sieges and ambushes of mine vehicles along the approach roads.

Ed peered around at the thick vegetation crowding to the side of the road and noted places where it was thickest and overhanging. He remembered Chiri arriving at the mine offices in only a single vehicle because his other two had been stolen or destroyed in a Galamsey attack.

Then they were out into the blinding tropical sun and speeding along a treeless, barren landscape toward barbed wire and guards. Dust flew up from the wheels as they rattled into the Exploration headquarters and came to rest next to two other pickups. No sign of Chiri's vehicle; he and his acolytes must still be in Lomax, at the mine, Ed reflected.

"Back again," sighed Allen, alighting and looking around. "Doesn't seem to change."

The Exploration headquarters were low prisoner of war style huts that were pulled into a series of rectangles with central, grassed courtyards. "These buildings are bullet-proofed," whispered Allen pointing at the windows that looked out onto the jungle. "Cost a fortune, but the Galamsey like to take pot shots from the edges of the clearing."

Glancing over his shoulder, Ed noticed that beyond the tall razor wire that surrounded the Exploration compound there was a hundred metres where all trees had been felled and vegetation cleared. It provided a way for Chiri and his acolytes to monitor Galamsey activity close to their headquarters and prevent surprise attack. "Great shooting range," Ed said, squinting to see if he could see any movement at the edge of the clearing.

They hurried up the nearest steps and into a dark corridor in which creosote hung on the air. Allen kept up his commentary for Ed's benefit. "I asked Chiri where our Wolf Man was staying. Apparently, they've put him in my old room." Ed knew that this meant he would be found at the far end of the complex, as far from Chiri's office as it was possible to get.

The Exploration headquarters were huge, built at a time when there'd been ambitions to hugely expand production of the mine. But its location in the forest, surrounded by hostile Galamsey, had meant that the scope of operations had been scaled back, until now only Chiri and his acolytes remained.

Moving through the complex on raised wooden board walks, Ed noticed how the courtyard grass became longer and the condition of the paint on buildings more scrappy the further they went from Chiri's heartland. In the remotest corner there was an air of dereliction, the courtyard grass grew knee high, vegetation draped down from gutters and burst out from between slats in the walkway. Doors to offices were missing, broken furniture abandoned; a sense that Mother Nature was reclaiming it for her own.

This was where they found the Wolf Man, lying in a hammock that he'd erected between two struts that supported a portico roof. He was bare-chested and a thin plume of smoke rose lazily from a roll-up wedged in the side of his mouth. In the middle of the grassed courtyard a billycan bubbled away above a small camp fire. The atmosphere was hot, full of wood smoke that hinted at barbequed meat.

The Wolf Man pushed his hat above his eyes when he heard their boots on the walkway. He swivelled his head to look at them. Ed turned away, pretending to be interested in the thin vapour emanating from the billycan, but Allen shouted a greeting and started to walk forward, more warily than before. His movement reminded Ed of a keeper of dangerous animals. No sudden motions or noises, nothing to alarm the unpredictable creature in its Kookaburra hat.

There were white objects suspended from the roof above the Wolf Man. For a moment Ed had trouble recognising them, but then he realised they were monkey skulls, bleached white by the sun, fangs bared as if in warning. When a light wind entered the courtyard, they swayed gently, rubbing up against tinkling wind chimes.

The Wolf Man's torso was covered in curling black hair that partially hid a series of skull tattoos, and on his face there was a long gouge mark, just as Chiri had described. Ed couldn't take his eyes from this latter feature, he kept thinking of finger nails. "To what do I owe this pleasure," the Wolf Man said to Allen, sarcasm etched on every syllable.

Before answering, Allen looked around. "You seem to have set yourself up real comfortable here."

Brett sneered. "A man needs to live by his own rules. I like to smoke and keep my own company." It was said like a credo.

"It's all over," said Allen. "You'll have to leave. The press have found out you're here. It won't be long before they arrive."

"So what," the Wolf Man replied. "Let them come."

"The Mine Manager has ordered me to send you and Billy Barker back to PNG. He wants you out of here before they arrive and start asking questions about how and why Alfie may have died. It'll not take them long to work out that you and he had a history." He stared hard at Brett's face. "They'll come looking for you and start wondering how you got that mark."

"Fell over one night, caught my head against the edge of the television in my room."

"You'll be out of here by tomorrow, on the mine service bus," said Allen, his voice full of authority. "I'll make sure Chiri and his men know what's expected." He gestured before turning and walking away down the boardwalk. "You can take your hammock and your skulls with you."

They said nothing to each other until nearly out of the complex. "He's insane," Allen said through the side of his mouth.

"Yes," said Ed.

Turning sharply, his face flushed with anger. "Do you really think I wanted him here?"

"I don't think you really knew what you were getting in the first place," said Ed. "I don't think you checked well enough. I'd like to think that if you'd known he was a psychopath you'd have walked away and left Billy to his fate."

"Well, you're dead right, I didn't know his true nature, only that he was a bit of a rough neck, that's all."

They climbed into the pickup and headed back to Lomax, silence filling the space between them as both watched the dark forest for signs of lurking danger. On reaching the compound Allen refused a drink in the bar; he said he'd had enough for the day, he wanted to get home to his villa so he could think about the day's events.

After a hasty meal Ed decided that he would try and find Billy, tell him the news that the Wolf Man had been given his marching orders as well. But Billy just shouted through the door that he wanted to be alone. His voice was slurred, like he'd been drinking, so Ed thought he'd leave him to it.

Billy Confesses

Next morning Ed woke early, the memories of his visit to the Wolf Man fresh in his mind. There were other thoughts, like the sight of Bismarck lying in bed or the triumphant face of Chiri when he'd burst into their room, armed militia and armoured cars at his back. But it was the raw insanity of the Wolf Man with his bleached monkey skulls hanging from the rafters that made him feel most uncomfortable. The smell of madness had hung in the air, Allen had smelled it and so had Ed, but neither wished to discuss what they had experienced, it was too unsettling, too near the bone. That was why Allen had decided to go straight off home and it was why Ed had not forced his way straight into Billy's room last night so he could try and comfort him.

He knocked on Billy's door before going down to breakfast. There was no answer; Ed suspected that he might be suffering from an almighty hangover so left him. The breakfast room was empty, the Faces had gone, telling the staff that they'd be back within the month when tempers might have calmed. Ed wondered whether he should be making plans to leave now that the situation was spiralling out of control. But he dismissed the idea, he wasn't here just to earn a living, he needed to discover why trilobites kept arriving in his farmhouse. If the solution wasn't to be found here, then he had no idea where else he could look. The thought of waiting for a knock on his kitchen door with God-knows-what menace waiting outside didn't appeal.

After a breakfast of tea, pineapple and toast he left a hefty tip for Moonlight the waitress and took a stroll outside. Frank was in the car park. "Mr Allen wants me to get Mr Walsh from Exploration," he said. "I'll be an hour, maybe longer. Mr Allen suspects it might take longer. I'm to wait until Mr Chiri arrives."

Ed nodded his understanding and decided to go back to call on Billy again. He banged on the door very loudly and shouted. A worry that had been tickling away at the back of his mind started to suddenly expand. He banged on the door again, even kicked the base of it. He was making enough noise to wake the dead, so why wasn't Billy responding?

He stepped back, foot raised, aiming at the door lock. They could charge him for the damage. Then he kicked his foot hard, the way they'd trained him in the army, and with a sound of splintering wood, the door flew open.

Billy lay in the foetus position facing away from the door, fully clothed. On the bed side table was an empty bottle of whisky, and resting against his back, in the well of the bed, was a bottle of pills, its top removed and discarded.

"Billy," he shouted, leaning over the bed and shaking him.

Even through the thick cotton of the mine clothes he could feel the coldness of the body. For one frantic moment he thought maybe Billy wasn't dead, he was just cold because of the air conditioner. He searched around the room looking for a blanket. "Billy wake up." He shook the body again, rubbing the skin to try and get some warmth back.

When he leaned over the body to take a look at the face he was met with two wide-open, lifeless eyes. No twinkle, no nervous glance or frightened stare, just a deathly curtain. On the floor, next to the bed, was a tapestry of the Australian Outback.

Standing up slowly he backed away, the horror creeping over him. He sat down heavily on a wooden chair, but a rushing of bile overcame him and he ran into the toilet where he was violently sick. When the waves of nausea subsided he emerged, amazed that he should have had such a visceral reaction. The room swam again, so he went to resume his place on the wooden chair, unable to bring himself to look at the body.

Eventually, even sitting in a chair was too much. He collapsed on the floor and knelt by the bed, elbows on the sheets, his hands covering his eyes so he didn't have to see. The room stopped moving and he felt his stomach relax, but he remained in the same position, praying for the first time since he was a child that God would understand why Billy had taken his own life.

For a long time he knelt, lost in the misery and the waste. A tightness in his chest moved up into his throat and he coughed, realising that tears were forming in his eyes. He tried to keep a hold of himself, if he gave in to his emotions he may not be able to stop. Then he sobbed long and bitterly, unsure if he was crying for Billy or himself.

And this was how Bernie found him when she arrived in a puff of scent. "Oh my God," she said in a small voice.

Ed didn't bother to answer, he wanted to seem like he was in control, but a fresh paroxysm of grief overcame him. He heard her sit in the wooden seat and uncork a bottle of whisky. "Keeps the emotions at arms' length," she said, handing him a glass.

Ed looked up at her through a bleary eye. Taking the glass he threw the liquid back in a single mouthful. "Thanks," he gasped. "Any more in there?"

"Sure there is," she said taking back the glass.

The fire of the whisky burned his insides, took his mind off the other hurt. When the burning subsided the feeling of desolation returned, but not so acutely. He took the opportunity to stand and walk across to a nearby soft seat where he collapsed, exhausted.

Bernie followed him across. "Try and sip it this time," she said handing him a full glass.

"I'm sorry," said Ed, tears starting to roll down his cheeks.

"For what?"

"I haven't cried much since I was child." He took a sip of the whisky. "What a waste," he spat.

"Sometimes it takes you like that, when you're not looking, suddenly the pointlessness creeps up and gets to you."

Ed looked at her in surprise, wondering whether she was being sarcastic. But there was no flicker of a grin across her face. "I had a partner who committed suicide," she said, "took me two whole years to recover and another year to dry out."

"I've only known Billy a few days," replied Ed, "but somehow I feel I've known him all my life. Is that a silly thing to say?"

She shrugged and then looked around the room. Her eye fell on a laptop on the bedside table next to a bottle of whisky. "Wonder if he left anything," she said to herself, leaning across Billy's body. She grabbed the device and placed it on the bed next to Billy's back. Ed felt sickened that she was not respecting Billy's privacy, always prying and looking for the story.

"No password," she said. "And look, he's left an application open on the desktop." She clicked a button and sat back in her seat.

From the speakers of the lap top came a hiss and then a cough. "The final testament of Billy Barker," said Billy's voice, slightly reedy with a hint of a Liverpool accent, "being the confessions of a geologist, a socialist and a murderer." In the background, there was the sound of whisky being poured into a glass. It was clear from the slightly slurred speech that Billy had already consumed quite a bit. "My family, such that remain, are Catholic and believe that suicide is a mortal sin and that you'll go straight to hell, do not pass go, do not collect £200." There was a pause while he drank. "But I don't believe in God, nor in organised religion, which Karl Marx rightly concluded to be the opium of the masses."

In the background, Ed could hear a clicking sound, and he realised with horror that it was Billy struggling to undo the safety cap on the bottle of pills which were now lying on the bed.

"But I always liked the thought of confession. Back in the day I once tried to persuade Allen that we should introduce it into our manifesto. Cadres would be able to confess their sins to one of the party elders, get their punishment and move on. I thought it might engender a spirit of openness in our new society." He cackled loudly, then the cackle turned into a wheezing laugh and finally a hysterical howl of grief.

For several moments there was nothing more. Ed looked up at Bernie questioningly. "There's more," she said, "much more."

A cough indicated that Billy had managed to control himself and was attempting to continue. "I was born in Liverpool. When I was eight my father went to sea and never came back and my mother struggled with alcoholism until I was twelve, when she finally managed to kill herself."

Ed stared across at the bed, it was like Billy was still alive, talking with his back to them.

"The mental asylum where my mother lived had a library and I would spend time in there waiting for her to come round. That's where my interest in geology and politics came from. I read obsessively and I scraped together enough exams to get into a polytechnic in London. When I arrived I was lost, I suppose I was in search of something to give order and meaning to my life, and revolutionary politics fitted the bill. This is where James Allen entered my life, he somehow managed to get funding for a research project which he offered to me when I graduated. It was the most wonderful feeling in the world, it was like I was floating on air, I would do anything for that man."

More gurgling from the whisky bottle.

"Over the two years when we worked closely together we recruited another ten people to the Crappers, not all of them suitable. Allen decided we needed to expand our operations beyond campus politics. He said he'd been contacted by a cultural attaché at the Russian embassy called Chumshkev who wanted to offer help in our struggle against Thatcher and her supporters in the ruling classes. Of course, we jumped at the chance, here was a way of hitting the State where it hurt."

In the background there were sounds of Billy moving around the room, a door squeaking on its hinges and then closing. When he returned to the microphone his voice was choked with emotion.

"I have a rug. It's made of a fine weave and I took great care to make it perfect."

Bernie stood very suddenly, sloshing her drink and

rushed around the end of the bed. "Look at this," she said. But Ed was too fixated with the voice coming out of the computer to get up from his seat. Billy had begun to move on from rugs and back to the main point of his confession.

"Very soon we began to run messages for him, leaving packages at post offices, keeping watch on various politicians. Allen met with him every month, sometimes more. On several occasions I was asked to attend."

There was a rattle of pills. He hadn't yet taken off the top of the bottle. Then there was a pause, a muffled knock in the background, Ed could hear his own voice asking if Billy wanted to talk.

"I want to be alone," Billy shouted.

There was another pause, Billy was waiting to make sure Ed had really gone. "Soon I began to realise that Allen was up to much more. He was in contact with a man from Downing Street, a senior man, Charles Cathcart, now Sir Charles Cathcart. He was in the Cabinet Office, still is. I only found out his name by accident when I was looking at the newspapers in Australia a few years back. He was trying to get the Australian government to accept a British nuclear facility on an offshore island." He stopped and sniffed. "What a monstrous bloody cheek. I almost went to somebody then and there to tell them he was a commie spy, a traitor, a betrayer of his own class."

The pill bottle was shaken again.

"But I didn't. Because the risk was too great. Since a child I've been afraid of locked doors and enclosed spaces. That's why the Outback was the best place in the world for me, lines of sight expanding away to the horizon. In PNG I got a taste of what prison would be like, hot and claustrophobic and locked away with people like the Wolf Man, a vision of hell. But when I take these pills I will imagine myself at dawn in the Outback, a massive cup of tea in my hand, the stars still visible above me and a newly made fire crackling away beside me. As I slip away I will place myself there, feeling the cool morning breeze on my face."

There was silence for a long minute before the voice came back.

"If I believed I could get back there I wouldn't be taking these pills and you would not know about Allen and his past." He sighed and took another slurp of whisky. "Allen shot Ledger in the head and I disposed of his body in a lake. Ledger had found out that Allen was a draft dodger and as a result had taken a very strong interest in the Crappers. As well as being a journalist Ledger sometimes contributed to the CIA. He was basically a lackey of the Americans, like much of the British press, even now. He'd got a sniff of what we were up to and was busy trying to prove that Allen had a contact inside the Cabinet Office. We couldn't allow that to continue so Allen hatched a plot to get rid of him. He was pretty sure Ledger was acting alone without reference to his superiors. He was a glory seeker, like one of those bounty hunters in old American films."

"We'd hoped to blame the murder on a looney who'd recently joined the Crappers. He was so extreme that we were sure he was insane. But Sonny turned out to be a police agent. Allen told me to run and keep running and that's what I've been doing."

The sound of pills pouring out of a bottle, the filling of the whisky glass.

"I have no earthly possessions except my clothes and my tapestries. Any money I made was given straight to charity before the Wolf Man could get his hands on it. I would like Ed to sell the tapestries and give the proceeds to a charity of his choice, or else keep them if he wants. You can do what you like with my story."

"Final thing, tell Joe I've hacked into Forge's account and had a look around, I've sent him an email."

There was a click and the recording stopped. Bernie, her head down, blonde hair covering her face, lost in thought, reached across and put the lid down on the laptop, then put it in her bag. Ed wasn't sure that was a good idea. "He'll have work for the mine on that machine," he said stretching his hand across.

But a deep voice broke through from the doorway. "He's killed himself then?" It was the Wolf Man, face unknowable, uncaring, "He threatened to do that," he said. "Surprised he didn't do it earlier, always threatening." A white smile appeared from behind the dark whiskers, crescent-like and pleased.

"Because of you," said Ed. "The thought of being with a murderer." His buried rage burned clear to the surface. "You made his life unliveable. Your violence is why he's dead, the knowledge he carried with him of your crimes was too much."

The smile widened, teeth bright and hard. So far he'd remained at the door, unwilling to advance across the threshold, it was like he was unsure whether a residue of Billy remained that might contaminate him. Death was probably something the Wolf Man believed was contagious. "Did he leave his confession? Always threatened to."

"That's right," replied Bernie. "We got the whole thing about the murder and how Allen pulled the trigger."

The smile vanished behind the whiskers. "I didn't know about that," he said. "Allen pulled the trigger you say?" He looked at Billy's back, eyes wide with astonishment. "He never told me that, said it was nothing to do with him. Said he'd been set up."

For several moments the implication of what the Wolf

Man had said didn't register. It was like a bomb had gone off in the middle of the room. Turning his head slowly Ed saw that Bernie was as motionless as a cat in long grass. "What confession were you talking about?" she asked.

The white crescent returned, Ed could see there were fast calculations being done, advantages assessed, next moves being planned. "The one that got us over here o' course."

Billy Speaks Again

"It isn't the same pattern," said Joe. He was holding a magnifying lens and studying a picture in a book.

It was later the same day and Ed had decided to come into the office, despite feeling sick. He needed to keep busy, to keep as normal as possible. He'd searched for Allen at Lomax 'A' and upstairs from the Drilling Office, without success. As he'd wandered along the balcony a helicopter flew over and landed at the Mine Manager's villa.

"What d'you mean?" he asked, distracted by thoughts of who might have been in the helicopter.

"The binary code, underneath the trilobite in Forge's book," said Joe, "it's on different colour paper and it doesn't match the pattern."

Ed looked blankly at him. "Sorry Joe, tell me again."

"Remember yesterday we were discussing the binary code on the sheets we found in the drilling volume?"

Ed nodded, wondering what Joe was trying to say.

"Well, Billy said that he thought the pattern in the picture, on the paper beneath the trilobite, was the same as on the sheets we found in the book and it's not, nowhere near."

Ed didn't react, the name of Billy, thrown out of Joe's mouth as if he was still alive, had wrenched his brain back to Billy's room and the aftermath. While Bernie had gone to inform the front desk that Billy had committed suicide, Ed had searched Billy's effects. In a large rucksack there were clothes, tapestry materials, a few books on tapestry techniques and patterns. There was also a large plastic roll containing fabrics propped against the back wall of the wardrobe. He'd removed everything and gone back to his room, aware that the Wolf Man might be on the prowl.

Joe tutted, frustrated by Ed's lack of reaction and turned away to continue looking through Forge's trilobite book. Ed gazed at the gate house; there were fewer armoured personnel carriers today, and the number of militia had thinned a bit. He wondered whether they'd realised the approaches to the gatehouse from within the mine were wide open.

When he'd left the compound, the Wolf Man had been sitting in the sun, hat over his eyes, smoking. He'd refused to say any more about what Billy had held back from his confession. But perhaps Billy hadn't held back, it was probably just that Bernie and Ed were concentrating on the facts that mattered to them. There'd been other names, Sir Charles Cathcart, a traitor who Allen had helped run for a Soviet diplomat called Chumsomething or other. He shut his eyes and thought hard. Chunschev, or Chumshkev. That was it, Chumshkev.

If the rest of the world learned that Allen had killed a fellow American, he would be a complete pariah. The only place he'd be able to find work would be inside one of the former Soviet states. Maybe this was why Allen was loyal to Lomax. Lomax knew of Allen's left wing, murderous past and had used that against him. But apparently, the murder was not the reason why Allen and Lomax had brought Billy and the Wolf Man all the way from PNG. So, what was the reason?

He remembered the Mine Manager before Miriam's

husband taking him aside. "Lomax generally has something on the people he trusts, it keeps them honest, means they don't ask too many questions, maintains loyalty."

No wonder Allen was so coy about telling Ed anything about his past, why he specialised in disseminating misinformation about himself. It was his way of creating doubt in peoples' minds, the equivalent of throwing dust into the air.

He gazed at Billy's desk and then at Joe who was still looking through a magnifying glass at pictures of trilobites, no doubt hoping that Forge had left vestiges of a clue in some of them. Billy had said he'd emailed Joe. There was only one computer in the office, on Joe's desk.

"Ed?" said a voice. It was Joe, his face full of concern. "You should go back to the compound. You've had a shock, you shouldn't be here."

Ed shook his head and turned back to the window. He reflected again on the names Cathcart and Chumshkev. He needed to find out a bit more about these two characters, work out if they were still around. Billy intimated that Cathcart was now a very senior figure in the Cabinet Office. It wouldn't take very long on the web to find out but he would have to circumvent the mine firewall. Perhaps he could forward Billy's confession to somebody he trusted, ask them to do a search.

He shook his head again. There was no surer or quicker ways of having Billy's confession broadcast throughout the mine. But the concept was okay, he thought. If he could send Billy's confession using a private email then there would be less chance of it being read by a Lomax operative.

"Joe, did you say you had a way of getting web mail?"

"Sure," he said keeping his head down.

"And the web, can you get onto the web?"

Joe looked up and smiled. "Perhaps," he said. "But it's

too easy to get caught."

"I need to send a message, something Billy wanted me to do, but I need to circumvent the mine email system."

Joe's eyes narrowed in suspicion. "Why?"

"It involves his family, he wanted them to know details of his will. It's not something he wanted broadcast, wanted to keep it confidential because it could still hurt the living. If I send it via the mine email it'll be common knowledge to everybody before tea time."

Reluctantly, Joe stood up and indicated with his hand that Ed should sit down in front of the computer.

"You're a gem, Joe, I owe you one."

A plethora of circulars loaded into his workspace when he logged in; engineering meetings, proposed changes to work patterns, the ongoing problems with the union. It was mostly chaff, the background noise of an organisation attempting to show that it was working efficiently. And there, right at the top of the list, was an email from Billy's Lomax account with an attached WAV file, Billy's suicide note. He downloaded the file and turned to Joe and nodded.

Joe leaned across. "You'll have to tell me your web mail provider," he said.

Before long all the mine emails were replaced with others inviting Ed to join a local gym, become a member of different credit card schemes, sign different online petitions. "Amazing how all this rubbish can accumulate, even after only a few days," he remarked to Joe, who nodded.

The emails continued flooding from the web server. He was able to see them scroll past his eyes and read their titles before disappearing down the window to be scrolled off the bottom.

An email from Alice, dated the day before and titled

'Gone on holiday' appeared at the top and was instantly shunted down. Ed attempted to click on it but kept missing.

"Wait," said Joe. "Can't be many more. You can read it when they've stopped downloading."

After another twenty or more emails arrived, the avalanche ceased and he was able to scroll down. Her email was short and to the point, still redolent with anger. *'You're right, I'm being watched. Gone on holiday.'*

There was no, 'love from Alice' or kisses, no 'hope you are well'. He sighed, clicked reply and then attached Billy's WAV file.

"Cathcart and Chumshkev," he wrote. *"Please can you find out details. Wouldn't ask unless I thought it was crucial."*

He sat back and wondered how she should send her reply. *"Email the answer to my personal email address then let me know you've sent it using my Lomax account."* He attached the Lomax account details and then sat back.

Worry fluttered around his stomach. Had she taken his advice and gone to Sophie's? What precautions had she taken to ensure she wasn't followed?

Joe was looking at some of Forge's trilobites. He tapped a sheet of paper on the desk. "Billy sent me an email before he died as well," he said lifting his eyes to look at him. "He suggests I look at pictures of trilobites on Forge's account. Have a read," he said, handing across a printed-out email.

Ed took the sheet and peered at the text:

'Leaving tomorrow. I've been thinking of our problem and I've decided that the answer lies in steganography. Forge saved pictures of his trilobites on the computer in his office; Calymene01 is his password. I hacked into his account from the compound. See attached programme, found in a secret folder in a hidden part of Forge's profile.'

"Steganography?" asked Ed. "Never heard of it."

"Neither had I until today," replied Joe. "It's the science of hiding messages within digital images."

"What was the attachment?"

"A small program Billy found on Forge's profile. It's called Stegamine, allows users to encrypt and decrypt messages using image files."

For several moments Ed said nothing, allowing the implication of this latest discovery to ruminate in his already over-tired and emotional brain. "On Forge's profile?"

"It was in a hidden folder, password protected."

"So why are you not searching through Forge's pictures? This must be the solution. This was how Forge was able to communicate with the outside, passing pictures of trilobites back and forth."

Joe tutted. "It's not that easy. There're literally thousands of trilobite pictures. It'll take years to go through each one."

"So we're no further forward," said Ed pushing his hair back in frustration.

"We are further forward," Joe corrected him. "We know Forge hid messages in full view. We just need to select the correct series of pictures. On his profile there are up to twenty pictures of each specimen he bought, taken from slightly different angles. I bet he printed off the correct one and put it in this book." He held up Forge's trilobite catalogue. "When he wanted to read the message again he looked in here to work out which was the correct one."

He took up his magnifying glass and started to look at the trilobite pictures again.

"Look at his Calymene pictures," said Ed with a sudden burst of enthusiasm. "Those were really important; those were the trilobites that the syndicate used."

Joe lifted his eyebrows and started to flick the pages.

"There are four pictures of Claymene," Ed said. "Forge

212

gave one specimen to each of the group. He bought them from a shop in London on the day of a crucial meeting with a man named Snodgrass."

Joe laid down his magnifying glass and folded his arms. "I'm not sure I want to go any further," he said, standing up and walking to the window. "There's too much heat in this thing, Chiri's a frightening man when he decides he doesn't like you." He muttered something under his breath which Ed could not quite hear. "And he's coming up the steps right now."

Ed's heart sank, Chiri must have learned of Billy's suicide and wanted information about his death bed confession. The thumping feet grew louder along the walkway and Ed braced himself for the invasion. And then the boots started to recede and Ed opened his eyes.

"Close one," he said to Joe.

"They're going up the stairs," said Joe. "Must be looking for Allen."

Realising that he had not yet shut down the computer, Ed pressed the off button and kept it depressed. Then he walked back across the room and sat down, listening intently for the return of Chiri.

Joe went back to examining the trilobite book.

In the silence, Ed's thoughts returned to Billy's suicide and its aftermath. After removing the rucksack and the scroll of tapestries, he'd gone back to Billy's room and found the Wolf Man searching through drawers. He'd asked him what he thought he was doing and had received a sneer in return. "He owes me money."

"Make a claim against his estate," Ed had replied and stared, feeling himself shake with anger.

The Wolf Man had continued opening drawers, and then turned to the wardrobe. "It's no good," said Ed, "I've taken his belongings to the front desk, the militia have them under guard until an investigation is made into the circumstances of his death."

"Investigation?" asked the Wolf Man, grinning.

"Like the investigation into Alfie's death," Ed had said. "I've let them know my suspicions."

The Wolf Man had chuckled to himself. "Good luck with that," he said and walked from the room.

Ed had collapsed against the wardrobe, his breathing hard, his head spinning. At his feet was Billy's tapestry of the Western Australian Outback. Beautifully executed, in less than five primary colours, it showed a view of open country from the eaves of a Eucalyptus wood. The sun was low, illuminating a low range of hills, and up in the sky was a firmament of stars.

As he took in the detail he was able to see a small figure in the middle ground, lost in the vastness of the landscape and the universe. A fire made the figure glow orange and yellow. Ed's head began to swim so that the figure moved, it turned its head and looked at him before continuing to gaze at the stars.

* * *

The sound of heavy boots banging down steps interrupted his reflections and brought him back to the Drilling Office and its rows of volumes lining the walls. "They're coming back," said Joe in a lead-heavy voice.

Sure enough, the door was thrown open and Chiri, with a smile several feet wide, walked inside followed by his acolytes. Since the Wolf Man had stopped joining them on their regular patrols they looked to have settled back into their old habit of filling any space that they entered.

Chiri was beside himself. "A communist agitator," he roared with barely suppressed glee. "I think the name of

Allen will go down in history: Lenin, Stalin, Trotsky and Allen." The room erupted in laughter. "Where is he? Plotting the revolution?"

"Still negotiating the return of the geology section as far as I'm aware," said Ed. "It's taking longer than he thought."

"There'll be nobody returning here. From now on I'll be choosing the geology section." He turned to Joe. "And after what we've just learned I think some of the more recent appointments will have to be reviewed."

"Joe's here because of the direct intervention of Lomax," said Ed defensively. "Or are you trying to imply that Lomax is a communist?"

"I'm saying that he was appointed because that's what Allen wanted and up until this morning nobody knew that Allen had been some kind of insurgent. I think we're all beginning to understand the origin of the union agitation that has blighted this mine. Ever since Comrade Allen arrived there's been nothing but trouble."

The trouble originated long before the arrival of Allen, but Ed let this detail pass. "Why don't you find him and ask him what he's been up to?"

"That's just what I'm trying to do, but he's disappeared. And no wonder." He looked around his acolytes and gave a huge grin. They reciprocated, as delighted as their master at the demise of Allen. Then he turned back to Ed. "Lomax has arrived. He phoned from Accra, wanting to speak with Allen as a matter of urgency. I've been trying to find him, even popped into the compound to see if he was there and that is where I met Brett."

"I suppose he told you about Billy's suicide?" asked Ed.

Chiri nodded his head, grin still fixed in place, "He told me about the truth Billy spoke before he died: communist, murderer and traitor. Lomax told me Allen was a draft dodger but I never imagined he was anything much more than a coward."

"You might find that Lomax knows about it and doesn't care, considers it all in the past."

Chiri's smile disappeared. "Maybe," he said. "We will see. I take it that you haven't seen Allen then?"

Ed shook his head. "I've been looking for him, trying to warn him what's coming. Nobody's seen him and he's not in any of his usual haunts. Haven't tried at home yet."

"That's where we're going next," said Chiri. "See if he's decided to try and hide in his hole." His manner turned menacing suddenly. "You shouldn't get comfortable here. You were appointed by Comrade Allen and that means I'll be coming back here for a longer chat. Perhaps we'll discuss why Herman was so keen to have you as an errand boy."

He swept from the room, his acolytes falling into his slip stream. Joe sat back, his lower lip trembling slightly. Ed felt a ringing in his ears, like he'd just been privy to a loud explosion and was waiting to find out if anything hurt. When he regained his heartbeat and felt like he'd returned to earth he looked out of the window. Chiri had climbed into a waiting pickup and was barking orders to his acolytes. Then the vehicle sped off through the gates and out into the town.

"Wait by the river long enough and you'll see the bodies of your enemies float past," said Ed aloud. He realised Joe was looking at him, confusion written across his face.

"One of Stalin's great quotes. Just about sums up Chiri's attitude to life as well. He's seen Kojo and Bismarck swept away and I think he's just seen Allen's body 'round the bend." He smiled apologetically at Joe. "I'm afraid he sees you as one of his enemies as well."

"And you," Joe said quickly.

Ed shrugged. If Chiri told him to go home, back to his lovely farmhouse on the top of a mountain then he would gladly pack his bags and leave. Joe couldn't do the same.

"Is Allen a communist?" asked Joe before Ed could ask him if he had an alternative chance of employment.

"No," said Ed. "But he used to be, and there's also an allegation of murder. It doesn't look good."

Joe nodded. "I guess I better not buy that new house I had my eye on."

"Perhaps not," said Ed. He thought for a while before giving his opinion. "If you find out about those images, it might save your job and be a great help to your future career, on the other hand it'll consolidate Chiri's opinion of you as real threat to his position."

Further debate was cut short when they heard a single set of footsteps clicking along the balcony. "Not a word about steganography to Bernie," he said, sitting back and fixing his gaze on the door.

Bernie had changed since the morning when she had been wearing a sombre green outfit similar to the mine's uniform. Now she was dressed in a flowing khaki cotton suit with white silk blouse and a hat sporting a leopard skin band. Quick, jerky movements showed she was simmering with excitement but didn't want to upset Ed's sensibilities by celebrating Allen's downfall too ostentatiously. On entering, she simpered, as if offering Ed her deepest condolences at this difficult time, then swept across the space and sat, uninvited, on Billy's old chair.

"Well, the shit's hit the fan," she said, trying to keep the edge from her voice. "Lomax has flown in from his London fortress and Allen has disappeared."

"I wonder why Lomax has chosen this moment?" said Ed. "He can't know of Billy's suicide and confession yet."

Bernie tutted. "He's come to lord it over his enemies of

course. He wants to find out from Bismarck what he's done with the money he stole."

"Good luck to him," said Ed. "If Herman and all his brutality couldn't drive it out of Bismarck I doubt Lomax will frighten him."

Ignoring him, Bernie ploughed on. "And he wants to speak with Herman now that he has the advantage. Always negotiate from strength, isn't that what they say? Now he has Herman in a lock up he can afford to show a bit of compassion. I daresay he will claim that the smashing of the union block and arrests were nothing to do with him, that he has reprimanded the people responsible and will release Herman and his executive if they agree to his terms."

"And that'll work?" asked Ed. "What'll happen if Herman says no to the terms?"

"Put him on trial for the murder of Alfie?" replied Bernie shrugging his shoulders. "Who knows, these tycoons generally have something up their sleeve." She looked across at Joe and smiled. "He'll probably offer to reinstate most or all of the people who were sacked for being in the union if Herman agrees his terms."

Joe ignored her, he was too busy looking at trilobites through his magnifying glass. "What are you doin' there, Joe?" Bernie asked walking over to his desk.

Ed cursed under his breath.

"Lookin' at trilobites," said Joe, unconcerned.

"Why would you be doing that?"

"Allen asked me to go through Forge's back catalogue and look for the more valuable ones," he replied. "I think he wants to do a fire sale. He said it had something to do with raising funds for something."

Bernie looked down on him and opened her mouth to say something, but Joe ploughed on. "Don't know why he asked me, I know nothing about trilobites and I wouldn't know a valuable trilobite from a dead wood louse."

The phone began to ring and Bernie forgot the question she was about to ask and leaned forward. "I think this is the call I've been waiting for." She picked up the instrument and spoke her name, then listened. There was a long reply during which Bernie looked searchingly at Ed. "We're both on our way," she said eventually and put the phone down. Returning her gaze to Ed she said, "We've been invited to dinner up at the Mine Manager's residence."

Allen Confesses

Ed felt a constant low level of adrenalin and every now and again his heart would skip a beat. His heightened senses registered he was hot but he did not connect the sweat running down his back to the temperature, only to his constant fear. Away in a far corner of his brain his waking mind told all his senses to cool down.

So, after they arrived on the hill top and Bernie had rushed into the Mine Manager's villa, presumably to meet up with Miriam and suck up to Lomax, Ed decided he needed time to think. There was no point staying in the pickup with Frank, who had developed the habit of asking inane questions, about Billy's death and the situation with Bismarck in the mine hospital, so he took himself off to tour the gardens.

None of the blousy blooms or large buzzing insects caught his attention, he was too busy trying to wind down the gears of his imagination, work out the difference between truth and falsehood. In his feverish state, he contemplated whether Lomax had deliberately brought the Wolf Man here to act as some kind of agent provocateur.

But that didn't make sense, the Wolf Man had come as part of a package, he was here because of Billy. And the reason Billy was here was because he had information that Allen wanted kept quiet, about his past as a Soviet agent helping to run a civil servant called Cathcart. The Wolf Man was incidental, he was along for the ride.

He could see why Allen would want to keep his past quiet, but why should Lomax care? If Lomax had found out that his favoured geologist in Africa was a former Soviet agent and murderer then surely he should have sacked him, not been complicit in the cover up.

With Kojo and Bismarck persona non-grata and Allen disgraced, Chiri would have a free reign. As Exploration Manager, he was quite powerful, but with his contacts in the militia and with the geology section as his power base he would be free to act as he wished and the Mine Manager would be helpless. This did not worry Ed very much, he would be leaving sooner or later, preferably sooner, but he felt for Joe and his friends who would be excluded from employment in a place they had called home for many years.

Joe would be gone by tomorrow, and what would that mean for finding the secret behind Forge's pictures? He stopped and swung around to look at the villa. His mind made up, he knew what he needed; it was time. He would dangle the promise of getting into Forge's code as a way of forcing Chiri to stay his hand. With an extra forty-eight hours or more he was sure things would start to resolve themselves, for good or ill. He walked toward the villa, his head clearer and feeling much less jumpy.

When he arrived in the house he heard a muffled conversation coming from the drawing room; Miriam and Bernie were in conference, probably deciding how best to slip the knife into Allen's ribs. Beyond the door stood a ginger-haired man, small and watchful. The man fixed him with a keen stare and moved forward, cat-like, forcing Ed's arms in the air so he could be frisked.

"Mr Lomax is in the dining room," he said when

finished, pointing down the corridor.

When Ed reached the end of the dark passage he knocked at the only door and waited for a muffled, 'come in,' before pushing the door handle.

He'd been in this room, before Miriam had become mistress of the villa. It had been decorated simply, a central polished dining table the only gesture to ostentation. Now the windows were covered in flowing silk and the walls were home to pictures of seascapes. Every surface had knickknacks, pictures of children, or vases of cut flowers. In the middle of the grotto sat Lomax, silver haired, sparkling blue eyes, skin folded by age and the sun, a favoured paisley neckerchief about his neck.

To Lomax's left sat another man, his face obscured by a large vase of flowers. Assuming this to be a body guard like the one in the hall, or a functionary that Lomax had brought from London, Ed waited to be introduced.

"Sit down, Ed," said Lomax. His voice was a rich baritone, part of the man's charisma.

The man from behind the vase leaned sideways. "Hello, Ed." It was Allen.

"Why am I not surprised to see you here," said Ed, feeling anger at Allen's mischievous grin. "The whole of the district is up in arms trying to be the first to bring you before Mr Lomax, and here you are."

He shrugged, then leaned back so his face was once again obscured.

Lomax cleared his throat and then went to the door where he called his bodyguard. There was a muffled conversation and then Lomax came back to his seat. "I've asked Bernie and Miriam to be here, they're the ones I've got to convince before tackling Chiri and the Mine Manager." A smile came to his lips. "Oh what a tangled web we weave when first we practice to deceive."

"Didn't take you as a Shakespeare man," said Allen from behind his barricade.

"I'm not, it's from a poem by Sir Walter Scott."

The clicking sound of heels could be heard coming down the corridor as Lomax leaned across to Allen. "You leave the talking to me, no more of your bullshit." He rose as Miriam and Bernie entered the room and became the genial host. He offered them both a seat and then crossed to the whisky decanter and poured five stiff measures which he then distributed, leaving Allen to the last. The appearance of Allen from around the flowers made Miriam gag on her first sip and spill a certain amount down the front of her flowing silk dress.

"Now, ladies, I believe you have a story to relate," said Lomax ignoring the startled looks, "about Allen."

Bernie was the first to recover. "You may not have heard yet, but Billy Barker, the man Allen appointed to inspect the drilling, committed suicide this morning."

"I had heard something of the sort," said Lomax, his manner uncharacteristically evasive.

"Then you'll probably know that he produced a confession before he died which was sent to me and Ed," she said, indicating Ed with her head. "He made a number of allegations about James Allen and his past, all of which are very serious."

"Go on."

Lomax's flash of interest flushed out Miriam. "At least one of these allegations has been verified independently," she said.

"That's right," said Bernie. "I'm sure Allen would seek to contest Billy's allegations, offer his own version of events, but we've instigated enquiries in England to find the truth."

"Which is?" said Lomax, his eyes half closed as if

listening intently.

"That Allen was a Soviet spy," said Bernie. "He helped a Soviet agent named Chumshkev to run a mole inside the Cabinet Office, called Charles Cathcart, now Sir Charles Cathcart."

"And?"

Lomax's casualness took the wind out of Bernie's sails, but she carried on. "As if that wasn't bad enough, he was responsible for the murder of a CIA operative named Ledger."

Lomax sunk back into his chair and took a sip of whisky. He eyed both of the women, his thoughts unknowable. "All of these events are a long time ago," he said. "We won in the end, didn't we? What would you say if we let sleeping dogs lie?"

Miriam looked scandalised. She drew herself up in her chair, chest puffed out. "He killed a man who was working for our own side; he killed one of his fellow countrymen." When Lomax still didn't react, she decided to embellish the point. "He's a traitor, capable of murder; he's a man who rejected his country at its time of need."

It was fortunate that Allen was hidden by flowers from Miriam's gaze. She was becoming increasingly angry at Lomax's refusal to express outrage at Allen's crimes. Ed was intrigued and decided to intervene. "Perhaps Allen could explain what went on," he said.

Lomax and Allen looked at each other, then Lomax turned back. "I've told Allen not to say anything."

Bernie took the floor again. "But that implies that you want to stand by your man despite the evidence of his treachery. He's introduced a multiple murderer into Lomax who's probably been responsible for killing an Australian driller."

Still no reaction.

"To say nothing of triggering Billy's suicide."

At this final statement, Lomax shifted in his chair and Allen's shoulders took on a much greater hunch. Ed felt the injustice of this last statement, "That's not strictly true," he said. "Allen had his hand forced by circumstances, it was the mine's decision to...."

Miriam decided to interject again. "Even if you think Mr Allen's crimes lie in the past, which I doubt given the amount of left wing activity we are presently experiencing, it is incumbent upon us to inform Her Majesty's government that they have a traitor in their midst. If Sir Charles Cathcart is not actively spying for a foreign power he has opened himself to blackmail. He must be forced to answer these allegations."

Lomax put his glass down on the table and leaned forward slightly. "What if I told you that the British government would not be interested in your story, and that I am personally acquainted with Sir Charles Cathcart?" Both women stared at him intently. "I was in school and university with him," he added.

Ed was the first to react. "Doesn't that give him the perfect profile for a spy? Private school and Oxbridge. Spies are generally the ones you least suspect, like Burgess and McLean, establishment figures."

Lomax smiled. "I can assure you, Sir Charles Cathcart is not a Soviet spy."

The two women stared in silence. Eventually Bernie spoke. "Well, I'm glad you can feel indifference about this, but as a journalist I can't let the matter lie." She put her glass down on the table and started to rise.

"Sit down," said Lomax.

"No point," replied Bernie advancing across the room. "I have rarely seen such a lack of backbone," she said flinging the door open.

"I talked to Sir Charles Cathcart an hour before boarding the plane to come out here."

Bernie stopped.

"He has authorised me to let you in on the truth, but with conditions."

"Which are?" she asked, still with her back to the room.

"That you don't publish a word."

"And what happens if I choose to ignore his condition?" she said, turning to face him.

Lomax smiled, showing very white teeth against his brown skin. "When you've heard the situation I think you'll have no problem struggling with your conscience. Chumshkev can be a very bad man to cross."

Bernie returned to her seat and took up her drink again. "Well?" she asked.

Lomax rose and filled his glass, offered the decanter around to the rest of the meeting, then he went and stood on the other side of the table, behind Allen. It was like he was showing his support. "First, let me assure you that we tried our best for Billy. When we understood that his identity was going to be discovered, Allen contacted me and I contacted Cathcart. We offered to use friends to set up a new identity, allow him to return to Australia under an alias, rub his name off police watch lists, have a word in the right place to stop the media chasing him."

He swilled his drink around his glass.

"I even talked to him on the damn phone when he was in Allen's office, but he was having none of it. I guess he couldn't get it into his head that people he'd considered enemies were trying to help him. The only condition we asked was that he should drop this damn story about Allen and himself killing Ledger and playing bookies runner for the Soviet embassy in London." He turned to the window and put his hands behind his back. "Poor sod."

Ed was unimpressed with Lomax's expression of sympathy. Some men who wield power like to feel the lives they touch and in so doing associate themselves with the struggle and hardships of little people; like the man who scores a goal and immediately feels sorry for the opposition.

Lomax sighed.

"I first met Allen in the United States, about two years after he'd fled Britain. He was in quite a parlous state. Wife had gone off with some preacher and joined a sect of lunatics called 'The Lord's Apocalypse' and taken their child with her."

He turned to his audience again, his face flushed with sadness, or anger, Ed couldn't say.

"When I returned to England I had a message from Cathcart asking whether I had a job going for Allen. Until that point I hadn't realised that the two men knew each other."

He swung around and looked at Bernie and Miriam before glancing at Ed and turning away. "Okay, I said, if he can make his way to London then I would certainly interview him." He found a chair on the far side of the room and sat down, taking a sip of his whisky. "Nothing happened for several months, until I went back to Cathcart and asked if he'd passed on my message. He replied that Allen was unwilling to travel across the Atlantic. Naturally I thought that would be the end of the matter."

Ed tried to shift around so he could see Allen's face. But Allen still had his head down, palms down on the table. He looked like a naughty schoolboy in the headmaster's study.

"When I returned to America on a business trip several months later, Allen met me at the airport. He seemed to know why I had returned, even though I wasn't going anywhere near The Lord's Apocalypse. Not only that, he had the low down on Sergei Chumshkev, a former Soviet KGB man who was now making a name for himself as a budding oligarch. He knew about the trouble I was having in the Far East with Chumshkev and said he could advise me on how best to tackle him.

Miriam let out a derisory sound. "He openly admitted that he knew this Soviet KGB man?"

"Yes he did, and what's more, so did Sir Charles Cathcart."

"Of course they knew each other," said Bernie, "This is more proof if any more were needed, of Allen's guilt."

"Please let me finish," said Lomax, raising his hand. "Like you, I was deeply suspicious, particularly when I did a bit of digging and learned about the death of this American Ledger and of the subsequent investigation and flight of Allen from Britain to America. There was also the strange story of his desertion from the American air force many years before. I confronted Cathcart and demanded to know what was going on."

Bernie had her arms crossed, looking unimpressed, Miriam was looking at Lomax, sitting in her chair as if riding side saddle, enthralled that she was being trusted with an important story. "Cathcart explained to me that Allen was part of a CIA-inspired initiative. There were any number of people like him shipped across to Europe; men and women who were told to go and lie low and wait for an activation signal. The Soviets had them as well, cells of revolutionaries, people buried deep in the civil service; it was only natural that our side should have them as well."

He suddenly laughed, as though at a joke only he saw and understood. "Allen's brief was to start a revolutionary communist cell and build links with the Russians. They made sure his cover story was good; a deserter who quoted the Nuremberg trials at his superiors, a man who hated his homeland enough to betray it and its allies."

Miriam bristled, her ram-rod back straighter than ever. "Outrageous."

Lomax shrugged. "Allen was perfect, he'd always been a maverick. It's part of the reason why he found it so difficult to fit back into the intelligence community when he was finally withdrawn back to America. He'd imbibed his cover too far, he'd become an ideological junky, always lecturing his superiors about their moral responsibility. The military likes the thought of liberty but not libertarianism."

At last Allen stirred. His head peeked around the flowers at Ed, face blank. Ed could tell Allen was uncomfortable, wanted to be miles away but was trapped.

"While he was in London, Allen took a wife, Caitlin, or Cat. She had no idea of Allen's links to the American military. She was a committed socialist. They had a child, which in the spirit of the age they called Kitten. They lived the life of a revolutionary couple, organising meetings, recruiting likely cadres. One of them was Billy Barker, a man newly arrived from Liverpool, already trained in the arts of revolution by his uncle. He and Allen became good friends. I believe Cat even had an affair with Billy." He looked down at Allen's back and hesitated. "Perhaps not a detail which should be developed here," he said, almost to himself. "But you get the point, they were a commune, an alternative to what they saw as the money-grabbing society of Margaret Thatcher."

There was a knock at the door which echoed around the wood panelled room and made everybody jump. The head of Lomax's guard appeared. "Chiri and his mates have arrived," he said.

"Tell them to wait in the drawing room," said Lomax, "we'll be about ten minutes." He fiddled with his neckerchief and straightened his clothes until the sound of his body guard disappearing down the hallway had gone. "Chumshkev had been a very reliable source for American intelligence for many years," continued Lomax. "Greedy and ruthless, he supplied secrets on a pro rata basis, payment on the nail. When he was promoted and moved to the Soviet embassy in London the Americans looked around for a way of servicing their agent and Allen's group bubbled to the surface."

"Allen had already developed the perfect cover by building up ties with East German cultural organisations. Therefore, meetings between Allen and Chumshkev would not look too far out of place. To make double sure, the Americans persuaded Cathcart to act as a double agent, pretending to be a Soviet traitor at the heart of the British establishment. Every month a top secret Whitehall committee would meet and decided what documents to release. Allen would pick up these documents and pass them to Chumshkev in return for documents detailing covert Soviet operations in Europe."

Lomax laughed again. "It was perfect, the only people who knew what was going on was Chumshkev, Allen and Cathcart's Whitehall committee. As far as Cat and Billy were concerned, Allen was running messages for the Soviet embassy, helping to hasten the overthrow of the imperialist state. If anybody from the Soviet embassy had investigated and asked questions, this would be the story they would find."

Lomax stopped and threw back the rest of his whisky and placed it on the table. "It was too perfect, turns out one of the C.R.A.P recruits was a police agent who got wind of what Allen was doing. He reported back to his superiors. Somewhere along the line Ledger got involved. Ledger was one of those occasional spies, a journalist who makes reports to the CIA but is ostensibly at arm's length. He didn't have a security rating so he could not be told the secret."

For the first time Lomax brought Allen into the conversation. "Have I got it mostly correct so far?"

Allen was surprised at being addressed and he looked up quickly. He considered Lomax's question for a few moments, Ed got the impression he hadn't been listening too attentively. "Just about," he said hoarsely.

"Good," said Lomax, turning back to his audience and exhaling some breath. "Ledger wouldn't leave well alone, couldn't accept the warnings. He went and confronted Allen with the facts as he saw them. Held a gun to his head and told him to come quietly. There was a struggle and Ledger's gun went off accidentally."

Bernie decided to intervene. "Why didn't you just go with him?" she asked Allen. "The whole thing would have been cleared up in an instant, why resist?"

Allen was sunk in thought and it took him a while to realise that Bernie was staring at him around the edge of the flowers. For a few seconds he considered what she had said. "I was being watched. If I'd gone with him, the Soviets would have known," he said eventually.

He sighed at the miscomprehension on the two women's faces. "My house was being watched. They'd have seen me leave with him, willingly, a gun to my back. The last thing they would've expected was for me to turn up the day after as if nothing had happened. They'd have smelled a rat, my cover would have been blown, I wouldn't have been able to carry on being a courier. They might have realised Chumshkev was one of ours." He rubbed his hands together nervously. "Ledger was such an amateur."

"So you killed him," insisted Bernie, "and then used Billy to clean up after you."

Allen hesitated and then nodded his head. "And Cat."

He swallowed and looked away. "Cat lied for me as well."

Lomax intervened quickly. "The police spy informed on them of course and the whole thing blew up in everybody's face. If the Americans did nothing, Allen would have gone to jail, on the other hand if they tried to protect him by invoking security of the state, the Soviets would have sniffed a rat, they would've realised Allen was working for us and not the other way around. So, the CIA smuggled Allen back to America and put him on ice. To protect their source Chumshkev."

"And Cat?" asked Ed, looking at Allen.

For the first time Allen looked miserable, almost close to tears. Ed was half tempted to reach across so he could touch his arm. The pretty blonde woman in the picture who Allen had pretended was his estranged sister forced itself into Ed's mind. Allen had betrayed her.

"Not best pleased as you might expect," continued Lomax. "First opportunity, she bunked off to join the looney sect. Couldn't go back to Britain where she was wanted for being an accessory to murder. And Billy spent the next decades hiding out in the Outback and PNG."

Bernie was still unimpressed. "If this story is true, and I'm still reserving judgement, what's the big deal in revealing the truth? The Cold War's a long way away. If Cathcart is innocent, he has nothing to fear. You haven't told us everything."

For the first time Lomax showed signs of annoyance, his famous temper was never too far away. "It's not Cathcart, it's Chumshkev who's keen for everything to be kept quiet, and no wonder, he has very close ties with the Kremlin. Many of the people around him have no idea about what he was doing in London all those years ago. If it became known that he was spying for us it could do his reputation huge harm. Anybody who casts any doubt on his integrity is likely to end up skinned and hanging from the nearest tree."

Bernie shook her head, "That still doesn't explain why it's such a big deal for you or Allen if everybody knows about this."

"Because, Miss Nosy Parker I have some important business dealings with Chumshkev which I do not want to have ruined by intrusive questioning."

There was a stunned silence. Allen poked his head around the vase and looked directly at Ed. Amusement had replaced misery for a few fleeting moments.

"Are you sure this is how it worked?" insisted Bernie, not willing to let go. "You've given me no direct evidence that Chumshkev was the spy and Allen the man who ran him. For all I know this might be a cunning story cooked up by Cathcart to keep his reputation intact."

Lomax had taken the opportunity of the silence to refill his glass. As Bernie spoke he added a splash of water and then took a sip before replying. His voice was calm, he was plainly trying hard to keep his temper in check. "Look at what you're saying," he suggested. "American intelligence pulled out all the stops to get him back from Britain when Ledger was killed. Would they do that if there was any doubt about him? The unfortunate business with Cat, when she found out he'd been working for the Americans all along, the fact that he worked as a Colonel of Intelligence for many years after he was redeployed. If he and Cathcart are still playing a double game then they've not only tricked me but also American intelligence."

From the look on Miriam's face, she was convinced. "A dirty business, but necessary," she said.

Lomax was less sanguine. "Allen's paid a high price, his wife took his daughter away from him, his betrayal of Billy he feels very strongly. He'll live in fear of Chumshkev for the rest of his life. Chumshkev appears not to know where to find Allen at the moment, but if this story blows up it'll be headline news. You can bet your bottom dollar he'll instruct his associates to start clearing up."

For the first time Allen contributed to the discussion voluntarily. "It's why we had to bring Billy and Brett across from PNG. They threatened to sell their story to an Australian newspaper. If it had got out into the public domain, Cathcart would have been forced to offer a public denial that he was a Soviet-era spy and the real story would have to come out."

Bernie looked like a cat who had had cream stolen from right under her nose. "So why employ him, Mr Lomax?"

For a moment Lomax looked perplexed. "Employ who? Brett and Billy you mean? Allen's just explained…"

"No, I mean why employ Allen? He's treacherous, you've said yourself, double-crossed his friends and his wife, he's not somebody I'd employ."

"I see what you mean," said Lomax. "Are you shocked?"

"Not shocked," replied Bernie, as if her badge of honour had been impugned. "But I'm not sure I'd like to employ somebody who'd got so used to the double life. You could never be sure which way he was facing."

Lomax narrowed his eyes. "I'd trust Allen beyond most of my other employees," he said, and could almost have pointed with his finger. "Other people are just as duplicitous. Besides, he has an expertise in the way ideology can be used, that's what he was doing for American Intelligence when I employed him, it's why he's here. You've seen all the trouble we've had in the mine with the union."

"Not my greatest work ever," said Allen in a low voice.

Lomax ignored this comment, his worries were more immediate. "I don't think any of what we've discussed should go beyond this room," he said, "least of all to Chiri. We don't want the entire district awash with rumour. I need suggestions for a cover story that will satisfy Chiri and anybody else who asks."

Allen's Remorse

Later that afternoon, Ed let himself back into an empty Drilling room. He wondered whether Joe had made any progress deciphering the images, then he sat down heavily at his desk and stared out of the window.

The meeting had terminated when they'd each agreed to keep to the same story; that Allen had been a communist in his time but was now reformed. Lomax had assured Chiri that Allen had been checked by the American military and he'd come back as clean. Ledger had been killed by a rival bunch of revolutionaries who wanted to frame Allen because he was American.

Chiri had looked deeply suspicious, and then frustrated as Lomax explained he'd originally employed Allen as an expert in counter insurgency to combat the left wing ideology that had become the bane of the mine. He hastened to assure Chiri that Allen had no residual left wing sympathies.

Yawning, Ed kicked his feet onto the desk and lay back. He wondered whether Lomax really believed, in his heart, that all the trouble at the mine was all down to left wing insurgents.

He looked down at the gate house with its armed guard

and thought about Herman the Helmet. He was a gangster, not an ideologue. He didn't have the moral conviction to do anything which was not in his own interest. Bismarck, on the other hand, was a very different matter.

The likes of Chiri and Bernie couldn't see the appeal of Bismarck, he was an intellectual, a no-hoper. But that was the face which Bismarck chose to show them. Ed knew better, he had dug a little deeper, found out what made Bismarck work, so had Allen. The man had a charisma and an intellectual reach that would have impressed even the most hard-bitten miner. And he was the product of the mine's callous disregard for its workers. A stream of anger, unbidden, came bubbling to the surface as Ed remembered stories about his grandfather's brother, killed in the Gresford mining disaster.

"The enemy within," that's what the British miners' union had been called by the government, the same government that Billy and Cat, Allen's nearest and dearest, had hated so much.

"Whisper it quietly," Allen had said to him once. "Lomax's family made money from the slave trade and then bought land which was found to have coal. You want somebody to hate? He's your man."

Walking across the room Ed looked down onto Billy's waiting desk. The fact of Billy's death hit him hard. "Poor Billy," he muttered. "A real sucker punch." What would be his epitaph, he wondered. "Here lies Billy Barker, a life spent in the shadows. A true believer who lost faith."

He would start making plans to leave the mine, and this time it would be forever, he promised himself. He'd come to understand why Allen had wanted him here, it was because he needed a spy who would reliably scent the wind. Well, Ed had scented the wind and he couldn't get out of this place fast enough. Worry about Alice flooded into his mind.

There was a respectful knock on the door and Frank walked in. "Mr Allen wants me to take you across to Lomax 'A' so you can have a chat."

Sighing, Ed nodded. Probably just as well, he mused, he'd be able to give his notice direct to Allen. They walked together down the steps and climbed into the pickup. "Fewer militia again today," said Ed.

Frank nodded. "They're gradually reducing the security, they probably hope nobody's noticing."

"Or maybe they're trying to tempt the opposition into an attack. That's more in Chiri's way of working. The more trouble the better."

Nothing else was said until they reached Lomax 'A'. The area surrounding the shaft was as busy as usual and Frank found difficulty negotiating his way through the crowd. "Wait here," said Ed. Now Billy was dead, Frank had no reason to go elsewhere.

Allen was behind his desk when Ed entered, his face in shadow. He didn't rise from his chair with a friendly greeting, or shout through to Adzo for coffee. "Thanks for coming," he said eventually, after Ed had sat down in a chair close to the desk.

There was a barrier between the two men, it was mental rather than physical, a friendship that would never be the same, which had to be remade. Leaning forward so his face became lit by the small beam of light from the narrow window, Allen's skin appeared white and pasty and his eyes were rimmed with red. "So now you know," he said in a husky voice. "The stories about me being a terrorist, a murderer and a fraudster are all true. You can add spy and betrayer to the list as well."

"I'm sure you did what you thought was necessary."

Allen sank back into the shadows. "In all my life I've

never loved another woman like Cat and I've never had a truer friend than Billy."

Ed couldn't think what to say. Maybe this was another reason why Allen had been keen to have him come to Lomax Mine; he was to be Allen's priest. "I understand why you didn't want to tell me anything," he assured Allen.

"Do you? Perhaps it would have been best to have told you straight away. It was shame that stopped me." He sighed. "And habit. Lying is a habit, it becomes a vice. I've told so many lies that I can't recognise fact from fiction any more. I think I lied to myself that Cat and Billy had known all along what I was doing when I was running backwards and forwards between Chumshkev and Cathcart. It was easy to convince myself that Billy had chosen to live in the Outback and PNG out of a lifestyle choice."

"You were carrying out your orders," said Ed. "People were relying on you."

A deep growl of anger emanated from somewhere in the darkness. Ed tensed, sensing danger, he felt the hairs on the back of his head stand up. But Allen remained seated, unmoving. "Cat was relying on me, so was Kitten, and Billy. Killing Ledger was the biggest mistake of my life. Once that trigger was pulled there was no way back."

The growl turned into a moan, a sound of misery which made Ed catch his breath. There was something he didn't get about Allen's grief. He was an American Intelligence officer, a man steeped in the arts of deception and double cross. He must have known what he was doing when he enmeshed himself in the life of a left-wing firebrand.

"When I returned to America after Ledger's death it was as if I'd landed in a foreign country. Once Cat found out about me she walked straight out of the door and out of my life. I tracked her down, but it was too late, she'd found her new religion and new set of weirdos."

He reached his head into the light again. "But my problem was that I'd come to believe in some kind of left-wing fantasy, that there might be a better way of living. Every time I went into the office and read reports on left wing activity in Africa, South America, Asia, I found myself sympathising. It led me into arguments with General Schwarl, my section head."

He disappeared back into the darkness again, this time there was a gurgle of laughter. "In our old house in London we had a problem with a mouse infestation. Cat, bless her, didn't like to think of killing the poor dear creatures, but eventually we put down traps. I'd have to reset them every ten minutes during the evening. We knew that the problem was the house and the way that we and the neighbours lived. But we weren't going to change, so I put down poison; that did the trick, for a while."

Ed listened, unsure where this was going. His confusion must have shown because Allen leaned forward again, and the light in his eyes had returned. "The habit of the left to speak in allegories is a hard habit to break," he said. "What I mean is that the mice are akin to insurgents, left wing revolutionaries, call them what you will. They breed well in places which are neglected. Me and Cat were content to kill but not willing to deal with the causes of the infestation." He leaned back into the darkness again. "A clumsy allegory, but one that I keep telling Lomax."

"And what does he say to that?" asked Ed.

Allen sniffed, then produced a posh English accent. "Knocking down slums and building smart apartments only makes economic sense if the slum dwellers have the money to pay for the rent on their new homes." He gurgled with laughter again. "It's Lomax trying to be cryptic and unknowable."

"What'll you do now?" asked Ed, "Will Lomax move

you on to another mine?"

"Doubt it, he'll keep me here for as long as he can. Tell you the truth I've had enough, I want to get out. The thought of Florida and fishing has its attractions; I could buy a boat and hire myself out."

"I think I've come to the end as well," said Ed. "I'm obliged to give you a couple of days' notice and that's what I'm doing as of now."

Allen didn't look surprised.

"There's no point me staying here," continued Ed. "Joe is more than capable of auditing the drilling. Once you get all those geologists back on board he'll have more than enough help."

"Any further forward in figuring out that binary?" asked Allen.

Ed hesitated, enough for Allen to lean forward so that his face was no longer in the shadows again.

"Before he died, Billy suggested that the binary code came from pictures of trilobites. He found a steganographic tool hidden in Forge's files."

Allen the intelligence officer did not have to be told about steganography. "And?" he asked.

"We think he may have been sending and receiving messages using pictures of trilobites. Forge has thousands of stored trilobite images."

"Might be useful to find out who was the main recipient of these images," said Allen. "Leave that to me."

"What about the Wolf Man?" asked Ed, "Is he going to be sent back?"

"Chiri'll make sure he gets to the airport, wouldn't do to have him hanging around."

Ed got to his feet. There seemed little else to discuss. "There's no real point in me staying for my notice period, Joe is more than capable of coping with everything. I'd like to get the first bus out."

"There's still Forge's binary code," replied Allen. "We need to know what these images mean. You should at least wait until that matter is resolved."

Ed was about to dismiss Allen's concern, but Allen cut across him. "That's why you're here, isn't it?" he asked. "To stop all those trilobites arriving? Maybe these messages of Forge will help you."

Shaking his head, Ed decided to walk toward the door. "I'm being manipulated, if not by Lomax then by Lomax's rival. If we discover where Forge put all the money belonging to the syndicate then I'm in the same position as before, only worse."

Allen looked at him quizzically. "But Lomax will be really grateful if you find the money, he'll protect you."

"Then why doesn't he protect me now?" demanded Ed. "What difference will having a few more tens of millions make to a man who's so rich?"

"You should tell him your concerns," said Allen. "He's coming over to my place tonight, around six o'clock; you should come as well."

Lomax Gives His Opinion

Back at the Drilling Office, Joe was sitting at his desk, his face a mask of concentration as he gazed at figures on a screen. He looked around when Ed entered the room and leaned back in his chair. "Meeting productive?"

"Fine," he said, "Allen's a bit down though."

"You mean they've found Allen?"

"That's right, he was with Lomax all the time."

"I suppose he's as shocked as us at Billy's suicide."

Ed smiled, realising that Joe was fishing for information. "They were both revolutionary communists long ago, that's how they met. They were in an organisation called the Campaign for Revolution and Peace, or CRAP for short."

"So what was the meeting about?"

"Lomax wanted to know about some murder that they were accused of committing, something about shooting a CIA agent. All a load of rubbish, but he had to have it all investigated."

"Wow," said Joe.

"I think Chiri's a bit upset, he thought he had Allen on toast." He suddenly wanted to be off the subject. "Any luck in decoding the images?" he asked.

"I think so," Joe replied, "but nothing that makes any sense. I've found a few of the images that have been modified and I've run them through the software but they've come back with rubbish. It's almost like the message was scrambled before being incorporated into the image. Definitely had something to hide."

"Well, whatever it is can wait for tomorrow, I'm off back to the compound."

Joe turned back to his screen. "I'll give this another hour or so, it's a question of luck, I'm not too far away."

"Keep me informed," said Ed walking to the door. "You got my personal email, company email's probably being monitored, best for Chiri not to know until the right time. In the meantime, Allen is checking who used to send Forge trilobite images. I doubt it'll show anything but you never know."

Later, as Ed dressed after his shower, Bernie arrived at his door. She had her usual small flask of whisky and was keen to talk. "Going back to Accra tomorrow," she said. "Everything seems to have started to calm down here so I thought I'd head back to the metropolis."

Ed grunted. 'Calm' was hardly the word he'd have employed.

"Lomax is giving me a ride back in his helicopter," she confided.

"What an honour," replied Ed.

She ignored his sarcasm, there were bigger fish to fry. "We've been a partnership, unmasking Allen's past and finding Billy's body."

Ed grunted. "Much good any of it did, you've got your story but you can't exactly publish any of it."

"True," she agreed. "But with Lomax's permission I'll publish a version of the events. All that matters is that Allen, Cathcart and the Russian are kept out." She tilted her head on one side. "I suppose I could report that the wanted criminal Brett Walsh, aka Wolf Man, has been seen in Lomax, and that the murdered driller was known to him once upon a time. I could also say that Billy Barker was with him. I'd certainly mention that Billy committed suicide before he could be arrested."

"And what about the Wolf Man?" asked Ed. "What'll you say about his whereabouts?"

"I'll tell them the truth, that he's gone on the run."

"On the run," asked Ed. "What do you mean?"

"Have you not heard? He's disappeared, last seen boarding the scheduled bus for Accra, but never arrived. The driver says he demanded his bag after they stopped for refreshment and then walked off. There's a bit of a man hunt going on at the moment."

Ed considered this piece of information and then shrugged. West Africa was not a place where a westerner could disappear easily, unless they had lots of money. "Interesting," he said, then looked at his watch. "If you don't mind I've got an appointment."

But Bernie was not keen to move just yet. "You talked with Allen quite a lot, did he ever mention Cat and Kitten?"

"Not interested, sorry," said Ed. "You want to dig the dirt you can go and find some grubby private detective."

Bernie pouted. "I'm only doing my job, it's what I get paid for, informing the public about stories of interest." She waited, expecting Ed to respond. "It's in the public interest," she continued, "knowing about the likes of Allen. I know I can't mention Chumshkev but there'll be an angle to this story that'll have legs. All that stuff about Cat having an affair with Billy, fascinating."

An anger from deep within Ed's soul started to inflate, he could feel it pressuring his stomach. "Nothing delights you more than the misery of other people," he said. There was a strange ringing in his ears. "You're a parasite, a flesh-eating zombie. I'd rather eat my own spleen than discuss Cat and Kitten with you."

"It's important for people to know," she insisted.

"Important for which people? Your fellow flesh-eating zombies who write? Or the dribbling morons who buy?"

She finished her drink and stood. "A shame," she said. "I'd really thought you'd be more sensible than this. You've chosen which side you're on, I can see that, and it's not my side, the side that seeks for truth and transparency." She walked to the door. "You don't want to make an enemy of me, or the papers I write for. I'm sure there are things in your closet which might need closer examination."

The door shut with a click and Ed was left alone with his anger. Outside he could hear the distant sound of thunder, its rumble echoing his own feelings. He couldn't wait to be gone from this place, but leaving might be harder than he'd thought. He'd overheard the remaining Faces at the bar say that there was a waiting list for flights back to London. Never mind, there was always the chance of standby.

He was going to be late for the dinner appointment with Lomax and Allen. He hurriedly finished dressing and made his way out. Frank was waiting for him in the car park, dark glasses and pork pie hat tilted at a jaunty angle. He was stretched across several of the seats with his music pitched loud enough to shake Ed's stomach.

Ed suddenly felt homesick for his farmhouse where the loudest sound was the oak coppice shaking its boughs in the wind. It may be cold and wet, and inconvenient for visitors like Alice, but at least he was in control. Perhaps it was the lack of control that he hated about Lomax, or maybe the lack of privacy. Either way, he would be glad to be rid of this place.

Off to the north he could see dark lightning-wreathed clouds sweeping in from the jungle, shaking scrub and young trees before them. Once more he had a vision of his own house high on the Welsh borders, where he was standing on the front doorstep watching forks of lightning strike the opposite hillside.

Frank sat up and turned down the music. "Mr Allen's?" he asked.

"Quite right," said Ed. "There's a bit of a party but I won't be much more than an hour." He shut the door and gazed at Frank as he started the engine. "Afraid I've got some bad news, I'm going home."

Frank showed no outward sign of concern, but Ed pressed on. "I'll give you two weeks' wages before I go. Anything else you want from me? Put in a good word with Lomax?"

Frank said nothing, his expression unreadable behind his glasses. Manoeuvring the vehicle in his usual reckless fashion, he bombed out of the gate. By the time they reached the outskirts of the town the rain had begun to fall in earnest, but Frank kept on his dark glasses, despite the gloom. He drove like a man possessed, bouncing out of potholes, beeping his horn at children who looked as if they might get in the way, shouting imprecations at other road users. By the time they reached the gates of the mine, Ed was under no illusions what the news that he was leaving meant to Frank.

"If you slow down, I'll tip you an extra week's wage," he said.

Frank hissed and tutted under his breath. "Not safe on the roads tonight, haven't you been watching? When we come back we'll take the long way 'round, not through Lomax town."

"But that'll take an extra hour," complained Ed. "And we'll be heading through Galamsey country in the dead of night."

Shrugging his shoulders, Frank said nothing for a

moment. "Best you stay at Mr Allen's then. My home's close to Mr Allen, I'll come and pick you up in the morning."

"What's going on? What have you seen?"

"Union men and Galamsey, hiding down alleys, peeking out of doorways. You must have seen them as well."

Ed had not seen them, but he was willing to believe that Frank was correct. "You think they're after trouble? Might they attack the mine?"

"Probably," replied Frank. "Best if you're not on the road tonight, they might decide a western contractor is a good target. You tell Mr Allen to lock his door and don't think of going anywhere tonight."

As they sped away from the mine gates along the main thoroughfare of Lomax, Ed started to see what Frank meant. Men stood at every intersection where small alleyways led off into the connective tissue of Lomax township. "Are you sure they're not just worried about the storm?" asked Ed.

"If they were that worried they'd have got into shelter by now," said Frank. "They're out here and keeping watch, not keeping dry."

By now they were reaching the part of town where Allen lived. After five further minutes in which the rain hammered down stronger than ever, Frank swung the pickup into a gateway and skidded to a halt next to a large, white four-wheel drive. For several seconds Ed looked out of the windscreen at splashes of water bouncing several centimetres into the air. A crack of thunder, so loud that it caused the pickup to vibrate, spurred him to throw the door open and make a run for the house.

The door was opened as he approached and Lomax's ginger-haired body guard pulled him in, expertly thrusting hands into the air. After a quick search, he nodded his head, indicating that Ed could enter the sitting room.

"Tis yourself," came Allen's unmistakable greeting.

On entering the room, he found Allen standing with a beer in his hand while Lomax sat stretched out on the sofa sipping a glass of whisky. Ed shook his hair and pulled the wet cotton shirt from his skin, shaking any excess moisture from its surface. "Quite a storm," he said.

"Has Frank gone?" asked Lomax.

Ed nodded, pretending not to be amazed at Lomax's ability to grasp detail. "He wants to get inside as soon as possible," he said. "He's of the opinion that it's not safe to be out tonight."

"Not surprised," said Allen. "A truly ferocious storm."

As if to emphasise the point, there was another vicious clap of thunder that caused all of the cups and plates in the kitchen to clash.

"Not just that," said Ed, "there's loads of union men on the street, hanging around on street corners, looking moody."

Lomax and Allen exchanged glances, then Lomax looked across at his bodyguard.

"He suggested that I stay the night here," Ed continued. "Reckons there'll be trouble in the town, better for a contractor to be off the road and locked away." He gazed hard at Lomax. "Perhaps they know that the owner of the mine is abroad."

Lomax smiled. "Thanks for the advice, when the storm clears, I'll call my helicopter to pick me up."

Allen returned from the kitchen, a beer in each hand. "Great you could come," he said. "We have quite a bit to discuss." Gone was the self-doubt and depression of earlier in the day. "Lomax wants to know how the investigation into Forge's drilling is progressing."

"You know how it's going," said Ed. "I've been

reporting to you every day. We've found these images Billy reckoned hid messages. Joe's investigating."

"And any further progress?" asked Lomax.

Ed looked directly into Lomax's eyes. "What about Bismarck, is he better?"

"Still in the hospital," replied Allen. "He's got dehydration and some bad infection from being kept in the cellar underneath Hermanville. He should be okay, they're pumping solution and antibiotics into him."

Another clash of thunder made them all stop talking and look up. Dust from the ceiling plaster came down and the central light shook on its flex. After a few moments, Ed took the initiative. "Any word what Bismarck and Kojo did with their share of the money? I mean, we're all keen to know how Forge disposed of his portion, what about the part that stayed in Africa?"

Lomax swilled the whisky in his glass and then put it on the table next to him. When he spoke, his baritone voice was commanding and his deep blue eyes bulged. "Easier to dispose of money in Africa," he said. "It's largely a cash economy, you can buy just about anything using US dollars and nobody asks any questions. But I understand they've been commissioning building work, buying vehicles, hiring their own thugs. Bismarck's children have been sent to Switzerland to be educated, their fees are paid in cash from a bank account serviced from Nigeria. They're busy, very busy."

"So what's your bet for what Forge did with the money?" asked Ed.

Lomax picked up his drink, savouring the atmosphere of dependence. "There are several things he could have done," he said with certainty. "Number one, he could have opened a bank account and stashed the money in there. I don't think that's very likely, banks are on the lookout for such things and they need to report suspicious activity. You can't just deposit millions of pounds unless there's a very good reason. Of course you could open lots of different bank accounts and deposit smaller amounts but that's a real ball-aching process."

He leaned forward and took a swig of his whisky before sitting back down again. A distant rumble of thunder indicated that the storm was passing away.

"He could have just converted the money to some other commodity, like gold or diamonds or pieces of art. Not very liquid though. You'd have to sell the gold and that would be noticed somewhere, and then he'd have to bank the cash or stuff it under the mattress. A million dollars is quite bulky to carry around and easily stolen."

"What about art then?" asked Ed. "Forge never seemed to me to be the arty type."

"True," replied Lomax, "But most people who invest in art never clap eyes on their purchases. The pictures and sculptures are kept inside tax free warehouses near airports. I know Snodgrass is an art lover, a genuine art lover, not just an investor. He's known to spend millions every year and he secretes the stuff away in a place he has down in south west Wales. It's rumoured there's a special room kept air conditioned and for his eyes only which has pictures of such quality that it would put many London galleries to shame."

"So Forge may have invested his money in art?" asked Ed.

"More than likely. With Snodgrass guiding him he could have purchased some Picassos or Rembrandts. All that's needed is a purchaser and a vendor company, the name of a person isn't even needed and if it was known Snodgrass was involved then none of the major auction houses would have batted an eyelid. Forge may have had a shell company.

None of the tax authorities would have known because any transaction would have taken place in one of the many offshore tax havens."

"In the end he'd have to bring the money onshore though," said Allen leaning forward eagerly. "When he sold the pictures and wanted to spend his money, he'd have to put it in a British bank."

Lomax gave a snort of derision. "Of course not. The company would have a credit card supplied by some offshore bank. Any purchase he'd want to make would be on that credit card and there would be nothing to suggest that Forge was the person doing the buying, only the name of his company would appear. There need be no involvement of a British high street bank. And what's more it would all be legitimate."

Nobody said anything. Ed thought of his own tax arrangements which were somewhat unconventional, involving a bank in the Isle of Man, but they were nothing on the scale of what Lomax was suggesting. "So for all we know the funds could have been released the moment we placed those trilobites in the shop window. But it would all go on behind a wall of secrecy so nobody would know what was happening."

Lomax nodded his head. "Except for a few lawyers maybe, or the person whose job it was to pull the trigger once the trilobites made an appearance. I've had my people looking and there's been no transfers involving any of the major City institutions using the name Forge. So, either it's all been done in some other jurisdiction or nothing has happened, yet."

"Is it likely that the bank would be in London?" asked Ed. "It's a bit close to home. Forge'd be more likely to have somewhere far away from prying eyes. And he wouldn't necessarily use the name Forge."

"Very true, although he'd need some kind of proof of identity," remarked Lomax. "Which is why we need to get to grips with these pictures. Forge will have been communicating with an intermediary. If we know the identity of that person and what they've been saying to one another we might be in a position to find out exactly where the money has gone."

Attack on the Jail House

Driving in the pickup the next day, Ed was struck by how clear the atmosphere had become. The rains of the previous day had driven away much of the murk that had settled over the town and while it hadn't exactly freshened the temperature it had made the air more breathable.

Frank was still wary, he'd heard things over night that had made him more convinced than ever that there was going to be a major incident. "Who was in the helicopter?" he asked. "I was just getting some sleep after the storm had stopped and it was like we'd been invaded."

"It was Lomax," said Ed. "He was at Allen's last night but didn't want to stay. I guess Allen's place is too much like a slum for him so he called his helicopter and went back to the hacienda on the hill."

Frank smiled. "The hacienda. I've seen such things in the movies. It is like a hacienda, you're right."

Ed started to look out the window at the passing crowds, trying to pick out the men on street corners that had been a feature of their drive last night. With the drier weather, there were far more people milling around. A few looked suspiciously at the pickup as they went past but other than that Ed found difficulty in seeing anything untoward.

"I don't recognise this street," he told Frank at one

point.

"I promised Joe I'd pick him up today. His pickup is being fixed. I think he lives up the hill. It's not far out of our way."

Ed nodded and turned back to the road. The rains overnight had filled the potholes to overflowing. In places, fresh ruts in the road had developed into canyons, their bare earth walls collapsing under the weight of passing traffic. As the road began to climb, the canyons became more pronounced and the water faster flowing. Frank had to pick his way carefully using every ounce of his expertise and the four-wheel drive traction.

Eventually, Frank pulled up next to a pleasant bungalow with a wide veranda on which three boys played football. Joe, briefcase in hand, ran out of the main door and immediately crashed into one of them. With a shout, he aimed a swipe at the nearest boy before scooping up the ball and taking it inside. Then he ran out again, shouting imprecations, before finally climbing into the back seat of the pickup behind Ed.

Frank turned the vehicle and made his way gingerly down the road. Ed was able to see the Lomax 'A' shaft far below in the valley through a fringe of tree fronds that had been bowed down by the night's rain. He listened with half an ear to Frank and Joe discuss the road clearance and how deep some of the ruts had become overnight. "On the other side of town the ruts are so deep a man could drown in them," Frank said enthusiastically.

A knock on the shoulder indicated that Joe wanted to talk to him. Ed swivelled in his seat and moved his face closer. "Message in your inbox, I cracked the code last night." His voice was low so that Frank could not easily overhear. Ed smiled and put his thumb up and then turned back to the road. Joe settled back in his seat, a look of delight on his face.

After a while the road levelled off again, the ruts became markedly less deep and Frank was able to speed up. Within about ten minutes they saw the watchtowers of the gate come into view above the corrugated iron of the shanty town roofs. Scout cars and heavily armed militia could be seen lining the street, and down the small alleyways that issued from within the Lomax town, men advanced en masse toward the main thoroughfare that led to the mine gates.

Frank and Joe, who had been talking animatedly, even joyfully, suddenly ceased their chatter and concentrated instead on staring out of the window. "We should go around via Lomax 'A'," said Joe eyeing the display of armour at the gate. "I've rarely seen the militia so jumpy."

Frank didn't need a second invitation, he turned right and headed down a road that ran parallel with the mine's defensive perimeter. They met several groups of men, none of them talking, all looking sombre. The tension in the air was palpable, like the humidity before a lightning storm. "No children playing," said Frank, "That means trouble."

As they approached Lomax 'A' they were amazed to see only young lads guarding the gate. After a cursory glance they were waved through so that they found themselves on the mine road heading to the gate house and the Drilling Office. Nobody spoke, each kept their eyes scanning the horizon and any dark corners in the scrub that kept close to the road.

"Why are we doing this?" asked Ed eventually, turning in his seat to fix Joe in the eye.

Joe shrugged. "What else should we be doing?"

"Getting well away from here. Going back to the compound."

They'd reached the well-kept golf course and saw, not so

far away, the Drilling Office rising up above the gatehouse.

"Perhaps we were imagining things," said Joe.

"Are you joking?" replied Ed. "Those men in the town did not look like they were heading for work."

As the pickup approached the road that led to the mine gates, Frank slowed down. There were a lot of men standing close to the junction, keeping out of sight of the militia at the gate. None of them wore mine uniform and most had a watchful look, eyes focussed on the pickup. Just beyond them, hidden in high shrubs that encroached close to the road, were lookouts, bending low and staring intently at the gatehouse one hundred metres away.

"Galamsey," breathed Joe.

"Turn around, for God's sake," shouted Ed.

Frank screeched to a halt and attempted to swing the vehicle to the right, away from the gatehouse and toward the Mine Manager's residence, but the road was blocked by an old army truck, its canvas cover fluttering in the wind. The men in the cab were dressed in vests and dark glasses, not standard militia uniform. Frank tried again and swung the vehicle to point back the way they had come, but the men at the junction had spread across the road and some had produced guns.

The lorry with the canvas cover revved its engine and started to move forward. It was heavy and could only move very slowly at first.

"We'll have to take our chances at the gate," said Joe watching one of the men raise his AK-47.

Frank swung the wheel again and they were off, dashing the final one hundred metres in only a few seconds. Ed felt his chest tighten with anxiety, he longed to get off this road so he could get somewhere safer. He thought of the Drilling Office. Of course, it depended what these men were after. If they wanted hostages with which they could bargain for the return of the union leaders then Ed would be a great prize. On the other hand, if it was an all-out assault on the gatehouse then hiding under his desk would be as safe a place as any.

As the pickup skidded into the car park and came to rest in front of two scout cars next to the gatehouse, Ed threw open his door. He could hear panicked shouting from the militia, and in the distance he heard the sound of the lorry. It was still in high gear, the engine screaming in agony.

Some of the militia at the gate shouted to get the scout cars turned around. Up in the watch towers men worked frantically to turn the heavy machine guns around so they pointed in toward the mine, not out at the town. One of the scout cars next to Ed tried to start its engine, there was some coughing and spluttering, black diesel fumes and a bang, then nothing.

The lorry was only thirty metres away, still accelerating, the noise of its engine increasingly agonised. To Ed's terror he saw there was no longer anybody in the cab, the drivers in vests must have jumped out or were hiding beneath the dashboard.

Twenty metres and Ed decided that the best place to hide was behind the armoured scout car that was still attempting to start its engine. He called across to Frank and Joe and then ran for all he was worth. Glancing back, he saw Frank follow him, but Joe was mesmerised by the scene and had not yet got out of the pickup. The crackle of machine guns and small arms fire split the air as the militia attempted to prevent the lorry coming any closer.

Ten metres and the militia started to break and run, only a few were left to try and stop the lorry making its inexorable way toward the gatehouse. Ed shouted for Joe to come quickly, he felt a jerk as Frank grabbed him by the collar and threw him behind the scout car. They slid into a ditch that ran alongside the edge of the fence and landed in stinking water from last night's rain. Ed thought of snakes and looked around expecting to see a rearing head and sharp fangs.

The screaming of the lorry engine reached a crescendo, then started to change its note as it drew level to the ditch. A calmness gathered for a split second as the lorry entered the gatehouse. It must have hit a building or a scout car because the note of the engine remained the same. And Joe still hadn't joined them from the middle of the coming conflagration. Panic gripped Ed as he started to scrabble up the sides of the ditch. A hand grabbed him again and he recognised Frank hauling him down.

Then the lorry exploded. It was as loud a sound as Ed had ever heard. The earth around him began to quiver in shock and he felt the mud on which he was lying start to soften and then liquefy. He felt he was being drawn down, as if the earth itself was moving toward an underground cavern. Not wanting to take his hands off his head he pushed himself up onto his knees and felt his legs slip beneath the earth. The ditch was on the move, its walls were collapsing, something hard and hot hit him in the head and back. He fell forward, desperate to keep fighting so he could extricate himself from the soup of mud and debris that was pulling him down into the depths. Another intense bang on the back of his head caused him to slump forward. He looked around and saw Frank's body disappear, only his head remained above ground, eyes popping with fear. The mouth opened to scream but mud flowed quickly to fill the gap so that the scream turned quickly into a gurgle. And then the head disappeared into the flowing mud and Ed was left alone, paralysed with terror.

He moved sideways, scrabbling in the slurry for a hand

or an arm. The pain in his head increased, he could feel his senses slipping away on a wave of pain and horror. A wooden crate appeared and bumped his shoulder. Like a drowning man grabs a life jacket, Ed clung onto the wooden slats and pulled himself up, enough to keep his head above the soup. But his mind was functioning on borrowed time, another intense pain, this time in his rib cage, caused him to finally sink into the blackness.

Morning in the Hospital

He opened his anguished eyes and felt an agonising throb that emanated from the middle of his brain and followed spiralling tentacles down to his arms and legs. He shut his eyes again so he could shut out the light and the torment.

"I'll shut the curtains," said a familiar Irish American voice.

The brightness of the room dimmed and Ed could hear a pair of feet shuffling around. A chair was pulled out, the sound of its legs scraping on the floor reverberated around his fragile skull. A smell of stinking mud entered his nostrils, mixing unpleasantly with the scent of hospital detergent. He tried clenching his hands and then moving his feet. The bed sheets rustled.

Lifting his head off the sheets he felt a hand push him down. "Don't try and move," said Allen. "If you have a relapse they'll never let me come in again."

Visions of mud came flying back into his mind. At the same time he realised that this was not the first time he'd been awake. Vague memories of a helicopter lifting off, an oxygen mask over his face. An ambulance, some kind of operating theatre with people telling him he was going to be okay.

"Where am I?" he asked looking around. It definitely wasn't the mine hospital, there were too many machines, too much gleaming chrome. "Am I in Accra?"

Allen cackled. "You're in London, a guest of Lucky Lomax. This is the hospital he attends when he wants to have a nip and tuck."

"I don't understand," said Ed. "How long have I been out?"

"About three days, long enough for you to be airlifted back here and undergo surgery to remove shrapnel. But now you're awake I'm told you can look forward to a miraculous recovery, when the drugs wear off. You'll be up on your feet in a day and out of here in two or three, back to your sweet little farmhouse in the hills. Your leg got badly twisted, but that'll heal in time."

"Where's Frank and Joe?" asked Ed. "Did they get out?"

Even in the darkness, Allen's expression of sadness was hard to miss. "They pulled Frank out after they dug you out. You were buried up to the shoulders but somehow you managed to wedge your hands and head into wooden slats. When the mud solidified, you were stuck fast but easily rescuable. Frank was about ten centimetres down."

"He was just too far away," said Ed. "I could've reached out and grabbed him." His voice started to break as he saw Frank's terrified eyes staring out at him as he disappeared beneath the oily soup.

"May as well have tried to stretch across the Atlantic Ocean," said Allen soothingly. "There was nothing you could have done."

Ed hesitated before asking his next questions. "And Joe?"

"Not a chance, too close to the lorry when it exploded. The gatehouse doesn't exist anymore, it's just a big hole in the ground. Anybody within a few tens of metres ceased to exist. Fortunately, many of the militia got out and threw themselves behind sand bags and the like. It was just the inmates and a few people not quick enough getting away that died."

"Poor Joe," said Ed. "Just when things were going right for him. He had a family, I saw his kids."

Allen shook his head sadly. "Afraid not, Joe lived with his sister, those would have been his sister's kids."

Pondering this, Ed slipped further into his pillows. "That's something at least."

"Yeah," snorted Allen. "Must have been a real comfort as the blast wave hit him."

Ed tutted. "You know what I mean. And what about you?" His eyes had grown used to the light and he could see Allen quite distinctly. "I take it you were miles away when the blast happened."

"That's right, I was at the Miners' Diner with your friend Bernie. She wanted to pump me for information regarding yourself and Alice. I told her where she could sling her hook."

"She really is the limit," said Ed with enough heat to hurt the stitches in his shoulder. "She came to see me as well on the night I met you and Lomax. She wanted information about Cat and Kitten. I told her where she could stick her pen. Got a sermon about the public's right to know."

For several seconds Allen was quiet, looking at the machine readout next to Ed's bed. "Thanks," he said.

"You're welcome."

When Allen seemed disinclined to continue the conversation, Ed leaned over onto one side and whispered. "So the union's dead. I bet Lomax is pleased."

Allen took some time to consider this. "On the whole, I think he's very displeased."

"How d'you make that out?"

"The union boss is dead, long live the union boss," said

Allen cryptically before giving a smile. "At the same time as everybody in the hospital was running toward the scene of the devastation, a group of armed Galamsey were heading for Bismarck. There were no guards to stop them, no nursing staff, the place was completely deserted. They carried Bismarck to a waiting vehicle and rushed him away."

Allen stopped talking and let Ed fill in the blanks.

"You mean the lorry was a diversion?"

"Looks like it," said Allen. "Quite a big diversion as well, with the extra bonus that it disposed of the union leadership at the same time. It was well planned, executed with military precision. Of course, Kojo had been in the army before he went into gold mining."

"So Bismarck and Kojo have a clear field."

"And several million bucks to play with. But now the Ghanaian army are all over the place. They've chucked the militia out. I'd say Kojo's bitten off more than he can chew. I saw the soldiers arrive, efficient, no nonsense combat troops. If I was Kojo and Bismarck I'd call it quits and head out. Meanwhile there's to be an investigation into how the mine has been dealing with its employees."

The door opened and a middle-aged nurse arrived. "Visiting time is at an end," she announced.

"I'm going back to Ghana tomorrow," announced Allen getting to his feet. "So I guess this is goodbye. You know you'll always have a job at the mine while I'm Manager of Geology." He smiled at Ed's expression and walked toward the door. He paused for a moment then looked back. "You're a good man, Edryd Evans."

* * *

Ed slept fitfully for the rest of the day, waking only

when the nurse arrived to offer him some refreshment. Billy visited his dreams, sucking on his pipe, staring up into the sky. Then Joe would appear, head down, staring at sheets of binary code. Frank, in the pickup truck, sleeping amid music that made the ground thump, causing it to liquefy and swallow him whole.

In the evening the nurse encouraged him to stand and walk a few steps. He achieved his first goal of sitting in the chair at the side of the room and then he managed to enter the bathroom. "Small steps at first," said the nurse. "In a couple of days you'll be as right as rain. You'll be able to go home. Have you any family who might come and get you?"

Ed shook his head.

"Shame," replied the nurse. "I'm sure we could call you a taxi or something, where d'you live?"

"North Wales."

She paused for a few seconds. "Perhaps we could get you a taxi to the train station and you can make your way from there." Then she turned to leave the room. "Are you sure you have nobody you can contact?" she asked.

Ed was on the verge of saying no when a thought occurred to him. "I do as a matter of fact."

The nurse beamed in approval.

"But I only have their email address. To contact them I'll have to get access to the internet."

"I suppose you lost your tablet in the explosion," she said to him.

"That's right," said Ed not wanting to confess that he didn't usually carry any computing device, small or large.

"I'll see what we can do," she said and left the room.

For the next hour Ed practised walking between bed and chair, chair and bathroom and bathroom to bed. The pain he felt when he stretched his muscles made him remember certain events.

The murder of Alfie the Driller which had caused the mine to take drastic action against the union; the death of Billy in an act of despair; Frank arriving at his shoulder the very minute he'd arrived in Lomax. Had Frank known he'd be arriving on that bus? His staring eyes would haunt his dreams for as long as he lived. Kojo's warning, its meaning now very clear.

He lay down on the bed and stared at the ceiling, seeing Joe talking happily about the code in Forge's pictures of the trilobites.

The nurse walked back in with a laptop and placed it on the bedside table. "I've borrowed this from our office, you can access the internet." She smiled and walked to the door. "Good luck," she said.

When the door had shut, Ed booted the computer into life and then typed the web address of his email provider and logged in. An avalanche of emails buried one another so that he was only able to see titles and addresses fleetingly as they zipped down the page. By the time the avalanche stopped he had already spotted Joe's message and knew it was buried beneath fifty others.

He scrolled down carefully, looking for any hint from Alice. Nothing.

"Serial number of the trilobite is the cipher," wrote Joe. "First message reads: 'Pictures transferred to the name of Walesby, now in Geneva, awaiting instruction'."

A blankness spread around Ed's mind. At first sight this did not look very informative. He'd expected bank accounts, details of maps with X mark the spot, not a message about who owned bits of art. He remembered Lucky Lomax discussing how the syndicate might have stored their wealth as gold or diamonds, or pieces of art.

Looking down at the email he wondered about the significance of the name Walesby. Could he have been a friend of Forge?

Walesby was quite a rare name, he was sure he had only seen it once. His mind flooded with images of a card that had been left in Hardacre's small shop in Horncastle. It had been left for people who might be interested in buying some early twentieth century decanters. Ed would have dismissed this recollection if it had not been in the same place where Forge's Calymene trilobites had been placed. As he recollected, Lomax had bought the decanters from a Mr Walesby in order to clear a space for the trilobites in the window.

By now Ed was standing up and limping around the room, ignoring his stitches and the aches in his shoulder. He had to decide quickly what he should do next.

Mr Walesby in Horncastle

Sitting patiently on the bench in the town square of Horncastle, Ed considered his options. He'd gone to examine the shop where Forge's Calymene trilobites were still displayed in the window. There they were, waiting patiently for somebody to notice them. Then he'd walked around the shop looking at decanters, carefully examining cards on shelves to see if they gave any hint of a Mr Walesby and his address. Finally, he'd approached the proprietor of the shop, a large man with comb-over hair dressed in old denims. He'd looked up, across a counter of curios, and enquired grumpily if Ed wanted anything. He'd hesitated before replying, wondering if he was making a big mistake by showing his hand. "I was here a while ago, there were some lovely decanters displayed in your window."

The man looked at him blankly, waiting. "And?" he asked.

"I believe it was a Mr Walesby who owned them. They've been sold and there's some trilobites in the window in their place."

"That space in the window is for rent," explained the shopkeeper, "people can pay me for it, nothing to do with me what's in there."

"I know that," Ed said. "It's just that I wanted to know whether he had other examples of those decanters. I'd like to contact him."

The shopkeeper shook his head. "I generally burn all the business cards when the items are sold or the rental of the window space runs out." He looked at Ed and seemed to take pity on him. "Mr Walesby comes in here from time to time, he's what's known as a local character. You can generally find him in the market square doing the Lord's work. Just sit on the bench by the war memorial, he'll be along presently. He's a large man, stocky, bald-headed like me but without the Bobby Charlton hair style." He grinned and indicated his head.

So, Ed had waited for much of the rest of the morning, looking for somebody fitting the shopkeeper's description. There were plenty who could be Mr Walesby, the town seemed to be crammed full. He decided to say 'Mr Walesby' in the hearing of any man who was slightly balding. He got a few startled looks, but none of them stopped.

Eventually he decided that he needed to return to the shop to question the proprietor more closely about Mr Walesby's appearance. Standing up, he felt his shoulder twinge and his leg give way slightly, but he managed to steady himself. He waited a few seconds until the pain subsided and he was able to focus again. A passer-by stopped, noticing his discomfort, and asked if he was okay.

"Fine," replied Ed, turning to the voice.

For several moments, he wondered if he was halluc-inating. Standing in front of him, gazing concernedly into his face, was a man whom he knew. The face was so familiar to him that for several moments he couldn't place to whom it belonged. Even more confusingly, the man showed no sign that he recognised Ed.

Then with a nod, the man bid him, 'good day' and began

to walk away.

"Mr Walesby," said Ed.

The man turned again and this time Ed could see him in more detail. He had a large head and no neck with a small crown of hair that was so close cropped that he looked entirely bald. Large bulging blue eyes peered out from a face that was largely featureless, like a smooth glass wall, except for a wide protuberant nose. A large belly held his thick arms at a distance from his body. An outsized wooden cross hung from his neck.

He was a mirror image of Paul Forge, the only feature he lacked was the hard, searching eyes and the curling lip. "Can I help you brother?" he asked.

Slightly flummoxed by being referred to as his brother, Ed gathered himself together and summoned a smile. "I'm glad I bumped into you," he said holding out his hand. "I was interested in those decanters you had in Hardacre's shop window a few months ago. I understand you've sold them now. I wonder if you have any more like it?"

Walesby looked down at the proffered hand and then up into Ed's face. There was suspicion, a dawning realisation. Pleased by this reaction, Ed dived head first. "Why have you not responded to the Calymene?"

"I don't know what you mean," Walesby said trying hard to appear casual.

"I think you do. Are you Paul's twin?"

Walesby dropped his gaze and turned around, about to walk off, but Ed stopped him by grabbing his shoulder. An arm flew out and hit Ed hard around the face, causing him to topple backwards slightly and sit down on the bench. When he looked up Walesby was running. "You can run, but you can't hide," called Ed to his retreating back. Then louder, "You can get me at the hotel, I'm your only chance."

There was no use in chasing after him, Ed's leg and shoulder were too weak and he could feel his head spin. As the feeling of disorientation subsided he rose to his feet once more. He could see Walesby's back disappear around the far corner. If the man did not turn up at the hotel tonight he'd have to tell Lomax and his heavy brigade, they would not be gentle.

The excitement of discovering Forge's brother sent shivers through Ed's body as he trudged back to his hotel. For an hour he hobbled around his room, thoughts racing through his mind about why Forge's brother had a different surname, why he was living in Lincolnshire's Horncastle – he was certain Forge was a Londoner – and above all what arrangements Forge had made with his brother.

He slept for hours, a side-effect of the painkilling drugs. On waking, the phone was ringing on his bedside table and the clock registered half past ten. He'd been dreaming of Alice, wondering where she was and why there'd been no word from her. He'd rung her flat in Liverpool twice and the hospital where she worked once; nobody had seen her for a week or more, not since she'd left the note on Ed's email. The thought that she'd fallen into Snodgrass's hands made him feel sick with worry. In his more sanguine moments he realised that if Snodgrass had taken her then surely he'd have let Ed know about it by now.

"Hello?" he said into the mouthpiece.

"Reception, we have a Mr Walesby here for you."

Interesting, thought Ed through his mind-fog, he must know who I am if he's able to tell the front desk who to phone. "Tell him I'll be straight down."

Walesby was sitting in a small seating area close to the main doors. He was partially hidden by several potted plants. As Ed approached, he had a mutinous look, and his hand held the wooden cross as if warding off evil spirits.

Ed sat down in the chair opposite and leaned forward, feeling the stitches in his shoulder.

"How did you know?" said Walesby his bulging eyes boring wood.

"Steganography," said Ed.

Walesby looked at him as if he'd gone mad.

"The science of concealing messages in pictures. The first image we analysed from your brother's account contained the name Walesby. It's very distinctive and I remembered it from when I was investigating up here. You had several decanters in Hardacre's window."

"I never knew it was a type of 'ography. Paul gave me the impression it was a little-known branch of secret codes."

"Not at all," Ed reassured him. "It's a fairly standard technique. What gave us the problem was that you'd encrypted the message before encoding it in the picture."

"How many more images have you managed to decipher?" Walesby's voice was strange, it wasn't the reedy tenor of Forge, it was more Alto in its quality and his accent wasn't London either, it was softer, more BBC and educated than his brother.

"Nothing more," said Ed. "The man who deciphered it died. But it won't take long to do the others. I expect Allen is having them all checked as we speak."

"Allen," said Walesby closing his eyes. "My brother sometimes talked about him. He wasn't very kind, used to go out of his way to make himself a nuisance. Then there was a man called Dave with whom he shared an office, a compulsive fornicator, and Greg. He didn't mind Greg so much."

"And what about me?" asked Ed. "I expect he had nothing very nice to say about me."

"A nosy parker, too clever by half, too friendly with

Allen. You were a friend of Greg's I believe. You shared the same girlfriend and Greg won, he married her while you were away, missing on some expedition."

"Is that what Forge told you?" asked Ed, not at all pleased that so much of his past was known.

Walesby nodded. "He would communicate quite often using those images of trilobites, tell me all the gossip. I think it gave him a thrill knowing that he knew everything about everybody and they knew nothing about him at all, not even that he had a twin brother and that his real name was Walesby."

Very true, thought Ed. Forge was a hoarder of information, a man who gained power way beyond his official position through knowing about other people. It had been his undoing in the end. When men like Jeremy and Snodgrass came looking he was their go-to man. He had his finger on all the data collection systems and he knew where each could be circumvented.

"You sent your brother a note, you said 'the art is now in the name of Walesby', and then there was something else about it being kept in Geneva."

Walesby shifted from one buttock to the next and leaned forward. "Not sure that's anything to do with you," he said. "That's entirely between me and my brother."

"Not entirely," said Ed smiling mirthlessly. "Your brother stole that money from the Lomax Mine; if it belongs to anybody, it's Lucky Lomax." He paused to let this information sink in. "And he's very keen to get this money back."

"But I don't have it," he replied, an edge of panic in his voice. "When those trilobites appeared in Hardacre's window I sent the emails, as agreed."

"Who to?"

"Some lawyer in Geneva, the one who's been acting for

my brother. I was to send him the registration numbers of the companies."

"Sorry? Registration numbers?"

"Serial numbers on the base of the trilobites. I sent these to the lawyer and then the lawyer was to sell the pictures."

Ed held up his hand. "Lucky Lomax will want to know everything. You've already lost me. What are these pictures all about?"

"Paul said he'd made an arrangement with some man in London to buy these pictures for him. He said he'd been in a position to do this man some good, a bit of insider trading. He said this man was so grateful he'd bought him a series of pictures. They were kept in some place in Geneva."

"He didn't happen to mention the name of the man, the one who bought him the pictures?"

"Why?"

"Lucky Lomax is sure to want to know."

Walesby grabbed his cross so hard that his knuckles turned white, then he shut his eyes. "No, he never said."

Scoffing, Ed leaned back in his chair. "Yes he did, of course he did, the name was Snodgrass."

Walesby's eyes shot open and he blanched slightly. Clearly Forge had explained to his brother the nature of Snodgrass. "Don't worry," said Ed, "Your secret is safe with me. Lomax knows about Snodgrass." He leaned forward again and tapped his nose conspiratorially. Despite himself he was enjoying the conversation with Forge's brother. "Did he say how much these paintings were worth?"

"A few hundred thousand quid," replied Walesby. "I thought at the time that Snodgrass must have made quite a killing on the shares my brother tipped him."

"Indeed," said Ed. "So tell me what happened after

these paintings had been bought."

For several seconds Walesby shut his eyes, thinking. "Are you saying that my brother stole this money?"

Ed started to open his mouth to tell him yes but then decided to tell a lie. There may be no telling what Walesby might do, particularly if he was as devout as his cross suggested. "I'm not sure what went on. All I know is that Lucky Lomax feels he's been the victim of some kind of racket and he believes your brother was involved." This information hovered for a moment, like an apparition. "Perhaps you should tell me what happened after your brother had these paintings transferred."

Still a bit distracted, Walesby took a gulp of air. "He told me that he'd agreed to divide the money equally between the people he worked with." A pause as he reached for some kind of explanation. "I suppose they were his accomplices in the insider trading. Some man named Stone, another called Smith, and your friend Greg. He sent me pictures of four trilobites and said each had a serial number on the bottom. These were the registered numbers of companies based in the British Virgin Islands, shell companies or something, he said. If any of these trilobites appeared in Hardacre's window I was to send the serial number of the trilobite off to the man in Geneva and he would sell the pictures and transfer the proceeds into the company."

"There have been four trilobites sitting in Hardacre's; have you sent the serial numbers yet?" asked Ed.

Walesby nodded. "The day after they appeared I sent the email."

"Have the pictures been sold?"

A nod of the head. "I had confirmation last week, the pictures have new owners and the shell companies in the British Virgin Islands have received the cash. The credit cards attached to the accounts have to go to an address but you don't need an id to use them, anybody could take one down to their local supermarket and use it. Only the name of the company will appear, not the real owner of the account."

"Did the confirmations show how much money was involved?" Ed brought his gaze from the street outside and stared directly at Walesby.

There was a vigorous shake of the head. "I haven't opened any of my brother's correspondence."

"So when would the syndicate start getting their credit cards?" Ed asked.

"During the last week or two," replied Frank.

For several seconds Ed stared at him, his mind unable to take it in. He reflected that there was no need for criminals to bury their treasure anymore, they could just pick up the phone and talk to their friendly international banker who would bury it for them. And Lomax had known how it might have worked, he'd given Ed a hint at Allen's party. He must have realised there was no pot of gold buried at a place marked 'X'.

"When did you learn that your brother was dead?" asked Ed.

"I was there at the hospital. He died peacefully in his sleep. The Lord be praised."

"And yet you decided to go ahead and disperse the money."

Walesby looked confused.

"I mean," said Ed, "that when you saw the trilobites in the window of the shop it must have been around the time that Paul was dead or dying, and yet you still went ahead with contacting the Swiss banker."

"I promised him, that whatever happened I would follow his instructions."

Leaning forward, Ed started to tap the wood of the table that separated both men. "So a burglar could get the card, or somebody could use coercion to get the card?"

Walesby shrugged. "Nothing to stop intimidation I suppose."

"Greg Boston's card, where was his home address?"

"Can't remember off hand, two of the addresses were in London, one in New Zealand and one in Wales."

The two in London would have been Forge and his friend Stone, the old Health and Safety Manager at Lomax Mine, Ed thought. The address in New Zealand would have been Dave Smith's. "No address in Liverpool? That's where Greg Boston lived."

Walesby shook his head.

"What was the address in Wales?"

Again, Walesby shrugged. "Something unpronounceable."

"Was it Llanfair Farmhouse?"

Walesby jerked in surprise before mastering himself and giving one of his characteristic shrugs. Not as good at concealing the truth as his twin brother, thought Ed. Suddenly the trilobites left around his house before he had gone back to Africa made sense. They had not been a warning of impending doom. They were aimed at forcing him out of his farmhouse so that the mail could be intercepted and the credit card stolen without Ed knowing what had happened.

And Ed had been called away by Allen's urgent message. He suddenly became still as the implication hit him. Had Allen's plea for him to return to Lomax been genuine? Or was it part of the scheme to drive him out of the farmhouse? And if it was, what did this say about how much Lomax and Allen knew?

He put his fingers to his eyes and pressed. Why would

Greg use Llanfair Farmhouse? In a crazy kind of way, it made sense. Greg's last act had been to send Alice the trilobite with instructions about the window in which the trilobite was to be placed. He had not said what would happen if she placed it there, maybe because Alice already knew. Maybe Greg was worried that Alice would simply take the money and run.

Back in his room, Ed picked up the phone again. His talk with Walesby had unsettled him, given him a streak of paranoia that was gnawing away at his mind. He wanted to speak to Alice and ask if she had known about the arrangement with the trilobite and if she had been stringing him along.

He dredged Sophie Scrape's number from the depths of his mind, the neighbour who lived down the hill from Llanfair, Alice's auntie. He couldn't believe he hadn't thought of contacting her before. Maybe Alice had taken his advice and gone to stay with her. She'd undertaken to collect Ed's mail from the post office and keep it for him.

The phone rang several times and was picked up. "Hello?" asked Sophie in her vaguely Liverpool accent. "I have no chickens for sale, you should ring back later when I might have a few running around." She sounded clipped, on the edge.

"Sophie, it's me, Ed."

A short silence. "I don't know anybody of that name, you've got the wrong number, Fred, I'd be more careful when punching those numbers if I were you." Her voice rose as she was talking, like she was on the verge of losing control.

"No, No, it's …"

"I heard you the first time, and I still don't know anybody of that name. And don't you go accusing me of being senile neither."

She rang off.

Ed put the phone down. Sophie had sounded deranged, like she was out of her wits with worry. Why would she think somebody named Fred was ringing her to order eggs at midnight?

Sophie never lost control like that. She mocked people who showed exaggerated emotion or sentimentality.

Ed was suddenly worried.

Sophie's House

Forewarned is forearmed, or so they say. But Ed's mind, as he travelled across from Lincolnshire on the coach, was consumed by doubt. It was very unlike Sophie to be so panicked. During her working life, she'd been a nurse then social worker, a champion of women's rights. Something was amiss.

By the time he reached Birmingham, he'd had enough of slow-stop transport and decided to rent a car. It would not get him up the track to his farmhouse but would at least get him close. He wondered whether he should go straight to Sophie's. On the whole, he thought stealth would be best. He would approach her house from his own.

Several times he'd been on the verge of stopping to call Allen and request help. He'd have to contact him through the Lomax office and that would take time. Perhaps he could get help from Lucky Lomax, he mused at one point before dismissing the idea. In Lucky Lomax's world Ed was an irritating fly, somebody who he tolerated only because it suited his purposes. It may even be a henchman of Lucky Lomax who was terrorising Sophie.

As he drove north and west he bashed the steering wheel in frustration, urging the car to go faster along the narrow country lanes, cursing every time he intersected a tractor or a slow-moving tourist.

There was an old track that went over the mountain close to his house. He could drive to a spot several miles from his farmhouse and then drop down into the valley. There would still be a scramble of several hundred metres across rough country that would be punishing for his leg.

He'd called Sophie's house a couple of times from the few remaining call boxes found at service stations along the way. The lack of answer served to heighten his apprehension that something had gone terribly wrong.

In Oswestry he'd stopped, bought a few supplies including food, a torch and an old fashioned walking stick that would serve as a prop for the forthcoming march. Then he drove to the place where the track climbed to the top of the mountain along a series of streams and waterfalls. Thick clouds and a thin drizzle reduced the early evening light to a damp gloominess. He put his waterproof and torch in a small rucksack and climbed across a style, eyes peeled for movement on the horizon.

Ten minutes later he crested the top of the mountain and stared down to see his farmhouse. The thin drizzle had turned into a persistent heavy rain, it penetrated his flimsy waterproofs and dribbled down his back. The injuries from the blast complained at the cold, he wanted to lie down and have a rest but knew he must keep going.

There was no sign of human habitation at his farmhouse, no sudden movement or smoke rising from the chimney, nor from Sophie's cottage, several hundred metres further on. Dropping quickly down the slope he was relieved to feel the wind drop so that the rain felt less like a deluge. Several times he slipped on the sheep-clipped grass and was only able to stop himself by lying flat on the waterlogged turf. He finally reached a fence line that contoured the hillside. He would follow this feature and then enter an old oak coppice that ran down to meet the back of his house.

After twenty minutes of hard slog in which he was cut by barbed wire and bruised from falling over exposed tree roots, he reached a log pile that commanded an excellent view of his kitchen and living room. Pulling off the covering tarpaulin sheet he fell on the logs and dragged the sheeting over him. For a minute or two he winced at the pain in his shoulder and panted until his lungs felt like they were once again able to take in air. Then, becoming aware of his surroundings, he realised his breathing was like an old puffer train. He mastered his heaving chest and listened to the sounds of the woods. There was little he could hear beyond the thrumming of rain on plastic.

Within half an hour he was cold and uncomfortable enough to chance a move closer to the house. Slipping out of the plastic sheet he propped himself up onto his knees and looked around. Nothing moved save for the limbs of the oak trees. No unnatural sound disturbed the constant hiss of rain and wind.

Moving close to the ground he slid down the last bank and onto a gravel path that skirted around the kitchen window. The rain intensified, drumming on the windows and on the tin roof of the old utility room, disguising the crunching of his feet. He pressed his nose to the kitchen window and stared inside. It looked exactly as he had left it, trilobites staring down from the mantelpiece.

Sinking down behind the lintel he moved along the gravel path and looked in the living room. Nothing disturbed in here.

He entered Taid's old store room where he found the spare key under a large black metal box. Then, picking up a pick axe handle that he'd bought three weeks earlier, before the call from Allen, he moved toward the kitchen door, eyes and ears straining for movement. As the door swung open the match sticks he'd left in the jam on leaving for Africa fell to the floor. The kitchen was reassuringly cold and musty. He moved swiftly to the sitting-room door, it was locked, the match sticks still in place.

He relaxed. The cold and wetness began to penetrate to his conscious, the shrapnel injury in his back began to ache. Slumping down on one of the kitchen chairs he listened to the noises of the house. No sound of creaking stairs or shuffling feet, no clicking of a door opening or squeaking floorboards. The house was as quiet as a tomb.

Half an hour later he had changed into new clothes and was sitting in the darkness of his kitchen with an old army blanket around his shoulders, sipping a cup of tea, worrying about how he would approach Sophie's house and what he would find there.

* * *

Sophie was his postman; she had agreed to pick up his mail from the post office in town and keep it until he arrived back. In case she was out when Ed arrived back she had said she would place it in an old sealed plastic box in her potting shed.

Tiredness coursed through his veins, it made him think of lying down and waiting 'til morning. He remembered the conversation he'd had with Sophie before leaving for Africa. "I always knew Greg would come to a sticky end," she'd said. Sophie'd been correct about that, but her clairvoyance had not stretched far enough to see how Greg's acquisitiveness might impact on her.

Sighing, he took a sharp knife from a hook on the wall and cut a hole in his blanket through which he could stick his head. His coat was useless in the sort of rain falling outside and the blanket would provide better protection. It would also be soundless and camouflaged. He smuggled his pick axe handle beneath its cover.

As he crossed the stile that led down to Sophie's cottage his weak leg gave way and he stumbled. Cursing, he remained crouched for several moments hoping that the violent movement had not opened the stitches in his back. Eventually he leaned against the stile-post and looked down at his feet. He saw small white rectangles on the grass, in between sprigs of heather. Stooping to pick one up he became aware that his senses had suddenly exploded into life again. Every swish of grass and drip of water sounded menacing. Holding one of the rectangles to his nose he smelled tobacco that was redolent with bleached-white monkey skulls, tropical wood smoke and sweat-stained kookaburra hats.

He wanted to be away from this place, leave Sophie to her fate. The farmhouse was no longer his sanctuary; it had been sullied by the presence of evil. Forever more he would feel unsafe here, the shadow and threat of the wolf would hang around its walls and paths. He should have realised that Sophie's terror on the phone might mean that the Wolf Man had arrived.

His mind rebelled against what he knew to be true. How had the Wolf Man found where he lived and made it here from Africa so quickly? There was no way he could be here, it was impossible. It must be a local man who used the same strange tobacco.

Leaning more heavily against the stile, he looked into the gathering night, heard the wind in his ears and the surrounding grass. The trees in the neighbouring coppice creaked alarmingly, their canopy swaying like seaweed in a flowing tide. On a night like this only a mad man would be skulking around, so what did that make Ed?

He hefted the pick axe for balance and peered more

closely at the gathering gloom. At the moment, Sophie's assailant, whoever he was, held the advantage; he was probably watching Ed's every move from a carefully chosen vantage point. But Ed knew the country around here, this was his home. He levered himself from the stile and set off slowly down the hill along the path Alice had used many years ago when she visited Ed and Greg in Taid's farmhouse. There were many hiding places where a man might lie in ambush for an unwary traveller. Ed knew them all, was able to avoid them by running quickly through, the better to avoid a hasty blow, or else bring his weapon down in an arcing blow to smash concealing bushes.

The stream that ran past Sophie's house was in spate, its cobble-strewn bed growling as Ed waded knee-deep across a ford that would normally cover the souls of his shoes. Once across the stream he crested a small rise and entered a wood that Sophie maintained as her source of firewood. In ancient days Taid had coppiced for her, but now the trees were overgrown and the undergrowth lengthy, plenty of places for a madman to hide. He staggered through toward Sophie's gloomy house, tripping on exposed tree roots.

There was an abandoned cigarette stub on the floor close to the edge of the wood. Stooping to pick it up, he sniffed its still-fresh scent. He saw the Wolf Man sitting in his office confronted by Chiri and his men, hat across his eyes. He really was here; somehow he'd made it to Britain and then come up here to seek out Ed.

This was crazy, he thought to himself, he must get away from here and call the police, tell them the Wolf Man was on the loose in the hills around his home. But that wouldn't help Sophie. By the time he'd explained who the Wolf Man was and why he was prowling the area, she would be dead. And why was the Wolf Man prowling the area? Why come all this way from Africa?

He stopped breathing, all thought of his surroundings forgotten as he turned a nascent theory around in his head. Would it be insane to believe that the Wolf Man knew about the credit cards? The only other people who knew of the arrangement made by Forge were the members of the syndicate: Paul Forge, Jon Stone (aka Golf Club), Dave Smith, Greg Boston. He ticked off what he knew about each of them: Paul Forge was dead due to injuries sustained from a beating by the miners' union, Jon Stone was dead from head injuries (killed by his own golf club on orders from the union), Dave Smith was dead as well, Ed had seen the body (killed by the miners' union), and finally Greg Boston who was presumed dead (killed by the miners' union).

Perhaps these were not the only four who knew how the money was distributed, perhaps others had guessed. Snodgrass might have known that Forge's real name was Walesby and had already rung the story from his brother, in which case the Wolf Man could be working for him, trying to sweep up the pieces.

But that didn't make sense either, it was only a few days since the Wolf Man had left Africa, not enough time to set up a meeting with Snodgrass and agree terms. A cold feeling in the pit of his stomach tightened as his theorising crystallised. The Wolf Man might have been working for Snodgrass all along. His mind raced, fitting all the pieces into place. The Wolf Man had killed Alfie as part of a pre-meditated act to disrupt production at the mine, a flame to the powder keg that was Lomax township.

Could Kojo have known about Snodgrass's intention with the Wolf Man and tried to warn Ed about what was coming? Perhaps the Wolf Man's original target had been Ed.

The rushing wind in the trees came roaring back. He

was on a track heading through a small coppice of trees toward a cottage where a psychotic killer lurked, a man who he now theorised was in the pay of a gangland criminal. Even if by some miracle Ed managed to survive the night there would be others who would come, stealthy and lethal in the darkness.

He resumed his careful progress through the trees, seeing every dark shape as a potential madman with an axe. On reaching Sophie's dilapidated wicker fence he stopped to listen and watch. The house was small, a two up and two down with a kitchen built onto the back, an easy place to reconnoitre.

Sophie kept a dog, a small and suspicious Jack Russell named Katy that barked whenever anybody came near her mistress's property. He wondered about the dog's silence.

Stepping over the fence he crept around the house, gazing into the darkness of the ground floor sitting rooms. They all looked undisturbed, crockery on shelves were intact, cushions and upholstery ordered. He crept around the back and discovered light showing through tiny cracks in the kitchen shutters.

Conscious that his attention had been entirely focussed on the house, he looked over his shoulder. Katy the Jack Russell gazed at him from only a few metres away, her lolling tongue motionless. His breath caught in his chest as he waited for the explosion of noise, but Katy uttered no sound, nor did she advance to challenge him.

He whispered soft words of comfort to her, consorting her to remain silent so as not to give the game away. Katy appeared not to have seen him, her doggy focus was on something over his shoulder, beyond the window of the kitchen. He turned and looked at what she was seeing, but there was nothing.

The blowing wind intensified, exciting the waving trees,

and Katy moved slightly. He took a couple of steps closer, knowing that something was terribly amiss. Her head yielded to his touch far too easily. Repulsed by the coldness of her, he withdrew his hand and Katy's decapitated head swung forward, then back, then forward again. Stepping away, stomach tightening from waves of nausea, he whipped around and peered into the wild, gloomy night, searching for signs of a Kookaburra hat. The Wolf Man was close-by, this was his signature, his calling card.

After several seconds of desperate search, he was satisfied that he was in no immediate danger, so he returned his attention to the kitchen windows. Leaning forward he gazed through the cracks in the shutters, fearing what he might see inside. There was nothing except unwashed plates and cups and Sophie's tea pot on the table, its lid removed.

Then a man moved into view, tall and rangy with curly blonde hair, he removed the kettle from its stand and poured water into the tea pot before sitting down, his back to the windows. Ed staggered back, mind unable to comprehend the presence of THAT man in this kitchen. He had been certain THAT man was dead, he'd assured Alice that there was no way HE was coming back. And yet here HE was, calmly making tea in Sophie's kitchen with Sophie nowhere to be found and her dog's decapitated head swinging freely from a nearby tree.

For a minute or more he gazed blankly at the kitchen windows, the storm raging around him, thoughts becoming ever more confused. Greg Boston would not have killed Sophie's dog in such a sadistic fashion and then placed her head so as to be clearly visible from the kitchen windows. Greg may dislike Sophie for the way in which she always picked on him, but not enough to do that to her beloved dog. Unless he'd become deranged by his experiences at the

Lomax Gold Mine.

He wondered how Greg had gained access into Sophie's house, he could not have known about the spare key that Sophie kept under one of her flower pots. There'd been no signs of a break in when Ed had reconnoitred, and Sophie was not in the habit of leaving doors unlocked. Perhaps Sophie was upstairs, bound and gagged.

Which brought Ed to reflect on what Greg was doing in Sophie's kitchen in the first place, casually helping himself to Sophie's tea. He was surely here to find the credit card, the one that would give him access to the offshore account. Sophie must have collected it with the rest of Ed's mail and placed it in the plastic box in her greenhouse. And presumably Sophie had refused to tell Greg where she'd arranged to place Ed's correspondence. Otherwise Greg wouldn't be casually sipping tea in her kitchen. He'd be down the road wondering how he was going to spend several million quid.

Had Greg decapitated Katy the dog in an attempt to wheedle the location of Ed's mail out of Sophie? Ed's mind rebelled, it yelled that Greg had been brought up on Taid's farm, he'd loved animals and dogs.

Falling back from the window, he ran at a crouch across Sophie's small lawn and slid open the greenhouse door. There was no light from Sophie's kitchen to guide him in here, he must feel along the warm, musty ground to find the plastic box containing his mail. After several seconds his hand hit something hard, it moved slightly as if completely empty. He threw his hand inside and found nothing, all the mail had been removed.

Crouching on the floor he had an urge to shut the greenhouse door and sleep. It was warm, his stitches were complaining, his muscles ached and nothing in this world made sense. He fell forward and shut his eyes, wondering how he would confront Greg and find out why he was still here when he must have possession of the credit card.

A male voice near at hand whispered, "Ed, is that you?"

Lying motionless on the ground holding his breath, his skin tingling with fright, Ed felt the pickaxe handle nestle in his left hand.

"I know it's you," came the familiar voice. "I saw you run in here, I'd know that gait anywhere."

Rolling over onto his back, Ed looked up at the dark frizzy profile framed in the greenhouse doorway. No doubt Greg was grinning at him in the way that always made Ed feel small. He felt like bringing the pickaxe onto his head.

"Ed, what are you doing in here?" Greg asked.

"Potting some plants," replied Ed. "What the hell d'you think I'm doing."

"I dunno," said Greg. "You've been out here for hours, I've been calling for you to come in an' talk, have a cup of tea and stuff."

Ed leapt to his feet and pushed past Greg, into the middle of Sophie's small lawn, away from concealing bushes and overhanging trees. He held the pickaxe ready in his hand, circling around while Greg followed him, his voice bewildered. "Come inside and warm up, you must be freezing, I can explain everything."

After an interval, Ed allowed himself to be led inside. He stood in the middle of the kitchen dripping onto the tiled floor, staring around at the used cups and plates, his mind unable to assess what had happened in the last hour. When he'd set off across the hilltop to rescue Sophie, never in his wildest dreams would he have expected to end the evening being offered tea in her kitchen by a man who was supposed to be dead.

"Where's Sophie?" he asked, ignoring Greg's inane chatter about the inclemency of the weather.

"Dunno," he replied. "I came here this afternoon and she was nowhere around. I knocked on her door and it swung open."

"So you thought you'd just walk in and help yourself to her facilities," said Ed.

"Something like that," admitted Greg.

"In that case you won't mind if I go upstairs and have a look around, make sure she's definitely not hiding?"

"Why would she do that?" asked Greg.

"Perhaps because a dead man is walking around her kitchen using her facilities."

"Be my guest," replied Greg. "A dead man's not likely to scare her, other way around more like." He smiled and flicked the switch on the kettle. "I'll make another pot of tea. I've found her store of brandy, perhaps I'll add a measure. It'll be ready when you come down again."

Climbing the stairs Ed had to rid himself of age-old feelings about invading somebody's privacy. He'd never been up here before and as far as he was aware nobody else had either (except maybe Taid). One room was her bedroom - bed showed no signs of being used - and the other a bathroom. He checked in a wardrobe, under the bed, behind the shower curtain, no sign of Sophie anywhere.

He crept downstairs again.

"She wasn't here when you arrived?" he asked, much calmer now that he'd also confirmed that the Wolf Man had not entered the house while they'd both been outside in the garden.

"That's right, nor that horrible yappy dog she keeps," he said stirring the tea pot.

"You know about Katy then?" Ed asked, surprised.

The stirring ceased suddenly and Greg's tone became more matter-of-fact. "Met it when I visited a while ago."

He hesitated. "You know, with Alice." He turned 'round and looked at Ed, but his smile had become more fixed.

Nothing had changed in the thin, angular face since the last time they'd met. Still the long, thin nose, the clear blue eyes, bushy blonde hair, waxy youthful skin that could not take a full growth of beard. And the same cheeky grin that could be guaranteed to have people falling over to forgive and forget.

"Why are you here?" Ed asked, although several other questions popped into his mind at the same time.

Greg handed across the tea laced with brandy and then sat down. "I'm here because I've come to claim my winnings," he said, "I want my company credit card."

"What makes you think I have it?" said Ed.

"I was advised by Snodgrass that you were on your way back here and that you had learned how the syndicate dispersed its money. He advised that I persuade you to cough up the credit card."

Ed took a sip of his tea, the brandy was warming and agreeable. "You nominated Llanfair Farmhouse. A bit of a risk, I might have cut it up and thrown it in the Rayburn, it's what I generally do to unsolicited cards that come through my post box." Then he stopped, cup half way to his lips. "It was you who placed all those trilobites around my house."

Greg smiled and nodded. "I did think of contacting you," he replied, "but announcing that I was still alive and needed your help might not have produced the result I wanted." He paused again and looked shifty. "All things considered, it was better to get you away from your house. That way I could hang around without worrying that you might intersect the package and do a runner."

His smile vanished. "Snodgrass suggested that I place trilobites around your house as a first phase. He thought it would spook you, soften you up so that you'd be ready to leave when the next phase of the operation started. But we never had to start the next phase, you took yourself off to Africa." He stopped, expecting Ed to explain why he had taken himself off.

But Ed was not about to explain. "So you're working for Snodgrass."

Greg shook his head. "I have a business relationship with him, we collaborate in areas of mutual interest."

Ed took a sip of his warming tea to prevent himself from laughing. To claim a business relationship with a shark like Snodgrass was pretty conceited, even for Greg. "And what about Snodgrass's Wolf Man?" he asked. "Is he part of your care package? Or an assassin in case I don't cooperate."

"The Wolf Man?" asked Greg without deceit, it was clear that he knew nothing about the psychopath wandering around outside. Then he shook his head and leaned forward, brushing away Ed's attempt to divert him. "We can do a deal. If you hand over the company credit card, I'll promise to give you half."

This time Ed really did laugh, but without much humour. The thought of the Wolf Man outside precluded merriment. "I suppose you'll have the credit card for the first half of the year and then you'll post it from your hideaway and I'll have it for the second half?"

Greg looked genuinely hurt. "Look, I know things haven't worked out the way either of us would have wished, but we need to pull together now, there's a lot of money at stake, more money than either of us ever dreamed of earning as exploration geologists." His tone was wheedling, he was putting forth all his charm. It might have worked a few years ago.

Stretching his muscles to dispel some of the stiffness,

Ed half thought of removing the blanket that was still draped around his shoulders. It had absorbed quite a bit of water on his trip down to Sophie's cottage and his shoulders were beginning to ache. He feared cramp developing in his calf muscles, so he stood and started to pace around the kitchen. "If I had the card, d'you really think I'd be out here in the middle of the night in an old blanket?" he asked.

"No," conceded Greg, "but you may know where the card can be found." He paused, eyes gleaming. "That's why you're here isn't it? You've come to lay your hands on the card."

"I came here to rescue Sophie," Ed explained. "I rang her last night and she was in terror. I got here as quick as I could hoping to help her, but then I found small cigarette tabs on the path down to her cottage and the head of her dog swinging in the wind outside her kitchen window." He paused for dramatic effect. "The place reeks of the Wolf Man."

"Who is this Wolf Man?" Greg said, annoyed that Ed kept attempting to divert the conversation.

"He's Snodgrass's killer, he worked at the Lomax Mine, a seriously nasty piece of work. He's left a trail of murder and mayhem across New Zealand and Australia and probably murdered a contract driller in Lomax a couple of weeks ago."

"And he's here?" Greg asked, incredulity etched in every syllable. "And he's beheaded Katy?"

"Take a look if you don't believe me," said Ed, "Only I'd take my pickaxe handle in case he appears out of the darkness. He's quick and used to killing so I wouldn't hang around once you verify the head for yourself." He pointed at the window that was closest to the dog's head. "Alternatively you can just pull the blind and take a look."

Greg walked quickly to the window and pulled the blind. There was a moment's silence as he focused on the scene outside, then he swore very loudly and stepped back. "Is that Katy?" He swayed a little, face fixed in an expression of disgust. "She wasn't there when I shut the blinds half an hour ago, I swear."

"Then the Wolf Man must be somewhere close," Ed said matter-of-factly. Greg staggered back to his seat. He took hold of Sophie's brandy. "Have you any notion why he might be here?" he asked.

"Why else would he be here?" replied Ed. "He's after the credit card. If he's managed to capture Sophie she would have told him quite quickly..." His voice trailed off into silence. A nasty thought had crossed his mind, one that made him feel cold inside. His distress must have shown because Greg leaned across.

"What?" he asked.

"When you found me, I'd just discovered the box she uses to store my letters is empty."

"Empty?" echoed Greg. "Then we're too late." His face contorted into anger. "That's my money."

"But if he has the credit card why did he string Katy's head from a tree less than thirty minutes ago?"

Greg blinked, once, twice, three times as he began to understand the implications. Ed tried to help his thought process, "Why is he still walking around when logic dictates that he should have departed long ago?"

The inference was glaringly obvious, even to Greg, and caused him to leap up. "We'll bar the doors, turn this place into a fortress. In the morning we'll get down the hill to my car." He leapt from the table, grabbed a large cupboard and started to haul it toward the back door. "Give me a hand," he called.

But Ed remained where he was. "No good," he said,

"we can't block the windows, nor secure the roof, it'll take him a few seconds to get in. We need to get somewhere more secure, where there's no windows and a concrete roof."

"Is he so dangerous?" asked Greg, pausing for a moment in his exertion. "If he's stupid enough to break in here there'll be two of us armed with knives and pick axe handles."

"He had a face-off with ten Australian drillers," explained Ed patiently. "He only backed down because it suited his purposes, and because there were armed guards at the gates. He's psychotic." He walked across to the back door. "Taid's pantry's the only place that's secure, we need to get back up the hill, lock ourselves inside and wait till morning."

"But if he's that dangerous he'll kill you on the way."

Ed stopped, intrigued by Greg's use of the singular. "You think he's come only for me?" he asked.

Greg had recovered his poise, "I have an arrangement with Snodgrass, he wouldn't kill me, we've got plans to develop our own exploration company..." He stopped and gave Ed a sheepish grin, like he'd accidentally spilled the beans.

"Please yourself," said Ed and turned on his heel, his mind racing. Maybe Greg was right, the Wolf Man had come for him and him alone. In which case he needed a place of safety where he could work out the bigger picture.

He wondered what had happened to Sophie. He hoped she'd managed to escape. But in all probability, she was dead and he would soon find her body, throat cut or decapitated.

Taid's pantry was a small, box-like bunker with a concrete roof and steel door where farm chemicals had been kept in times gone by. Taid had claimed that it was built by the army during the war, when they'd run exercises across the hills and mountains in the area. In more recent times Ed had used it as a store room for all of the rubbish he didn't want to throw away, bags of concrete, half used tins of paint, concrete slabs. There wasn't a lock on the door, but he'd be able to wedge it shut.

When Ed reached for the kitchen door, Greg grabbed his hand. "You've got to be crazy," he said, his voice a desperate hiss. "There're a million and one places out there he could be waiting." His deep blue eyes were full of a fright that Ed knew must be in his own.

"I don't want to wait in here for the end, I'd rather meet him outside where I'll have room to swing my bat."

Greg squeezed his hand harder. "But there're two of us in here, if we stay together we've got a better chance." He started to try and drag Ed back from the door, his voice no longer a hiss. He was speaking as if trying to calm the insane.

Ed snatched back his arm and pushed Greg away from him. "You can stay here, after all it's me he wants." He was becoming suspicious that Greg wanted him to stay, suspicious that he knew more than he was letting on.

Greg came toward him again but Ed raised his pick axe handle and shoved it in his chest. "If you're right and you've nothing to fear from the Wolf Man, stay here. Or even better, go and find your car and head home. I'm going to Taid's pantry and locking myself in."

"Okay, then," said Greg. "I'll come with you, if we're together he'll have to think twice."

"No," said Ed not lowering his pickaxe handle. "You and he are both Snodgrass's men." He backed toward the door keeping his eyes fixed on Greg. "I'll need to keep my eyes open for the Wolf Man, can't be worrying about what you're up to as well."

The look of hurt innocence on Greg's face produced a flame of anger. "Keep away from me," he said and turned to unlock the door.

Greg remained where he was. "Please," he said, "We need to stay together."

"No," insisted Ed, turning the key. The door swung open and he plunged into the stormy night, uncaring that the Wolf Man might be waiting for him on Sophie's roof or in Katy's tree. Through the small gate he ran, and then onto the path that led through the small wood toward the stream. A moving target would be harder to hit with a bullet or a knife and might cause the Wolf Man to botch his attack. He was sure his stitches had split, and by the time he reached the edge of the wood the pain in his back and leg had returned in full fury.

Standing by the edge of the wood, gasping for air, waiting for his panicky heartbeat to subside, he looked across the creek which was now in full spate. He listened to the rushing water and heard the low grumble of grinding cobbles in the river bed. At least it was dark, he mused, and the rain was not as intense as it had been when he'd entered Sophie's kitchen.

He took a tentative step out of the protection of the woods, then decided he had nothing to lose by running again. He reached the edge of the roaring torrent and plunged the end of the pickaxe handle into the water. When he stepped in, his leg was almost swept from under him; he pushed hard on the pick axe and stamped down so that his weight acted to keep him balanced. The level of the water had risen to mid-thigh level and for a fleeting second he considered turning back.

He placed his other leg in the torrent and hastily moved the staff into deeper water, levering his body around its pivot so he was not washed away. He made progress slowly, feeling carefully with his feet for rocks that would cause him to trip. After several breathless minutes during which he twice narrowly avoided catastrophe, he threw himself onto the opposite bank, legs and back aching and heart pumping with adrenalin.

The moon appeared momentarily from behind thinning cloud, signalling that the storm was over for the time being. He looked across the river and saw its turbulent surface reflect the silvery light. A furtive figure was waiting on the bank, Greg had decided to follow him.

"Hoi!" Greg called and waved. "Wait there." He produced a stick and plunged it into the water, intending to mimic Ed's feat.

"Go back," shouted Ed, waving his hand up and down to emphasise his meaning.

But Greg kept coming, slowly at first and then with more confidence. Ed made off into the night, stopping after ten seconds when a scream and a shout muffled by the roar of the water indicated that all was not well. He hesitated, the last thing he wanted was to take Greg with him to Taid's pantry. On the other hand, if the man was in trouble….

He legged it back to find Greg in mid-stream, waving what remained of his stick and shouting for help. Forgetting his instinctive distrust, Ed walked back into the rush of water and made his way slowly and steadily to the figure. He grasped Greg's jacket and told him to put one hand on his shoulder and the other on the stick. With both locked together they were able to return back to shore.

"What the hell are you doing?" asked Ed after they'd climbed out of the river. "You'll be much better off in Sophie's cottage." He paused for a moment, catching his breath. "You aren't coming with me into Taid's pantry."

"Where else can I go?" Greg asked, looking across the

gurgling and rushing river.

"Anywhere, but not with me," replied Ed swinging his staff up to Greg's chin. "You follow me and I'll be forced to give you a clout around the ears." He stepped away from him and then turned and limped to the small rise where the path took off to his farmhouse. He knew Greg would be compelled to follow because he had nowhere else to go and he probably still believed Ed held the key to finding his precious money.

Exhaustion wasn't just gnawing him around the edges, it had invaded his whole soul with the compulsion to stop and lie down. Soon he'd reached the stile at the bottom of the small pasture that led up to his farmhouse. He rested against its welcoming step and looked back the way he had come. The rain had completely stopped and the moon was ever present, bathing the entire landscape in its cold glow. A hundred metres away Greg's profile looked around at the undergrowth that crowded the path.

He inhaled deeply, hoping to fill his tired lungs with the mountain air zipping past his nose. A vague scent on the wind caused his senses to heighten, reminding him that he was not yet safe. It had an unmistakeable herbal quality, like burnt lavender, and evoked memories of the compound bar. Somewhere close-by the Wolf Man was smoking.

He'd reached the zone of maximum danger; the Wolf Man might even have guessed at Ed's plan and was lying in wait somewhere up ahead. Through the thoughts that crowded his mind he wondered why the Wolf Man had decided to smoke and thereby warn Ed of his presence. Maybe it was an attempt to sow panic, keep the hunted moving.

He began to climb the stile, his eyes scanning every dark shape. With the moon high in the sky there were few hiding places left for the Wolf Man, only the odd tree close to the house and a ruined outhouse.

He began stepping cautiously forward, thoughts of running now a distant memory. A snort close at hand made him turn to see Greg standing at the stile. He'd made good progress, must have run the last few tens of metres. Ed gave a warning swing of his staff, cursing Greg for never taking no for an answer.

Then he saw what he was looking for; it was poking up from the top of an old, ruined wall next to his farmhouse. The top of a kookaburra hat. For a moment, he stood still with fright, unsure how he would be able to approach Taid's pantry without being seen. In his mind, he traced routes across the landscape and concluded there was only one way of avoiding the wall. He would have to skirt the edge of the field and arrive close to the house under the eaves of a couple of trees. From there it would be a simple dash to the door.

He felt his heart flutter with excitement as he crouched down and scuttled sideways like a crab, keeping the thicket of trees through which he had just emerged to his back. Then he walked quickly up a small fence and around the back of the wall behind which the Wolf Man squatted. Looking back he saw Greg following him, only ten metres behind. He felt like marching down the field, staff raised over his head, demanding that he be left in peace. But the strength of the Wolf Man's tobacco had now reached a peak, reminding him that his main priority was to seek safety.

Emerging from the cover of the trees, he saw the heavy door of Taid's pantry less than ten metres away; he picked up his feet and made a dash. He'd crossed two thirds of the space when there was a loud crack like a tree branch breaking, followed by a thump. Greg's voice was raised in a scream, there was a second, sickening snap, then silence.

Not stopping to find out what was happening, Ed hit the metal door of Taid's pantry. Rather than yielding easily to his shoulder, he was thrown back a metre and landed heavily. For several moments he lay on the ground wondering what had happened, feeling the shoulder that had impacted against the door. Then he pulled himself up and turned 'round to look at where the cracking noise had originated. The tall, bald silhouette of the Wolf Man was getting to his feet, and beneath him lay the motionless body of Greg.

"I warn you, I'm armed," Ed shouted, bringing up the staff and pretending to aim. He placed his back against the metal door and pushed. It remained as tightly shut as if locked. But there was no lock.

Even in the dim light of the moon Ed could see a sneer spread across the Wolf Man's face as he calmly took something out of his breast pocket. A light illuminated a black and red beard before being quickly extinguished, then the sweet scent of freshly burnt tobacco drifted across to him. The Wolf Man was in no hurry, he appeared content to remain under the trees beside Greg's motionless body, almost like he was waiting for something else to happen.

Above the rushing wind Ed heard a scraping sound, it was coming from behind Taid's pantry door. He stepped aside, raised his staff, ready to strike.

"Ed?" came a voice from the darkness.

With a great rush of relief he recognised Sophie's voice, weaker than he remembered but definitely her. Without a word he dived into the dimly-lit room beyond. The door slammed on the moonlit night and the lurking insanity, and he was plunged into darkness.

"Help me push this back," came Sophie's urgent voice. A light from a small torch illuminated large metal wedges that had been rammed under the door. Sophie was attempting to push a huge metal cabinet full of old cement and rubble. Together they hauled the obstruction into place, plus a great deal more besides. Ed slumped to the floor, exhausted.

Wolf Man Tidies Up

"Who is that man?" Sophie asked, a slight tremor in her voice. A light flared and her face came into view, pale and frightened with thin strands of hair falling across her face. "Who screamed?" she asked.

Ed didn't answer immediately, his head was spinning with exhaustion. Images of flooded rivers, dead dogs and shadowy undergrowth flitted across his feverish mind. Levering himself up onto his elbow, he could see that she'd somehow found a candle. Its flame flickered and cast shadows into the corners of the room. The place was exactly how he remembered, three metre square and filled with old paint pots, metal poles, fence posts and wire. Sophie had made herself a bed from tarpaulin and a stack of mouldy old curtain fabric.

"It was Greg who screamed," he said quietly. For the moment it was better not to openly talk of the Wolf Man, not until he'd been able to screw up his courage.

Her grey eyes flicked across his face looking for signs of deceit. "He's alive then, I always thought he might be." Her voice was full of self-satisfaction, as if a long-foretold event had come to pass.

"Was alive," corrected Ed. "I think he's definitely dead. And if he's not, he'll soon wish he was."

Sophie ignored him. "I knew it was him, he's been

wandering around your place ever since you went back to Africa. At first I couldn't be sure because I could only get a distant view during dusk, and I didn't want to stare and let him know that I'd seen him."

Ed lay back on the floor and took a deep breath. "Where did you put my mail?" he asked.

"Your mail?" asked Sophie. "What the hell d'you want to know about that for?"

He looked at her without raising his head. "Greg was after my mail, it wasn't in the box in your greenhouse."

"You're damn right it wasn't in there. It's in the heavy metal box Taid used to store his bits and bobs, in the old store house out the back."

"The old store house?" asked Ed. "You mean the place where I keep the spare key?" She nodded her head and Ed felt his head spin again. He'd actually put his hand on Taid's old metal box earlier that evening.

"And how do I open the box?"

She dived into the pocket of her coat and then unfurled her hand to reveal a key. Ed stared at it for a moment before nodding his head. "You keep it for now."

Sophie stuffed it back in her pocket and then turned to him, eyes bright in the candlelight. "What's going on?" she asked. "Who is that man out there?"

Ed turned onto his front and then pushed himself to his feet. He could feel warm liquid trickling down his back, his limbs ached, his skin felt as if it was drawn too tight in places. He staggered across to Sophie's makeshift bed and collapsed.

"Who is that man?" asked Sophie. "He appeared last night, just before you phoned."

Ed cut across her. "Have you talked to Alice?" he asked. "I had an email saying she was going away, that she was being followed or something."

"That's right," said Sophie, "When Greg appeared and was stalking around the place I naturally rang her to say she mustn't come down here at any cost. To tell you the truth I don't think it had ever crossed her mind to do so."

"So she's nowhere near here?" Ed asked.

Sophie shook her head. "Up north, with a friend. I told her that there were suspicious people prowling around your farmhouse and that she should think about getting out of her flat for a while."

He could not get comfortable, whatever position he adopted on the small bed was painful. Sophie noticed his discomfort and came closer with her candle. "Are you hurt?"

Ed looked up into the lined old face with its strands of hair out of place and wondered what to say. "Did you tell her that you thought Greg was back from the dead?"

For several seconds Sophie hesitated, long enough for Ed to fill in the blanks. He shut his eyes and clenched his fists.

"She already knew," said Sophie in a rush. "She asked me straight out if it was Greg who was prowling around, she said she thought she'd seen him in the park opposite her flat."

Ed said nothing, he wondered what Alice had thought once she realised Greg was alive. He felt a touch on his arm.

"Last night, just before you rang, Katy ran out of the house in pursuit of that man out there. I haven't seen her since." She went silent, looking into his eyes, asking a question she dare not articulate.

Her hand was cold when he reached for it. He looked away from her and squeezed, then he shook his head.

"Who is he?" she asked, voice surprisingly strong. "What the hell does he want?"

Ed cleared his throat. "Up until a few moments ago I would have said that he wanted to kill me," he said. "But now I'm not so sure. He could have easily killed me back there, but instead he chose to go for Greg."

Sophie thought for several seconds, tapping her forehead. "He killed my cockerel and hung it in the tree outside my kitchen window. That was when Katy went off barking. I could hear her running around in the bushes, then there was a noise like shears snapping together and there was silence."

She was silent, lost in thought about her beloved dog and cockerel. Ed couldn't think what to say. Sophie was the innocent bystander caught in the cross fire. He opened his mouth to apologise but she cut across him.

"All night long he thumped up and down, knocking on my windows, howling like a wolf. I had no means of communication in or out; he cut my landline just after you called, and I don't keep a mobile phone. By the end of the night I was at my wits' end, I couldn't think of staying in my cottage. I ran out of my front door and down the path toward my old car, but he was there." She swallowed. "Or at least his spirit was there. All of my chickens were hung by their necks across the path. I turned around and ran back, the smell of his awful tobacco in my nose. I couldn't get away from it, couldn't think of going back into my house, so I made my way up to your farmhouse. I remembered Taid saying that his pantry was the most secure place on his farm,;he'd often joked about it being his panic room."

Her monologue finished, she looked into Ed's eyes. "Who is he?"

Ed sighed, the fright he had felt when he'd thrown himself into Taid's pantry was subsiding. They were safe for a few hours, until thirst forced them out, by which time he might have a plan. Perhaps discussing recent events would help. Sophie knew about Snodgrass and Lomax and he had discussed the reasons for Greg's disappearance with her on previous occasions.

"His name's Brett Walsh, AKA the Wolf Man, a psychotic killer," he said, hoping that this would be the last time he'd have to explain. "He's followed me from Africa, for what reason I can't begin to explain except that he enjoys terrorising and killing. He may be working alone, perhaps he sees me as being an easy target, a bit of entertainment."

Sophie gaped at him. "So you know him?" she asked. "Actually spoken to him?"

Ed considered her question before replying. "Yes. He arrived at Lomax Mine at the invitation of Lucky Lomax and James Allen…"

"So he's working for them?" she asked, not letting him finish.

"If he's working for anybody I'd say it must be Snodgrass." He paused for a moment. "But that doesn't make sense because Greg confessed that he had a business relationship with Snodgrass. So, unless Snodgrass has decided to do a bit of sweeping up it makes no sense for the Wolf Man to have killed Greg."

"So he must be working for Lomax, then," replied Sophie.

Ed shook his head. "He murdered one of Lomax's contractors, a driller named Alfie. It caused chaos, virtually closed Lomax Mine. Why would Lomax want to damage his own mine? It makes far more sense if he's working for Snodgrass. Besides, Lomax has no idea of how the syndicate disbursed its funds." He was beginning to talk to himself, to reason his way through what was happening. "Lomax has no idea that I was worried by trilobites. Only

Allen..."

He stopped and looked into the darkness of Taid's pantry; a new thought had entered his mind that kindled a flame of anger. Allen had been the real reason why he'd left the farmhouse, not the storm of trilobites sent by Greg. Allen had rung him up in a fit of panic and demanded that he must return to Africa. All through the week or so at Lomax Mine Ed had been unable to clearly establish why Allen had been so insistent.

What if Lomax had known that the credit card was being delivered to Ed's farmhouse? He might have been just as keen for Ed to move out as Snodgrass. Was that why Allen had been so adamant that Ed should return to Africa? Maybe it was Allen's way of trying to protect Ed.

Sophie interrupted again, she was getting frustrated and her voice was sharp. "I don't understand," she said. "Tell me what's going on." She grabbed Ed by the lapel and shook it angrily. "What syndicate? What funds?"

Ed looked up. It was safe to talk with Sophie. He reminded her about the fraud he'd uncovered the last time he'd gone to Lomax Mine and the part played by Greg. "You had to put some trilobites in a window in Horncastle as I recall," said Sophie nodding.

"Last night I discovered how it worked. Turns out that placing a trilobite in the window triggered the sale of artworks and disbursement of proceeds into the account of an offshore company. On receipt of funds a management company issued a credit card in the company name and then sent it to a pre-arranged address. Greg had put Llanfair Farmhouse as the business address for his company. Those trilobites that kept appearing around my house came from Greg, he was following orders from Snodgrass. They wanted me out of the way so they could check my mail."

Sophie fell back on her haunches. She'd definitely grown stronger since Ed had arrived. The tremor had gone from her voice and her face was no longer grey. Most people who had just experienced the terrors of the Wolf Man would have been lying on the floor suffering catatonia, but Sophie had always possessed an irrepressible strength of will. Taid had once confided to him that she was tough, beyond what might be expected in a normal person. He'd thought it was this facet of her personality that had caused her to remain alone all her life. In his opinion nobody would want to attach themselves to her knowing that they could never have their own way in anything.

Ed was glad she was with him in the pantry, she would be a formidable foe, even for the Wolf Man.

She sensed Ed watching her. "Doesn't make sense," she said, fixing him in the eye. "If Greg or Snodgrass wanted the card, all they had to do was send the boys around. No need for the subterfuge."

"I know," said Ed. "Seems strange. I suppose they wanted to get the card secretly. Snodgrass must have got three of the four syndicate credit cards already. If they'd taken Greg's card from me with menace then it would have given the game away, put Lomax on the trail."

She thought about this for a while and nodded before glancing at the door. "I wonder what the Wolf Man'll do next," she said.

They both sat and worried. Minutes turned into hours and there was no sign that the Wolf Man wanted to get into Taid's pantry. Ed recounted what had happened on his short trip to Africa. They discussed what they might do if the Wolf Man forced an entry, and whether they would be able to make a run for it. "When it's daylight," remarked Ed. "Perhaps we can make an attempt to get water."

He must have fallen asleep because he was shaken

awake by Sophie. He was disorientated and annoyed with himself. Every muscle in his body had seized up and his shirt stuck to his back. Then he realised why Sophie had woken him. Daylight was coming through the bottom of the metal door and there was a smell of tobacco.

They waited, tensed for the slightest noise. A whispering voice came across the air. "Come out little piggies." This was followed by a loud, raucous laugh which made them both jump.

"I'm going now," said the Wolf Man. "Lomax'll contact you soon, to tidy up the loose ends."

Ed heard, but couldn't believe. "You're working for Lomax?" He'd wanted to remain quiet, but the Wolf Man's statement had forced him to speak.

"Sure I am," said the Wolf Man, and Ed thought he could detect a sneer as he said the words. "Chiri can be a very persuasive man." A pause. "Lomax wants the card. If he doesn't get it he'll assume you're Snodgrass's man." He stopped speaking. Ed thought he must be waiting for a reply. "One more thing before I go," he said, "don't look too hard for your mate's body." There was a sound of feet retreating from the door.

Neither Ed nor Sophie said anything for the next few minutes. Ed realised his throat was constricted and his chest compressed. "Is it a trap?" asked Sophie eventually. "Is he waiting for us to remove all the stuff from the door?"

For the next few hours they waited, continuing their discussion about what to do next. Sophie wanted to inform the police of what had happened. "I've never found them particularly effective," she intoned. "But there's more than enough evidence here, even for their limited imagination."

Ed was less sure. "I don't think we need to act so quickly."

After all, he mused to himself, they would want to know why Greg had come to the farmhouse. From there an explanation of the credit card would be required, and inevitably this would lead to the fraud that had taken place at Lomax Mine. He felt sure Snodgrass would want to prevent the story emerging. By the time Snodgrass's mates in the media had finished with Ed's character, nothing he said would be believed.

And what about Lomax? If Ed started telling the police about the Wolf Man, there would be the possibility that the circumstances of Billy's suicide might be examined and that could lead to Cathcart and Chumshkev.

Sophie continued, getting angry that Ed wouldn't listen. She even punched his arm when he ignored her.

"D'you want the Wolf Man back?" he said. "Because that's what'll happen if you tell anybody."

"But he's killed Greg," insisted Sophie. "Sure, Greg was a shit, but he was still a human being." She sought out a conquering argument. "If we don't tell the police, this Wolf Man will be at liberty to kill again."

"You heard him, he's working for Lomax. If we tell the police we'll also have to implicate Snodgrass and Lomax." He could see that in Sophie's terrier-like mind, something stirred. "D'you really want them as your enemies?" he asked.

"But what about Greg?" she said. "Surely he deserves better?"

Ed sighed, knowing that Sophie was weakening, for once in her life. "He's officially a missing person," he said, "presumed dead - in Africa. Nobody's looking for him, he'll not be missed."

* * *

They crept out of Taid's pantry, armed with staves and metal bars that were lying around on the floor. But the Wolf Man had gone, leaving little trace of what had happened over the last twenty-four hours. All the cigarette butts had been retrieved, Katy's head had thankfully been removed, and the carcasses of Sophie's chickens were nowhere.

After some sleep, Ed eventually agreed to attend accident and emergency, where he told the nurse he had fallen over on the farm and rolled down the hill. She had looked at him suspiciously and then shrugged her shoulders before getting scissors to cut his shirt away from the stitched wound. The doctor had arrived and questioned him closely before stitching him back up and discharging.

Sophie was waiting when he emerged. She'd come along in her own car to give Ed a lift back after he returned his rental one. "You going to post the credit card to Lomax?" she asked.

"Not likely," said Ed. "I'll be placing it in his hand and asking him exactly why he employed somebody like the Wolf Man. There are a few other details I want cleared up as well."

"Such as?"

"He could have warned me about what might be waiting for me. He must have known about the credit cards."

He looked into Sophie's tired eyes and felt an urge to put his arm around her shoulders, but he wasn't too sure if this was something she'd appreciate.

"You can't know that," she said.

"Then how come the Wolf Man turned up at my farmhouse on his orders? How else should we interpret the Wolf Man's comment about the credit card? I think that's why Allen contacted me and pulled me back to Lomax Gold Mine. He knew I was in danger. It was the only way he could think of warning me without giving the game away."

He slumped sideways, bumping into Sophie's slight form. But instead of pushing him away with one of her famous acerbic comments, which is what he'd expected, Sophie put her arm around his waist and reached up to give him a kiss on the cheek. He felt wetness on his face and realised that she was crying. He pulled her into an embrace; she felt like a small quivering bird.

For a few moments, they held onto one another, while staff and patients passed.

A loud beep on a car horn made them break apart like startled rabbits. Sophie looked up into his face and he could tell from the glint in her eye that she had re-found her previous steel.

"Excuse me," she said to Ed, turning to look at the motorist, who had wound his window down so he could tell Ed to go and grope grandma somewhere else. He was around fifty, with a suit and a small, clipped beard and moustache.

"Sophie," Ed said, trying to layer warning into his tone.

"This is a nice car," she said walking toward the motorist. "Is it a BMW or some-such?" The man was nonplussed, remarks about his car was the last thing he was expecting.

"Of course not, it's an Audi," he said.

"Is it water resistant?" she asked.

"What sort of question is that?" he asked, narrowing his eyes, voice full of contempt.

Sophie was standing beside his open window by now, hands resting on the top of the door. Something caught her attention and she stepped back, an expression of fear on her face. As the motorist turned to look at what she had spotted, she ducked her head down and reappeared a second later holding the ignition key. The car engine sputtered and died.

"You daft bitch…."

His keys followed an arcing trajectory toward the memorial fountain, and landed with a satisfying plop.

"Come," Sophie said to Ed, walking away and ignoring the man's angry shouting. "Our work is finished here."

The man leapt from the car and moved toward Sophie, but Ed stepped forward and blocked his path. The motorist looked up into his scarred face and the eyes that still held anger from the previous night.

"You need to keep her on a leash," he shouted.

Ed stood his ground and said nothing.

The man glared at Sophie, who was climbing into the driver's seat of her car, unconcerned. Then he turned and stalked off toward the fountain so he could retrieve his keys.

Ed climbed in beside her. "What'll you tell Alice?" he said as if nothing had just happened.

Sophie scratched her nose and pretended to look in the rear-view mirror. "She knows that Greg's returned," she said eventually. "She'll be wondering where he's gone. She'll need to be told that he's dead."

"D'you think she's spoken with him?"

"Who knows?" Sophie replied.

Ed was silent for a moment, he hoped his next question would not provoke a furious response. Sophie may see herself as Ed's friend, grandson of Taid, but she was also Alice's aunt. "Why do you think Greg nominated Llanfair Farmhouse rather than the flat he shared with Alice in Liverpool as the place where the credit card should be delivered?"

"Could be any number of reasons," she replied slowly. She'd picked up on his thoughtfulness and glanced sideways, taking her eyes off the car park. "What are you trying to say?"

But Ed had lost courage. Expressing his fears out loud to Sophie was unwise. Instead he decided another tack. "If she thinks Greg is still alive, then it means trouble for our relationship."

She turned her face back to the car park. "For a moment there I thought you might be on the verge of accusing her." She sucked her teeth, a sure sign she was thinking. "I've wondered for a while about how much she knew about Greg's activities at Lomax. After all, she was married to him, they must have discussed stuff."

Shifting uncomfortably in his seat, Ed decided to give voice to what was bothering him. "The problem is that with Greg dead I've no way of establishing the extent of her involvement. And if the pieces are being swept…."

"You mean she might be in danger?" asked Sophie.

"All the other conspirators are dead," he said, "either killed by the miners' union, no doubt at the request of Snodgrass, or by the Wolf Man."

"You need to warn her," said Sophie, her voice raised in agitation.

"But if she really is involved then she'll more than likely be aware of the dangers."

"And what if she's not involved?"

Ed bit his lip before answering. "I don't want to be the one to question her closely. After all the trouble she's been through. She's likely to throw me out of her flat again and this time forbid me to darken her door again."

"You could always ask Lomax if she was involved," she suggested. "He's bound to have a view."

"And make him aware of our suspicions?" He bit his lip again. "Not likely."

Both sat looking out of the windscreen, lost in thought.

Eventually Ed said, "Allen called me away to Africa, he made it sound really urgent. He knew that it might not be safe for me to stay at my farmhouse. He must have known about the arrangements with the credit cards all along, which means that Lomax knew as well. Lomax probably has a spy in Snodgrass's camp, he may have known from the very start what was going on and whether Alice has been involved."

Sophie shrugged, then started the car and pulled out of the parking space. The motorist had rolled up his trousers and was wading through the fountain toward his keys. He made a rude gesture as they passed. Sophie smiled and waved, pleased that she had cause the man so much trouble.

"You'll need a damn good rest before going down to London," she said, turning her head away from the fountain. "I know I'll be sleeping for a week."

Finally, Alice

The mirrors of the lift which transported him to the nineteenth floor of Lomax Towers had been dark. They'd made him feel like he was entering a twilight world. He'd been met by Lomax's red-haired security guard who'd steered him through an x-ray scanner before escorting him to the twentieth floor.

Lomax's flat was Spartan and wooden, with large glass windows that looked out across the City. When he'd handed over the envelope containing Greg's card, Lomax had thrown it on a table as if it meant nothing to him. He'd then invited Ed to sit on a large sofa which served as his hub for informal meetings.

Ed wondered how to engage in small talk with a tycoon; they could hardly compare notes on the size of each other's yacht. Lomax had pressed a button and a manservant had appeared, feet squeaking on the parquet floor. "Fish," Lomax had shouted enthusiastically, "whatever's freshest."

Over the proceeding hours, Ed had been too pre-occupied to notice food, he'd been busy turning Lomax's words around in his head and seeing if they made any sense.

"Glad you decided to choose me above Snodgrass," he'd said, handing Ed a whisky. "He's been the bane of my life recently, hatching plots at a distance, colluding with business rivals. Not a man I'd have chosen to have as my enemy. But we can't always choose our enemies like we can friends."

Ed had asked whether it was true that he'd employed the Wolf Man.

"Didn't you realise?" Lomax replied, smiling. "I wouldn't have touched him with a barge pole unless it'd been absolutely necessary. It was Allen's idea to turn him around and point him back at Snodgrass. I called on Chiri for help." He'd suddenly laughed, a great bark that was unlike his usual silk-like tones. "Chiri could frighten Satan himself."

A shudder emanated from Ed as he remembered a night when the Galamsay were beating their drums and it was so hot that sweat had saturated his sheets. Chiri had appeared, stealthy in the night, smelling of death.

"And then I offered double what Snodgrass was paying," Lomax had continued. "A perfect job in my opinion, you can always rely on Chiri if there's any persuasion to be done."

"You've probably guessed by now that Snodgrass is connected to various parts of the media in this country. He was well placed when the Wolf Man went to a British newspaper correspondent in PNG and tried to create a bidding war for the story of Cathcart and Chumshkev. Snodgrass had no idea that it was Chumshkev who was the traitor, as far as I'm aware he's still ignorant of how the whole scheme worked. All he wanted was a way of embarrassing me. We had no choice but to offer both Billy and the Wolf Man employment so we could keep them quiet. I believe that Snodgrass offered the Wolf Man a supplementary payment if he could engineer industrial unrest at Lomax Gold Mine. I don't think Snodgrass meant him to kill a white contractor."

Ed was less sanguine than Lomax, he was certain the Wolf Man had Ed in his sights all along. It was only his thirst to fulfil a vendetta against Alfie that had saved Ed's life.

"And what about Kojo and Bismarck?" Ed had asked when the fish was being served.

"I've decided to make peace with them. They have the money and the education to cause a serious mess if I push. Good luck to 'em. All I ask is that they don't make deals with Snodgrass. In the meantime, The Union Is Dead, Long Live The Union." He raised his glass in the air as if to toast its demise. Ed hadn't followed him.

"As for yourself," said Lomax, "I think we need to make sure you're safe. Yes, indeed we do. Until the Snodgrass issue has been brought to a conclusion, you need to be kept on ice."

* * *

As Ed packed woollen jumpers, waterproofs and thermals into his rucksack he could see the reassuring sight of a thin plume of smoke rising from Sophie's cottage.

She'd taken the death of her dog much harder than Ed had initially realised. Her distress had manifested itself in a tendency to pick fights. On a trip to town she'd shouted at the postmaster, shaken her stick at the assistant in Boots the chemist and virtually done a citizen's arrest on a boy who had dropped some litter.

Ed had found a sign in the newsagents advertising Jack Russell puppies and had insisted that she visit. He'd paid several hundred pounds for one covered with black spots and set up an account at the vets so she'd have no worries about the expense of a new pet.

The district could breathe a sigh of relief.

Only when she'd got the puppy home (christened, Smotyn) and drunk several cups of tea laced with brandy had he broken the news that he was off again, at the behest of Lomax.

There'd been a predictable explosion.

Ed walked down the stairs and looked out of the kitchen window. He was expecting Sophie to arrive that afternoon. He'd been slow cooking a leg of lamb in the Rayburn for her. Now rosemary and the soft smell of roasting meat mingled with wood smoke. It invoked memories of when Taid had cooked his mutton broth in this kitchen.

His mind drifted again, to the subject that had become his monomania; Alice. He'd visited Alice's flat a couple of weeks ago. He'd been greeted by a tall woman who had been instantly suspicious. When she'd discovered his name was Ed, she'd slammed the door in his face. Hardly auspicious, Ed had reflected on the journey back. By the time he'd reached home, his spirits had been lower than at any time since the visit of the Wolf Man.

Sophie had taken up the batten and had rung the hospital in Liverpool where Alice worked. She'd discovered, somehow, that Alice had been signed off with stress. According to the hospital it was 'a delayed reaction to the loss of her husband'.

He gazed disconsolately out of the window, at the sweep of the valley. He would not be able to see her before leaving for Canada. The thought made him feel depressed and lonely. Sophie promised that she would continue her search.

He was about to turn away when a bashed old Mitsubishi turned into the road at the bottom of the hill and stopped. Ed's mind was still focussed so it took several moments before he registered the colour and the make. With a sudden jolt he realised it was Alice's. He strained his eyes through the distorting kitchen window, focussing on the figure in the driver's seat until he was certain it was her.

Adrenalin shot through his veins.

She was making her way up the track toward his house, already over half way up. He could see it was definitely Alice, her eyes fixed on the muddy track, hands clasped to the steering wheel, face set in a determined expression.

He walked outside to greet her and stood beneath the trees where the Wolf Man had hidden. Turning into the gate she stopped close to where he was standing and smiled through her open window. They looked at each other for a few moments while Ed rummaged through his mind for something to say. "Easy trip?" he asked.

She nodded and got out of the car. She was a picture of auburn delight, a wardrobe of chestnut colours, picked to display her long bushy hair to its best. Ed was keenly aware of the shortcomings of his own attire which was a patchwork of red and blue cottons that neither matched nor fitted particularly well.

Despite the effort she'd made, Ed could see in her eyes the tiredness of a soldier who had been living too long under the strain of battle. They lingered too long on one place, showed that the controlling brain was preoccupied and tired. Alice was reaching her breaking point, had maybe reached it.

But it wasn't just her eyes that gave away her inner turmoil. Where once she had beautiful sensuous curves, now there was bone. Ed gulped and stared.

She gave him a hug, the harsh words of a month ago when Ed had announced he was returning to Africa, had long since been forgotten. "Let's get in before it rains," she said as it became obvious that Ed was not going to say anything further.

He tried switching on lights to banish gloom from the

kitchen, but the fuse instantly blew. "I need to upgrade all the electrics," he said. "All the work I've been doing for Lomax will be enough to completely transform this place."

"Looks like it's candles then," she said, fishing in the cupboard where they were kept.

"It's either that or messing about with bits of fuse wire in the dark," Ed agreed.

With the candles flickering under the influence of strong drafts from the warped and ill-fitted windows, he retrieved vegetables from his store and started to chop and peel. He felt awkward and was unsure what to say. There was so much he wanted to get off his chest that he hardly knew where to start.

Alice decided to break the awkward silence. "I got the information about Chumshkev and Cathcart," she said, then laughed at Ed's look of shock. "The email you sent from Africa, with Billy Barker's suicide note, remember?"

So much had happened that he'd completely forgotten his request for her help. It had been the act of a man under pressure, grasping at straws.

"I've printed off a summary of what I found," she said, handing across a folder. "Quite a story."

Putting down the knife with which he had been chopping potatoes, he turned and looked her in the eye. "I wouldn't tell anybody about what Billy confessed."

"You're dead right," said Alice.

"It's not quite as it seems, nothing ever is when Lomax is involved." He turned back to the sink and continued preparing his potatoes. "If I told you what it was all about, I'd have to shoot you and then eat you," he said.

Alice didn't laugh.

"All top secret," he continued, "a fiendish plot by Johnny Foreigner to destabilise our way of life." He was trying to make light of the situation and he was failing badly.

"Had it anything to do with Greg?" she asked.

Ed didn't answer, he could feel Alice getting annoyed by his silence. "He was here a couple of weeks or so ago," he said eventually, as if Greg had popped in for a friendly chat and a cup of coffee.

"Sophie said he'd been hanging around."

Ed continued peeling potatoes feeling her eyes on his back.

"A few days after you left, he called my flat," she said. "Sandra took the message. He called himself Ed. That's why Sandra slammed the door in your face when you called the other day, she thought you were Greg."

Ed nodded his understanding and then threw the last potato into the pot before moving across to the Rayburn. He could tell Alice wanted to tell him something and the best way he could help her was to carry on as normal. In the back of the store room he had some red wine; he unscrewed the top and poured two glasses while Alice struggled to find the words.

"I'm guessing he offered you a deal," he said eventually, when she seemed incapable of moving forward with her story.

She nodded, and then took a sip. "He said that you had stolen his money. He wanted me to help him get it back."

"And how were you supposed to do that?" Ed asked, although he thought he knew.

"He wanted me to steal a credit card. He said he'd split the balance with me."

There was a long silence. Alice looked toward the window where the Wolf Man's tree was silhouetted. Ed swilled the blood-red wine in his glass. "I didn't steal anything from him," he said eventually.

Alice charged on as if Ed hadn't spoken. "He said he'd

return the next day for my answer." Her voice began to break. "I was in a panic, I fled." Ed leaned across and touched the hand clutching the wine glass. Alice did not move her hand away, she was too intent. "He said he was working for Snodgrass," she said, voice cracking.

Withdrawing his hand, Ed rose to his feet and walked around the table until he was directly next to her. "Have you talked to Sophie about what happened here, when Greg arrived and tried to get the credit card?"

Alice looked up at him, eyes shining with tears. "No," she said, her voice a tremolo. "I haven't talked to her."

"Then I would. She'd be more than happy to fill you in. You shouldn't worry that Greg will be calling."

"And did you steal from him?"

Ed shook his head. "It's quite simple, Greg nominated Llanfair Farmhouse as the business premises for his company. That's why the credit card was sent here. I knew nothing about it."

She looked at him in astonishment. "So it's all settled now?"

"There are several loose ends to tie up. I need to go to Canada for a month while it's all sorted."

"You mean you're off again?" she asked, he could tell she was annoyed.

"Just for a while."

"But why?"

"I gave Greg's card to Lomax. Lomax thinks I should go somewhere far out of the way where Snodgrass can't get to me. I have to go tomorrow."

She gazed up at him, eyes wide with fear. "Who knows you're here?" he asked.

Alice shook her head. "Nobody."

"Then I'd like you to stay with Sophie," he said. "She knows what's going on, she's had experience of this sort of thing. She can protect you."

Alice opened her mouth to object, but Ed jumped in quickly. "It's me Snodgrass wants, but Lomax seems to think anybody associated with this business might be in trouble." He tapped the table, thinking hard, it was on the tip of his tongue to say he would cancel his trip. It was hardly noble to leave Alice to face the wrath of Snodgrass while he jetted off to safety. But then he shook his head. "It'll only be for a month, and after the first week or so and the all-clear comes from Lomax, then you can come up to the farmhouse and live."

Silence.

"And what if Greg turns up?" she asked.

"I told you," said Ed urgently, leaning forward and squeezing her hand. "You shouldn't worry about Greg turning up anymore."

She looked at him intently, searching his face, trying to work out why he was so certain.

"Because..." he hesitated, long enough for Alice to bridle.

"Because?" she said. "You mean you're wanting me to take your word for it? You've told me once before that Greg was never going to be returning. I took your word for it then, I was glad to be away from him." She suddenly broke down and started to cry in earnest.

He took her hand. "I thought we agreed that we would both draw a line under what happened and move on," he said.

"We can't move on," she insisted face flushed with anger, "not when Greg is still walking around, he'll be a constant reminder of what's happened to us. He'll do his best to make our lives miserable, especially now you've given away his precious credit card."

Ed waited patiently until she'd blown herself out.

"And what if he's no longer around?" he asked eventually.

She let out a hiss, frustrated that he had apparently not been listening.

He rose and took her hand, pulling her gently out of the door and walking toward the trees from which the Wolf Man had dropped onto Greg's head. He explained what had happened the night he had returned, how he had gone down to Sophie's and discovered Greg sitting at her kitchen table. How he had decided to come back up and discovered the Kookaburra hat perched on the wall and smelled the tobacco. He then walked her over to Taid's pantry and said how he had looked back to see Greg lying on the floor, neck apparently broken, and the Wolf Man standing over him, leering.

"Then Sophie opened the door and let me in," he said.

Alice was white again, she looked into his eyes searching for signs of deceit. He shook his head and turned away. "I didn't inspect Greg's body or take a pulse, but I did hear the crack as his neck broke," he said.

Alice said nothing as she looked around the inside of Taid's pantry sniffing the damp, musty atmosphere.

"There's several piles of earth up in the oak coppice, and a horrible smell comes from Taid's old coal adit. He shook his head again. "Greg hated working down that hole, ironic that he'll spend eternity down there."

She looked up at the old oak coppice and visibly shuddered. Could have been the chill wind in the farmyard, or maybe she'd sensed Ed was telling the truth and Greg's shadow had passed from her. "I'm not glad he's dead," she said, as if trying to convince herself. "He was a tiresome sneak. I'd rather he'd just left me." She stopped and hugged herself. "Left us - in peace. Just crawled under his rock and stayed there until we were all old and none of this mattered." She turned and looked at him full in the face. "But that was never his way."

"No," agreed Ed. "Never his way."

"You got any boots?" she asked. "I'd like to walk, build up an appetite for lunch. I can tell you're going to try and force feed me."

* * *

They'd gone down the hill to Sophie's, past the stream that had almost washed Greg away. It was back in its bed and barely came up beyond the soles of their boots. Ed had paused and looked back towards his own house which was lost behind a coppice of trees. He saw himself going up the path, followed by Greg, walking wide-eyed into a trap.

Sophie had been reserved when she saw Alice, eyeing her sparse frame with eyebrow-hooded disapproval. They'd drunk tea with brandy and munched on barbecued chicken wings while talking of events past and future. They'd all agreed that nothing need be decided until tomorrow when Ed was due to leave.

Walking back up the hill to the farmhouse, Alice had stopped in the spot where Greg had died and looked up into the tree. "What's that?" she said pointing up into the tree canopy.

Ed lifted his head and squinted. The lowest branch had been hacked about, leaving deep white grooves that were easily picked out against the darkness of the bark. "Looks like some kind of carving," he said.

"Like a wolf's head," Alice said.

Ed quickly looked away, a shiver going down his spine. Forever more this tree would be associated with the Wolf Man. He could imagine his children (if he ever had any) staring up and wondering who had created the carving and for what purpose. One thing was for certain, he would not enlighten them.

He pressed on toward the kitchen door. Only time would tell whether the farmhouse would ever be rid of the Wolf Man, whether time and the ravages of the weather up here on the mountain would sanitise the stench of evil.

But for now, he was going to enjoy the moment when he had Alice's undivided attention. The day had become windy and cold, uncharacteristically cold for early summer. In contrast the kitchen was warm, fuggy and aromatic.

He would force merriment, create a bubble around them so that in this place and at this time, all rumour of the Wolf Man, and memory of Greg, would be banished.

"Do you remember when we started to go out?" he asked.

She looked at him, clearly wondering whether he was referring to the time when they had been young in this farm, when Taid had been alive and Sophie had been a regular visitor to the kitchen where they now both sat. But that was not what Ed meant.

"You'd invited me to some house party," he continued. "When I arrived there were people hanging out of windows and the music was pitched to wake the dead."

She smiled coyly. "I remember," she said. "You lurked. I watched you for a full five minutes from an upstairs window."

Ed nodded. "I built enough courage to come up the path and was stopped by some gorilla on the door who asked me for an invitation. Then you appeared in that small black dress you used to wear and took my hand and walked me down the path. Do you remember what you said to me?"

She narrowed her eyes. "Let's go to the pub, or something?"

"That's right, you said, 'let's go to the pub and then you can take me out for dinner'."

She looked at him, bemused. "What's your point?"

He looked at her, the smile growing on his face. Then he turned to the Rayburn and pulled open the oven door and checked the lamb. "It was a great night," he said. "We had a load to drink and then I carried you upstairs to the flat."

He could sense her smiling at his back. "That's right," she said quietly.

Time passed, Alice's cheeks became rosy under the influence of wine, lamb and a warm kitchen. They talked about what would happen when Ed returned home from Labrador. She suggested lending an old car and touring, spending only cash and keeping to the back roads, away from road cameras.

"I'm paranoid," she said when Ed suggested that they just go abroad. "They'll know from the plane tickets where we've gone. If we stay in this country, we'll not have to show a passport or any form of identity."

Ed shrugged.

Silence.

"Before I left for Scotland, Sophie said she'd been investigating your family history."

Ed turned his head in surprise.

"That's right, the old wolverine has her teeth into your family tree."

"And?"

She hesitated, then sat back in her chair. He could see that she was regretting her words. "I think she was trying to find the relationship between Greg and Snodgrass."

Ed narrowed his eyes. "Greg isn't related to me, can't be. His mother and father are from Manchester, we've never had relatives from there." The cosy atmosphere had disappeared. He could feel frustration bubble to the surface. "Sophie said nothing to me about investigating my family."

Alice crossed her arms and closed her eyes. She shook her head. "I can't believe I said it. It's the wine. I'm not thinking straight. Please don't ask me to explain. I'm sorry for bringing it up." She put her glass down on the table. He could tell she was on the edge, about to burst into tears. "It was something Taid told her about your family. She seemed to think that it would explain how Greg came to know Snodgrass." She opened her eyes. "I don't want to tell you." She blinked a few times and then pulled herself up. "I won't tell you. If you must know, ask Sophie."

Ed retreated. The thought that there was a secret about the Evans' family that only Sophie and Alice knew did not surprise him very much. Sophie seemed to know everything about everybody. He smiled. "I've never been one for family history. It can wait."

Alice nodded, relieved.

When night fell, they both felt drowsy and climbed the stairs, leaving the warm fug of the kitchen behind and entering the cold dampness of Ed's bedroom. Drunk as they were Ed felt coy. He hadn't told her of the explosion at Lomax Mine and therefore she knew nothing of his wounds. She picked up on his apprehension, always able to see straight through him.

"I heard about the explosion on the news. I guessed you would have been somewhere near." Her voice was matter-of-fact, like she was accusing him of provocation. "There were a few people killed I hear, anybody you knew?"

He wondered whether to tell the truth as he got into the bed, but then decided it wouldn't do any good. "Only vaguely," he said. "One was a driver named Frank and the other was a geologist who worked in the same office."

"So long as you're safe," she said sleepily, lying fully

clothed on the bed. The food and wine had done the trick, she was already on the edge of oblivion. Ed watched as her eyes closed and her breathing became heavy. He'd been told babies have the trick of falling asleep instantly, but he'd never seen it in an adult. She must have a lot of sleep to catch up on, he supposed.

* * *

She insisted on driving him to the airport early the next morning. They stopped at a service station for a quick breakfast and Ed refuelled her Mitsubishi. As they approached the drop off at the airport departure terminal Ed turned to her. "Decision time," he said. "Are you going back to Sophie's?"

She said nothing until the tricky parking manoeuvre had been achieved, then she twisted in her seat. "No," she said. "I couldn't stand it."

Ed opened his mouth to protest, but she told him to hush. "I haven't finished. I would like to stay at your farmhouse. It's summer so it won't be too cold. I think Sophie should stay with me up there. We're near to Taid's pantry. Perhaps I can kit it out as a serious panic room when I get back."

"That's something you'll have to discuss with Sophie," said Ed, relieved that she was not intending to disappear. "You know where everything is stored in the house. I made an arrangement with the local stores in the event that you turned up. Sophie can buy food and anything else and it'll all go on my tab."

He leaned across and kissed her, before she could express her thanks. "Be careful," he said. "Perhaps you should think of putting extra locks on the doors and putting furniture against your door. You could even rig up a tent inside Taid's pantry..."

He looked at his watch, he was late for booking into the Newfoundland flight. "I'll ring you," he said jumping from the vehicle with his rucksack. He ran through the large glass doors, turning to look at her every now and then. She waved a few times, but by the time he had checked his rucksack into the flight, she had gone. He looked at where her vehicle had been waiting, wishing that he had given into her insistence that she parked and joined him. But on the other hand, he felt better that she was on her way back to the farmhouse and not trying to negotiate her way through shadowy concourses and dark, low-ceilinged car parks.

He walked through into the departure lounge and waited, there were no seats available and there were people milling around, waiting for the final call. He was hung over and tired from the previous evening so he sat down on the floor and leaned against the wall, pulling his legs toward him so nobody would accidentally trip.

On a whim, he pulled open his hand luggage and produced a large document wallet from which he pulled a schedule for his trip to Labrador. He was to de-plane at St John's and then fly to a town called Base before taking a float plane at the earliest possible opportunity up the coast. He was to be based on Dog Island out in the Labrador Sea, tens of kilometres from Nain, the northernmost permanent Inuit settlement in Labrador.

His companions were a young woman, Trudy, who was to be the organiser of the camp, and two Americans based out of Vancouver, Mullberry and John. In the notes, Lomax had made special mention that the expedition was funded by Lomax Enterprises, but all of the personnel had been chosen by a university professor called Hofflaar who was the nominated fund holder for the scientific project.

During their lunch, when Lomax had proposed the

Labrador trip, Ed had been provided with pen portraits for each member of the group. Mullberry he described as 'a good ol' boy', John was 'frightened of his own shadow', and Trudy was 'like one of the old Hudson Bay fur trappers'.

The call came for him to board the plane and he stood up, feeling the stiffness in his joints. As he limped toward the embarkation corridor and boarded the plane, he reflected that the place he was going was so isolated that Snodgrass would never be able to lay hands on him. And Lomax promised that by the time he returned Snodgrass would have been dealt with.

The expedition companions sounded eccentric, but he would be on the island for less than a month. Before he knew it he would be boarding a plane home, back to Alice and the prospect of several months holiday in which he would have her undivided attention. He put his luggage in the overhead locker and then sat down in his seat. He was feeling hopeful about the future, and as the plane moved off towards the runway he leaned back and felt the beginnings of excitement bubble in his chest.

Even the thought that Sophie had been investigating his family didn't ruffle his calmness. Whatever she'd found couldn't be that important. So what if Greg had known Snodgrass through some tenuous Evans family connection? Greg was dead, the connection was closed, it couldn't possibly affect him now.

Could it?

ACKNOWLEDGEMENTS

Thanks goes to Sue Miller (editing), Alan Jones (cover) and all at TeamAuthorUK for your support. Rachel Harris and Noreen Harris for providing feedback on earlier drafts. My children for listening excitedly to stories of Africa. Those who read and enjoyed the first Lomax Gold Mine book, Dead Man's Gold, and encouraged me to keep going.

ABOUT THE AUTHOR

Mendus Harris has been writing conspiracy thrillers for the last ten years. His latest books are based in a fictional gold mine named Lomax and draw on his extensive experience as an exploration geologist. Very few people appreciate how a large gold mine in Africa functions and those that do may not be keen for the truth to be told.

His writing conjures images which are redolent with the sights and sounds of West African gold mines, the characters who inhabit them and the political conflicts which can threaten to rip them apart. Here is an author who has been there and seen that and has a view on what he has experienced.

For More Information:

mendusharris.co.uk

davidmendusharris@gmail.com

www.facebook.com/authormendusharris

Book 1 in the Lomax Gold Mine Series

Dead Man's Gold
Available Now from Amazon

COMING IN 2017...

Ice Bound –
Book 3 of the Lomax Gold Mine Series

At the behest of Lucky Lomax, wealthy tycoon and owner of Lomax Gold Mine, Ed undertakes a hazardous journey to the wilderness of Canada's eastern coast where he joins an exploration crew prospecting in an isolated corner of the Labrador Sea.

They are stranded on a remote island after an enormous storm tracks south down the Davis Strait and cuts their line of communication. When the crew investigate the best way to escape they spot a man on a remote hillside. At first they take him for a lone adventurer out in the wilderness trapping and shooting game, but soon his malevolent intentions become clear.

As the days pass, the morale of the crew disintegrates and a story of a cruel conspiracy emerges that gradually comes to explain the presence of the man on the island. Events at Lomax Gold Mine reverberate, even here.

When Ed returns home, he is determined to put a stop to those who have dogged his steps for so long. It's kill or be killed.